Praise fo

"An ambitious first novel. [...]
edgeable meddling, [Klale's] attempts to get inside Blade's head
trigger a redemption process that forms the most satisfying thread
of this complex narrative—a technologically aware and emotionally wrenching twist on the old tale of Beauty and the Beast."
—*The New York Times Book Review*

"Science fiction tends to be Romantic with a capital R, and so do
the readers. This book delivers all the Romanticism you could
want—dark secrets, hidden pasts, desperate odds, a violent and
grungy yet curiously beautiful world, surprises and disguises,
heroes who have been bad, villains who could have been great . . .
all in a nicely imagined, scary but exciting future. So, buy it."
—John Barnes, author of *The Merchants of Souls*

"Her crisp narrative moves along at a cracking pace, and, while
West Coasters will enjoy the references to a familiar landscape
rendered weird, there's a universal quality to the story that makes
that landscape and its bizarre inhabitants accessible to readers
anywhere. McMahon has fashioned quite an attention-grabber
and *Dance of Knives* makes for an auspicious first book."
—Stephen Hume, *The Vancouver Sun*

"I always enjoy discovering a new writer who gets everything
right the first time out. Donna McMahon doesn't just show promise with *Dance of Knives*, she delivers the real goods from the
first page through to the last.

"What gives the book its heart are the deft interactions that
connect Klale, the dangerous Blade, and the bartender Toni. The
triangle formed by these three is what captures a reader's interest
and holds it there, all the way through to the book's surprising
and satisfying conclusion.

"McMahon, for all that she's a new author, has the writing
chops of a seasoned pro. This is a wonderful debut."
—Charles de Lint, *The Magazine of Fantasy & Science Fiction*

DANCE OF KNIVES

DONNA MCMAHON

TOR®

A TOM DOHERTY ASSOCIATES BOOK
NEW YORK

DANCE OF KNIVES

Copyright © 2001 by Donna McMahon

This book is printed on acid-free paper.

A Tor Book
Published by Tom Doherty Associates, LLC
175 Fifth Avenue
New York, NY 10010

www.tor.com

Tor® is a registered trademark of Tom Doherty Associates, LLC.

Library of Congress Cataloging-in-Publication Data

McMahon, Donna.
    Dance of knives / Donna McMahon.
        p. cm.
    "A Tom Doherty Associates book."
    ISBN 0-312-87431-6 (hc)
    ISBN 0-312-87536-3 (pbk)
    1. Vancouver (B.C.)—Fiction. I. Title.

PR9199.3.M33465 D36 2001
813'.54—dc21   00-031795

First Hardcover Edition: May 2001
First Trade Paperback Edition: June 2001

Printed in the United States of America

0 9 8 7 6 5 4 3 2 1

In memory of some good fan friends
(and some great convention parties):

Paul Simms
Evelyn Beheshti Hildebrandt
Robert Hahn

ACKNOWLEDGMENTS

Thanks to the following people for their advice, assistance, and encouragement (and apologies to anybody I forgot to name): David Andrien, AJ Budrys, Ed Beauregard, Jordan Brooks, Nancy Campbell, Howard Davidson, Jim Fiscus, Robert Hahn, Eugene James, Vince Kohler, Shar McCallum, Jeanne Robinson, Lisa Smedman, and of course my sweetie, Clint.

DANCE OF KNIVES

PROLOGUE

The boy danced on shimmering moonlight across a glass sea, spin-ning joyously, stretching to trail his fingers through the silver black ceiling of storm clouds. At the edge of his vision, ripples . . .

Blade glanced quickly to confirm the identity of the slight figure approaching along the old float—Linden Chan, operative for the Viet Ching—then he ducked his head beneath the level of the boat's rail and exhaled underneath his infrared-masking serape, waiting for Chan to complete her surveillance scan. No motion disturbed his hiding place. In the cabin below, a water taxi family huddled in rigid terror, knowing he would kill them if any sound or movement be-trayed him. Since securing them some hours ago he had lain prone on the water taxi deck under a heap of tarps, waiting to observe Chan's drop. The intercepted Viet Ching message had given a time, but no other details.

He raised his head, risking a glance. Chan stood just three meters in front of him, her back turned, scanning the harbor and surround-ing boats for electronic or human surveillance. At the top of the ramp leading to the Pender Street wharf, two figures stood silhouetted against distant lights—Chan's henches. The drop must be so discreet that she didn't want them to observe the details. Interesting.

Blade slid his goggles over his eyes, switched to enhanced am-bient light and began recording. Chan, now clearly visible to him, finished her scan, then walked to the pilings anchoring the end of the float and crouched down under the sign which read RESERVED 24 HOURS FOR HARBOR PATROL. The end of the old float sagged low in the water, its lichen-encrusted foot-rails half rotted away. Beyond, nav hazard lights blinked, marking drowned buildings. An old elevator shaft jutted skeletally out of black seawater.

Blade zoomed in on Chan's gloved hands and saw her remove a sealed plastiche pouch from her coat pocket. A length of fishing line trailed from it. Chan dropped the pouch into the water, then looped the end of the fish line around a steel cleat and stood up.

Blade ducked down again and counted off a minute. When he looked up, the float and the wharf lay deserted. He scanned the area with his goggles, then tagged the sequence he'd recorded to Chan's dossier and began his wait for the pick-up....

The little boy rushed back out to his glorious dance floor, flipping onto his hands and waggling his feet in the air, his palms walking the mirror-sheened water. He loved his wonderful night stillness, the seductive promise that he could flee along the moon's path and leave the ugly, twisted ghoul behind him. A chill of fear clutched at his limbs and he looked unwillingly back at the float, searching the shadowed water taxi for a glimpse of that stone-frozen skull.

Instead he saw a fish boat . . .

Blade began recording again and focused on the craft. It was a standard Fisher vessel, about ten meters long, with modern trolling gear retrofitted on an antique aluminum hull. It chugged toward the Patrol float, slowing and swinging broadside. Navigation lights shone from the mast, but the captain wasn't using the wheelhouse spotlight for this landing. Glowing yellow biolume letters on the bow spelled *Urchin*.

Several figures stepped out of the wheelhouse and moved toward the stern. They waited as the boat drifted closer, then one person jumped lightly over to the float. Someone else threw a large bag and the first figure caught it, then waved, and Blade saw the soft infrared puff of a shout. The boat heeled gently and began pulling away.

Movement caught Blade's gaze and he turned to see a tall figure in a Harbor Patrol parka striding down the boat ramp. Unexpected. He zoomed in on the officer's face, noting dark hair tied back in a standard patrol queue and facial features—heavy but distinctly female. He queried his database. A second later, text flashed up in the periphery of his vision: MATCH 92% PROBABILITY: CAPTAIN BALJEET DHILLON, COMMANDING PBOAT7. Most interesting. If she wasn't with her boat, she must be off duty, and in that case he could think of no legitimate reason for her to be alone on foot in the slums of old Downtown.

Dhillon strode toward the newcomer, frowning and opening her mouth. Blade cued his directional microphone, and text unrolled along the bottom of his field of vision.

". . . reserved float!"

The Fisher turned toward Dhillon and Blade saw her face clearly. She had pale, freckled skin and looked to be in her twenties, but his database could not ID her.

"Sorry, captain, but it's no big spill. Just some friends dropping me off. Didn't take a second. See, I'm almost gone already . . ." She headed for the ramp, heavy duffel bag slung over one shoulder. She did not glance back toward the piling where Chan's packet lay hidden.

"Hold it, Citizen! This is a fineable offense!"

The Fisher swung around and aimed a broad grin at Dhillon's scowl.

"So fine the Guild! It's no rain on me. I just left. The Fishers Guild can suck seawater. I'm not!"

Laughing, she turned and sprinted up the ramp. At the top she tossed down her duffel bag, flung both hands up over her head, and started jumping up and down. Then she threw herself sideways . . .

The boy stared, open-mouthed with delight as the Fisher woman cartwheeled across the wharf, boots arching through the air, heavy sweater flapping wildly. Two, three, four cartwheels, then she hopped in an ecstatic circle, arms windmilling, hair flying wildly around her head. The boy rushed up to join her, only to be disappointed when she stopped to catch her breath. He'd never seen anybody dance on a wharf before, only the greedy-eyed, raucous seagulls who whirled up into the dizzy freedom of the sky. He watched the girl hopefully, but she only brushed her hands off on her pants, and then shouldered her bag and walked off toward Pender Street. . . .

A shadow fell across Blade. He ducked automatically as Dhillon walked past him toward the end of the float, then he refocused his goggles, tagging this recording to his master's attention, high priority. The Harbor Patrol were customarily paid off by the Kung Lok. If Dhillon was also transacting with their rivals, the Viet Ching, evidence of her actions would be highly salable.

He glanced back at the wharf to confirm that the Fisher girl had departed and instead saw another Harbor Patrol officer approaching down the ramp. A collaborator? Dhillon was kneeling, retrieving the packet when she evidently heard footsteps. She jumped to her feet, letting the packet fall back into the water as the other officer stepped onto the float. Blade queried the new arrival's identity. The database had difficulty discerning his shadowed features, but one possible hit was Dhillon's first mate, Officer Gill.

". . . just go and leave it behind," the man was saying. The text crawl's red hue indicated agitation in his voice, but Dhillon's reply was gray.

"I don't know what you're talking about."

"Bullshit you don't! Look, a little palm grease, OK, no smog, everyone does it, but you're diving too deep, gonna get all of us in trouble!"

"You sneak around following me at night and you think I'm a problem? Well, I don't slag my own crew."

"I'm not slagging, I'm scared! There's rumors going around the flots. You got to clean up, talk to Command before somebody else does."

There was a pause. Dhillon looked down at the hidden packet.

"I can't leave this here."

"OK, so we take it. And get rid of it somehow."

Dhillon hesitated. The other officer stepped past her and knelt down. "Here . . ."

Dhillon reached under her coat, pulled a pistol, reversed her grip and struck his skull with the gun butt. The man pitched toward the water, but she grabbed his arms and hauled him back, staggering under his weight. She looked around urgently and Blade glimpsed her calculating expression in the dim light from the wharf.

For several seconds Dhillon stood holding her slumped comrade, then she shifted her grip on his arms and laid him out facedown on the float with his head and shoulders hanging out over the water.

After one last glance around her, she knelt over him, knees on either side of his buttocks, gripped his wrists in one hand, and then lowered his head into the water. The man's legs kicked convulsively. Little waves rippled out across the calm water, bubbles bobbing in their wake.

Dhillon held him under for a long moment, then she sat back, grabbed his legs and slid the body slowly and quietly into the water. Trapped air bubbles swelled the man's parka, then boiled out as he began to sink.

Dhillon turned and retrieved Chan's package, cramming the wet fishing line deep into an inside pocket of her parka. Then she looked down into the dark water and smiled.

1

TUESDAY, SEPT. 12, 2108

I should have arrived in the daytime, thought Klale ruefully, staring into the inky darkness beyond the lone streetlight at the end of the Pender Street Wharf. But she'd had no idea that downtown streets would be deserted at ten-thirty at night or so damned dark!

A raindrop splashed on her head, leaking cold rivulets through her hair onto her scalp, then two more followed in quick succession. Klale sighed and started rooting in her duffel bag for her rain cape. Trust the thunderstorm to arrive now.

It would have been smarter to catch a ferry from Nanaimo to Vancouver tomorrow, but the free ride on *Urchin* had seemed just too good to pass up. And she'd asked to be dropped off on the island of Downtown, despite the crew's warnings, because she hadn't wanted to be caught wandering Vancouver streets after curfew and interrogated by some petty Watch Patroller who'd want to know why she wasn't staying at a Fisher hostel. Downtown lay outside of Guild law and had no Watch to bother Klale. Unfortunately, it hadn't any street lights either.

Well, there had to be a bright side, she told herself. Surely the rain would keep beggars and bludgers inside. Then she heard footsteps.

Klale tensed, heart pounding, then caught sight of the Harbor Patrol Officer. Ten minutes ago the officious woman had irritated her. Now she felt a wave of relief.

"Evening, Captain," she called out.

The officer looked at Klale and changed course to meet her.

"Evening." The dark-haired officer summoned up a smile, though it didn't meet her eyes. "Guild hostels are all over in Vancouver."

"I'm looking for a public hostel instead," said Klale firmly.

"Uh huh. Really left your Guild, eh?"

"Sure. It's not the twenty-first century anymore, you know. People move around. I'll find another one," she said, hoping she sounded a hell of a lot more confident than she felt. Seven hundred kilometers up the coast her plan had seemed simple. But now she had the sinking feeling it wouldn't be anywhere near that easy.

"Walking?"

"Yeah," said Klale wondering what the alternative might be. Did Downtown have buses? Cabs? Abruptly she wished she'd spent more of the trip doing research. Or any of it.

"I'm going to Granville Street. Come along if you want."

"Sure, thanks," said Klale, too relieved to care about the officer's ungracious manner.

As she shouldered her duffel bag and stepped out to follow the Patroller, the downpour started in earnest. Klale pulled the hood of the rain cape low over her eyes and hurried forward, grateful that she wasn't alone. The street was inky dark, there were no signs, and anyway it took most of her concentration just keeping her feet under her. She couldn't see potholes until she splashed into them. In these eerie surroundings all the stories she'd heard about Downtown started coming back to her: roamers who'd kill citizens for a phone, packs of rabid dogs, street gangs . . .

Something glowed blue in a recess between two buildings. Klale turned to look and found herself staring into the biolumed faces of three gang members with half-shaved, half-furred heads. Ghost Shadows. She'd seen pix of them on the net. Grotesque blue-lumed skin-art spilled from their eyes, noses, and ears. They were leaning against a wall smoking, and Klale caught the distinctive tobacco/marijuana scent of Fireweed. They straightened and looked her way.

Alarmed, she hurried forward. Abruptly, the captain stopped, then spoke over her shoulder, pointing to her right.

"There's hostels over there," she announced. "I'm going the other way. Good night."

There was an ominous undertone of satisfaction in her voice. Klale stood frozen in disbelief for a crucial instant as the officer strode off, then she started after the woman yelling: "Hey, you can't leave me here!"

The captain didn't stop or turn. She stepped into deep shadows beside a building, then her footsteps ceased. Klale, stumbling blindly behind, stopped to listen. She heard a click, then two seconds later, a bang, and she realized with sudden horror that she'd heard a door shutting. Too late, she remembered the light on her phone and shone it ahead. There was a door there, all right. And it was locked.

She turned, heart pounding, and realized that she'd made another mistake. Bobbing blue glows were homing in on her light. She flicked it off and hurried away, trying to make no noise, but the Ghost Shadows followed. One ran ahead much faster than she dared run in the dark, and then stopped, blocking Klale's path while two others came up behind. She had to halt. The man in front shone a dazzling light in her face for a few seconds, then flicked it off and Klale cursed silently. She hadn't closed her eyes fast enough. She was temporarily blinded.

"Where you think you're going, Zitty bitch?"

"To a hostel," she said flatly, trying to keep fear out of her voice and posture. She was unarmed and outnumbered, and could only pray that they didn't want to bludge her.

"This is Kung Lok territory. Lo fahn gotta pay toll. You paid your toll, dzo gai?" The Shadows laughed unpleasantly while the first man reached over and grabbed her chin. Klale forced herself not to duck or flinch from his stinking breath, knowing she'd be seized from behind. For the first time it occurred to her that she might be raped.

"Normally we charge fifty, but for you we give a special deal, eh?"

One of his eyes was hidden behind a night lens; the other shone ferally, its red iris contrasting with the corpse-blue horror-art crawling on his face. Klale tensed, centering herself. If she got in a couple of fast, hard blows they might decide she was too much trouble. Then, abruptly, the man holding Klale's chin looked over her shoulder, let go, and stepped back, reaching under his coat. The gang members on either side spun and Klale heard heavy steps crunch directly behind her. There was a frozen pause in which she could hear her own ragged breathing and the spatter of rain on her hood. Then the gang leader motioned and the Ghost Shadows backed away a few paces, turned and walked up the street.

Klale drew a deep breath and swung around, starting to say "thank you," then the air stopped in her throat. A gigantic figure towered over her, silhouetted against a faint, distant glow from the waterfront. She had a sudden urgent sense of menace and froze, gripped by the fear that running might trigger an attack reflex—like running from a bear. When the figure abruptly moved she flinched, but the man stepped past her, and she realized he was walking away. He was leaving her, too!

"Hey!" Without thinking she grabbed his arm. The giant man whirled, throwing her off roughly, and she stumbled back, heart pounding as she caught a glimpse of a distorted, skull-like face and twisted ear. What in the hell?!

Maybe she was better off with the Ghost Shadows. . . . No!

She took a breath and shouted over the rain. "Sir, can you take me to a hostel? Please!"

He stood like a massive statue, utterly unresponsive, so Klale repeated herself, this time gesturing with shaking hands although she doubted he could see in the dark.

Abruptly the man turned and strode off. Had he understood? wondered Klale desperately. She hesitated a second, then ran after him, muttering to herself: "Please don't be going some place worse than this!" Then, feeling the edges of hysteria: "It's OK, Klale, everything will be all right."

The roaring rainstorm seemed to have swallowed any trace of light and drowned all but muffled bytes of sound. Klale caught only snatches of distant shouts, a baby wailing, and one chilling scream. Within seconds she was completely lost. The huge man plunged into a twisting alley and then another and she followed, jogging to keep up with his long stride. He picked his way surely around potholes and piles of debris, but she tripped several times and nearly fell. After the second stumble she closed the gap between them, realizing that if she fell she might lose him utterly.

Klale smelled smoke, then passed a doorway where a small group of men huddled over a tiny flame. They'd lit a fire for heat or cooking, she realized with a tiny shock. And there must be hundreds more illicit fires fouling the air Downtown. The shabby men looked at her companion, then quickly turned away.

Finally, they rounded another corner and Klale caught sight of a big red K shining dimly through the rain. She gasped in relief. Everybody on the coast knew about the KlonDyke. Its giant red K, perched atop the ruins of a rotary restaurant, was a Vancouver landmark. And the bar's erotic floor shows were popular on CoastNet—especially with bored Fishers on long winter runs. She stumbled forward, warm tears of relief flowing into the cold rain on her cheeks.

A little to her surprise, the big man headed straight for the KlonDyke, strode up brightly lit stairs and entered white double doors. Klale, who had fallen behind, got only an impression of a sweeping dark serape before he vanished inside. She paused for a second, despite the rain, to stare at the antique neon sign over the door. It read LADIES AND ESCORTS, and a new lume sign below it announced:

THE KLONDYKE, EST. 2068
VISIBLE WEAPONS WILL BE CONFISCATED
ABSOLUTELY NO PLUGS, PIMPS, OR MISSIONARIES

Klale walked up red-carpeted steps and doors swung open releasing a familiar tumult of voices, music, and the smell of warm food, old beer, and Fireweed. She took a few paces inside, then slid her duffel bag off her aching shoulder. Behind her, the doors drifted silently shut.

A vast room stretched into dimness, three levels curving around a stage on which a jazzmer group played. The audience sat in a mayhem of battered, mismatched furniture—tables, desks, and chairs gleaned from abandoned office towers. In contrast, the long bar beside the stage gleamed with antique polished wood, brass rails, and tall, mirror-backed shelves.

Klale dug in her pocket with cold stiff fingers, pulling out a fistful of bronze and silver coins, worn almost smooth with age. As a parting present *Urchin*'s crew had given her thirty cash dollars in loonies, toonies, beavers, and eagles, and until she could sort out her banking problems, it was all she had. She hefted her bag again and approached the bar doubtfully. Hell, even the worst bars up the coast refused cash. But a sign posted on the till read: CASH SALES MINIMUM $10.

Relieved, she joined the short lineup, studying the pix on the walls as she waited. They were oil paintings of nude women, clumsily executed. Well, the Klondike Gold Rush wasn't remembered for its art, she thought, grinning to herself. Her grin faded when her order totaled $24 cash. She knew cash wasn't worth much, but this seemed outrageous. She would have to nurse her beer. And as for a hostel . . .

Well, no point worrying about it now. She grabbed her platter in one hand, and a mug in the other, and surveyed the jumble of tables for a seat. On the far side of the room the patrons were almost all women, many sitting arm in arm, and some with children. Directly opposite the stage in a railed-off section sat groups of men wearing ensilk suits—probably the gangsters the 'Dyke was so famous for. The people nearest Klale were mostly Guild. Some looked like dockers just off shift while others were dressed like tourists in neat casuals, with stylish phones hanging from their necks or clipped to sweaters. Lots of plastic here, thought Klale, wondering grimly whether the rest of the city was this expensive.

A couple rose from seats near the stage and Klale hurried over to nab their delaminating office desk. She sat on an ancient creaky chair, pushed aside dirty glasses and sampled her meal. The beer slid cool and rich over her tongue, the spicy chili tasted of real meat, and the pompommes were perfect—slices of potato and apple deep-fried to an even, golden brown. She blew on one and bit in, reveling in the crisp salty exterior and the burst of hot sweetness inside.

She was digging into the chili when she realized that the chatter around her had hushed, except for one loud, angry voice.

"What'd you say, turd? You wanna tell everyone?"

She turned. A big group of men and women sat nearby around several tables. They wore long hair in queues cinched back with silver insignia clips. Harbor Patrol officers. Some were in uniform. A big

Patroller stood, hands on hips, staring belligerently at two thin sullen Guildless men. One looked anxious to leave, but the other turned and faced the Patroller, speaking with an American accent so heavy that Klale had to strain to understand.

"I said: *Know what you call a port pig ten meters under water?*"

Silence fell across the bar and Klale saw customers turning around in alarm.

"*A clean-up!*"

Another Patroller, burly and red-faced, jumped up, grabbed the man's arm, and twisted it behind his back.

"You wanna slag the Patrol, dogshit, I'll show ya funny!"

He was drunk, realized Klale with alarm. She watched, frozen with shock, as he shoved the Guildless man to the floor. Even after her encounter with the captain she could hardly believe she was seeing Patrollers behave like this. She looked around the tables, then felt a jolt of horror as she recognized the captain who had just abandoned her Downtown. The woman sat with her arms crossed watching the altercation with narrowed eyes.

"Lick it, dogshit! *Lick it!*" the big Patroller was yelling.

Klale saw a small Afroid woman stride over from behind the bar, glaring and waving her arms in a "stop" gesture. Where are the bouncers? Klale wondered, scanning the crowd, then she spotted two muscular women in yellow shirts hurrying from the other side of the room.

Her eyes were on the bouncers when the fight started so she didn't see the first blow. When she looked back, the two flots were trying to get away. Other Patrollers leaped up to block them, shoving furniture roughly to one side.

A blue-uniformed pair of buttocks slammed against Klale's desk, shooting her meal onto the floor and toppling her chair. Klale rolled as she fell and bounced up, furious. She grabbed her bowl off the floor, scooped up spilled chili, then spotted the Patrol captain. With a red flash of rage she flung the scalding mess straight at her. The captain screamed. Patrollers whirled to stare at Klale.

"Oh, shit," she thought in sudden panic. This wasn't Prince Rupert where a third of the bar were Fishers. She was alone and there must be fifteen Patrollers.

The captain frantically swiped gobs of chili off her face, then looked at Klale with dawning recognition. Klale edged back, eyes locked with half a dozen angry Patrollers. Behind them, she saw the little bartender wave at her to back off. *No smog!* thought Klale desperately, but a pack of tables and spectators blocked her retreat. The captain lunged at Klale, slipped in the chili and lurched into a table, swearing.

Now! thought Klale. *Run!* She started to turn, then saw a fist slam into the bartender from behind, spilling the small woman to the floor. Klale reacted automatically, reversing direction and leaping straight past the captain. She landed an elbow in the surprised officer's stomach as she dove past to the bartender, who was on her knees, gasping for air. When Klale grabbed her arm, she struggled.

"Hey! Friend! I'm helping you!" yelled Klale.

The woman quit resisting and Klale gripped her arm firmly, towing her toward a large desk. A heavy boot kicked out, but Klale yanked hard and the bartender skidded across the tiles out of reach. She pushed the woman under the desk well and scooted after her, feeling a flash of exultation.

Things were improving. A defensible position and twice the odds—two against fifteen.

The bartender was still panting for air, but she turned, braced herself, and kicked out. Klale caught a flash of steel on the bottom of her boot as it smacked into an ankle, then heard a satisfying bellow. Good idea, thought Klale. She positioned her right workboot and looked for a target, but abruptly the desk above her heaved. Klale grabbed and tried to hold it down, but expert hands caught her shirt and dragged her up, then pinned her arms painfully behind her. A Patroller grabbed the bartender's boots and hauled her out upside down. Behind him Klale saw a livid, chili-streaked face.

Klale was just feeling the first edges of panic when something whistled past her face and hit the man holding the bartender. He jerked backward, dropping the bartender as he clutched his shoulder, then spun to look beyond Klale. His face slackened in terror. The grip on Klale's arms released suddenly and she staggered forward, then whirled.

Striding straight at them was a genuine tong enforcer, over two meters tall and massively built, with a shaved head, masklike altered features, and a wide, puckered scar running down over one grotesquely burned ear. A Chinese character had been seared into his forehead with a branding iron. Customers scrambled out of his path. The wounded Patroller gazed around with panic-stricken eyes as his comrades melted away. Blood rained from his shoulder, spattering the floor.

He's going to be killed! Klale thought, backing off a few steps as the sick realization hit her that bar fights here didn't end with bruises and contusions. Then a muscular woman in a yellow shirt ran between the Patroller and the enforcer and threw up her arms.

"*Freeze!*" she bellowed. "Everyone freeze, *now!*" She made a slashing gesture at the enforcer.

Christ, she's got guts, thought Klale. The bouncer was big, but the enforcer towered a head over her and his narrowed eyes were fixed on the wounded Patroller. Then Klale felt cold shock as she recognized the enforcer's profile. This was the huge man she had followed to the bar.

Then the bartender staggered up from the floor, gesturing urgently. If the bouncer seemed small in front of the enforcer, the bartender looked like a midget, but the giant glanced at her, then halted. For just an instant the bouncer looked extremely relieved. Then she turned and viewed the Patrollers.

"Who's the ranking officer?"

Those were the right words. The Patrollers glowered, but the chili-stained captain stepped forward.

"Captain Dhillon, you have one minute to get your people the hell out of this bar. That means every member of the Harbor Patrol, in uniform or not."

Klale could barely hear the reply, spoken in a cold, furious whisper.

"Mica's wounded."

"We'll med him and pass him out to you. Now get out!"

Klale couldn't see the captain's face, but remembering the livid expression well enough she stepped back several paces into a knot of other customers, hoping to escape notice. Several seconds stretched out, then the captain turned and beckoned her comrades.

Several were limping. Three were unconscious and had to be carried to the exit. Klale was surprised at that, then remembered hearing the hiss of knockout spray when the bouncers arrived.

When she looked back at the scene of the fight, bouncers had stripped off the wounded Patroller's shirt and were spraying disinfectant/sealing foam on his shoulder. Klale couldn't see the flots. The head bouncer stood watching, hands on hips, then she strode to the bar, bent down, and searched along the front of the polished wood until she found what she was looking for. She needed both hands to yank it out, and when she handed it to the enforcer Klale realized that it was a moledged throwing knife. It had been hurled with enough force to slice right through the Patroller's shoulder and then into the bar up to its hilt. Klale blanched. She'd used molecular-edged knives on fish boats, but she hated handling them. They were too damned dangerous. Knowing that one had flown past her face made her stomach twist.

The enforcer wiped his blade on a bar cloth and resheathed it. When he turned, people again hurried to clear his path. Klale stared at the brand on his forehead. Why would anyone. . . . ? Then it hit her with another sick shock. The enforcer must be a slave. She'd heard stories of slavery among the Guildless, of course, but somehow she'd never really believed them.

As the enforcer strode to the back of the room, murmurs of conversation rose. Music resumed and patrons took their seats. Klale walked back to her overturned desk and stared at the mess on the floor, starting to shake with the aftermath of adrenaline on an empty stomach. She knew she was lucky to be alive, but all she could think was that she didn't have enough cash for another meal, never mind for a place to stay. She knelt to wipe beer and chili off her duffel bag, tears stinging in her eyes.

"Excuse me."

The voice had spoken twice, Klale realized abruptly. She looked up with apprehension. A well-dressed Guild man peered down at her in friendly concern.

"Are you all right, Citizen?"

"Fine," muttered Klale, clearing her throat, "thank you, sir. The only casualty was my dinner."

The man held out his hand. He had dark good looks and curly hair, but something about his eyes hinted that he was older than his appearance. Forty at least, she guessed.

"Cedar de Groot, City Services Guild. My friends and I sit over there. We'd be pleased if you'd share our hospitality."

"Klale Renhardt, Fisher," she returned, wiping her hand awkwardly on her work pants and standing to accept his handshake. "Thank you for your kindness, Citizen," she said automatically, looking where he pointed. About a dozen men and women sat around two long tables. Most were middle aged and casually dressed, Guild-style. Several smiled in her direction. They looked like neighbors back home. She hesitated.

"Honestly, I'm very grateful, Mister de Groot, but . . ."

"Please call me Cedar. First-naming is a custom Downtown, you know. And we're all friends here at the 'Dyke. Believe it or not there are hardly ever any fights—I mean, that's the first one I've seen."

Klale shrugged ruefully. "I attract mayhem."

"Oh, it had nothing to do with you," said de Groot earnestly. "There's been bad smog on the harbor lately and people are still taxed about it, but Captain Dhillon's a pyro captain and . . ." Then it seemed to occur to him for the first time that Klale might have been joking. He peered at her, then produced a nervous chuckle. "Must be your lucky night."

Klale smiled some more, but sighed inwardly. Another thick sense of humor. Still, there was no way in hell she was going back outside. She picked up her bag and followed him.

"This is the Wooden Boat Club," he said proudly, then began introductions. Klale shook hands a dozen more times, keeping careful track of names and Guilds. No other Fishers, thank gods. De Groot pulled over a chair and wedged it in next to a lean old man with deep wrinkles and laugh creases around his eyes who introduced himself as "Ron McCaskill, City Services retired, and you look like you could use a drink, my dear."

McCaskill's hair was bleached white with age and his fingers felt old and knobby, but his shake was firm and Klale saw genuine warmth in his faded-blue eyes.

"Up coast we always say a real welcome is one you can drink," she told him, sitting down.

McCaskill laughed. De Groot looked around for a server. Several were cleaning up the overturned tables. De Groot waved at them, then stood up and called out.

"Toni!"

A woman turned and Klale recognized the small bartender from the fight. As she walked over Klale saw she was a light-skinned Afroid, with graying, close-cropped hair and a handsome, authoritative face. She looked about fifty—probably her true age, since Guildless people Downtown surely couldn't afford juvving treatments. She wore art on her left cheek and upper arms. Smears of blood were drying on her hands and leather vest, but she seemed unhurt.

"Toni, we were so worried about you!" De Groot rushed at her with outstretched arms and Klale saw a flicker of distaste cross the bartender's face.

"I'm just fine, Cedar." She removed herself from his hug. "None of you got hurt, did you? Ron?"

"Fine, dear. But Miz Renhardt lost her meal."

Toni focused on Klale with sudden recognition, and stepped forward, hand extended.

"Thank you for your help, Citizen—I'm debted to you." She gave a rueful sigh. "I'm sorry it was necessary. I should know better than to walk into a brawl."

"Uh . . . so should I," Klale admitted, shaking hands.

"Well, on behalf of the KlonDyke, I'd like to apologize for the disturbance," said Toni briskly. "We'll certainly replace your meal. Can I get you anything else?"

"A job," said Klale impulsively.

Toni's eyebrows rose and Klale flushed a little, but held the woman's sharp gaze. She needed money to live on, and she wouldn't get it from her Guild—not anymore. She expected Toni to ask if she was joking, but the bartender just gave a small nod.

"You'll have to talk to the boss tomorrow. Now, you had a pint of NarAle and what?"

"Chili." She grinned. "I gave mine to the captain."

Toni didn't return the smile. She eyed Klale gravely.

"Defiling a Revised Sikh with pork is a serious insult. I wouldn't take it lightly."

"Oh . . ."

That hadn't occurred to Klale. Not that she regretted insulting someone who'd nearly got her killed, but it was yet another jar of dislocation. Even people that looked familiar, like the Harbor Patrol, were alien here. And when Toni turned to go back to the bar she got another small shock.

A bald patch shaped like a rose had been etched into Toni's short, curly hair with follicle suppressant. Inside it, a scarlet rose was drawn on the skull, and below the rose a dollar-sized skull leaked two luminescent drops of blood down the back of her neck. The blood glistened wetly, seeming to flow with Toni's movements. Was the bartender a wirehead? But the sign outside prohibited neural plugs. Was this a souvenir, then?

Klale sat down uneasily, wondering why in hell she'd asked for a job. She wasn't this desperate. Not yet.

"I'm sure she's not devout," said de Groot.

"What?" said Klale blankly.

"Captain Dhillon. After all, she does come into the bar. She wouldn't hold anything against you. She's a fine woman, very fine."

Klale refrained from comment.

"She's my vice president on the Free Vancouver League, you know. Have you heard of the League?"

"Something to do with the Maglev proposal, isn't it?" Klale said, trying to remember what she'd heard about the railway. Promoters wanted to run a track from Vancouver through Seattle and Portland to Sacramento, where it would meet *Train Americas* with links as far south as Santiago, Chile. The power costs alone of operating such a line seemed wildly improbable to Klale, but the proposal was serious.

"We're opposing the Maglev, of course! If they open up easy travel it'll undercut local markets and ruin our Guilds, not to mention the plague vectors!"

Klale nodded. Her own mother had died in an epidemic and de Groot was old enough to remember the pandemics.

"Here." He reached out and Klale noticed a pile of leaflets on the table. He handed her one. It was from "Farmers for Better Food."

"Cheap imports may sound tempting but they threaten your health. The Farmers Guild guarantees you top bio-enhanced fresh food and medicinals. Don't risk your family's health on natural or contaminated products from foreign farms. Eat the best, and support your neighbors as we support you! Call your Guild exec today and tell them NO!"

Prominent on the bottom of the document was the logo of the Free Vancouver League.

De Groot was still talking.

". . . and Vancouver's recovering because we're independent! But selling our city—our whole coast—to a lot of . . ." he spat the word out, "businessmen, is taking us back to what ruined the whole planet."

"Enough!" interrupted a burly, glowering woman across the table. Klale mentally paged back through the introductions. Sage Hendry, an artisan from Construction Trades. "This is the Wooden Boat Club and we're here to talk about boats!"

De Groot frowned. "Come on, Sage, don't be like that! This is important. And you've got to stop closing your eyes about . . ."

The woman slammed down her glass.

"*Scut it, de Groot!* You've been spewing your Freevie politics at us for weeks and I've had it! If you want to stay here, talk boats! If you don't want to talk boats, take yourself and your bloody pamphlets to another table!"

Klale stared open-mouthed at the woman's public rudeness. In Prince Rupert, accusing another citizen of politics was inviting Guild censure, or at least a fight. De Groot sputtered, red-faced. Klale edged her chair backward.

Then old Mr. McCaskill stood up and put his hand gently on de Groot's shoulder.

"Come on, Cedar. Let me buy you a drink at the bar."

"This is my club, too! I don't see anybody else being told what they can say!"

But McCaskill had de Groot's arm in a firm grip, and his voice carried authority. "Let's give everyone a chance to unruffle, eh?"

They belonged to the same Guild, remembered Klale. Of course, in a city as big as Vancouver, that might not mean much, but these two men seemed to know each other well. As they walked away, de Groot still protesting plaintively, an awkward silence fell at the table. Klale wondered if she should leave, too; then her meal arrived.

Perhaps out of embarrassment, the remaining club members became very friendly and plunged into boat talk, apparently assuming that a Fisher would be fascinated. All of them owned wooden boats, they explained, and Sage built baidarkas. De Groot and three others had shares in a schooner. Ron McCaskill—and this even caused Klale's eyebrows to rise—owned an original clinkerbuilt skiff, its two-century-old wood lovingly enzyme-preserved.

Klale listened and tried to look interested. As far as she was concerned, a boat was a thing she worked on which was cold and uncomfortable in winter, hot and uncomfortable in summer, and inevitably broke down at the most inconvenient or dangerous time. But she asked a few polite questions, and the group eagerly aired their favorite stories. Klale had expected city people to be snobbish, but their casual acceptance relaxed her. The beer didn't hurt either.

Eventually, the floor show rescued her from a discussion of bilge pumps, and Klale discovered that the crowd was there for amateur night auditions, rated by live and CoastNet response. Many performers were very polished, building portfolios in hopes of breaking into the notoriously high-gated Entertainment Guild. And most of their numbers were erotic, ranging from suggestive to explicit, with one live sex act between two women.

Klale found the sex act intriguing at first because she'd never seen anyone try to orgasm in 6/8 time, but she quickly grew bored and studied the audience instead. It did appear that the Harbor Patrol's behavior was exceptional. The crowd was vocal but more sedate than many Fisher/Logger pubs at home. At least two-thirds of the audience was women, she noticed. She wondered if it made any difference.

"I believe I promised you a drink," said a quiet voice near Klale's shoulder, and she looked up into Mr. McCaskill's disarming smile. The old gentleman set two pints down and pulled up a chair. Klale smiled her thanks, then leaned over, keeping her voice low.

"How is Mister de Groot?"

"Upset, but he's found some friends to talk to. He asked me to apologize to you for that little parliament."

"Well it was . . . interesting. Are manners in Vancouver always this, uh, relaxed?"

Unexpectedly, McCaskill frowned. "Not in Vancouver, but Downtown isn't Guild country and when citizens come here they often behave . . . well, less courteously than they would at home." He sighed and looked over at Klale. "I'm ashamed to say that my grandson was in that brawl earlier tonight. He's about your age, just joined the Harbor Patrol. I was hoping a Patrol hitch would do him good, level him out . . ."

He trailed off somberly and Klale cast around for a less awkward topic.

"Uh, nice show."

McCaskill's expression lightened. "How do you like the dancers?" he asked.

Klale had caught the twinkle in his eye and made a show of studying the stage thoughtfully before she answered.

"Drab. Seen better in Rupert."

McCaskill grinned. But Klale had spoken loudly and across the table Sage Hendry swiveled in her chair to give Klale an indignant glare.

"Better vampers in Prince Rupert? You must be fogging. Who, for instance?"

"Me!" said Klale impulsively. She folded her arms and leaned back in her chair.

"Uh huh." Sage folded her arms, too. They were very big arms and not fat, noticed Klale suddenly. "Then why don't you show us, girl? It's a slow night. I'm sure they can find a slot."

Beside Klale, Ron McCaskill was chuckling, his face creased into deep wrinkles around keen blue eyes. Klale couldn't back down in front of those eyes.

"Taken!" she said. She reached for her phone. "Where do I sign up?"

"Stage door," said Sage, smirking as she pointed.

"Strat."

Klale put her phone away, rose, and marched over to the indicated door, feeling a ridiculous grin of exhilaration stretch across her face. It had been ages since she'd done something this tilted—since before her father's death. And she wasn't in Rupert anymore. She didn't care if she made a cret of herself. She was free.

To her surprise, the stage manager slotted her for the end of the current set. Klale logged in and selected music on the stagehand panel. Many Guild bars had banned the piece she wanted, but she wasn't surprised to find that the 'Dyke would play it. Then she took a hurried inventory of her clothes. She was wearing a long-sleeved workshirt, a pair of scrubbies, and workboots, all clean but stained and smelling faintly of fish boats. Most of the working Guilds wore clothes like that, so with a few props she could pass for a Fisher, Forester, or Builder. Or a docker, she thought with sudden inspiration. She went back into the bar and looked around for the nearest table of dockers, then walked over and asked them for a tool belt and hat. They handed the items over, apparently too surprised to refuse.

Backstage again, Klale joined a glittering herd of biolumed, sequined, and feathered dancers. They stared openly at her dockers' gear, so she batted her eyes and wiggled a hip at them, winning a few giggles. Then she concentrated on trying to remember the act she'd done over a year ago.

Her cue came much too soon, and she felt a queasy lurch of nerves. She pulled on her Cowichan sweater, tucked her hair under the Longshore touque and pulled it low on her forehead, and then took a deep breath and swaggered onto the stage. Her boots clumped loudly in the hush and she heard some murmurs in the audience. With her broad face and bulky clothes Klale looked like a man, and it wasn't hard to appear tired, sweaty, and a bit drunk. Luckily, under the hot glare of stage lights, she couldn't see the faces staring at her. The music hadn't started, so she stopped in the middle of the stage, wiped the back of her hand across her nose, hoisted her pants, scratched her crotch, and spat. She heard a couple of chuckles, then the first booming chords of the song. She whipped off her hat and yelled with the opening chorus:

"Fuck the Guild!"

The pounding party tune picked up Klale's feet. She stomped in pantomimed rage, shook her fist, and sang with the chorus:

Don't want no rules!
Don't want no tools!
Don't want no walls!
Don't want no Halls!
Fuck the Guild!

On the last word Klale jumped with both feet. Her boots smacked down resoundingly, then skidded on the slick stage. She managed to save herself by turning the skid into a spin and then shrugged her heavy sweater off her shoulders—not a moment too soon because she was roasting. She twirled the sweater by one arm and whacked it against the floor, more or less in time with the verse:

Gonna hit that long dusty road
Turn my back on the town and walk on to the stars
Gonna sing and love and build and play
My own song, my own way

The audience began clapping in time. Great! Just what Klale had hoped for. She tore off her work shirt next and flung it down in mock disgust, then she tugged off her boots and tossed them. They careened over the edge of the stage and she winced, expecting a crash or a scream.

Not your slave
Chained womb to grave
Won't toil and bleed
For my ancestors' greed
Fuck the Guild!

Pulling off her pants and dancing at the same time was difficult and she had no trouble looking ridiculous. But she managed to extricate herself, then pranced along the stage edge, vamping the audience in her Guild issue thermal underwear. She's lost the last of her nervousness and cavorted with delight, buoyed by the throbbing music.

Abruptly she realized that she was running out of tune. Oops.

This was as far as she'd stripped at the Prince Rupert Amateur Benefit Show, in front of glowering Guild execs and cheering youngers. As the final chorus began, she wiggled her ass at the audience, stepped out of her shorts, and swung them around her head. Then she peeled her bandeau off, dropped it, and danced a tattoo on top. She threw her arms in the air and spun with one foot on the underwear, catching a glimpse of herself in the mirrored stage backdrop. Her square-built, muscular body gleamed white, except for the dark Fisher's tan on her face and lower arms, and the wild tangle of red hair flying around her head. Damn, she'd forgotten to comb it.

> No more fears!
> No more walls!
> Time to choose!
> Time to leave!
> A new world to build
> Fuck the Guild!

At the last bars, she threw out her arms, and bowed, laughing, panting, and exuberantly naked except for her navy wool socks.

2

Toni the bartender put away the last of the condiments, gave the bar's surface a final unnecessary wipe, and looked around to see that everything was in place. But she couldn't concentrate.

She felt more shaken by that fight than she liked to admit. It was a harsh reminder that she wasn't twenty-five or thirty anymore. And—apparently—that she hadn't learned much in the intervening years. Walking into a scrum at any time would have been stupid, but now was a particularly bad time to make cretting mistakes. The Maglev issue had ignited old feuds and the KlonDyke would need both caution and luck to maintain its precarious neutrality.

She sighed and trundled out the cranky, ancient coin sorter—a big metal gizmo on screeching casters which had apparently been cobbled together from an ancient fare box. She hated this job the most and always put it off until last. She scooped handfuls of coins from the till into the hopper where they slid, with loud rattles and *chings*, through slots and cogwheels and then dropped into stacks. After a few minutes and one jam caused by a worn coin, Toni had five stacks to reconcile with cash sales. Of course, her totals almost never matched. The sorter made mistakes and so did the bartenders. Well, she shouldn't have a big recount tonight. The fight and the rain had damped trade down.

Footsteps crossed the stage, echoing in the empty bar, then boots thumped loudly as the security chief jumped off onto the main floor.

"Locked tight," she called out, walking toward Toni. With a heavy coat that emphasized her broad shoulders, and her black watch cap pulled down over her short, blonde hair, Alberta looked every inch a soldier. She halted in front of the bar.

"I told the Boss to ban the Patrol. Permanently. Arrogant, poxing shits."

Alberta sounded angry, but not very hopeful. She knew the KlonDyke was in no position to offend the Harbor Patrol. Toni just nodded as she checked the sorter's sums against the till. By some miracle the totals agreed. She pulled her attention away for a second and poured Alberta a half pint, sliding it across the bar. Then she unclipped the loonie rack, grabbed some tubes, and started stacking coins into the first tube.

Alberta held up her glass and stared into the dark amber ale.

"And I want de Groot and his goddamned Freevies out, too! Mary's wasting her time trying to smooth things between de Groot's league and her Downtown friends. That fight was nothing. We're gonna see slagging over that damned Maglev."

Toni nodded again. Alberta took a deep draught, then put the glass back down on the bar and gave Toni a wary glance.

"You all right?" Alberta asked.

"Yeah. But I'm lucky that Zit kid pulled me out. She asked for a job, by the way."

"Here?" Alberta looked startled. "She lesbian?"

"Didn't ask."

"Well, it doesn't matter," said Alberta, shrugging. "A Guild kid wouldn't last."

"You did."

Alberta bristled. "I was army and this is work I know. Anyway, you don't want a brawler. Girl was lucky not to get hurt."

"So was I," said Toni dryly.

The bouncer made a rueful face.

"Yeah. No thanks to me, nursing a goddamned puking drunk in the toilet. I got no love for that ghoul of Choi's, but he came in useful tonight." She gave Toni a piercing look. "Defending you."

Toni ignored the edge in Alberta's voice and kept her face bland as she snapped together a tube of twenty-five loonies and dropped it in the cash safe. She didn't blame Alberta for loathing the enforcer. But Alberta must be upset. She rarely mentioned Blade or his owner, Choi, within Toni's earshot. Maybe she believed the rumors that Toni worked for Choi.

Abruptly Alberta spoke. "Boss thinks the 'Dyke is being tapped."

Toni was startled into looking up at her.

"*What?*"

"Yeah. But she's got no proof. Just a 'bad feeling.' "

Toni felt prickles of worry in her gut. From most people she'd dismiss "bad feelings," but not from the KlonDyke's manager. Mary had uncanny intuition.

"If you're asking my opinion, I'd pay attention. Mary has good instincts."

"Yeah, well, she got me worried. Anybody taps tong meetings here they got hot plastic data. But I've gone over the meeting rooms with a third level and checked every goddamn signal going in and out of the building. Nothing. Now Mary's bringing in a datadoc to look for a snare inside. And she wants me to watch all the sets."

"All of them?" said Toni incredulously. "There must be two dozen."

"Thirty-one," scowled Alberta. "I'm supposed to watch for 'suspicious activity,' whatever the hell that is."

So why was Alberta telling her this? Toni wondered uneasily.

"It's gotta be Choi," said Alberta.

Toni felt herself tense. That was why. She realized that she'd caught her breath and resumed packing coins before she spoke, keeping her voice calm and level.

"Choi makes sense. I'm sure he wants to know what happens at Consortium meetings. He's also devious as hell. I can see him setting a very sophisticated tap and then using the data so carefully he doesn't get caught."

"That's what I figured."

"Any other suspects?"

Alberta snorted.

"Sure. Screaming Eagles. Any of the independents. Factions inside the tongs. Cascadia Rail for all the hell I know." She looked over at Toni, then said abruptly: "I raked your apartment today—checked your set and then did a level three search."

Toni's gaze snapped up. Her apartment! She never let anybody in there! She pictured Alberta intruding on her sanctuary and a wave of white rage hit her. Dimly, underneath her wrath, she knew that Alberta was only doing her job, but it didn't change how she felt. She had to wait long seconds, forcing her breath in and out, before she could speak through clenched teeth.

"What did you find?"

Alberta shifted uncomfortably on her stool. "Nothing. You're clean, far as I can tell. Look, I'm sorry, but I had to check. I think our tapper is Choi and I think he's using someone." She took a deep breath. "I especially don't trust Blade and I don't want you letting him in here anymore after hours."

Toni's heart pounded in her ears. She held herself very, very still. "Are those Mary's orders?"

"No." Alberta scowled. "She 'trusts your judgment.' But I don't."

"Then run fucking surveillance on him!"

"Done it!" snapped Alberta. "And I've checked that office, floor to ceiling, practically taken the set apart. But I don't want Blade here. Anywhere. Anytime. And that's what I'll keep telling the Boss."

"Fine. You do that!" hissed Toni. She leaned down and slammed the cash safe shut, then kicked the coin sorter back under the bar. She looked up at Alberta. "You planning to try to stop me?"

Even to her own ears, Toni's voice sounded dangerous. Alberta looked at her for long seconds, then let out a hissing breath.

"Not tonight. Anyway, your damn ghoul's here already, waiting in the back." She stepped stiffly away from the bar and zipped her coat up. "You sure got him well trained."

Abruptly Toni's self-control snapped.

"I don't 'train' anyone!" she yelled. She whirled, grabbing her coffee mug, and stomped off toward the office. At the side door she turned and spat back over her shoulder, "And you fucking stay out of my apartment!"

Hot coffee slopped out of the mug, splashing Toni's hand and the lobby carpet as she crossed to the office, cursing steadily. Her own shrill words echoed in her head, making her all too aware that she'd made a fool of herself. Goddamn Alberta! And goddamn her own cretting temper!

In the office, she hurled herself into the chair and pounded the desk a few times. Then she leaned back, massaging her temples, and tried to assemble some calm. Don't think about the apartment, she told herself. Or the brawl. Or Downtown. But it was hard not to. Toni knew where her rage came from—fear. Fear that it was all falling apart.

Lately she'd been dreaming about her childhood again. She'd grown up with gang war: bombs spewing dust and shrapnel and blood onto the streets, children maimed in sudden crossfire, whole tenements wiped out by broadly aimed biologicals. She still remembered the stench from a block where contaminated bodies were left to rot because no one dared go near. The smell permeated her whole building for weeks and seeped into her nightmares.

This is not Chicago, she told herself, then sat back in the chair, slowed her breathing and focused on how the mountains had looked outside her window this morning. Row upon row of trees, on mountain after mountain, fading into infinity . . .

It was an old meditation routine and after a few minutes she began to level out. When she felt stable she booted the set and started the daily report.

A moment later the office door opened, but Toni didn't look up. She moved her chair slightly closer to the desk, making more space on her right between the chair and the curtained windows. Blade came up behind her, kneeled down next to the chair and waited. It was always an odd sensation. The giant enforcer, sitting back on his heels on the floor, still matched her height in the chair.

She switched the set to voice mode and took her coffee cup in her left hand, placing her right hand on the chair's armrest, palm up. Blade placed his left hand beside hers. She turned her hand over, then moved it on top of his. There was a pause, then very slowly and cautiously he curled up his fingers, engulfing her hand in his.

As she sat in the semidarkness listening to the whispering set and watching gaudy graphs flow up and down, Toni finally felt her anger and fear fade. Holding hands was comforting. Ironic, really, since she'd designed the routine for him. She blinked, then realized that she'd almost nodded off. That outburst of temper had drained her. She pulled herself awake with an effort and refocused her attention on analyses and supply orders.

She didn't look at Blade's face. After so many years she didn't have to. When emotions leaked out from behind that inhuman mask there was pain, anguish, and a deep, pathetic helplessness. She didn't like to look anymore. It reminded her too much of the others she'd worked on. And it never changed. He always looked the same, never varied the routine.

Alberta was right not to trust Toni. Toni couldn't be trusted by anyone, even Blade. Especially Blade. She had trained him, just as certainly as she had trained the others. And she wouldn't hesitate to use him just as callously as his master did.

3

Klale woke to cold air brushing her face, the harsh scream of seagulls, and chickens clucking. For a moment she thought she was back on her fish boat. But the hard surface under her shoulder didn't rock, and . . . chickens?

She opened her eyes to find herself lying on a dirty concrete floor amid a litter of old plaster and paint flakes. Bright morning light and air poured through a big opening which had once held sliding glass doors. Beyond was a tiny, cement-railed ledge, too small to be called a balcony. Twentieth century, Klale decided, sitting up cautiously, and running a hand over her throbbing temples. Nothing else except emergency shelters used so much ugly bare concrete.

She crawled stiffly to her feet, trying to ignore her headache. She'd slept in her roll with all her clothes on, and she felt hot and sweaty despite the cool air. She padded to the window in her socks and looked over the rail.

Her eyes widened in surprised delight. The decrepit towers around her were enveloped in vibrant green life. Planters projected precariously everywhere, balconies and windows spilled vines and blossoms into the air, and bird netting draped everything. Shafts of morning sunlight fell between the jungled buildings, sending up plumes of steam from the kitchen gardens and a cacophony of sounds: traffic, voices, music, chickens, goats, babies. She looked straight down. She was on the fifth or sixth floor of the KlonDyke, she decided—the only naked concrete tower in the area.

She looked along the street, trying to get her bearings, and caught a glimpse of blue harbor and mountains to her right. That was north. The street itself was a dirt and gravel trench, half choked with vendor carts and sheds. It ran between old buildings and piles of quake rubble overbuilt with crude shanties. Klale remembered the cooking fires last night with a thrill of strangeness. In Prince Rupert the Collapse was ancient history, but here she felt as if she'd thrown back fifty years. Poverty, natural disasters, and violence were suddenly immediate. So were the smells, she noticed abruptly. Under the cooking smells was the unmistakable whiff of chicken shit and human excrement. It made her suddenly queasy.

She moved back in from the balcony, trying to force her muzzy brain to work. What was she doing here anyway? She concentrated hard, then pieces of last night started returning with unnatural lethargy.

The Wooden Boat Club had toasted Klale's performance with another round of beer, then the dance floor had opened and she'd had at least one dance with everyone. She even had a dim recollection of pulling old Mr. McCaskill out onto the floor. It wasn't until two A.M. that she had remembered she still didn't have a place to stay. When she confessed her problem to Cedar de Groot, he offered to pay for a tatami room on the third floor and then got himself into an anxious, tangled explanation of how he wasn't propositioning her. He would absolutely never do that, well, no, actually he didn't mean that—she was a very attractive woman and he certainly would like to do that, that is, if he were the type of man who did that, which he wasn't. Well he was, he meant, he wasn't the other kind, except that . . . Klale was rescued by Toni, the bartender, who gave her permission to camp on a vacant floor in the tower. It had struck Klale as an adventure at the time, but in daylight the room looked sordid. Holes in the floor and walls revealed where wiring, plumbing, and even bolts had been stripped out. She saw a scattering of ashes where someone had built a fire, and a stain against one wall which looked suspiciously like piss. A roach scuttled across the floor and Klale shuddered. She immediately shook her sleeves and pant legs, then bent over and ran her hands through her hair. Nothing fell out, but she still felt polluted.

She needed a shower. And money. Damn the Fisher Bank. Well, she'd just have to keep calling them until they fixed her account.

She pulled her phone out of her shirt and entered a query, then waited. There was no response. Huh? She tried again, then checked diagnostics. Her phone said it was sending fine, but it wasn't receiving. Great, she had a broken phone, too!

In a real rasp now, she looked around for her boots. Her duffel bag lay on the floor next to her roll, but there were no boots in it. She tried to think back. The last time she could remember seeing her boots was when she threw them off the stage. Damn, damn, damn! She looked futilely around the empty room once more, then crammed her sleeping roll into her bag, shouldered it, and padded out of the room in stocking feet.

An empty door frame led into a rough concrete stairwell. She walked gingerly down several flights to a fire door. Beyond it, the stairwell was freshly painted, with carpeted runners. She descended another four flights, and tried the door marked GROUND. It opened onto a red-carpeted lobby with old-fashioned chairs and potted plants.

The door shut behind her with a sharp click. Klale whirled and grabbed the handle, but it had locked. Damn her groggy brain! She looked around. The street door was barred with a wrought-iron gate, so she started trying other doors. The second one opened.

This was a side entrance into the bar. The big room stood silent and dim. A few harsh shafts of sunshine fell through ornately barred windows, spotlighting pieces of furniture and floor that looked somehow grubbier than they had last night. Klale hesitated, wondering what to do, then caught sight of Toni working at the till. She let the door close behind her and walked over to the bar.

"Good morning, Miz, uh . . ."

"They're never good," growled Toni without looking up. Klale hesitated, taken aback, then tried again.

"I'm sorry, but we weren't really introduced."

"One name only. Toni," the woman informed her. Her clothes looked like the same ones she'd been wearing last night, though the blood was gone. Was she still up? Toni entered commands at the till with one hand and gripped a large mug with the other.

"Klale Renhardt," said Klale, wondering how she could politely address a person with only one name. Informally, she decided. "Please call me Klale. That's K-L-A-L-E. Rhymes with daily and ukulele."

Toni grunted. Klale studied her apprehensively, wondering if she was annoyed or if this was normal Downtown behavior.

A black cat leaped onto the polished bar, stepped delicately over to Klale and gave her an expectant yellow-eyed stare, so Klale reached out and scratched its silky head. She got an immediate rumbling response.

"And who are you?" she asked the cat.

"She's a goddamned nuisance."

"Awww," said Klale, grinning as she decided that Toni just had a gruff style. "What's her name?"

"Pauline Johnson," said Toni. She made a few more entries, then bent over and came up holding a pair of boots.

"I believe these are yours."

"Oh, thank you!"

Toni viewed Klale's delight through narrow eyes as she slid the boots across the bar.

"Guild boots are popular. Be careful where you throw them."

Klale stared at her blankly for a second, then Toni's meaning sunk in.

"You mean people Downtown steal clothes?"

"And food and anything else they can get."

Klale flushed, feeling suddenly very naive. She grabbed her boots and bent over. A stab of pain shot through her head and she groaned.

"Hangover?" asked Toni.

"Yeah. I got swilled last night—but I thought I was doing OK until Mister de Groot bought me that fruit thing."

"Cup of Dreams?"

"Yeah. What's in that?"

"Fruit, spices, honey, and hash oil."

Klale groaned again. "I thought he was fogging me."

Toni's mouth twitched slightly at the corners. "Coffee?"

"Sure."

Klale preferred tea, but anything hot and strong would help. Hash! No wonder her brain felt so slow.

Toni reached back, pulled a mug from the shelf, and filled it from a thermal flask by the till. She pushed the cat out of the way, slid the cup over to Klale, and dug out cream and honey with practiced motions. Klale pulled up a stool and inhaled, then looked up in surprise.

"It's real coffee!"

"The best. Jamaican. It's my own, but the KlonDyke's is good, too. Despite what you may have seen last night, this is a lume establishment."

She turned back to the till and Klale sat quietly, savoring the rich flavor. She didn't much like chicory coffee, but this liquid was coiting all over her taste buds.

As she sipped, she studied Toni. The bartender must have been a stunning young woman. A natural, too—at least Klale didn't recognize any common features from old face-sculpting menus. Toni still had high cheekbones, long-lashed dark eyes, and smooth brown skin, but she also wore evidence of a hard life. Her nose had been broken and there were faint scars along her jaws and around one eye. The scars and her clothes—sleeveless shirt, well worn leather vest and hempen pants tucked into tall boots—made her look American and very tough, but she spoke educated English with no accent. Klale knew there were a few Americans in Vancouver Guilds but Toni wouldn't be at the 'Dyke if she was Guild. Was she an outcast? Klale looked surreptitiously at the inside of Toni's arms and thought she spotted faint drug stains. And the art on the back of her head hinted at a neural plug. Those were certainly reasons for being expelled.

Toni looked up.

"Pass over your phone."

"Sure, but I'm empty," Klale said awkwardly, then remembered that Toni would know that from last night. She unlocked the cord around her neck and passed the phone over. Toni ran it past the till's validator and handed it back. Klale stared at the GD$11 credit on the read-out, then looked at Toni in confusion.

"Your cut of the earnings from amateur night," said Toni. "You get fifty percent of the first thousand downloads, then seventy-five percent after that, paid weekly until your act is dropped from the local library. You'll get an automatic credit from now on."

"Strat!" said Klale with delight, thumbing confirmation and then slinging the phone back around her neck. She'd been wondering how to manage until she could sort out the mix-up with her banking.

"You didn't know about that?" asked Toni.

"Hell, no. I only got into town last night. And I sure wasn't planning to come here and throw my clothes off."

"Or ask for a job?"

"Job? Oh, right!" said Klale, startled. She'd completely forgotten. Hell. She wasn't so sure she wanted it. And she wasn't prepared for an interview.

"Ready to meet the boss?"

"Sure," Klale told her. "Well, in a minute." She put her coffee down, dug a comb out of her pocket, and tried to force her hair into some kind of order. As usual, the comb got stuck in her wiry waves, and hair jutted out in all directions, so Klale finally tied it back. That would hold for a while, although it always worked loose eventually. She gulped down the rest of her coffee and stood, tucking her shirt nervously into her pants, then followed Toni through the lobby to a door labeled OFFICE.

Klale half expected some squalid cubicle with a sleazy business-man inside, but the office was a big, homey room. On her right, a couch and old-fashioned upholstered chairs surrounded a coffee table. To her left against the curtained windows, stood a big desk. Behind the desk a plump Native Indian woman with a deeply seamed brown face looked up from the netset. She wore her hair mostly gray and she'd let her face age. She looked about sixty. When she stood and came around the desk, Klale was vividly reminded of the Tsimshian elders back home. A bone medallion hung on a leather thong around her neck, and her flowing crimson smock suit gave a regal air to her walk. She clasped Klale's hand with a warm, steady grip, and brown eyes gazed at her with shrewd assessment.

"*Klahowya,*" tried Klale.

The woman's face creased into a sparkling smile.

"*Klahowya.* And I'm afraid that's all the Chinook I know. I'm Mary Tungsten Smarch, manager of the KlonDyke. Everyone calls me Mary or the Boss."

Her warmth was contagious and Klale smiled back.

"Klale Renhardt." She nearly added Fisher, but bit the word back in time and hurried on. "Well, actually my registered name is Margaret, but I chose Klale. It rhymes with 'ukulele' and it means blue in Chinook. Sort of a joke about my hair . . ."

I'm babbling, thought Klale nervously. The Boss gestured, and Klale hastily took an old armchair. Toni sat on the couch, propping her boots on the battered coffee table. The comfortably shabby furniture reminded Klale of home. The crocheted throw on the back of the chair even smelled faintly of cat.

"Toni says you're from Prince Rupert," said the Boss. It was a routine opening, but her eyes and voice showed genuine interest. "I don't suppose you know Francesca George?"

Klale glowed with unexpected delight.

"Sure I do! She taught me fifth grade. We have integrated schools in Rupert—the two big Guilds and the Natives—and I used to spin with the Gitksan kids a lot. Do you have family there?"

"A few friends. I'm Tlingit from Teslin, up in the Yukon."

"Everybody says Teslin's beautiful," said Klale truthfully. "But I haven't been there . . . or anywhere that's not a seaport."

The Boss's smile took on an edge of wistfulness. "Teslin's very beautiful and I miss it. But I've been down here thirty years now. I don't think I'll ever move back."

Does she feel at home here? Klale wondered suddenly. How did she cope with moving from a tiny community like Teslin to a big city where she was always surrounded by *holoima tilikum*—strangers?

"So what brings a Fisher from Prince Rupert to Vancouver's notorious lesbian/bent bar?"

Klale took a deep breath. "I left my Guild." Now that she actually said the words aloud they scared her.

"And you came to the city looking for an independent job," said Mary. She exchanged a weary look with Toni.

"People say you can get them down here," said Klale hearing the uncertainty in her own voice.

"Some small merchants over in Vancouver hire help," said Mary. "The competition is very steep. The KlonDyke hires servers, but we don't pay wages, Klale. Our servers get meals and tips, and free rent if they want to live in the tower."

"Oh," said Klale, taken aback. "Uh, what do tips come to?"

"I'd say the average is eight hundred cash dollars a month."

Klale's eyebrows rose. That was far more money than she'd ever earned, she thought in puzzlement, then remembered that cash dollars were worth far less than real ones. Well, if it only added up to two hundred dollars, that was still close to a Guild stipend. Was it enough to live on? Abruptly she realized that she had no idea. Her Guild had always covered her living expenses. Still, if she squeezed in all the work hours she could, it might be enough.

"Dancers earn more, of course," said Toni. "Your audition was good enough to earn you two spots a week, but you'd have to work hard to keep your ratings up."

"I could do that," said Klale, hope rising. The dance spot had paid Global Dollars.

"What did you do for your Guild?" the Boss asked.

"I worked the boats—got my first mate's ticket for inside waters two years ago, and just wrote my mate's ticket for deep water boats—and I also worked maintenance and fish farm in the off-season. I have some cafeteria experience, too. All members take shifts. And I've helped run socials. I have a good memory, I'm strong, and . . ." she groped for something else that might be relevant and finished, a little desperately, "I'm good with numbers."

The Boss looked amused.

"We *do* have pads," she noted, and Klale blushed, hoping that her hair hadn't worked loose yet and that she didn't look too slovenly. Klale liked her own wide, freckled features, but she knew she wasn't beautiful or glamorous and she'd noticed that most of the 'Dyke's servers were.

"Some of our servers also sell fucks upstairs when they're off duty," put in Toni in a neutral voice.

Klale looked at her with alarm.

"I won't do that," she said, wondering if that had been an offer. Hell, for all she knew, these women were pimps. But the Boss was smiling. She exchanged a cryptic look with Toni, like friends who'd worked together so long they didn't have to talk, then turned back to Klale.

"It's been busy lately and we're a bit shorthanded. I'll take you on trial for two weeks, if that's acceptable."

Klale gaped.

"Miz . . . Mary? Are you saying that I'm hired?"

"If you pass the health exam, yes."

"That's it? No formware?"

"That's it."

For a second she was at a loss for words, then she broke into a delighted grin. She'd found a job already!

"Pyro! Thank you! I always dreamed of a work assignment with no fish!"

Even Toni smiled faintly at her enthusiasm. Then Mary became serious.

"Now, this is our map, Klale. The KlonDyke is run by SisOpp, a venture of Sisters Residential Co-op. This is not a Guild. Income isn't shared. There are no work teams. We don't provide any services. Exchanging cash tips is your problem—we aren't money changers. Download fees and plastic tips are paid out every Sunday by myself or Toni. You provide the money card—or in your case we can credit your net account. The backstage manager assigns dance slots on Monday. Toni assigns server shifts. Hours are unpredictable and can be very long. If trade is slow, we close early. If it's busy, we stay open all night.

"We enforce our house rules. No plugs, no preaching, and no picking up tricks or freefucks on our time. You're expected to be on time and sober. The bartenders, the stage manager, and the bouncers will give you orders, and I back them up."

"And talking of bouncers . . ." she locked eyes with Klale's, "we expect you not to apply chili to our customers, even rude ones."

Klale nodded sheepishly, impressed that the Boss knew about that.

Mary stood and Klale followed suit, holding out her hand. They shook Guild-brother style—hand to elbow.

"Now, remind me, Klale. What's Chinook for 'welcome'?"

"Kloshe tumtum mika chako."

"Ah . . . hmm. Exactly. Welcome to the KlonDyke."

Klale left in a happy daze. She followed Toni back into the bar and begged more coffee, then perched on the bar stool while Toni poured.

"Still have your citizenship?" Toni asked suddenly.

"Huh? Oh yeah. People leave Rupert all the time—itchy feet—and they usually end up back home sooner or later. It's not a big crash anymore. It's just that without work credits I don't get a stipend." She gave Toni an anxious glance, wondering if Guild expulsion was a touchy subject for the bartender. She couldn't see any sign of it on Toni's face; still she'd rather find another topic.

"Guess you don't speak Chinook," she tried.

"I don't know any Native languages."

"Chinook's not a language, really—just a trading pidgin from the early days on the coast," Klale told her, warming to the subject. "It died out, then revived as a fad with Nations kids. It's very easy to learn and there's no real-time phone translation available so it's like having a secret language. And the words are fun. Like *muckamuck*. That's the noun food, or the verb eat. Your head cook is the *tyee muckamuck*—food chief. And you," she shot Toni a wide grin, "are the *tyee lum*. And last night I was *pahtl-lum*—drunk."

Toni smiled a little.

"See, that's the strat thing about Chinook," Klale continued buoyantly. "There's just a few hundred words, but it covers all the basics—drinking, gambling, insults, deceit. . . . You can't explain how to repair a boat in Chinook, but you can steal the boat, traffic it, and then hold a big party."

"Sounds useful," said Toni dryly. Then, giving her a sharp look: "Know where you're going to live?"

"Uh . . . no."

"People who work here can stay in the tower. This used to be Sisters' Co-op before they built the new one, and they tore out everything salvageable. But with some work you can fix a room and hook up to the building's power and water. SisOpp charges a monthly fee for those, but it's cheaper than local rents."

I could do that, thought Klale. Then something struck her.

"Rents? I thought everyone Downtown was squatting."

Toni snorted.

"Tongs and gangs collect rent. And lomo—protection money. If you plan to sleep in the tower again tonight, ask for security clearance on the doors."

"I may have to," said Klale, sighing. "I've got to sort out some bank bugs, but my phone's not working this morning."

"It wouldn't be. The 'Dyke is jammed."

"What?" said Klale stupidly.

"This is Downtown's lumest gangster bar, or didn't you know that either?" Toni sipped her coffee, looking amused.

"Uh, well, yeah, I'd heard something, but I didn't realize. . . ."

"All the tongs come here to traffic, so we have a highly toxic jamming field. No remotes of any kind work on site, or for about a block around. Everything is hard-wired. If you want to call out, you have to use a pay phone."

Klale had noticed a dozen antiquated pay phones near the toilets and wondered at their popularity.

She ran a hand through her hair, accidentally tugging big tufts loose from the tie. She sighed and pulled it all loose, then slid off the stool and picked up her duffel bag.

"I really should go and let you get back to work."

"Come back at four."

"Oh . . . right!"

"And get some clothes."

"Clothes?" she said, looking down at herself. Did she look that bad?

"You're dressed like a citizen. Get a cheap shirt and pants. Any street vendor. Pay cash if you can and save your plastic."

"Right."

"And never wear your phone to work, even under your shirt. You can't use it here anyway and it marks you as Guild."

"OK. Thanks."

Impulsively she dropped her bag, walked around behind the bar, and gave Toni a big hug.

"Thank you! Thank you for the place to stay and the job and the advice and everything!"

Toni's shoulders felt like stone. Oops, thought Klale. She doesn't like to be touched. She unwrapped herself carefully and backed off a step.

"Sorry," she said. "I didn't mean to attack you. It's just that you're my first new friend in Vancouver and you've been apex. I really didn't expect the job, you know."

"I know," said Toni. Did she look just the faintest bit flustered? She picked up her coffee mug and regained her stool. "I liked your looks."

Klale stared a second, then raised a questioning eyebrow. Toni met her gaze, but didn't flirt back.

"You'll be a change of pace around here," she said brusquely, then turned back to her work.

4

"You starting Klale tonight?"

"Yes," said Toni neutrally, wondering why Mary had called her back to the office. Was she upset by Toni's apparent interest in Klale? It seemed unlikely. Toni poured coffee from her thermal mug and passed a cup to Mary, giving her an assessing glance. Mary looked worried. She dragged the office chair around to the front of the desk and sat down next to Toni.

"Heard the news about the Harbor Patrol?"

"No."

"Dhillon's first officer is missing. There's a big search on, and lots of spec he was killed by smugglers."

"Oh, hell," said Toni with feeling.

"Exactly. I've been working so hard to improve relations between the Patrol and the flots. This could put us back years." Mary sighed. "And it gets worse. If I don't ban the Patrol from the bar after that fight, I lose face. I want an apology and damages, but I can't afford to demand that when I'm not going to get it. Not right now, anyway. And I don't dare ban them when we've got bigger brews coming."

"Bigger?" asked Toni, suddenly apprehensive.

"Tong brews." Mary's face turned grim. "I'm afraid the Consortium is going to splinter over the Maglev."

Toni felt her stomach sink. The alliance between the three big tongs had kept peace Downtown for decades. If it fractured, there would be war.

"I thought they all oppose the Maglev. If we get the railroad, we also get the Guilds back."

"The Viet Ching are certainly opposed," said Mary. "When the city takes over, they'll step on scab factories, drugs, plugs, and pimping. But I hear rumors that the Sun Yee On is trying to lay legal claim to the Downtown property they've been slumlording for decades. They could make a huge profit. And the Kung Lok might go for it if they thought they could expand their smuggling operations onto the Maglev . . ."

Toni frowned worriedly at Mary.

"It sounds like you think the railroad's coming."

In the ensuing pause she could hear traffic noise from Robson Street, faint cries of hawkers, and a loud wheezy rumble from Pauline Johnson, curled up in Mary's lap. Mary stroked the cat automatically, without looking, and her voice was low and troubled.

"Toni, my reading of the portents is that the Maglev will go through. Older people are afraid of losing everything they fought and starved for, but young people are eager for change."

Mary's face usually glowed with an inner serenity that drew people to her, but now she looked tired, worried, and every bit her age. Toni found it unexpectedly frightening. She relied a great deal on Mary's stability. Also, she respected Mary's shrewdness. If Mary foresaw the Maglev, it was coming. And if she foresaw tong war . . . Toni nearly shuddered, then realized that Mary was watching and pulled herself under control.

"What are you going to do?" she asked.

"Fight for the Guildless, of course. We must get the Vancouver Council of Guilds and Cascadia Rail to agree to jobs and housing now—before they close any agreement—or the flots and squats will be trampled."

Toni nodded and Mary continued.

"Even without the Maglev it's only a matter of time before Downtown is redeveloped. And we need that. The population's doubled since I moved here, and the buildings are falling apart. The

Council of Guilds *must* recognize their community responsibility."

Then she gave a long sigh.

"Sorry. You've heard that speech. I shouldn't let this rasp me so much." She looked down in her lap and scratched the cat's chin. "Worrying doesn't do me any good, does it, Pauline?"

The purrs grew louder. Toni rolled her eyes. She'd never understood Guild people's gushing sentimentality about animals, especially dangerous ones like dogs. Where she grew up, you killed animals before they attacked you or stole your food. The KlonDyke's cat was useful for catching vermin, but there was no need to make a pet of it.

She leaned forward and refilled her coffee cup while Mary googled and fussed. When Toni looked back, Mary was studying Toni's face.

"You look tired, dear. You've been filling in for me too much lately, and I'm afraid it's just going to get worse." She leaned forward with gentle urgency. "Why not take the title of assistant manager? And the share in SisOpp?"

Toni shook her head brusquely.

"Sorry. Being a bartender is all I want." She paused, trying to find something more to say to the disappointment in Mary's eyes. She wished like hell Mary hadn't asked again. It always seemed that Mary wanted more than she was willing to give—or able to. More commitment. More involvement. More intimacy.

Mary looked like she wanted to pursue it further, but the netset chimed with a priority call. Mary rolled her chair backward and reached for the audio tab.

"Mary Smarch."

"Good morning, Miz Smarch."

It was a man's voice, very formal, with a slight Chinese accent. A tong exec, guessed Toni, seeing wariness shadow Mary's face. Mary shooed the cat off her lap.

"Good morning, Mr. Choi."

The blackmailer! No wonder his voice was unfamiliar. Toni had heard a great deal about Choi Shung Wai, but it was all secondhand. He never went out in public and on the rare occasions he phoned the 'Dyke he dealt directly with Mary.

Toni stood up quietly. Choi would insist on privacy, and she certainly didn't want to interfere. It had been Blade, Choi's slave, who delivered Toni to the KlonDyke ten years before and she still had no idea why, or even how much Choi knew about her. He hadn't attempted blackmail, so it was possible that he hadn't traced her past, but he could have done so and decided to reserve the data for some future use—a possibility that made her very afraid. She had no desire to remind him of her existence.

"It was most obliging of you to make yourself available so promptly, Miz Smarch."

"I am always pleased to talk to you, Mr. Choi," said Mary smoothly. "I was just meeting with my head bartender. I assume you would prefer to speak to me alone?"

"I understand that you place great confidence in Miz Toni as a valued employee."

Toni was three steps away from the desk, but stopped abruptly when she heard her name and looked back at Mary with alarm. Mary raised her eyebrows and shrugged helplessly. She hadn't been expecting it either.

"I trust her implicitly," she told Mr. Choi.

"Very well. She may remain."

Damn, thought Toni, feeling fear twist in her stomach. Undoubtedly Choi had dossiers on the 'Dyke's staff, but he'd never paid attention to anyone except the Boss before.

Mary passed her a spare headset from the desk drawer and snicked the hard-wire jack into place. Then she moved her chair around beside Toni's and widened the scanner field to encompass both of them. Toni sat, took a deep breath, and slid the headset over her eyes and ears.

She sat in a traditional Chinese room with paper-screened walls and a polished hardwood floor. It should have felt serene, but it seemed severe instead. The only decoration in the spacious room was a calligraphy scroll, and the only furnishings were an elaborately inlaid antique cabinet, and a large mahogany desk, which she and Mary faced.

Behind the desk sat Choi Shung Wai, looking like a classical Chinese painting of an elderly man in a high-collared black silk tunic.

His only visible concession to the twenty-second century was an elaborate gold inlay phone hanging around his neck. It looked like an antique medallion. Arranged meticulously on the highly polished surface in front of him were a sheet of rice paper, a set of calligraphy brushes, and a black porcelain tea service. The netset wasn't visible— probably edited out of the image, decided Toni. To her left, carved lattice windows opened onto a courtyard. The bamboo-fringed yard looked convincing in every detail, but it was almost certainly a simulation. Mr. Choi lived in an underground bunker.

A formal smile folded sharp creases into Choi's parchment skin, but his eyes remained icy. He gave Toni an assessing gaze for a second too long before turning his attention to Mary.

"Perhaps you will forgive me if I drink tea in front of you?"

"In fact, we were just having coffee," said Mary. "Perhaps we could join you."

"By all means."

While Mr. Choi poured steaming tea from his pot, Toni snapped up her right goggle, fetched their coffee mugs, then slid the eyepiece into place again.

"May I inquire about trade at the KlonDyke, Miz Smarch?"

"Trade is very good, thank you, Mr. Choi. I trust you are also prospering."

"I make modest gains, thank you."

While they continued with the formalities, Toni studied Choi's hands, trying to estimate his age. Seventy, at least, but he could easily be forty or fifty years older. His kind of money could buy extensive rejuvenation treatments. On the other hand, a man who lived alone in a fortified bunker might not trust doctors that much. Choi's thin, long-nailed fingertips closed precisely on a fragile teacup. He sipped some pale tea. The tension beneath his controlled movements gave Toni a sharp sense of menace and she had to concentrate to keep her face bland. The sim scanner portrayed facial expression very accurately.

"I understand that you had a regrettable disturbance in the bar last night," said Choi.

"True," replied Mary. "And I must thank you for your servant's assistance." She looked at Choi very cautiously, then added. "It's something of a running joke that we should add him to our security team."

Blade would certainly make some bouncer, thought Toni dryly, then blinked in astonishment at Mr. Choi's next words.

"It would please me if you make use of him when he is at the KlonDyke. I will contract with you for a nominal fee and order him to receive your instructions."

For a split second Mary looked astounded, then she recovered and thanked Mr. Choi graciously. What the hell was he up to? fretted Toni. Did he want to put Mary in his debt? Or did he want to ensure Blade's continued access to the bar?

"I read your financial statements for last year with considerable interest." Mr. Choi poured himself more tea and put the pot back down in precisely the same position as before. His voice was cold, almost without inflection. "The KlonDyke continues to perform very well under your guidance."

Mary thanked him again.

"I was, however, concerned by your reference to the building's state of disrepair. I take it that renovations are not feasible."

Mary shook her head. "Upgrading would be far more expensive than constructing a new building."

Those details had been in the appendix to the financial report, thought Toni. What was Choi leading up to?

"Do you intend to rebuild?"

"No. We don't have the capital, and without legal title to the property, there's no way to raise it. SisOpp gambled on building the residence here because our need was so urgent, but we can't risk any more investment Downtown."

"Understandable," said Mr. Choi. He finished his second cup of tea and folded his hands on the desk. Getting to the point, guessed Toni, and his next words confirmed that.

"Perhaps I could interest you in a proposal of mutual benefit."

Mary nodded, her face showing nothing but polite expectation. Her mug of coffee sat cooling on her knee.

"I may be in a position to acquire recognized title to the land under the KlonDyke. I would be willing to offer a fifty-year lease to SisOpp in return for a share in the venture and a percentage of

KlonDyke revenues. The present tower would be demolished, of course, and I would advance capital toward a new structure. This would meet the KlonDyke's long-term space requirements and also make it easier for you to acquire status as a registered venture when Downtown is reabsorbed by Vancouver City. In addition, there would be considerable income from renting out space."

Mary sat frozen for a few seconds. Her composure was good, but Toni could tell that she'd been caught off balance.

"Mr. Choi, this is a very impressive and substantial offer. I'll have to consider it at length and consult with the SisOpp Board."

"Naturally. And you will require more information. I have a detailed proposal ready to send you. However, I expect you and your board to treat this offer with absolute confidence." His piercing gaze held an unmistakable threat.

"Of course."

Mr. Choi viewed her a second longer, then moved smoothly to the briefest form of closing pleasantries. Mary had regained her aplomb, and concluded the conversation with grace while Toni held very still. Choi had ignored her, but just before the transmission ended she saw his gaze flick toward her and their eyes met for an instant. Then the signal cut, and she was sitting in darkness with a chill knot of dread in her stomach. She had to concentrate to keep her hands steady as she lifted off her headset. Choi was toying with her. Why?

For the thousandth time she wished futilely that she knew what had happened during those missing months before she turned up at the KlonDyke. But she had only a few disconnected images that felt like snatches of nightmares. Throwing up on a street. Panhandling for another fix. Waking up naked in a stinking room with two strange men fucking her. But nothing about Choi and no explanation of why Blade had dumped her at the KlonDyke's back door. She'd even tried asking Blade but, predictably, got no response. Considering his probable level of neural damage, there was a good chance he didn't remember anyway.

Mary stared into the distance, preoccupied and Toni took a few seconds to concentrate on calming herself. When she spoke, she had her voice under control.

"Was that an offer or a threat?"

"Both, I think. By the Mother, he's a real businessman." Mary's tone was grim as she moved her chair to face Toni's. "The KlonDyke's existing reputation, plus a new building . . . we could do very well by the Second Coming."

"I thought that all land titles in Downtown were suspended," said Toni doubtfully. "And what about Cascadia Rail?"

"Thankfully, Cascadia doesn't want this property. In theory, we have an excellent claim for title when the City comes in, but now I'm not sure about our chances. This will be the biggest land transfer in Vancouver in centuries and Choi isn't the only vulture circling. Bribes have been passing under the table for years."

"What will you do?"

"Refuse, of course, but I'll string it out as long as I can. Ultimately, if he gets the land title, we'll have to deal with him whether we want to or not." Mary's hands were clasped in her lap, fingers knotted together tensely. "We don't have the money either to move or to pay him off. We spent every last dollar building the rez and we borrowed from members, too. We'll pay out member loans next year, thanks to 'Dyke revenues, but that leaves us empty."

Toni absently turned her mug around in her hands as she tried to make sense of the situation.

"But why now? And why would he go after SisOpp?"

"I can only guess, Toni. He may have struck some sort of deal with the tongs that allows him a foothold here. He may even be fronting for one of them. Or he may be maneuvering behind their backs. The 'Dyke is one of the few properties not under any tong's control."

"What about his own place?"

Mary raised her eyebrows.

"That's a good question. They say he lives under the old Bentall Towers, in Kung Lok territory. Those towers are sure to be demolished. Maybe he's looking to build a bolt-hole under a new building."

"I prefer the sort of basement vermin we can send Pauline Johnson after," said Toni acidly. The edge in her voice was too intense. She took a slow breath and then ventured another question.

"How old do you think he is?"

Mary shrugged distractedly.

"No idea. I could never tell in person either. He always looked ageless."

"In person?" said Toni, startled. "You've seen him?"

"Sure. He used to come around for meetings. But that was a long time ago—twenty or twenty-five years."

"Then you don't cred the spin that he's really been dead for years and that's just a replica?"

Mary shook her head dismissively. "No. That's him—I'm sure. Besides, if he left a replica running, the tongs' surveillance programs would have flagged it."

Toni nodded. It made sense, and she trusted Mary's instincts.

"What was he like?" she asked, curiously.

"Just what you saw. Meticulous. Viciously polite, with an aura like an arctic wind. He hates people. And he's vector phobic. He used to make sure his tool kept everyone at least a meter away. Even brought his own tea service so he didn't have to touch anything of ours." As Mary remembered her face had taken on an uncharacteristic scowl. "That man has only two interests in life—making money, and getting revenge." Then she looked up and caught Toni's eyes with intensity. "He's insane, love. Leaves a path like a snake in mud."

Toni didn't like to think about that. She looked away.

"What are you going to do about Choi's offer of Blade?" she asked, keeping her voice casual with effort.

After a few seconds Mary sighed.

"I hope it was just a negotiating gesture and he'll withdraw it when we don't accept his deal. But I'm afraid that he already sees the KlonDyke as his, and he wants Blade here keeping an eye on it."

And on the bartender, thought Toni grimly.

Mary looked at her, then reached out and put a hand on Toni's shoulder and spoke softly.

"Dear, I'm very sorry about your apartment. I know how much it means to you. But Alberta was right. We had to search without notice."

Toni felt herself stiffen with a fresh flood of anger. She had just spent the whole night cleaning with frantic, irrational fury, then she'd gone out and bought another deadbolt, but it would be a long time before she could feel settled again. Mary leaned toward her for a comforting hug, but Toni pulled back. Then she gave an internal sigh. Damn! Mary tried so hard with her and Toni could never seem to stop shoving her away.

"Anything else on the agenda?" she heard herself ask.

"I think that was plenty," said Mary. Her voice was cheerful, but Toni knew her well enough to detect the undercurrent of sadness. She paused a second, then when Toni didn't say anything more, she stood up and rolled her chair back around the desk to the netset. "Thanks for the coffee."

"Any time," Toni told her.

She left, closing the office door quietly behind her. In the back hall across from the kitchen, she entered the security code that let her into the storeroom. Lights flickered on, revealing shelves loaded with bricks of irradiated food, and hanging nets of fresh potatoes, apples, and garlic. As the heavy door swung shut, Toni leaned against a shelf and gave in to the wave of near panic.

The Maglev was coming. The 'Dyke would be demolished.

Why didn't I see it? she wanted to wail, but she knew why. She'd wanted to believe that Downtown was isolated, unchanging. But the outside world was poised to invade. This building would be destroyed, and with it her apartment—the first home she'd ever allowed herself to love.

How could I have been so stupid as to build a home in a condemned building? she asked savagely, but for once she couldn't flay herself into anger. A small terrified voice inside her was crying: Where will I go?

I've started a new life before, she told herself, but the words were hollow. Yeah, she'd run away three times, and the last time was nearly fatal. If it hadn't been for Mary she'd be dead.

She was fifty years old and alone. Nowhere to go. No family. No Guild. No money. And she was still in danger from bents like Choi who'd use her ruthlessly if they uncovered her secret. For a few sick, dizzy seconds she contemplated running—stowing on a tramp ship, living on the streets again—then she forcibly pulled herself together. Being young and poor had been hell enough; she had no intention of living to be old and destitute.

She straightened up, tugging the carryall strap higher on her shoulder. She would stay as long as she could. After all, she was debted to Mary. And then . . . well, there was always one other option.

She straightened and left the storeroom, letting the door thud shut behind her.

5

"CHARITY, CITIZEN!"

Yeah, I could use some, Klale felt like telling the beggar who blocked her way into the KlonDyke, but when she met the tiny woman's eyes the words froze in her mouth. The woman stood no taller than Klale's waist, even propped upright on crutches. Beside her a young man with no legs sat on a roll-board. He beamed Klale the beatific smile of a juice addict.

Klale shook her head and walked past them, appalled at their public shame, then repulsed by the waft of acrid stench, and finally ashamed at her own feelings. She couldn't get used to the raucous hubbub of pleas from dirty children, thin women with wailing babies, and even old people. In Prince Rupert no one was Guildless. Drifters who couldn't prove status or family were run out of town by the Watch. It had never before occurred to Klale to wonder where they went.

Just how stupid had it been to leave Prince Rupert? she wondered uneasily. A day of trekking around Downtown had left her weary and frustrated. Several phone calls to the Fisher Bank had got her nowhere. She'd foolishly kept all her savings in the family's boat account, and it was frozen pending settlement of her father's estate. So she took the money from her audition, converted it to cash, and went to shop for a shirt. And that was when she discovered that everything in Downtown—clothes, food, medicine, *everything*—had to be purchased in person in a maze of unindexed shops and stalls

where the prices varied from one place to the next. Nobody even
took body scans—the clothes were presewn.

Worst of all, she couldn't get decent net access. When she'd called
navsat for local street directions her phone had informed her that
she was "outside the service area." That stunned her. Klale had used
navsat everywhere from Prince Rupert to the mid-Pacific.

The KlonDyke doors opened onto a dim stew of noise. Bright
clothes and biolume jewelry seethed weirdly in a fog of Fireweed
smoke that had overwhelmed the air scrubbers. Servers wore black
aprons with a luminous red "K," but they hardly stood out in this
crowd. Klale crammed her Guild sweater into her duffel bag, then
walked over to the bar in her scratchy new hempen shirt and dropped
her bag in front of the till. The new shirt fit poorly. She'd bought it
off a rack where shirts were "small," "medium," and "large." No
wonder everyone Downtown looked like they were wearing somebody else's hand-me-downs.

The bartender was a young woman with green biolumed,
static-charged hair that flowed around her head, casting a flickering
green glow in all directions. It looked like seaweed underwater.

"Excuse me. Is Toni in?"

The bartender fixed emerald eyes on Klale and flicked unnatural
lashes.

"*I'm* around now, hon, and I'm *much* warmer." She learned forward thrusting her nipples up out of her bodice, and said in a throaty
voice: "Can I help you?"

"Actually, I'm here to help you. I'm the new server."

The bartender looked her up and down and sniffed.

"Sure and I'm Dai Lo of the Ghost Shadows."

She spun dismissively on her heel and minced away, leaving Klale
staring. The bartender wore sequined panties that matched her lace-
up bodice, a translucent body stocking which gave her skin an emerald sheen, and glowing heels that chimed as she moved. When she
turned back, Klale was really startled. Clearly outlined in the panties
was a penis and testicles. She was a he.

Well . . . maybe. The figure was boyishly thin except for large
breasts, and the hips were slender, but the bartender's face looked
feminine. And the hands . . . could be a man's or woman's.

As the bartender approached she tried again.

"Look, Toni and Mary hired me yesterday."

The bartender smirked.

"What for, darling?"

"For throwing chili on a customer," retorted Klale.

Glowing eyebrows rose, then she (or he) broke into a wicked smile.

"Oh, so *you* grimed Baljeet! Why didn't you say so? Did you really get the bitch in the face? What's your name, sweetbush?"

Klale had just opened her mouth when Toni hurried through from the kitchen carrying a tray of garnishes.

"About time," she told Klale. "We're busy. Drop your bag in the back hall, then grab an apron from that rack."

Toni was moving at full speed. She thrust an order pad at Klale and rattled off instructions while she filled steins. Klale was to take net accounts first, then the table number and order. Because of the jammer, orders had to be logged by physical upload to a till or the kitchen terminal. They were tagged by table number and flashed up on the bar and pass-through readouts when ready.

"And don't put more on a tray than you're sure you can manage," Toni added brusquely. "The first spill's on the house; after that it comes out of your pocket."

The next three hours sped by in a blur as Klale struggled to keep up with drinks, food, and customers. Her biggest unexpected hurdle was customers who ordered in Sign. In desperation she asked another server for translation, but the woman simply glowered at her and stalked off, leaving Klale wondering what she'd said wrong. The customers weren't unfriendly, but they treated Klale so incuriously that she began to realize how accustomed they were to strange faces. In Prince Rupert newcomers attracted attention, but here Klale was no novelty, and as a server she was invisible except when a glass was empty.

By the time the first dance set started, she felt sweaty, harassed, and very grateful for a lull. She'd planned to watch the show, but now all she wanted to do was sit down and breathe deeply. She was just trying to figure out how to do that when Toni waved her over, then turned and called:

"Bracken!"

Luminescent green hair floated in their direction, accompanied by a distinct whiff of spearmint. Flavored, too? wondered Klale.

"Klale, Bracken. Bracken, Klale's new to Downtown, so please try to give her some *useful* information."

"Oooh, I like Zitty virgins!" announced Bracken, batting his or her eyes at Klale, then asking baldly: "Where are you from?"

"Prince Rupert," said Klale, trying not to stare at those bulging breasts and genitals. How old was Bracken under all that makeup? Her own age?

"Bet they don't grow them like me where you come from!"

"No," said Klale firmly, and grinned. "Definitely not."

Bracken chuckled. "I'm a hermy, dear—the genuine article. Ask me nicely, I might demonstrate some time." Then Bracken glanced over Klale's shoulder, and his/her face crumpled into a scowl. "Ghoul," s/he told Toni.

Toni didn't look; she just reached over to the till and entered an order, then started filling a stein, but Klale turned. Walking toward the bar was the enforcer she'd seen the night before. Klale remembered his throwing knife and swallowed.

Close up he seemed even taller than she remembered, and his face looked more disturbingly skull-like. He had light brown skin and dark brown eyes with what might be a slight epicanthic fold. He could have been any mix of Native Indian, Afroid, Asian, or Mediterranean. The skin was pulled so tight across his skull that she wondered if he was even capable of showing an emotion. She realized that he probably hadn't chosen that horrible face and felt a stab of pity.

Bracken grabbed Klale's elbow and jerked her away.

"Don't stare!" There was no trace of theatrics in Bracken's voice now. "Don't you know how to treat tools?"

"Uh, no."

"Don't look at them, don't talk to them, and stay the hell out of their way."

"I wouldn't worry too much, Klale," came Toni's calm voice from behind her. Klale looked around. The enforcer had picked up his drink and was walking to a table at the back of the room. "He's the only tool you'll ever see in the KlonDyke."

"Yeah, he's the house tool," said Bracken acidly. She gave Toni a glare which hinted at old quarrels, then strutted away.

Klale looked at the enforcer again. A couple of citizens stared, but everyone else in the bar looked away as he strode heavily through the tables. A man with his back to the bar pushed out his chair to stand up just as the enforcer approached. Klale caught her breath, but the giant made a fast sidestep to the right and kept going, missing the chair by maybe a centimeter. The man turned, almost collided with him, and jumped backward, blanching.

Klale blinked. She would never have expected such swift motion from that immense, lumbering man. She turned to Toni.

"What's his name?"

"Tools don't have names, Klale. But we call him Blade." She processed a cash order at the till as she spoke. "We give him a pint and a large order of fries when he arrives. Charge it to the overhead code." Her eyes held Klale's for a long second, then moved back to the readout. "Please remember that Blade is every bit as dangerous as he looks, but he has orders to behave in here and he does."

"There are just a few basic rules. He's a deaf-mute, and he uses Slang only. Never walk up behind him. Never startle him. Keep your distance. If he scares you, call me or security."

Preferably Toni, thought Klale, remembering how he'd stopped on her orders last night. Christ, what would have happened if he hadn't?

"Klale?"

She realized suddenly that Toni had asked a question.

"Sorry, could you repeat that?"

"Do you understand Slang?"

She shook her head. "Only a few signs."

"Well, you'll have to learn enough to take orders and staff signals. It's the problem with remotes again—we rely a lot on Slang."

She made her hand into a fist, then extended her thumb and little finger and raised the hand toward her lips as if her hand were a tankard. "That's beer, and it means a pint of Granville unless they specify something else." Then she ran through the signs for types of beers, glasses, pints, and pitchers while Klale watched, trying to take them all in. It was hitting her again just how much she had to learn.

Toni's readout pinged quietly, and she glanced at the kitchen pass-through. "Take those fries over to Blade, please."

Klale put them on her tray, took a deep breath, and walked over.

The enforcer sat at his table like a statue of death, back to the wall, staring straight ahead. He'd tossed his gray serape on the chair next to him and underneath he wore a dark, long-sleeved shirt. Klale approached nervously, but Blade didn't look at her, so she studied his disturbing face. He had no hair at all, not even eyelashes, and his stretched skin looked synthetic, but the burn scars and the horrible brand on his forehead showed all too clearly that it was real.

What kind of a human being lived behind that face? she wondered suddenly. She put the fries down in front of him, then stood waiting, feeling adrenaline pulse through her body. For ten seconds or more he did nothing, then his eyes flicked quickly past her. Not enough, thought Klale. She stood still, scared but determined. A minute passed, then two minutes. Finally his dark eyes met hers for a long second, then he shifted his gaze away.

"Klale?" Klale jumped at Toni's voice and spun around. Toni looked furious. She Slanged rapidly at Blade, then grabbed Klale's shoulder and steered her roughly away.

When they reached a quiet corner, Toni stopped, put her hands on her hips, and hissed:

"What in hell were you doing?!"

Klale did her best to explain, feeling more and more foolish under the bartender's icy gaze.

"And what impression did you get?" Toni asked acidly.

Klale ignored her sarcasm, and thought back.

"I'm not sure. He wasn't angry, but there was definitely something . . ." She concentrated, picturing his eyes, and suddenly had it. "He was scared." She looked at Toni, startled at her own words. "At least that's what I think I saw . . ." Already she felt doubtful. "Is that tilted?"

Toni stared at Klale in surprise, then her tense shoulders sagged and her eyes seemed suddenly very old.

"No," she said quietly. She turned away, but Klale caught at her elbow.

"What did you say to him?"

Toni shook her off with exasperation.

"I told him that I own you because he'll understand that and he has instructions to respect the KlonDyke staff. But," Toni wheeled and glared up into Klale's eyes, "I can't guarantee your safety if you take cretting risks! If you want to work here, you will give him his food and get out! Do you understand?"

"Yes," said Klale meekly.

It seemed like a good idea to stay out of Toni's way for a while, so Klale made another round of her section, this time focusing more closely on her customers. She was working the lesbian side of the floor, and many of the women there looked Guild or ex-Guild. Two tables were playing mahjong with yellowing plastic tiles that clacked deafeningly when shuffled. The lesbians segued into a sort of artistes' ghetto with young trendies who bought cheap drinks and nursed them for hours. They were tox tippers but Klale was busy enough to be thankful for tables that didn't want much.

By the time the next stage show started, the smell of food had her starving. She marched up to the bar and looked Bracken straight in the eyes.

"Should I call you he or she?"

"Oh darling, yes!"

Klale sighed. Bracken laughed in warm gusts of spearmint while his/her fingers deftly arranged sliced fruit in glass goblets for Cups of Dreams.

"Take your pick, sweets. The Sisters mostly call me 'he' and men usually call me 'she.' I believe it's a way of saying . . ." Bracken thrust out a dramatic strawberry, " ' . . . that creature's not one of *us*.' "

"Mmmm." Klale studied Bracken, then settled on "she." Maybe it was too many years in a Fisher town, but she couldn't quite bring herself to call somebody with breasts bigger than her own "he."

"What do I do about meals?" she asked.

"Order them on your tip code. Here." Bracken pushed an order of pyrogies nearer to Klale. "I'll never finish all this."

Klale hesitated, then reminded herself sharply that all the KlonDyke staff took weekly contagion screenings. She reached out and picked up a pyrogy with her fingers, hoping that Bracken hadn't noticed her hesitation.

"So where are you from, Bracken?"

Bracken looked at her narrowly.

"And what makes you think I come from anywhere?"

"Well . . . nothing, actually. I was just asking."

"Mmmm." Bracken stretched with artful casualness, making eye contact with a woman walking past the bar, then pulled her attention back to Klale. "It's not wise to ask people about their pasts, darling. Ask somebody else about them. At least you'll hear lots of pulsing spec."

"Oh. Then I should ask you about Toni."

"Toni!" Bracken's eyes sparkled. "Well, she appeared in a puff of smoke ten years ago—nobody knows where from. There are rumors, of course. Some say she belonged to Choi Shung Wai, the blackmailer. Some say she still does."

That didn't mean much to Klale. She tried:

"Was Toni a joy addict?"

"Hell, no," said Bracken disdainfully. "They never stay clean. She was a smut, sweets. At least, that's what she says, and she certainly knows enough about whoring. She was also a trip junkie—still has the marks. But she dried out, pulled the wire, and she doesn't coit anybody, even for free." She nodded at a table of garishly dressed women. "The hookers here are all clean. The boss doesn't allow plugs. But it's the same show—they just fake the ooh-ahs instead of renting the 'on' button."

Klale looked away, flushing uncomfortably. She had served those women and hadn't even realized they were prostitutes. How many of these people led desperate lives? Toni evidently had, and Bracken's bravado hinted at old wounds. But the Boss had seemed so normal. . . .

"Embarrassed, sweetbush?"

"I was just trying to picture dens of iniquity in Teslin," said Klale. "Never mind."

Bracken gave her an odd glance, and said in a brittle voice: "Little hells are the worst." She dropped cherries in four Cups of Dreams, added a dollop of whipped cream, and regained her normal tone. "The Boss has no secrets, but Toni does, and she bites."

She flicked her eyelashes and leaned closer. "Talking of biting, do tell me, Klale—do you prefer men or women?"

Klale grinned.

"Bracken, the problem with you is that whatever I say, I'm in trouble. Why don't I just get back to work?"

Bracken made a shooing motion.

"Take a break! Why don't you go over there," she gestured, "and talk to de Groot before he pees himself trying to catch your eye."

Klale turned around and immediately saw the man from the Wooden Boat Club. He waved with such enthusiasm that she had to turn back quickly to hide her laughter.

"Ask him all about Downtown. He's an expert."

Bracken's tone was sly, observed Klale, but she took the proffered beer and the pyrogies and weaved through the seats to Cedar's table. De Groot dressed plainly compared to the crowd, but his blue Z-shirt with reflective trim and matching earpieces looked good on him. He sat with a round-faced chubby man whom he introduced as Tommy Yip, local restaurateur and treasurer of the Free Vancouver League. Interesting, thought Klale. Yip might run a Downtown restaurant, but he certainly wasn't poor judging by the heavy gold chain that gleamed at the open neck of his hand-embroidered ensilk shirt.

Yip beamed her a jovial smile that Klale instantly mistrusted. She pulled up a chair on the opposite side of de Groot who leaned over and spoke close to her ear above the noise of the floor show.

"So you're working here now?"

A real gift for the obvious, thought Klale, then squelched the uncharitable thought. He'd been kind when she was in trouble.

"Yes." He was paying no attention to the show, so she decided to try for some information. "Bracken said you're an expert on Downtown."

De Groot scowled.

"That was a joke. I'm vice president of the City Services Guild."

Klale tried to cover her surprise. De Groot didn't look like a Guild exec to her. On the other hand, it wasn't unusual for Guilds to vote in compromise candidates too ineffectual to offend anyone.

"I'm impressed," she said, and he beamed at her with reassured self-importance. "Maybe you can tell me something," she continued. "Why hasn't the city reclaimed Downtown?"

"Too expensive. We'd have to demolish all these old buildings and reconstruct everything from minus thirty meters up, plus there's cleansing the contaminated sites and then putting in new infrastructure. We're talking a lot of money and just try to get all the Guilds on Council to agree about anything! They can't even pass a dog bylaw. Anyway, we don't have the capital. We're running everything pay-as-we-go, and there's hundreds of backlisted projects."

Klale nodded. She knew all too well about the chronic shortage of capital that hobbled the economy. It had taken the Fishers twelve years to build their last fish farm and irradiation plant, even with investment from the Gitksan Nation, Mariner's Guild and the Merchant's Association.

"NetSys says there aren't any utilities or permanent net connects Downtown," she said. "But . . ." She waved a pyrogy at the room.

"Oh, the KlonDyke has its own solar/water/biogas plant," explained Cedar, "and they buy drinking water when they don't collect enough in the roof cisterns. The residential co-ops and casinos do the same thing. And they're big enough to operate their own net nodes."

Sudden anxiety crossed his face.

"You aren't planning to live Downtown, are you?"

"Well, yes I am."

"By yourself?" he asked, horrified.

"Yes."

"You can't!" His loud protest attracted looks, so he lowered his voice and spoke urgently. "Miz Renhardt, it's dangerous! There's fires and collapses all the time, and these old buildings are full of tilties and bludgers and plagues. Get a rez with your Guild."

Klale opened her mouth to say what she thought of her Guild, then held back.

"I'll think about it," she said instead and started to rise. De Groot jumped to his feet, oblivious of blocking people's views.

"Uh, look, you could stay with me. That is, I mean . . . just until you find somewhere else. Just for a little while . . ." Was he blushing? Klale peered closely as he took a deep breath and plunged in again.

"I live in the City Services Co-op on Twelfth Avenue and I've got room—just have to clean up a few things first."

"Well, thank you, but . . ."

"The KlonDyke tower is a hundred and fifty years old, you know. If we had another earthquake it would come right down."

"I really didn't want to know that," Klale shot back with annoyance. "Look, I'm going back to work."

But de Groot's words began to haunt Klale as the crowd thinned and the hours dragged out. Bracken quit at midnight and departed arm in arm with a bemused-looking man. Klale ate another meal, then started polishing glasses out of desperation for something to do, but she couldn't stop glancing apprehensively up at the ceiling. Finally Toni gave the last call at three, then at three-twenty flashed the lights and chased the last few customers out.

Once the doors were shut, the bouncers started a methodical security check and Toni did a walk-through to make sure everything was cleaned away. Klale tagged along for a tour of the kitchen, downroom, cold room, storage room, office, and backstage, and she returned impressed by the overall neatness and efficiency.

Most of the other staff had already left. Klale finished wiping down the tables in her section and took her order pad to Toni who checked and cleared it at the till. Then, while Toni began emptying coins into a noisy machine behind the bar, Klale counted her tips.

"So how was your first night?"

"OK. Ummm . . . Thirty-one dollars, not counting two tips I got on plastic." She hung up her apron and walked over beside Toni. "That makes about eight real dollars . . ."

"Five," corrected Toni.

"*What?*" Klale stared at her. "I bought some cash today from a money changer. The rate was four to one."

"That's the buying rate. For tourists. The selling rate is six to one, seven to one at Undersell All stores. Which, incidentally, is why they're called Plunder and Maul."

"Oh hell," said Klale bleakly as it sank in. Even with download fees from dancing she'd be hard put to survive. And she'd have no choice about staying in the wrecked KlonDyke tower—she couldn't afford anything else.

Toni gave her an assessing glance.

"You OK?"

"Yeah," said Klale, sighing. She took a deep breath and tried to think of something cheerful. "At least I'm glad you told me to get a cheap shirt. I spilled beer all down it."

She managed a grin, then impulsively reached an arm around the smaller woman's shoulders and squeezed her gently.

"Thank you for the advice. And I'm sorry I upset you."

Footsteps approached and Klale turned to see a large woman in a bouncer shirt staring at them with raised eyebrows. Toni pulled away from Klale, picked up a half pint glass and put it under the ale tap.

"Klale, this is Alberta, chief of security," she said curtly. "Alberta, Klale Renhardt."

Alberta nodded at Klale, eyes sharp with speculation. She held out her hand and Klale shook it.

"Name's Patricia Clarke, but everybody calls me Alberta. You might as well, too."

The security chief took her beer and pulled over a stool. She was in her early or mid thirties, judged Klale, with straight, close-cropped blonde hair, a square face and heavily muscled shoulders. She stood half a head taller than Klale and she walked with a heavy, no-nonsense stride.

"Do you come from Alberta?" Klale asked, remembering Bracken's warning a split second too late, but the bouncer didn't seem to mind the question.

"Yeah, I'm named after the Calgary regiment. Got a father, uncle, and brother named Patrick. We're the Pats' Pats." She looked Klale over, then said bluntly. "I hear you left your Guild."

"Uh huh." Klale wasn't anxious to elaborate. She cast around for another subject, then remembered something she'd wondered about earlier. "Could you tell me about tongs? They're Chinese ventures, aren't they?"

Alberta shook her head.

"Around here 'tong' means any big, organized group of bent sleazes. The Sun Yee On and the Kung Lok are offshoots of Chinese triads. The Viet Ching are the Vietnamese/Italian mafia. That's the big three. They own the Pan Pacific Consortium and run smuggling, gambling, drugs, plugs, slavery, and everything else toxic."

"Do they fight a lot?" asked Klale.

Alberta snorted. "Hell no, they'd crease their suits. They carved up Downtown decades ago. Now they call themselves Merchants, live in big tree neighborhoods, and send their kids to payschool."

"And they come here to drink?"

"Yeah. And for board meetings. Pan Pacific invested in our renovations—that's why we're neutral."

Alberta didn't sound happy about it.

"The tongs do a lot more," interjected Toni. "They fund clinics, schools, housing co-ops, and the fire brigade, and they do some basic policing. They provide the only services the flots and squats have."

"If you call Black Cross a service," snapped Alberta. She glowered. "The tongs are goddamn jackals, chewing on everybody's guts."

Toni met her glower coolly.

"Without the jackals we'd have nothing."

The sorter stopped clinking. In the awkward silence that followed, a buzzer went off and a door slammed in the back. Klale heard distant footsteps, then a tall, slim woman walked out from backstage. She had long, straight brown hair and a pretty smile.

"Hey, Toni! You through with my wife yet?" she called.

"Take her home to bed, Rill."

Alberta stood and greeted the other woman with a kiss and a frown. "You shouldn't walk over alone!"

"It's just a block! Besides, we haven't seen God's gonads in weeks." She looked at Klale and put out her hand. "Rill Clarke."

"Klale Renhardt, Fisher's Guild," she responded automatically, then kicked herself. She had to get out of that habit. "Uh, God's gonads . . . ?"

"Religious bigots," said Alberta grimly. "Sisters does DNA splicing. We want babies that are really ours—both of ours. And some shit-for-brains spluts call our kids abominations."

Rill grinned at her.

"Two years until we're paid up for our own little abomination."

Alberta looked embarrassed. She drained the last of her beer and put the glass back on the bar. "You got more questions?"

"No," said Klale. "Yes. Is Bracken really a hermaphrodite?"

Rill laughed. Alberta scowled.

"He's sure as hell a major fucker," she said shortly.

Rill said good night, still chuckling, and the two of them left arm in arm. Klale turned back to Toni, who was stacking coins on the bar.

"About Bracken . . ."

Toni counted under her breath, entered something on the till, and then nodded.

"Yeah, he is. Of course, he's had some cosmetic tweaking, like breast enlargement."

"Is that common here—hermaphroditism?"

"Probably. The flots and squats have high toxin levels. But Bracken's not local."

Environmental toxins, thought Klale, with a fresh twinge of alarm. Anything could be in these buildings or under them. She'd already seen squats using banned plastics to carry drinking water.

Suddenly her mind flashed back to the bar fight. What would the Patrol have done to those flots if there hadn't been Guild witnesses? Hell, look what Dhillon had done to Klale when they were alone. She felt a rush of anger. The Patrol was Guild. They shouldn't be allowed to get away with it!

"How would I find those two flots?" she asked suddenly. "You know, from the fight last night."

"Why?"

Klale told her about the incident with Dhillon, then said: "I want to report her. But it's just my word against hers. So I thought I could find the flots and get them to file a complaint about the fight. The Patrol was way out of line and there were lots of witnesses."

"The flots can't file a complaint, Klale. They aren't citizens."

"But . . . ! Then they could make a public posting. Let people know what happened."

"Sure, using their phones and their net accounts."

"But there's free public . . . !"

"Look, Klale, flots don't complain. It's too dangerous, and anyway citizens don't give a damn what happens to them."

"Yes they do. They would. If they knew!"

"Of course they know!" Toni snapped harshly. "The Guilds just don't want to pay the price of fixing 'the refugee problem,' so they've been hoping for fifty years that it'll just vanish." She glared over at Klale with sudden fury. "The only way the problem is going to vanish is if we all die, like we were supposed to do in the inner cities and the 'relocation camps.' But unfortunately some of us scum survived and the problem didn't end. Except in Atlanta, of course."

Klale stared at her, shocked.

"That was an accident!"

"Like hell it was," said Toni bitterly. She slammed a cupboard shut, then started toward the kitchen. Klale hurried around the bar and blocked her path.

"Toni, you don't think something like the Atlanta biologicals would happen here, do you?" she asked urgently, hearing the tinny edge of fear in her voice.

Toni took a steadying breath, then spoke calmly.

"This isn't Atlanta, Klale. The situation here is bad, but it's nothing compared to what happened in the big cities in Old America." Then she caught Klale's gaze and held it intensely. "However, if you're smart you'll go back to your Guild before you get hurt."

Abruptly Klale's temper flared.

"I am *not* going back! Not after those bent nespots hounded my father to death and took our boat and threw it back into the common pool the day after he died! And I am not going to live in that horrible town and turn into one of those horrible people who spent their whole life in a place they hate doing work assignments they hate until they're all crippled up with bitterness and terrified to do anything different."

She started to stomp away, then whirled back.

"And I *am* going to university! I earned it! I've finished three quarters of my degree already—all I need is my team study year—but those bastards kept putting me off and putting me off for *years!* They were never going to send me! So I'll do it myself! I've saved money and I'll pay the tuition myself and I hope they all *drown!*"

Now that she had started, the words poured out. "And I *am* going to find those flots and help them file a complaint against the Patrol. Because somebody's got to!"

Fury sped her feet up the tower stairs, but it faded rapidly to apprehension. Klale had decided to go higher in the tower this time, hoping to get above the roaches and street smells, but as she climbed she found more and more stairwell lights were missing. She hesitated, then nerved herself to keep climbing into the shadows. In the dank, oppressive shaft her mind flashed back to de Groot's words. In an earthquake, dozens of storeys of concrete would pancake down, crushing her. . . .

She stopped abruptly, fighting a panicked urge to run back downstairs. She wanted to flee the building, but there was no escape outside, just a maze of lethal streets. Tears burned at the back of her eyes.

God, I miss you, Dad, she thought suddenly, and then she did cry, standing in the cold black stairway.

Maybe she should swallow her pride and go back. Even as the thought occurred to her, Klale recoiled in horror. How could she give up? How could she go back?

She gulped back tears, and trudged upward.

The fifteenth floor was empty, but the shadows seemed menacing, so Klale humored her fears by shining her handlight behind every pillar to make sure she was alone. The concrete floor shone wetly on the windward side but the east corner was dry. She laid out her roll, then kicked off her boots and sat down, wrapping her arms around her knees. She felt cold.

"Bold yourself, Klale!" she said out loud. "You're perfectly safe, OK?"

No, it wasn't OK. She'd never felt so alone in her life. She couldn't use her phone to call for help and the nearest thing she had to a weapon was her pocket knife. She found herself longing for her old bed at home, but the house was somebody else's now—snatched back, like their boat "Big Fry"—and she could never return.

Oh hell, she was crying *again*! She pulled off her clothes, bundled them in the bottom of her sleeping bag, and crawled in, keeping her pocket knife near her hand. It took her a very long time to get warm, despite the heating panels, and even longer to fall asleep. There were too many noises. The buffeting wind set off creaks and bangs in the old building, and occasional yells echoed up from the street. Every time Klale began to doze off a sound would jerk her awake, heart pounding. She tried to distract herself from her fears by remembering happy times, but her thoughts kept slipping to darker images.

Finally, after what seemed like hours, she fell into a restless sleep. She dreamed of black, rain drenched streets, then of Blade's death-mask face looming out of the shadows, and she woke up sweating in terror.

6

The automated Longshore freight hauler careened around the corner in a spray of dust, heading straight for a broken-kneed beggar. Klale caught her breath, but the beggar threw himself out of the way just in time. A rear wheel rumbled over one of his crutches, snapping the shaft. He lay on the pavement for a moment in the morning sunshine, screaming at the departing truck, then began to pull himself up.

Klale vaulted over the concrete barrier and retrieved the man's remaining crutch, grimacing as his stench hit her. The beggar rewarded her efforts with a glare and a stream of incoherent curses. She tried to prop the crutch under him, then gave up and retreated hastily, wiping her hands on her pants.

"Did he thank you for your citizenship?" came a sardonic voice, and Klale turned to see the chief bouncer, Alberta, looking like an ad for the Eco Rangers in khaki shirt and shorts, sturdy boots and an equipment belt with a canteen. Beside her stood another even taller woman whose crossed brown arms bulged with muscle.

"Pum," indicated Alberta, gesturing at her. "C'mon with us."

"What are you doing here?"

"Keeping you from getting slagged," said Alberta darkly. "You can thank Toni." She started to move away, then looked back. "You got a subdermal emergency transmitter?"

"Sure. All boat crews do," said Klale, surprised. "In fact, I just had mine upgraded when I wrote my deep water ticket."

"Good. Give me the code. Just in case. I got Mary wearing a transmitter, too—no big sweat to cover one more."

It seemed melodramatic, but Klale obediently looked up the code on her phone and sent it. Then she scrambled to catch up with Alberta and Pum as they strode along Smithe Street, part of the Guild-maintained haulage route between Pier B-C and the old Cambie Bridge. In stark contrast to other Downtown streets, this road was wide, fresh-paved, and empty. By looking up and squinting to blur the faces of the old office towers, Klale could almost imagine herself back a hundred years.

"Where are we going?" she called.

"Granville. It's neutral turf. We can talk to anybody, no smog. Anyway, I got a lead on your flots."

Granville Street teemed with hawkers, shoppers, addicts, tourists, guards-for-hire, beggars, money changers, and buskers. It was impossible to hurry through the noisy press, so Klale stared around in fascination. Store signs and conversations were in more languages than she could recognize, and she saw a lot of Slang, too. The local version of sign language was clearly a lingua franca Downtown, and she wished she could follow the speeding fingers, but with translation available by phone, languages had always seemed like a waste of time.

Although it wasn't yet ten A.M., the spuddy carts were already lined up, vendors bellowing offers of hash browns and onions for a loonie, and beer or water for another two coins. Signs proclaimed SAFE TO DRINK! OUR WATER FILTERED AND BOILED TEN MINUTES! At one cart a red-faced woman grabbed a wiggling guinea pig, bashed its head against a block, then eviscerated it with swift strokes. Klale winced.

"Kind of takes my appetite away," she told Alberta.

"Good. Food here is grown in random dirt—lousy nutrition. And don't eat from a cart unless you want cholera."

That finished Klale's appetite.

"And be careful about vectors. If you get a cut or scrape, treat it fast and if it's not healing clean within twenty-four hours, run to a clinic."

Klale nodded. She was already in that habit from the boats and the processing plant where virulent strains of staph and strep were constant threats. Despite precautions, people still occasionally died from Bloom—necrotizing bacterial infections that spread so fast they could kill before they were identified and treated. She wondered how common Bloom was Downtown, then put the thought aside with a shudder.

A cluster of power bikes snorted past, ridden by toughs in black leathers. "Tigers—the Viet Ching's gang," Alberta told her. Then Klale glimpsed unmistakable half-furred, half-shaved skulls. "Ghost Shadows. They're the Kung Lok's gang," said Alberta. As the gang members strutted past, Klale fell in behind the two bouncers. She didn't think she'd be recognized, but why take chances?

Alberta led them into a skin-art store whose grimy windows advertised surgery and dental extractions. Inside, a thin, sallow-faced man sat in a dentist chair, noisily eating spuddies and watching soccer on an old ceiling-suspended screen. As they walked in, he shoved his greasy plate onto the instrument tray and stood up, twisting his face into a rictus smile.

"Finest art, Citizens . . ." he started.

"Looking for a girl," said Alberta, planting her feet.

The man's smile faded to a nervous scowl.

"No girls here."

"Just want a quarter hour." She dug some coins out of her pocket, and held them up. "Ten."

"No girls here."

Pum tapped Alberta's shoulder and stepped forward menacingly.

"We're looking for Shar and we're gonna see her. Be nice and we pay ten."

"Don't take cash," said the man sullenly.

"Yeah you do. Catch."

She took Alberta's money and began tossing coins one at a time. The man glowered, but caught them deftly out of the air, then threw something shiny back at Pum. She caught it and stepped past him to a threadbare curtain at the back of the shop. Alberta took Klale's shoulder and steered her forward.

Beyond the curtain a flight of stairs led up to a dingy room which reminded Klale absurdly of a water taxi waiting booth. A young Afroid girl sat huddled on an old couch wearing a headset. When Pum tapped her shoulder she took it off, revealing sleepy, sullen eyes. For a second Klale thought she must be the man's child, then she saw the heavy makeup and tight clothes and realized that the girl was a prostitute. She looked about twelve.

"You Shar?"

"No."

"I'm looking for Shar."

"No Shar here."

"I'm here for talk, not fucking," Pum told her. "Wanna know how to find Hassim and Drake."

The girl shook her head.

Pum held up a shiny metal tube, about the size of half a cigarette.

"Hassim and Drake. Tell us; it's yours, we leave."

The girl's eyes followed the tube as Pum waved it. She squirmed uneasily on the couch. Pum held up a coin next to the tube. When the girl showed no reaction she held up a second coin.

"Last chance."

"Hassim got a room at Dick's."

"Yeah, and how come you know?"

"He my cuz," said the girl sullenly.

"You Shar?"

"Not no more." She stuck her chin out. "I'm Galadriella Morn-ingstar."

Pum tossed her the coins and tube. The girl caught the objects deftly in cupped hands, shoved the coins in a pocket, and then reached up with both hands to the back of her neck. She gasped, arched, and her face stretched into an ecstatic smile, then she sagged back on the couch, grinning vacantly.

"What's that?" Klale asked softly.

"Fifteen-minute booster," said Pum. She didn't bother lowering her voice. She beckoned Klale, walked around the back of the couch, pushed the girl's head forward and parted her hair. Under it Klale saw the booster tube plugged directly into a thalamic jack.

"It goes right through her skin!" said Klale in horror, looking at the inflamed site.

"Transdermal jack," said Alberta grimly behind her. "Cheap death. Vectors everything."

The girl gave a sudden throaty moan. She twisted around, reaching for Pum's hand with an eager smile. Pum pulled away. The girl lifted up her shirt and moved her gaze to Alberta, stroking and squeezing her tiny breasts while staring fixedly into Alberta's eyes. She was so thin her ribs stood out. Klale felt her face flame.

Alberta grabbed Klale's arm.

"We're outta here."

She moved toward the stairs, but the girl lurched up off the couch, and blocked their path. She was breathing urgently, and under her beatific smile Klale sensed sudden desperation.

"This way," called Pum. They turned and hurried after her along a hall and down back stairs which led into an alley lined with shacks. Alberta marched at top speed until they reached the nearest street, then she stopped and wiped her forehead.

"Jesus. Watching that gives me the heaves. Another minute and she'll be screwing anything she can get between her legs."

Klale stood, looking back down the alley with a cold, sick knot in her gut.

"Toni was wired like that, wasn't she?"

"She was wired better'n that or she'd be dead," said Alberta. "You had enough yet?"

Klale put her hands on her hips and set her face stubbornly.

"I came here to find those flots. But I didn't ask you to help. Give me the address and I'll go on my own."

Alberta snorted.

"Yeah right."

She turned and started walking. Klale followed, hoping like hell Alberta would stick around. She no longer had any desire to try this alone.

The "Richards Private Residence" had once been an office tower with wraparound plate glass windows which were now an expanse of crudely nailed boards, broken only by a reinforced steel door with a faded vacancy sign. Inside the tiny lobby they were stopped by an ancient man with a shiny new tracking pistol. He accepted Alberta's bribe and pointed to a filthy stairwell. They climbed up fifteen floors and emerged in a narrow, dim maze of corridors, heavy with the sour smell of humans. Pum and Alberta started knocking on unmarked doors. When they got an answer they flashed coins, but few people were home and no one had much to say. One small kid claimed Hassim had lived there but moved away weeks ago. Klale wondered if he was lying to get a coin. Eventually they reached a communal kitchen, its walls streaked with swatted roaches.

"Makes the 'Dyke look like a palace," Klale said. "What's the rent?"

"Twenty bucks a week for a room with no windows," said Alberta. "Most of these people are blissers, working the Viet Ching factories. Pay's rigged so they never get out of debt, but blissers don't care. Just want to plug back into the job, maybe work faster and earn a little joy bonus."

Footsteps approached along a blind hallway. Alberta and Pum spun, clutching at their armpits. They were wearing shoulder holsters, Klale realized suddenly. An old man rounded a corner, and stopped, blinking at them from rheumy eyes sunk deeply into a gray face. He backed off and scuttled away.

Klale suppressed a shudder. He looked more dead than Blade, she thought. Alberta let out a long breath and straightened up, brushing off her shirt.

"We're getting nowhere. C'mon."

When they emerged onto a crowded sidewalk in the glare of the hot sun, Klale took deep breaths of clean air to steady herself. Her feet felt damp and swollen in her heavy boots, and she was very thirsty. She tugged at her shirt, fanning air underneath and looked over at the others. Were they willing to continue? Alberta looked annoyed. Pum looked bored. Klale had just opened her mouth, when four very large Americans stepped out of the crowd. One pointed an automatic weapon directly at the KlonDyke women.

Alberta and Pum froze, only their eyes moving. For long seconds nobody spoke. Klale stared.

The gang members wore identical gray hempen overalls tucked into black, steel-toed boots, wide leather bandoliers slung over their shoulders and leather knuckle gloves with armored wristcuffs. All of them were Pum's size or bigger and had very dark skin, so identical in shade that Klale suspected enhanced pigmentation. They wore close-cropped hair elaborately etched with follicle suppressant and cicatrices carved in distinctive patterns across their foreheads, cheeks, upper arms, and chests.

Klale felt her stomach do a panicked fish-flop and fought to keep her face calm. She had grown up with games and ficvids full of violent, crazed American refugees.

One, the only woman, stepped forward and smiled coldly. Her white teeth were filed into points.

"Bloods hear you lookin' for Drake and Hassim."

"Yeah?" said Alberta.

"Yeah. They 'Mercan people. What you want with them?"

"Nothin'. No brews, no smog." said Alberta stonily. "We're leaving."

"No we aren't!" blurted Klale.

Everyone stared at her.

"Look," she stammered, regretting too late that she'd opened her mouth, "I don't mean to be discourteous." She held out her hands placatingly and tried to look harmless. "I just want to find them so I can help them out. That's all."

The Blood woman smirked.

"They don't be takin' no help from no Zitty twat."

"But it's important!" Klale took a nervous breath and avoided Alberta's poisonous glare. She could hear her own blood pounding in her ears. "It's about the Harbor Patrol."

Klale had the Bloods' full attention now—four sets of very white eyes fixed on her from very dark faces. The woman with the filed teeth seemed to be considering something.

"You wanna talk to Lincoln," she said finally. She turned and walked away. The man pointing the automatic waved at them to follow.

"Where are you taking us?" asked Alberta loudly. She stood with her feet planted, arms loose by her side.

The Blood woman turned back, eyes glinting.

"You want I truss you like roast dog, or you come nice?"

"Nice," volunteered Klale.

"Shut up," hissed Alberta. But she followed, with Pum and Klale behind her and the other Bloods behind them.

As the Bloods escorted them into a narrow alley, Klale had time to regret her impulsiveness and consider just how much danger they were in. What if the Bloods simply killed them? She shoved her hands deep in her pockets and tried to look as impassive as Alberta and Pum, but it was everything she could do not to tremble.

After a few blocks they emerged near the False Creek waterfront beside a public waterstation—one of the last relics of the '62 earthquake, erected shortly before City Services abandoned Downtown. A line of silent, gaunt-faced people, mostly very old or very young, stood with mute resignation in the hot sun, holding bags and buckets. Despite the glare, few of them wore lenses or hats and Klale wondered how many flots got cancer.

The Bloods turned down a steep ramp onto a float lined with ramshackle boats and barges, many as small as three meters. Some were no more than crude rafts kept afloat with pieces of wood, ancient chunks of Styrofoam, or empty jugs. The noahs near shore were bumping bottom. At lower tides they would be grounded, thought Klale. In some places even the floats were foundering. Pum stepped on a corner of sidewalk and plunged to her ankles in muddy seawater, jumping back with such alarm that Klale guessed she couldn't swim. Klale squeezed her shoulder reassuringly and received a glare for her trouble.

Pum's movement had attracted attention. Eyes watched surreptitiously from all sides and Klale felt immensely conspicuous with her pale Zit skin. In the West End, the racial mix was heavily European, East Asian, and Oriental, but here most people were Afroid, with skin tones ranging from creamy coffee to black. Even brown-skinned Pum looked out of place with her distinctly Punjabi features.

A strange nasal chant, distorted by cheap amplifiers, began echoing through the noahs and the Bloods abruptly stopped at the intersection of two floats. Three of them put down their weapons, leaving only the woman armed. As Klale watched in puzzlement, they lifted cigar-shaped bundles off their shoulders and began unrolling them. Prayer rugs, she realized suddenly. All around them men emerged from noahs and laid down rugs on decks and floats. The female Blood gestured them back, and they sat down a little distance away, watching the Muslim prayers.

Men's voices droned, then they knelt in a wave, rocking the float. A hush had fallen over the din of voices, babies crying, and strains of popular music. The floats smelled intensely of old sweat, cooking, low tide, and the inevitable chickens. Klale swatted at a fly, then looked up to see a Longshore freight truck crossing the span of the Cambie Bridge. It was only a hundred meters away, yet in a different world.

Impulsively Klale touched Pum's arm and whispered: "Thank you for coming with me."

"I owe Toni," said Pum curtly.

"What for?"

The big bouncer hesitated, then replied.

"My teeth. I wasn't going to no butcher but real Zit dentists want plastic. Boss paid some but I was short. Toni loan me the rest."

"Oh," said Klale faintly, looking away. She'd heard of dental disease from the old days. The idea of teeth rotting inside Pum's mouth made her queasy.

When prayers ended the Bloods rolled up their rugs, picked up their weapons, and continued. Klale was beginning to feel that they were lost in the maze of noahs when she looked ahead and saw an anomaly amid the jumbled squalor: a freshly painted blue and white catamaran about fifteen meters long. A Red Cross flag flew from the mast, and a crowd of people were lined up on the float beside it.

Their Blood escort walked past the line-up and onto a modern, immaculately clean ship. The afterdeck held a medical reception area, but they were led around to the foredeck where a table and chairs had been arranged under an awning and an American man sat alone, casually sipping coffee. It would have been a peaceful scene except for his two Blood bodyguards, automatic weapons held loosely in their hands.

The man put down his coffee cup and stood gracefully, extending a pink-palmed hand.

"I'm Lincoln," he announced, flashing perfect white teeth. "I believe you have already met Atlanta, Malcolm, King, and Juju." He waved behind him. "Ali, Resolve."

Klale stared, startled by Lincoln's deep, resonant voice. She had vaguely imagined, the Bloods' commander as some combat-scarred toxgut, but this man was strikingly handsome. Lincoln dressed like the Bloods, but his hempen overalls were tailored to flatter his athletic figure, and they tucked into polished leather boots. Gold earcuffs and a gold spiral band on his upper arm gleamed richly against his dark chocolate skin. He had short unadorned hair and no facial art, though Klale glimpsed cicatrices on his chest and arms. She couldn't guess his age. When he smiled into her eyes, she caught her breath.

Alberta introduced the three KlonDyke women, then Lincoln waved the Blood escort away, and indicated chairs. Klale sat, uncomfortably aware of the two bodyguards and their weapons just behind her. A clinic staffer in medical whites hurried over with a pot of fresh coffee and cups. Behind him Klale caught a distant glimpse of the south shore of False Creek, with a newly built sea walk fronting on neatly trimmed Guild rezzes and merchant blocks.

She suddenly realized that Lincoln was speaking.

". . . new clinic is the pride of the Screaming Eagles. With it we are able to serve the poorest residents of Downtown. And the medics, nurses, and dentist aboard are all local people, sent to school on Screaming Eagles scholarships."

He smiled at her again, and Klale felt the assault of his charisma.

"Great," she managed. Lincoln gestured behind her.

"Do you see the black and silver bag hanging from the rigging?"

"Huh? I mean, yes. Uh . . ." She looked over at a nearby noah, shading her eyes. "Oh, the solar desalination unit?"

He raised an eyebrow, then favored her with an approving smile.

"Of course, you're a Fisher. You know about them."

"Emergency gear on all our boats. They can be opened out for rainwater collection, too," she said, relieved to hit on a topic she knew something about. Then it occurred to her to wonder how he knew she was a Fisher. That hadn't been in Alberta's introduction. Lincoln must have run a personal query on her while the Bloods were escorting them. Her sense of alarm returned.

"These units are provided free by the Screaming Eagles," said Lincoln proudly. "There are only six public taps along this part of the waterfront, but one of these units produces up to two liters of drinking water a day."

He pointed at a shed some distance away.

"We also build and maintain community toilets and wash sheds which are serviced by our own biogas barges. The fuel produced is sold back at cost for cooking and heating."

Klale nodded, impressed in spite of herself. Pum and Alberta sat stolidly, not touching their coffee, but Lincoln ignored them. He leaned back looking genial and unhurried, then he cut straight to the point with a directness that took Klale's breath away.

"I understand, Miz Renhardt, that you're looking for two Americans who were involved in a brawl at the KlonDyke. Might I ask why?"

She gathered her wits.

"I was hoping to persuade them to file a public complaint against the Harbor Patrol. I saw what happened and so did lots of other witnesses." Klale's genuine indignation helped her gather steam. "The Patrol has no jurisdiction on dry land, and they certainly have no right to treat anybody the way they did, citizen or not."

"Your enthusiasm is admirable. But I'm afraid that you will not find many Guildless who share it."

"Well, don't you care?" shot back Klale, suddenly angry. "The refugees are your people. Isn't your tong supposed to protect them?"

"The Screaming Eagles is not a tong," said Lincoln, his voice and eyes instantly hard.

His swift changeability alarmed Klale. Out of the corner of her eyes she saw the Bloods stiffen.

"I'm sorry," she said hastily. "I'm new to Vancouver and I'm still learning."

"Ignorance can be very hazardous," observed Lincoln.

"So can too much knowledge," pointed out Klale. She forced a grin.

Lincoln answered it with a sudden, sunny smile.

"It's a delicate balance, isn't it?" He put down his coffee cup.

Instantly the clinic staffer appeared at his elbow and refilled it.

"Very well, for your information, the Screaming Eagles is an association of residents dedicated to improving conditions for the Guildless. I'm the president, which is an *elected* position. I also belong to the community militia, nicknamed the Bloods, which polices and protects our people. And I would suggest you remember not to call us 'refugees.' Most of us were born here, just like you citizens."

Klale nodded.

"How do you get along with the Harbor Patrol?" she asked, trying to imitate his coolness.

Amusement flickered in Lincoln's eyes.

"Harmoniously, of course. So long as we commit no dire crimes such as fishing from the floats or urinating in the harbor. In those cases, offenders who cannot pay the necessary fines have their homes seized and scrapped. The Screaming Eagles mediates disputes for our people and we're often able to help."

They pay the Patrol off, translated Klale, a little amused at her own newly acquired cynicism.

"Drake and Hassim?" interrupted Alberta.

Lincoln made a regretful gesture.

"I am sorry. I understand they are not willing to speak against the Patrol and I certainly couldn't advise them to take such a risk. Nonetheless, I admire your objective. Do please feel free to call me if you need assistance."

"Assistance?" retorted Klale, annoyed. "You just said you wouldn't help us."

"Then perhaps I should make myself clear," said Lincoln and there was sudden steel under his smooth voice. "I have an interest in the Harbor Patrol and particularly Captain Dhillon, who has blamed the drowning of her first officer on Americans and is making trouble for us. I intend to do what I can to ensure that the trouble stops."

Klale glanced behind him and caught his Blood bodyguards exchanging brief, savage smiles. They chilled her.

"Call me any time," Lincoln continued. He produced a phone from under his coveralls and Klale had to struggle not to gape. It was gold biometal—a substance she'd heard of but never expected to see. She fumbled her own clunky Guild-issue alumplast phone out of her pocket and exchanged IDs.

Abruptly Lincoln stood. The others scrambled to follow. As Klale started to rise she found Lincoln's hand in front of her. She took it nervously and he helped her up, then bent forward slightly to put his mouth near her ear. She caught the faint scent of cologne.

"I viewed your audition. Very amusing."

"Thank you," managed Klale, trying not to look completely rattled.

She felt Lincoln's warm, hard grip for a long time afterward.

7

When Bracken whistled from the other end of the bar, Toni looked up in annoyance, expecting to see his hand signal for Blade. Instead, he pointed at the tong exec tables where a hench stood waving for service.

Damn Thursdays! thought Toni irritably, but she watched the Slanged order and waved acknowledgment. She had to run downstairs for a bottle of cognac, then decant it into an engraved flask in the kitchen while Val loaded a candle tray with silver saki cups, slices of fruit, nuts, red-embossed moon cakes, and steaming bamboo containers of dim sum.

Toni delivered the heavy tray herself to Mr. Kwong, who sat at the head of the table, erect and impeccable in a hand-tailored suit. As he gave her a slight nod, she was struck yet again by the oddness of his cold green-gray eyes in an Oriental face. Kwong's ancestry was Russian, but it was fashionable in the Sun Yee On to be Chinese.

She passed the flask to the subordinate on Kwong's right, who poured drinks. Toni could tell by their intensity that some sort of deal was in progress, but she couldn't guess what. The Chinese tongs used ancient hand signals for bargaining. According to Mary, it was all in how they held their chopsticks, or put their fingers around a cup—impossible for outsiders to read. And what about Blade? she wondered again. Toni knew that the enforcer could read lips, but did he know the hand signals, too? Is that what Choi used him for?

Then it struck her, and she glanced casually around, pretending to check her servers. Blade wasn't at his usual table. Strange. He always showed up at the bar on tong meeting nights.

Mr. Kwong grasped the tiny silver cup delicately between gold-ringed fingers, swirled, sniffed, sipped, then nodded. Toni was dismissed.

As she made her way back to the bar, Toni scanned the room. They had almost a full house tonight. On the far side of the room, a big group from Sisters rez toasted a new mother and her baby. At front center, a dozen dockers were spending heavy—either a gambling win or Longshore graft. Alberta was keeping a close eye on them. In the Zit section, a table of out-of-town Guild execs stared furtively around and tried to look urbane.

As Toni reached the bar a motion caught her attention and she glanced over. Lily again. She'd backed into Klale's path, almost colliding with her. The first time she'd tried that trick, Klale had lost a tray full of drinks, but Lily hadn't caught her a second time. At least Klale had the sense not to complain. The Guild girl would have to settle with the other servers on her own.

"One fire eats for the barkeep!" bellowed Val from the kitchen.

Toni flinched at her volume but took the meal off the ledge with thanks, then sat on her stool. Usually she ate in the downroom, but right now she was too hungry to bother. She balanced the warm chili dish on her knee and took a spoonful, enjoying the burn in her mouth and sinuses as the peppers made contact. Tasting the food made her suddenly ravenous. Several mouthfuls later she looked out of the corner of her eye at the far section.

Lily was heading back to the bar with empties. Was she limping? Yes, and she looked angry. Toni stifled a smile. Klale must have kicked her. Good. A few more and Lily would back off. Klale was bigger.

A puff of cinnamon wafted over her chili and she looked up to find herself nose-to-tit with Bracken's cinnamon sprinkled aureoles, poking out of a floor-length, translucent brown dress. Toni jabbed her fork toward the nearest breast and Bracken hopped back a step, then nodded to the main door and scowled.

"I thought we banned that tight-legged hyena!"

Toni followed his gaze to see Cedar de Groot coming in with his

Freevie friends, including Tommy Yip and Captain Dhillon. Yip swept the room with an ingratiating smile and Toni felt stirrings of unease. Yip was dangerous. Cedar was looking around, too, then he located Klale and started trying to catch her eye. Interesting. He seemed to have a middle-aged pash on the girl. Toni turned back.

"We didn't have much choice," she told Bracken shortly.

Bracken scowled.

"I'm going to piss in Baljeet's beer. Cedar, too."

Good idea, thought Toni, but didn't let it show on her face. She washed down a mouthful of chili, letting cool nearbeer soothe the burn in her mouth, and determinedly ignored her flashing readout and the eyes on the other side of the bar while Bracken tended cash customers at the till.

The Boss arrived through the side door with a tall Oriental man behind her. Cedar de Groot jumped up and intercepted them. Mary introduced him to the other man and de Groot shook hands, but he proceeded to ignore the newcomer while he made an impassioned speech at Mary. Mary stood listening for several minutes, then made polite leaving motions. Cedar ignored her hints. Finally, Mary began walking. Cedar followed, coming into Toni's earshot.

"... and it's important that Downtowners understand the dangers..."

The Boss rolled her eyes at Toni. Toni put her dinner aside, poured a pint of Granville and set it up on the bar in front of Cedar.

"Mary, I know you have good intentions, but..."

Mary had reached her limit. She turned and spoke quietly. "Cedar, I'm going to offer you one piece of advice, and I won't repeat it."

He blinked. "Ah... what?"

"Change your executive."

"But it's a strat team! And Tommy's doing tremendous work as treasurer!"

I'll bet, thought Toni acidly. But Mary hadn't given up yet. She dropped her voice so low that Toni barely caught her words.

"Cedar, you're running a tong front group."

He puffed up with indignation.

"No, no! It's not that way at all! You know that people Downtown don't have a choice about paying tongs. Tommy pays the Kung Lok, but that doesn't mean he's bent." De Groot's voice was growing strident and people started looking around. The tall Oriental man stood behind Mary, watching with open amusement. Bracken sidled over, pretending to inspect orders in the pass-through window while he eavesdropped.

"Besides we have other people, too. Baljeet's a pyro vice president!"

The Boss greeted that one with dead silence, and Toni looked up long enough to fix Cedar with a flat stare. He blinked a couple of times, then belatedly remembered the fight and realized that he'd put his foot in it.

"Ah, well, usually I mean . . .

Mary let him flounder a few seconds, then took him by the shoulder in her most motherly manner.

"Enough, Cedar. You were right. We should agree to disagree, OK?"

Unexpectedly, it wasn't. He shook off her hand.

"You're treating me like a cret, but you're the fool, Mary! Those railroad promoters are the real businessmen! They'll promise you anything now, but they'll sell you out later!" He turned and stalked off, ignoring the beer Toni held out.

"He has a point," said Toni very quietly, as she put it back down.

Mary regarded her with grave eyes.

"I'm doing my best to put Cascadia Rail in a position where they can't dishonor their agreements."

I hope so, thought Toni.

Mary turned to the man behind her.

"Dr. Lau, please forgive the interruption. Toni, I want to introduce you to the new medic we've been needing so much. Dr. Amerigo Lau, Robson Street Clinic. Toni, my indispensible head bartender."

Dr. Lau stepped forward, smiling politely, hand held out, then his eyes focused on Toni and he froze with a startled expression. Toni's heart pounded with sudden alarm. Did he recognize her? She looked different than she had ten years ago, but not that different. Had her luck finally run out?

She quickly assessed him. Lau was a handsome man, over fifty she guessed from his neck and ears, though he looked forty—the age appearance most doctors chose because it allegedly inspired patient confidence. He had probably gone for cosmetic work when he graduated, and would maintain "doctor age" into his seventies or eighties. Artful touches of gray in his long hair and a charming smile, slightly intensified by subtle worry lines around his eyes, added to his presence. His clothes were expensive, and he wore them with confidence. Like a tong exec, she thought warily. But she couldn't remember ever having met him before.

He was returning her assessment with an odd intensity, so she decided to tackle him directly.

"Have we met before?"

"No," he said hastily. "I'm sure I would remember if we had." He twinkled his charming eyes at her. "I'm very sorry to be discourteous. You reminded me of someone I used to know."

"I see," said Toni, failing to return his smile. Her coolness didn't seem to ruffle him.

Mary gave Toni a quizzical glance, then put a friendly hand on Lau's shoulder.

"Doctor, we're desperate for more medics Downtown and we want to make you very welcome. Might I invite you by my office for a drink?"

"Thank you, I am delighted," said Lau, and looked it.

"Toni, do you have a moment?" asked Mary.

For a split second Toni thought of begging off, but she knew Mary hadn't made the invitation lightly.

"Of course," she said. She abandoned her half-eaten dinner and followed, ignoring Bracken's squawk of dismay behind her.

Mary had already set out one of her precious bottles of ice wine and three crystal glasses. They sat down around the coffee table, Lau fastidiously adjusting his coat and trousers. His shiny long hair was tied back with a gold clip, reminding Toni uncomfortably of the Harbor Patrol's queues. She tried to look pleasant, but she felt wary and tense, and Lau's sidelong glances didn't help. He might be comparing her to someone else. Or he might have lied. She wished Mary had warned her about him.

Mary led the conversation, conducting her usual velvet-gloved interrogation. But Lau was Mary's match, both in questions and charm. Before long Toni felt sickeningly like a spectator at a diplomatic Ping-Pong match.

"Dr. Lau, I've heard that you were greatly loved by your patients in Hong Kong. They must miss you so much. . . ."

"Why, thank you. But I hear that you are very much loved by the people Downtown, Miz Smarch. . . ."

Et cetera.

After a while Toni ignored the content and searched for oddities. Lau spoke fluent English with a faint Chinese accent, but despite his education and polished style, he said he was only a general medic. Was he slumming? How did he afford his taste in clothes on a Black Cross stipend? Still, she recognized his type very well: dedicated, energetic, and driven. He probably worked seven days a week, was adored by his patients and staff, and never found enough time for his family. When he mentioned a recent divorce, she gave herself a mental check mark.

After a few rounds, Mary abruptly abandoned subtlety.

"I understand that you used to live in Vancouver. Why did you come back?"

For the first time Lau hesitated and Toni's attention sharpened. He toyed with his glass, then looked at Mary.

"Let us be honest, Miz Smarch. You want to know if you can trust me and I want to know if I can trust you, true?"

Mary's smile deepened the creases in her brown face.

"Exactly true," she said.

He gave her a boyish grin, then sobered.

"Very well. The Sun Yee On paid for my medical education, so I am tong debted. I worked for them in Hong Kong and now I work for them here. But they bought my work, not me."

Mary was looking into his eyes intently, then she reached over and took his hand.

"That's not why you came here," she said softly. She patted the back of his hand. "You have a reason. A sad one, I think. Will you tell me?"

Toni had seen Mary follow hunches before, but it still amazed her. Lau looked astonished, then intrigued. Then he surprised Toni by taking Mary's hand in both of his.

"I *will* tell you. I had a father and a son once. They both died here." His voice grew rough. "I can never forget my guilt that I was not here to help them."

Mary nodded, still watching his eyes closely.

"They haunt you. You want to face them, then let them go."

He nodded, grief showing on his face.

Very touching, thought Toni cynically, leaning back in her chair. But she could think of much better reasons for the tong to bring Lau to Vancouver. He might be a surgeon or a trainer, sent to do non-consensual alterations on contract for the Viet Ching. Or he might be an assassin. He met that profile perfectly—a respected, sociable, well placed person whom others would instinctively trust. She knew that the tongs found likely candidates and implanted directives, then covered their memories and waited years or even decades before making use of them. She should warn Alberta.

"And of course I wish to assist you with the Downtown Residents Association."

Alarms went off in Toni's head and she put down her glass, but Mary immediately started talking about the D.R.A. Toni listened unhappily, realizing that Mary had taken a strong liking to Lau. But Mary's instincts wouldn't tell her if Lau was an assassin since he wouldn't know it himself. And Mary's instincts couldn't protect Toni if Lau had recognized her.

"I have to get back to work," she said, too abruptly. Lau rose and held out his hand.

"I am very pleased to have met you, Miz Toni. I hope we can talk another time."

"About what?" she asked sharply. Behind Lau, Mary frowned.

"About Downtown, of course," said Lau smoothly.

"Of course."

Back in the bar Toni tried to shake off her uneasiness by concentrating on the backlog of orders that had accumulated. She was pleased to see Bracken coping despite the flood. In four years he had made considerable progress from his early days of hysteria. His volley of melodramatic complaints was mostly habit now. She only wished he would learn to do pad audits and reconcile cash so he could close up the bar, but at any hint of increased responsibility he backed off like a skittish child.

As the workload eased, her worries and fears resurfaced. She found it unreasonably disturbing that she'd still seen no sign of Blade. Could it have anything to do with Choi's call? But what?

When Klale came over to chat, Toni was hoping for a diversion, so she heard Klale's first words with sinking dismay.

"Toni, Blade's not here tonight."

"He doesn't always come in," said Toni shortly. Klale was still fascinated by the enforcer. Damn.

Klale frowned at her, wrinkling her freckled forehead. A tuft of wiry red hair had worked loose from her hair tie and fell into her face. She kept pushing it back.

"Toni, I've been thinking about Blade. Everyone seems to hate him. But he's a person."

"No, he's not, Klale. He's a tool."

"I know he has a neural plug. But that doesn't mean he isn't human!"

Toni felt like groaning. She was in no mood to explain the facts of life to a Zit kid, but she could already see that Klale would pester her incessantly if she didn't. Or get into still more trouble.

"Klale," she said wearily. "Pull up a stool."

As the girl obeyed, she searched for an explanation that Klale might understand.

"Tools start as kids, usually thirteen, fourteen years old, bought or stolen from the streets. Trainers wipe their memories, then subject them to torture and disorientation techniques that destroy their personalities. Once they're completely malleable, new behaviors are taught and those new neural pathways are chemically cemented."

She paused, looking at Klale's incomprehension.

"Klale, tools literally don't know they're human. And they are altered so far from behavioral norms that they aren't, anymore. They're slaves conditioned to absolute obedience."

She wasn't sure she was getting through, but she pushed on.

"Blunted tools can't feel anything except what their masters dispense: pain as punishment, or pleasure as reward. Even their sexuality is redirected and used to reinforce behavior. As a simple example, a master can key his own voice commands. When he says "good" the tool gets a nice jolt, "very good" gives a bigger jolt, and "excellent" delivers an orgasm. If a tool becomes aroused, he simply feels more and more urgency to please his master."

For the first time, Klale glanced away, looking faintly sick.

"Could Blade be . . . untrained?" she asked.

"No." Toni made her voice hard. "Too much neural damage. Many tools aren't even clinically sentient—they're called 'corpses' in the business. Removed from their master they simply wait for orders until they die. They have no personality left, and aren't capable of regaining any."

"But . . ." Klale looked at her with urgent hazel eyes, "Blade isn't a corpse, is he?"

And that was the problem, thought Toni grimly. A corpse would be beyond pain . . . or help.

"No. And that makes him especially dangerous. Sentient tools are prone to episodes of intense rage. Occasionally they go berserk and have to be destroyed. That's why they have a fishhook—a remote-triggered explosive device implanted at the base of the skull next to the spinal column. It kills instantly. Certain tong members also have fishhooks. They're almost impossible to remove, so they ensure loyalty."

She fixed Klale with a cold gaze.

"Klale, surviving Downtown means developing a necessary callousness. There's nothing you can do for Blade. Or many others. You'll simply have to learn to accept that."

Klale sighed and pushed her hair back again.

"I don't know if I can. Especially after today. I keep thinking about that girl—'Galadriella.' "

"Who?" asked Toni.

Klale filled Toni in on her trip to the American floats. Toni had already heard most of it from Alberta, but she found herself amazed all over again. How could one Zit girl get into so much smog in so short a time? When she got to Lincoln, Toni asked:

"What did you think of Lincoln?"

Klale grinned.

"God, he looked better than the hero in *Manifest Destiny* and that was a biodesigned simstar." She paused and looked more thoughtful. "The Americans seem to love him."

"And fear him," said Toni. "He has a big upper-storey following, but he skims his own people worse than the Patrol does and he's ruthless. People who speak him down are doused with marine fuel and set on fire."

"Oh." Klale's face sobered, then she crossed her arms across her chest. "Well . . . I guess I'm going to have to report Captain Dhillon myself."

Toni stared at her, aghast.

"Report her? Klale, you're a Guild runaway. The Patrol isn't going to take your word against hers, and the last thing you want to do is make an enemy of her."

"Enemy? She already made an enemy of me!"

"You're living alone Downtown. It's too dangerous!"

"But I can't just let her do that to me—to anybody—and get away with it!"

Klale's voice quavered and for the first time Toni noticed smudges of weariness under the girl's eyes. She bit back the sharp words she had ready and instead said:

"You look tired."

"Well . . . I'm having trouble sleeping." Klale ran a hand through her unruly hair and tried to force a smile. "Partly the hours, I guess, but . . . well, I hate to admit it, but it's hard living where my phone doesn't work. At night I'm scared and in the daytime I keep missing my net service. And worrying. I mean, I want to review my old courses to get ready for university, but I can't study without a set!"

Klale, on the verge of tears, looked impossibly young, thought Toni. And watching her made Toni oddly wistful for a naiveté that she'd never had. She hesitated a long moment, then gave way to an impulse.

"Look, Klale, I have a full service netset. That's a secret, by the way—Mary agreed to piggyback me onto the 'Dyke's connect as a once-only, and she doesn't want word getting around. But I'd be willing to let you use it."

She hadn't even disentangled herself from Klale's ecstatic hug before she regretted the impulse. In ten years the only person she'd invited into her apartment was Mary. And she'd been furious at Alberta for violating her hermitage. So why Klale?

Could it be sexual attraction? Doubtful. More likely her yearnings for companionship were a symptom of age, she thought cynically. And isolation. Certainly there was no point contemplating Klale. Nice Zit girls didn't fuck old smuts.

No, it was much simpler. Toni envied Klale's happy spontaneity and that unmistakable mark of Guild security—optimism. Rich people jumped for their dreams, thought Toni. Poor people grabbed in terror to keep from sliding to the bottom. Klale didn't understand that. She kept making friendly overtures to the Guildless servers, and then retreating from their rebuffs in puzzlement, not comprehending why they hated her perfect teeth, perfect eyes, perfect health, and easy self-confidence.

Well, Toni wouldn't have an apartment much longer. And she'd intended for a long time to reach out more, establish friendships. Why not Klale?

Still, second thoughts nagged her as the night dragged on. Bracken and most of the servers went off shift when the crowd thinned, but the tong execs remained, and Toni began to think they would stay all night. Finally, around half past four, they rose and left. She sighed in relief and gave the last call.

The staff rushed through close-up, and even Alberta departed before Toni had finished her pad audits. As usual when she was tired, everything seemed to crawl and the infernal coin counter kept jamming. By the time Toni finally took her routine walk around the back, she was half asleep.

Fear snapped her awake when a shadow moved in the dark hallway. Toni froze at the kitchen door, knowing that the staff had gone and the place should be empty. She was in trouble. The hall had only one old hard-wired light switch down at the other end. Worse, she was unarmed. She took a slow backward step into the kitchen where she could grab a knife.

"Who's there?" she yelled.

No answer. She took another step backward, preparing to jump

back into the kitchen and slam the door shut behind her. Then the
shadows moved again and a gigantic figure stepped forward. Blade.

For an instant Toni felt relieved, then Blade swayed and leaned
against the wall, crossing his arms protectively against his chest. He
was shaking. She felt a chill of terror. That's what she would expect
a tool to look like just before he went berserk.

Don't alarm him, she told herself urgently. Follow the usual routine. She took a deep breath and snapped off the kitchen lights, then
walked slowly down the dark hall toward the office. He let her pass,
then followed.

Inside the office she crossed to the desk and switched on a lamp,
then after a slight hesitation, wakened the netset and sat down. Blade
didn't wait for anything more—he fell on his knees at her side and
reached up immediately. When she put her hand on his enormous
one, he closed his fingers tightly.

Bad, bad, bad! Tools never varied routine. Toni took a few seconds to assemble her old professional detachment. Then she risked
a direct look at his face.

She felt a stab of alarm. His altered features were actually twisted
into an agonized grimace, and his clinging hand, usually warm, felt
ice cold. Sticky, too. She glanced down. It was caked with blood.

She almost flinched with revulsion, then made herself focus. First
question: whose blood? She looked Blade over as carefully as she
could without touching him. His sleeves and shirt front were splashed
with congealed blood, but she couldn't see any rips in the fabric or
fresh bleeding. Probably not his own, then. Had he already gone
berserk? No, of course not—once berserk he wouldn't stop killing.

Had he been punished? She bent forward slowly and studied his
eyes. His pupils were dilated, but she saw none of the bruising that
characterized prolonged stimulation of the pain center. Not a severe
punishment, at least. A spontaneous episode of violence, then. That
wasn't so bad. If he'd released some of his rage already, she should
be able to calm him.

She thought urgently, then pulled her hand out of his and signed
at him to stay put. In the kitchen she wet a cloth with hot water and
hurried back. He hadn't moved. She sat down, swiveling her chair to

face him, then took his left hand onto her lap and wiped it softly with the steaming cloth, letting heat soak in.

At the first stroke his eyes closed. At the next he winced and caught his breath.

"It's all right," she said soothingly. "You're safe now. Everything's all right." He made no threatening moves toward her, but his eyes stayed closed. Damn. No way to get through to him.

She finished with his left hand and he let her take the right. The taut skin at his temples quivered with each touch of the cloth, but he still wouldn't open his eyes. On impulse, she reached over and put a warm hand against his face. He whimpered. It was the first sound she'd ever heard from him.

"Damn it, Blade, let me in!"

She took his face gently in both hands. He gasped, then abruptly began to rock back and forth, breathing in jagged bursts, one arm clenched around his stomach, body rigid with unreleased anguish.

"Damn, damn, damn!" She was cursing out loud, she realized, and tears were pouring down her own cheeks. Damn the bastards who made him unable to cry!

Abruptly he turned his head toward her and opened his eyes. He wouldn't meet her gaze directly, but he stared at her wet cheeks, seeming mesmerized by them. She knew why.

"They're your tears," she told him. "I'm crying them for you."

Blade wanted something from her. She was certain of that. His eyes were begging, desperate. She tried touching his face again. She talked. She signed. She even gave him a notepad. Nothing. She couldn't coax any communication from him. After a while he closed his eyes again and went back to rocking.

For a long time Toni watched, trying futilely to think of anything more she could do. She grew cold and stiff in the chair, but she couldn't bring herself to pry his clinging fingers off her hand, so she sat, eventually falling into an exhausted doze.

When she woke it was daylight and she was alone.

8

When Klale phoned on Friday at noon, Toni had the vid switched off and her voice was a growl.

"Yeah?"

"Uh, Toni—it's Klale. You said to come by . . ."

"Oh. Right. I'll leave the door open."

Toni hit disconnect so fast that the last word was cut off, leaving Klale staring at the pay phone. It was almost twelve-thirty, but maybe she should have waited longer.

Oh well, too late now. She turned and went back to the stairs. She'd already walked up to twenty-one, only to discover that she couldn't get onto the floor from either stairwell and there was no com, so she'd had to trek back down to the bar's pay phones. Living in a jammed building wasn't only scary, it was bloody inconvenient.

By twenty-one Klale was panting, but the steel security door was now wedged open. She went through it into a hallway which ended in another security door, also open. She stepped inside with trepidation, thinking of the sordid living quarters she'd seen on other floors, then caught her breath.

A big living room stretched right across the building. On the north side, tall windows overlooked the sunlit harbor and mountains. On the south side, patio-style doors led onto a deep balcony garden. The floor was wood and the walls were ivory with ochre highlights. The room was sparsely furnished with a couch, a large work table, and bright patchwork rugs. Polished kitchen utensils hung on one wall above a counter. Music played quietly in the background, and Klale smelled fresh coffee.

"Toni?"

"Yeah." Toni stuck her head out a door on the west side of the room. In stark contrast to her usual tough bar clothes she wore a plushy red bathrobe. "Just getting up. Look around. Study's on the other side." She vanished again and Klale heard water running.

Klale left her boots at the door and explored. Her first impression had been that the apartment was lavish, but looking more closely she realized that it was built entirely from salvaged pre-Collapse materials. The big investment had been time. The old couch had been reupholstered, the windows assembled from odd-sized pieces of glass neatly fitted, and the flooring was scrap wood, painstakingly refinished. Even the framed prints had acid stains at the edges. The only new items were a few of the kitchen fixtures.

And the netset. Klale walked over and ran her hand across its surface with delight. It was a recent top speed model with a full wall screen, and optically maxed headset. Toni, she decided, was a woman with her priorities in the right place.

She peered through an open door on the east side of the living room and found a small study containing a desk, a terminal with headset, and a bookshelf partly filled with old paper books. They were too battered to be collector's items, and out of curiosity Klale knelt down to read the spines. She found volumes on home renovation and gardening, a few books in Spanish and *Legacy of Greed*—that gruesome history she'd suffered through in school. On the bottom shelf were several decks of tarot cards.

"Coffee?" called Toni.

Klale got to her feet hastily, embarrassed by her own nosiness and joined Toni at the kitchen counter. Toni, her hair damp, huddled around her cup. She looked tired.

"You did all the parquet woodwork in the study?" Klale asked.

"Uh huh." Toni grunted, but Klale caught the little flash of pride in her eyes. Klale kept looking at her, grinning, until Toni started to smile back in spite of herself. "It was slow work because I had to learn as I went. I'm still doing the bedroom."

"Toni, it's just beautiful," said Klale with genuine enthusiasm. Unable to resist the polished floor, she spun in her stocking feet and then stopped, laughing. Toni viewed her dourly.

"Are you always this cheerful in the morning?"

"Yup," admitted Klale. "After fishing, anything past four-thirty seems late."

She won an appalled look, then abruptly she remembered her visiting gift and hurried to get it out of her sac. She'd been baffled over what would be appropriate in Vancouver and finally settled on a jar of Guild-made apple chutney. It seemed suddenly very inadequate, but Toni thanked her and looked pleased.

As she sipped her coffee, Klale found herself drawn to the tall north windows. Yesterday's rain had washed the sky deep blue and left the mountains gleaming green. It made Klale yearn for forest trails, summer beaches, and idle afternoons.

"It's a *klahanie* day," she told Toni. "Makes me want to go out. I'm like our old dog—I want to press my nose against the window-pane and whine."

Toni stared at the view. In the bright light, Klale saw shadows under her eyes.

"It's long past time I took a day off and we're closing early tonight because of the picnic. . . ."

"Picnic?"

Toni smiled. "The annual staff picnic. Tomorrow. We leave at noon. But for today . . ." She hesitated, then said: "Would you like to come out with me for lunch? We can go to a restaurant. My treat."

"Sure! But . . ." Klale gestured at her work shirt. "I don't have anything to wear."

"I have a couple of loose summer robes that are long on me."

Robes? thought Klale. Toni?

She followed Toni to the bedroom closet where Toni picked out a seacrepe robe in cobalt blue, veined with green and gold. It cinched at Klale's waist with a sash, and the tail draped over her shoulder sari-style. Then Toni disappeared into the bathroom and came out five minutes later in a scarlet robe and brilliantly patterned head scarf that hid the gruesome skin-art on her neck. With long gold earcuffs and jangling bracelets she looked beautiful and wonderfully exotic.

"I don't have any shoes!" Klale exclaimed suddenly.

Toni looked down at her workboots.

"Well, I can't help with that. We'll buy you some sandals."

Klale nearly opened her mouth to say she couldn't afford them, then she shut it firmly again. To hell with it.

They headed out onto Robson Street, Klale laughing and clumping along in Toni's summery dress. At a cobbler's stall, Klale had her feet scanned and then she watched with delight as the antiquated machine laser-cut pieces of leathereen and bonded them together. She'd never seen shoes made before—just ordered them. The cobbler finished details by hand and gave her the sandals with a broad, gap-toothed smile. Under Toni's stern gaze, he charged a fiver.

They dropped Klale's boots back at the KlonDyke, then walked east, stopping at an art kiosk on Robson Street. Klale chose a scarlet sea dragon for her left cheek, with a tail that continued in biolume through her hair. Toni had an intricate flower design painted across her forehead, down her nose, and onto her cheekbones.

The discreet bistro Toni took them to catered to Guild patrons of a nearby casino. As a silver-haired server led them to seats on a patio overlooking the harbor, Klale tried hard to look blasé, but she had never eaten in such casually elegant surroundings. Prince Rupert only had one independent restaurant, and it was very creaky. She ordered beef from a fancy paper menu, then watched in delight as Toni ordered champagne and the server brought it out and popped the cork, just like in the ficpix.

Toni in her beautiful clothes was utterly different than Klale had seen her before—outgoing, witty, and intensely charming. She must be very well educated, thought Klale, and asked impulsively:

"Did you go to university?"

Toni's face turned cold.

"Some of my best customers were faculty," she snapped, then she looked at Klale's face and sighed. "Sorry, Klale. Old reflex. You didn't deserve that."

Klale grimaced.

"Sorry. I shouldn't have asked. I knew better." She paused, then took a small chance. "Bracken warned me that you bite."

"Yeah, well he got that right."

She'd ruined Toni's mood, thought Klale, annoyed at her own stupidity. Toni sat frowning, fingers curled tightly around the stem of her champagne glass, then she spoke with obvious effort.

"That's why I got my plug, Klale—to pay for university. On weekends my pimp rented me out to Guild bosses and traveling merchants and," her voice turned acid, "professors. I used euphoriates to feel good while strangers bought my passion and degraded me with it, and after a while I couldn't feel anything.

"I sold myself for a ticket out of the hell I lived in, and all I found was another hell where I hurt all the time, and hated the people around me because they'd had it so easy. I couldn't live there, either. Now that I look back, I realize I had other choices. I just didn't see them."

Abruptly she looked over at Klale.

"You have choices too, you know. Just don't . . . lock yourself onto one path."

Klale nodded, surprised and touched, but unsure what to say. Then dessert arrived and Toni reverted to trivial conversation. This time, though, Klale noticed how brittle and distracted she seemed underneath her cheerful words. Toni was upset, she decided, but she didn't seem to want to talk about it so Klale traded forkfuls of dessert and concentrated on making Toni laugh.

Much later, dawdling back along the street, Klale caught sight of Toni's bleak gaze in a shop window and took her hand. A little to her surprise, Toni held it, so they walked hand in hand in companionable silence, watching the sun sink low over the jungled ruin of Downtown. Wind rotors churned and smoke curled up from old elevator shafts into the evening sunshine. From a distance it looked enchanting, but close up the streets seethed with poverty and disease. How much would the price of their meals have bought some of these people? Klale wondered uncomfortably.

Loud bangs and shouts echoed through the buildings. Klale stopped in alarm, but Toni hurried eagerly forward.

"Got anything to burn?" Toni asked over her shoulder.

"Burn?" echoed Klale, wondering if she'd heard right.

Unexpectedly, Toni grinned, then she looked around and headed for a street stall where she bought two colorfully wrapped parcels that looked and hefted like pulp logs. She handed one to Klale and then pushed forward into the crowd gathering along the sides of Robson Street.

A bizarre band marched toward them, belting out a ruckus of music. The musicians were all ages, playing everything—guitars, recorders, old electronic minstrels, a one-stringed Chinese violin, a battered saxophone, and even pots and pans. Klale didn't recognize the tune, but many people in the crowd did, and they began singing along and clapping as the band approached. Others lit and threw firecrackers, which exploded in staccato bursts around the musicians.

Following the band were three bicycles, each towing a little cart. As the first one passed, Toni beckoned Klale and stepped forward, tossing her package into the cart. Klale copied her, peering inside, and was baffled to see wads of paper, broken bits of furniture and even driftwood. As she stepped back, the man peddling the next bicycle smiled gravely and nodded at her.

Other people were tossing logs and rubbish into the carts, too. Then there was a great deal of waving and whistling and the parade came to a halt as a stout shopkeeper approached carrying a heavy motor lube container. He gravely placed the container in a trailer, and then exchanged bows with the paraders. An old woman dressed all in white came forward and spoke to him, there was more bowing, then the parade started up again.

Klale watched as the old woman stepped back into a group of people also dressed in white. They were pulling a long, narrow cart, with a banner attached to the side, hand-lettered in Chinese, Cyrillic, and English. As it got nearer, Klale made out the English: "Abram Michael Wing." Then she saw the cart's contents: a man lying stretched out. Behind the cart were other similar carts, and a young couple dressed in black, walking together. The man carried a tiny coffin.

Finally the light dawned. She moved closer to Toni and spoke near her ear.

"This is a funeral!"

Toni nodded.

"The firecrackers keep evil spirits away."

"And the logs?"

"For the cremation. Fuel is expensive." She smiled without humor and added, "The Patrol turns a blind eye to smoke pollution from funeral pyres. Bodies in the inlet are more of a nuisance."

"Oh," said Klale, suddenly feeling very small. She'd never felt wealthy or privileged in Prince Rupert, but she did now.

People in the crowd crossed themselves and made other ritual gestures as the bodies passed. At the rear of the parade more bicycles towed fuel trailers and a big melee of children scoured the street, loudly soliciting bystanders for contributions. Toni was ready for them, too. She pulled wadded up papers from her pocket, gave a couple to Klale, then tossed the rest to the kids. Klale started to toss hers, then on a hunch smoothed out the paper enough to read "Farmers for Better Food." She laughed, screwed the paper up, and threw it.

They followed in the parade's wake to the KlonDyke, where the regular beggars sat at the bottom of the steps. To Klale's surprise, Toni stopped on the street to talk to them. They teased her raucously about her "Zitty rags," and Toni fired back in a heavy American dialect that Klale couldn't follow but the beggars clearly enjoyed. Since Toni seemed to know them, Klale asked for introductions. The tiny crippled woman with waist-long, gray-streaked red hair was Violet, and the legless boy gave his name as Juri. Klale swallowed hard and offered her hand. She got two defiant, grimy shakes.

Then they climbed up the long, long stairs to the twilit apartment where Toni put on music and made coffee while Klale scrubbed her hands and then wandered out to the balcony garden to look at slices of English Bay sunset between jungly towers. In a few minutes Toni came out with laced Jamaican coffee in spiral glass mugs and Klale sipped it, watching lights bloom in the towers around her.

"This is such an amazing apartment, Toni! I can't believe we're standing here drinking ambrosia, with funerals and beggars twenty-one storeys down. You know, this is the first place I've felt really safe Downtown."

"Yeah," said Toni. There was a harsh edge of grief in her voice, and Klale looked at her anxiously.

"Toni, is everything all right?"

The older woman nodded and put on a smile.

"Fine. I'm just not used to champagne anymore."

Well, there was no point pushing if Toni didn't want to talk, Klale decided. She thought back to the funeral band and gave a wistful smile.

"I liked that funeral. I wish my father's had been that much fun. Or so well attended."

"Or my mother's," said Toni, unexpectedly. "She never had one."

Klale looked over at her, surprised, then asked very softly:

"How did she die?"

Toni shrugged.

"On the wire, I guess. When she didn't come home for a few days I went out looking—checked all the bars and the joy houses. At one place they said she was dead." She looked out at the view, then added flatly, "I was twelve."

Klale dropped her gaze, appalled. Toni's life made her own problems look so trivial.

"My mother died when I was seven," said Klale. "She was the last person to die in the 2090 flu epidemic. People in Rupert always talk as if that's supposed to be some big consolation."

"And your father?"

"Pneumonia, just last month, but he was already weak from resistant TB. He was sick for years. I thought I'd just feel relieved when it was over, but . . ."

An unexpected surge of grief choked her and she had to stop until she could manage her voice.

"After mom died my brother Hans took care of me a lot. And then he left—applied to the Forester's Guild when he turned sixteen." She heard the anger in her voice and hastily added: "I can't blame him. Dad was a Governmentalist."

She shot Toni an anxious glance, but Toni didn't look scandalized. Well, it wasn't such a big tax down here.

"That must have been difficult," said Toni. "Was he the only one in town?"

"No. Just the only one stupid enough to stand up and say so in Guild meetings," Klale said bitterly, remembering the outrage and the constant rain of ridicule everywhere she went. She looked over at Toni rather desperately. "He was a good man, just hopelessly idealistic. He was very kind to us kids, but he couldn't even remember to order groceries. I did everything at home."

Abruptly tears came. Toni put an arm around her, and Klale cried, distantly aware of Toni's slippery silk robe, and the oddness of leaning her head against Toni's soft, woolly hair. It felt wonderful, though. Klale loved being touched and she missed it desperately. A little to her surprise, she realized she was getting aroused.

Almost as if she sensed that, Toni pulled away and offered Klale a handkerchief, then went to fetch more coffee. It was growing dark on the balcony, but there was still a luminescent blue sheen in the western sky, and English Bay glowed as if lit from beneath. Klale watched the light fade, feeling curiously buoyant after her tears. "Thank you for lunch. It was wonderful."

"Thank you for coming, Klale. I enjoyed myself very much." She gave Klale a sidelong glance, then asked quietly: "Did you file the complaint against Dhillon?"

Klale let out a gusty sigh.

"No. Not yet. I'm . . . I haven't got around to it."

Toni nodded without comment. There was a short silence. Then she said with strained casualness, "You're welcome to stay the night— if you'd like."

Klale looked at her, startled, and Toni gave a humorless smile.

"I'm not asking you to fuck me for the netset."

"I didn't think so!" retorted Klale sharply. Then, more softly: "I'd like to stay."

The rest of the apartment felt cool, but the bedroom was warm and smelled of freshly cut wood from where Toni had been working on the floor. Her bed was an unrolled futon, with a reader and a couple of paper books lying beside the pillow.

"You're welcome to share my bed or sleep on the couch," said Toni. She looked around contemplatively. "The one thing I could use is a tub for warm soaks on evenings like this, but water's too expensive. However, I do give a good massage."

Toni didn't seem drunk, but Klale was suddenly aware of pain lurking just beneath the brittle surface of her words. She wants to touch somebody, thought Klale suddenly. And she doesn't want to ask.

"I'd love one," she said.

Toni knelt and adjusted the bedside light to give a soft amber glow, then put her mug beside the bed and started to undress. Klale hung Toni's robe in the closet and left her underwear on top of the clothes she'd taken off that morning. She lay down on her stomach.

Toni warmed massage oil in her hands first. She started expertly at Klale's feet, eliciting little "oohs," then advanced up her legs, buttocks, back, and shoulders with strong, sure hands. Klale was melting with relaxation and simultaneously very aroused by the time Toni told her to roll over.

As Toni worked on Klale's left arm, Klale studied her. Toni's small breasts sagged and the skin around her stomach was loose, but otherwise her naked body looked young. Her arms and legs were wiry from hauling kegs and climbing stairs, and her brown skin felt soft. Something odd about one breast caught Klale's eyes and she stared, then abruptly realized that she was looking at a deep round burn scar which had partially destroyed the nipple.

She flinched deep inside and turned her head away, hoping that her horror hadn't shown. Thinking about the pain of that burn made her queasy. And it suddenly made Toni's past very real. No wonder Toni was always so guarded, so prickly. She must have far worse scars that didn't show.

I want to make love to Toni, Klale realized suddenly. Then: Is it safe? As soon as that thought struck her she felt a rush of shame. They all had to have clean health to work at the KlonDyke and anyway Toni was far too responsible to vector. If Toni had been a Guild friend in Rupert, the thought wouldn't have crossed her mind, she admitted to herself.

Toni had switched to Klale's stomach now, kneading the muscles gently. There wasn't anything deliberately seductive in her massage, yet the pull against Klale's crotch felt delicious. Impulsively she sat up and reached for Toni, then bent her head and kissed the scarred breast very tenderly. When she looked up, Toni's eyes were startled and—for just an instant—vulnerable.

They made love quietly and gently. Toni transformed the massage into something much more smoothly sensuous, eventually stroking Klale with a soft, steady tongue. She easily teased Klale's excitement into a fiery orgasm. Klale had much more difficulty reciprocating. Toni relaxed gradually under her caresses, but seemed distant and unresponsive, and Klale had to rely on her instructions. Eventually Toni gave a silent shudder and lay still for a long moment with her eyes tightly shut. Her expression was bleak.

Looking up at her face, Klale felt a wave of sadness. She could understand why Toni was like that, but it seemed terribly lonely. She moved up the bed and lay quietly next to her, feeling oddly protective. Perhaps it was that she was so much larger, and that Toni, thin and scarred, with her eyes closed, looked so very frail. Klale wanted to hold her, but instinctively knew that she had to wait for Toni to allow it.

When Toni opened her eyes and smiled a little, Klale smiled back and reached out. They cuddled, Klale spooning around Toni, with her arm around Toni's waist and her nose pressing softly against the bleeding skull on the back of her head.

9

Alberta's angry voice carried clearly and Klale leaned over the railing of the launch to get a better view of the small group of women on Cardero Wharf who were delaying the boat's noon departure. About two hundred KlonDyke staffers, Co-op residents, friends, and family had already boarded and were surging excitedly around the yacht's decks.

"Our families and children are coming to this picnic, and goddamn it, my security team deserves a break!" Alberta was talking to Toni and Mary, who were in a huddle at the edge of the wharf right below the launch. A few paces away three members of Alberta's security team were casting nervous glances at Blade, who stood at the foot of the gangplank. The rest of the staff had boarded the launch already.

Mary's soft voice was harder to overhear.

"I'm sorry, Pat, I don't know what else to do. I've told Blade to leave, but he won't stop following us. And Choi won't take my calls."

She turned to Toni, who shrugged helplessly.

"Choi may have ordered him to watch us, not knowing about the picnic. Or Blade may not understand what's going on. But there's no way to tell."

"We can't take him with us!" Alberta's voice was explosive with frustration.

"I think we have to," said Mary. "We certainly can't make him leave. And unless you think there's some serious danger, I'm not going to cancel the picnic."

Toni spoke with brisk practicality.

"We can manage. Blade hasn't caused any trouble at the bar and our people know to keep their distance. I'll stay with him, too."

Alberta swore. Mary put a hand on her arm and spoke to her softly. Klale's gaze shifted to Blade, towering expressionlessly over the bouncers. She couldn't tell from his blank face whether he was following their conversation or even aware of it.

They were the last passengers to board. A mate retracted the gangplank, the engines purred to life and the boat glided slowly away from the pier into the harbor. Indian summer sunshine sparkled on the calm water, and Klale felt a rush of delighted anticipation.

Toni had told Klale that the KlonDyke did up their Equinox picnic "Zit style," and she wasn't kidding, decided Klale. For instance, the "boat" leased by SisOpp for transport to the picnic was an immaculate forty meter yacht. Klale briefly considered finding Toni, but she'd be busy watching Blade, and besides Toni had been stiff and distant this morning—visibly unused to having an overnight visitor in her apartment. Instead, Klale squeezed through the crowd, then made her way up to the bridge and introduced herself as a Fisher. As she had hoped, the crisply uniformed yacht captain was happy to chat. Once across the busy center of the harbor, he left the bridge to his mate and led Klale out in front of the wheelhouse, where she got a bird's-eye view of the swirling tidal rips in the Second Narrows and fluorescent hazard buoys marking drowned industrial sites.

They followed Burrard Inlet east, then turned north up Indian Arm, where forested mountain slopes closed in around them. The float at Buntzen Landing was small, and the captain inched the big launch in slowly, using bow propellers to keep them from swinging with the tide. Klale watched with interest, then caught sight of Alberta, her wife Rill, Toni, and Blade already in position at the head of the gangplank. Three bouncers were with them: Pum, Sapphire, and Boston. Klale thanked the captain and rushed down from the bridge, pushing her way through to Toni's side. Toni gave her a sharp look, but didn't object.

Alberta marched the small group briskly up a narrow road which snaked past an old half-drowned gothic ruin with arched stone windows and then a new duratiled power station. They crossed and recrossed under a huge water pipe, rising steeply through a dense forest of firs, cedars, and pines. The rest of the KlonDyke crowd fell far behind and Klale reveled in the hush broken only by the crunch of feet on gravel and birdcalls echoing through the forest—glorious after the constant uproar of Downtown.

She turned to talk to Toni and saw Blade staring around him with uncharacteristically wide, mobile eyes. He seemed startled. No wonder, thought Klale. There was nothing like this Downtown. She smiled at Toni, but the older woman was watching Blade with a worried frown.

The road leveled out at the Buntzen Lake dam and then skirted the lakeshore to the picnic area where a hand-lettered sign announced the KlonDyke's picnic reservation. Beyond it stood picnic tables loaded with food and surrounded by everything from solar-cooled beer kegs and cookers to canoes and fishing rods. Klale stared in astonishment and raised her eyebrows at Toni.

"Sisters does this every year?"

"For more than thirty years."

Alberta gazed around the tree-ringed lawn, frowning, then said to Toni:

"I don't like to leave him here. All the kids will be here. But I've been thinking. We were planning to hike up Eagle Ridge. We could start now and take him with us. Keep him busy."

Klale saw unhappiness flicker across Toni's face.

"Steep hike, isn't it?"

"Yeah. Tire him out, maybe." Alberta looked down at Toni's feet. "I'd take you, Toni, but those aren't hiking boots."

Toni ran a hand through her hair.

"I don't like to let him out of my sight. But . . . Well, first let's see if he'll go with you." She turned and Slanged at Blade, ordering him to follow Alberta. Then she turned and walked away. Blade stayed where he was, looking at Alberta.

"Good," said Alberta. She sent Pum and Rill off to fetch food and water canteens, then signed to Blade that they were going up the mountain. He gave no response, but when Alberta turned away, Klale saw him throw a quick sideways glance at the precipitous green slope.

Klale looked at the mountains, too, and remembered how much she loved hiking.

"Alberta? I'd like to go," she said. "These are good boots."

Alberta hesitated.

"Check with Toni," she said finally.

When Klale repeated her request, Toni nodded.

"It should be OK. Just remember to keep your distance and don't startle him. But if you're worried *at all*, call me."

That wasn't entirely reassuring, thought Klale, but she shrugged it off and called the hiking board. She got a friendly interface that told her about conditions on the "unrelentingly steep" Halvor Lunden trail, and encouraged her to join the Belcarra Hiking Club. The hygiene instructions that followed she could have recited in her sleep, so she hung up and followed Alberta.

The trail was indeed steep, and Klale was just getting her second wind when it emerged at Swan Falls. She stepped out from the trees and looked around, open-mouthed with delight. They stood on an undulating slope of polished granite, with deep, round bowls, creek-carved into the rock surface. Klale jumped the narrow stream, climbed down the smooth rock to the lowest pool, and then crawled out to peer over the lip of the falls. The water cascaded straight down for seventy-five meters.

She would have loved to stay and admire the view, but Alberta wasn't much on sight-seeing, so they moved on briskly. The trail switched back and forth up a sheer slope of evergreens for a grueling hour, leveled out through muddy meadows, and then rose steeply again to a signed three-way fork on top of the ridge. They took the east trail to "Mount Beautiful" and finally reached the north viewpoint—a bare outcrop on a sharp ridge that plunged twelve hundred dizzy meters to Coquitlam Lake.

Klale stared out at rows of mountain peaks stretching into distant haze, and savored the cool breeze on her sweaty neck. A pair of eagles soared up on the thermals, passing the level of the peak and floating on up into the sky. Klale watched with delight, then remembered Blade and looked around. He stood a few paces away, staring wide-eyed at the panorama.

"I don't think he's seen anything like it," she said softly to Alberta.

"Probably never been out of Downtown," said Alberta, with grudging sympathy. She added grimly: "Gods only know what effect this will have on him."

She Slanged at the enforcer to sit and eat. He sat.

Klale sat down next to Alberta and Rill and dug out some lunch. Gray-feathered whiskey jacks flitted in the nearby trees, eyeing them greedily. Rill tore a piece of bread off her sandwich and tossed it on the ground a few feet away. Two birds swooped down.

"I saw old Mr. McCaskill on the boat," said Klale. "I'm glad he came. He's my favorite customer."

"Ron's a hell of a guy," said Alberta. "Best fire chief we ever had, too."

Klale raised her eyebrows. "I thought he was City Services."

"Yeah. Past president, even. Lives in Kitsilano. But he joined the Downtown fire brigade years ago, even opted for reduced Guild duties so he could take on being fire chief. Tough old bugger," she added admiringly. "Did that until he was eighty."

"Huh," said Klale. Alberta seemed to be in an expansive mood, so she decided to try for more information.

"What Guild is Captain Dhillon?"

"Merchant," said Rill.

"Yeah, a real value-added importer," added Alberta sourly.

Klale stared at her for a second, then got it.

"You mean she's skimming the flots?"

"They all do." Alberta chewed on her sandwich, ignoring the whiskey jacks. "She's near the end of her second hitch, too. Probably getting greedy to pad her accounts while she can. Two hitches is the max, then she's back to her Guild."

"Oh." Despite everything she'd seen Downtown, Klale still felt disillusioned. Every kid in Rupert dreamed of becoming a heroic Coast Patroller, rescuing drowning boaters and protecting coast waters from evil polluters. She'd never imagined they could be mercenary thugs.

Rill grinned teasingly at her.

"I bet Dhillon just doesn't like the way Cedar's been looking at you."

"Mr. de Groot?" said Klale, surprised.

Alberta snorted.

"Spin has it Dhillon figures on marrying him. He's the only one who hasn't heard."

"But he's a splut!"

Alberta shrugged. Rill frowned, then leaned forward.

"Look, you've got to understand that Dhillon's from a zealot family—Revised Sikh. Probably wants to line up a husband before her family finds one. She's close to thirty and they'll be pushing to marry her off as soon as her hitch is up. De Groot is a City Services exec—that's a good connection. And he'll do what she tells him."

Klale nodded thoughtfully, feeling some sympathy for Dhillon. Then she remembered the gang of burly Patrollers kicking two skinny flots in the KlonDyke. Her sympathy dissolved in a flood of new resolve. Somebody had to stand up to those bents. She *would* file a complaint.

But not right this instant. Her lunch finished, Klale spread out her jacket and lay back in the warm sun, tipping her hat over her face and feeling her whole body relax into the stillness. She actually missed fishing, she realized with a shock. Well, not fishing itself, but being out on the ocean. Sometimes she'd been able to cut the engine and just bob around out there, abandoning herself to the vibration of wind and waves. By contrast, Downtown was a discordant stew of noise that wore her down, day and night.

Her Gitksan friend Tolo would have enjoyed this, she thought suddenly, peeking under her hat at the blue sky. They'd called it *kwahnesum koosagh*—sky that soared forever—and on a day like this when they were just kids they'd sworn to be *kwahnesum tilikum*—eternal friends.

Just as she was reaching the horrible realization that she felt homesick, her thoughts were interrupted by a slithering crash and a scream. Klale jumped up, but Alberta was ahead of her, leaping through scarlet-leafed blueberry bushes.

"Stay back!" she yelled over her shoulder.

Klale stayed, heart pounding, and looked around for Blade. He sat silently on a rock some distance away. She relaxed a little. There was more crashing, some curses, and then Alberta called out: "Just a little accident. Rill, we need a hand."

A couple of minutes later, Rill and Alberta reappeared with a limping Sapphire between them.

"Slipped taking a piss," Saph muttered furiously.

"I think she sprained her ankle," added Alberta, and Klale stopped grinning. Sapphire was almost Alberta's height and much heavier. It was going to be hell getting her back down that trail.

They cut their break short and started back immediately, Blade following like a giant shadow. Sapphire gritted her teeth and did her best, but lowering her down the steep stretches of rock on the ridge was slow, difficult work. Around five o'clock, Toni called to check on their progress. When Alberta told her, she sounded very unhappy.

"I thought you'd be back by now," she told Alberta. "I'd like to get a meal into Blade. With his boosted metabolism and all that exercise, he should eat every three hours or he'll get hypoglycemic."

"Hypo what?"

"Nervous and unstable."

"Now you fucking tell me," muttered Alberta, giving Blade a sideways glance. "I've got some apple juice left."

"That'll help," said Toni. "But I'd feel better if you could get him down here faster."

"I could go ahead with him," suggested Klale.

"Too dangerous," snapped Alberta.

"No it isn't! Look, it'll only take an hour or so. I'll keep my distance. And Toni will meet us at the bottom."

Alberta didn't like the idea, but Toni did, so Alberta reluctantly agreed. She walked Klale back to where Blade waited, a little distance from the party, and for the first time Klale had second thoughts. She had rarely stood near the enforcer and she found herself startled again by just how huge he was—she didn't even come up to his shoulder. Up close she could see damp stains on his shirt and sweat trickling down his neck past his grotesquely burned left ear. Being curious about Blade was one thing—being alone with him was another. But she wasn't about to back out now.

The giant enforcer maintained his distance behind Klale and she soon became used to him. After fifteen minutes her knees started aching fiercely. She hadn't had any trouble climbing up, but downhill used different muscles. She started pausing occasionally. Blade stopped eight or ten paces behind her each time and waited impassively until she set out again.

The air got warmer as they lost altitude, and by the time they reached Swan Falls, Klale was hot and her knees were shaking. Time for a rest, she decided. She kneeled on warm granite and dipped her hot hands into the rushing stream, then looked at the circular, green-tinted pools with sudden temptation. She felt sticky and filthy, and here were glorious big bathtubs of crystal clear water. The lowest pool was too close to the edge of the cliff for her taste, but the one above it sparkled invitingly.

She glanced nervously at Blade, standing behind her in the trees. Was it safe to take a dip with him there? Then it occurred to her that if she was hot, he must be sweltering in his heavy clothes. Well, there were lots of pools.

She stood up, waved at Blade and then explained in an awkward jumble of Slang and pantomime that she was going to swim. She pointed up at the highest pool, well above her, and signed "You swim there." Then she turned and started pulling off her boots.

When she glanced up again, he was up beside the top pool with his back to her. She paused, boot in hand, unable to resist watching as he took off his shirt. She had already noticed that it was slit up the back seam so he could reach the knife between his shoulder blades. Now she saw the harness anchoring the knife sheath and below, at his waist, a gun belt. How many weapons did he have? she wondered nervously.

Blade's back and arms were ropy with muscle, although somehow slimmer than she'd expected. Pale burn scars spilled from the left side of his face down his neck and onto his brown shoulder. She focused on his bald skull and neck looking for some sign of the explosive implant Toni had mentioned. She thought she saw a small lump on the back of his neck, but she was too far away to be sure.

Klale shuddered a little and took off her socks, then looked up again. Blade was out of sight. She started to take her shirt off, then hesitated. She still didn't feel entirely safe, so she scrambled up twenty meters of steep granite ski slope and peeked over the lip. Blade stood next to the upper pool with his back to her. He still wore the pants and knife harness but seemed intent on going in. It was OK, she decided.

She climbed back down and finished stripping off, then sat for a minute enjoying the sensation of sun on her naked skin and warm rough rock against her buttocks. When she felt relaxed, she got up and stepped to the pool. No point dawdling, she thought. She braced herself, then jumped.

The shock of frigid water against her hot skin made Klale scream. She flailed wildly, then bobbed to her feet, gasping. Icy water lapped at her breasts, leaching her body heat right to the bone. The pool was much deeper than she had realized and much, *much* colder. She fought for breath, telling herself that she'd sure as hell cooled off. Time to get out.

She waded a step and a half to the edge, reached up, and then realized that the sides of the pool were worn into featureless smoothness like a granite teacup, and coated with slippery algae below water. It was difficult to stay on her feet, never mind find a handhold. She groped urgently along the edge with hands that were already turning numb. Icy pain stabbed at her legs, bringing tears to her eyes. Genuinely alarmed now, she looked up.

Blade was leaning over the edge of the rock, watching. She stared back nervously. She didn't want to call him down, but she couldn't see any other way out. She beckoned.

He started forward immediately, jumping lightly down the steep rock with bare feet while Klale bounced up and down, shivering and keeping up a steady stream of muttered commentary about her own stupidity. *Halo latet!*—no brain! Blade reached the pool and stopped uncertainly. Klale held out her hand. He hesitated an instant, then kneeled, reached forward, and grabbed it.

Klale flopped up onto the dry rock, skinning her leg and wincing at the pressure of Blade's hard grip. He let go and she crawled to her knees, then realized that he was still kneeling, staring at her pale goose-bumped body with strange lashless eyes.

Klale felt her stomach clench for a long paralyzed second, but Blade didn't move. His head was canted slightly to one side, lending him an oddly quizzical air. She took a deep breath and stared back. He'd had full follicle suppression, she decided. She saw no sign of hair on his chest or armpits. Oddly, he also had no nipples—not even scars on his chest where they should have been. It made him look like a life-sized mannequin, but he was so close that she could smell his sweat, and it was pungently male. He was wet, too, pant legs dripping on the granite. Must have been smart enough to choose a pool he could get out of, she thought sourly.

His eyes grazed her face. Abruptly he stood, backing away, and she had the sudden strong impression of fear. He turned and retreated swiftly up the rocks.

The sun had sunk behind the trees and Klale sat shivering on the cooling rock, trying to dry off a little before she put her clothes back on. Remembering Blade's muscular back moving up the rocks away from her, she found herself wondering what he would have looked like without the facial alterations, the scars, and that appalling brand.

She wrapped her arms around her knees, sickened. He might have been a very beautiful man, she thought—if that hadn't been done to him.

10

Toni pushed her way through the underbrush. A branch slapped her head and she swore softly. It had seemed so obvious in the daylight. She shone her light around, then saw the path she was looking for and headed for it, hearing twigs crunch behind her as Blade followed. Once on the path it was an easy walk to a small clearing on the lake shore which looked back over at the KlonDyke picnic's bonfire. The sound of voices carried clearly across the water.

She shut off her handlight and motioned Blade to sit. Faint moonlight illuminated the clearing, but the glare of the bonfire should make it hard for any of the 'Dyke picnickers to see them. Good.

So far, despite all her worries, Blade had remained stable. When Klale brought him down the trail, Toni parked him in an inconspicuous spot under the trees and fetched food for him. Then she waited several interminable hours for a chance to get him away, which didn't come until after Mary's recognition ceremony. Mary lined up the whole staff, looped a ribbon around each woman's neck and thanked her formally for her hard work all year. It seemed faintly silly, but many of the women were so touched they cried. That didn't surprise Toni. Most of those women had so little to be proud of, and Mary offered them success, stability, and belonging. No wonder they loved her so much.

When the picnickers congregated for the bonfire, Toni finally managed to steal Blade away. This was the first good chance she'd ever had to assess him and she didn't intend to miss it. She was sure he had orders not to talk to her at the KlonDyke, but tools were literal and Choi's orders might not cover other locations. Moreover, removing Blade from his usual surroundings might cause personality relics to surface.

She settled herself into a comfortable position against a tree and glanced over at Blade. He sat cross-legged like a statue, the distant flickering light of the bonfire making the brand on his forehead writhe like some demonic spider. His face was blank and his eyes looked flat and cold. Not good. She needed to relax him. Despite his anesthetized emotional state, he must have had a very stressful day.

She had to lead with her own body language, so she concentrated on relaxing her muscles and letting the tension drain away. She took a deep breath and released it slowly, concentrating on the cool evening air and the pungent scent of pine and cedar, then glanced at Blade out of the corner of her eye. It was hard to tell if he was relaxing. She placed her right hand on the ground beside her, palm up. There was a long pause when he seemed to take no notice, then his hand slid over beside hers, palm up. Excellent. She put her hand on top of his and squeezed, then watched for the subtle indicators. She saw a very quiet intake of breath, then he closed his eyes for a long moment. When he opened them again they had lost that disturbing automaton quality.

She held his hand for a few minutes, then pulled away gently, turned to face him, and Signed, "You were very good today." He looked at her hands without response. She hadn't expected one. Tools weren't praised, and there was a good chance that he didn't understand. But it couldn't hurt. She Signed: "I'm pleased."

Then she reached slowly into her belt purse and took out a small paper package. She'd tried something like this before, but Blade would only accept certain foods at the 'Dyke. Here, though, he'd already eaten everything she gave him for dinner. She unwrapped the package carefully, hoping that the ginger chocolates hadn't melted. They'd been expensive, but in her experience nothing worked better. Rough tools were kept on bland diets and with their accelerated metabolisms they craved sugars and oils.

She opened the paper out on her lap, releasing a cloud of sweet aroma, then raised her hands to Slang "Would you like a chocolate?" and realized with annoyance that she didn't know signs for either chocolate or candy. Damn, how stupid! Finally, she used the sign for food, then repeated the offer out loud, enunciating carefully.

Blade didn't move, so she sat very still, keeping her face unconcerned. She had just about decided to make the offer an order when he gave a very small shrug. He didn't know.

Well, that was a response, for a tool.

"Try one," she told him.

She put a candy in her own mouth, then handed one to him. He took it hesitantly. She made a show of sucking hers, enjoying the smooth dark chocolate and the bite of ginger on her tongue. He put the candy in his mouth, started to chew, and then the flavor hit him. His eyes went wide, and for a second he stared directly at her in astonishment. Then he ducked his head away, nervous, but still chewing.

Bingo! thought Toni with satisfaction. Watching him, she was suddenly reminded of Klale feeding squirrels by the picnic tables. Well, this was more like feeding a grizzly.

She let him finish, waited a minute, then signed: "Another?"

His eyes flicked uneasily past her, but he nodded with a betraying hint of eagerness. He tasted the second chocolate with intense concentration, and while he worked on it, she put the rest away, then offered her hand again. This time, he took it quickly and responded more openly. She even saw him glance down, so she reached out and stroked the back of his hand. He closed his eyes, then began to rock slightly in rhythm with her touch.

It reminded her with sudden vividness of his disturbing visit two nights before, and Toni felt a rush of pity. This was the moment she should start running tests and use the candy to reinforce his responses, but she found that she didn't want to let go of his hand.

She was mystified by that visit. She'd asked everywhere she could and heard no news of any violence involving a tool. Blade had reappeared the next evening and resumed his usual routine. However, Toni was almost sure she was seeing something, a flicker of movement, something, that was faintly out of character. This was certainly her chance to reach him. And she had to move quickly. There was no telling how long before Alberta missed her. She'd have to risk some intensive bonding work.

She moved over and leaned against Blade's side. He flinched and tensed. Moving with slow deliberation, she reached her right arm very gently around his waist and sat motionless, trying to project a tranquil presence. She felt tiny sitting next to his hard bulk, her head barely reaching his armpit. After a very long minute his anxious breathing evened out and his taut muscles gradually relaxed. Good.

She gave him another few minutes to get used to her, then withdrew her arm, leaned back, and looked directly up into his eyes. He glanced down. Putting all the gentleness and affection in her face that she could, she Signed, "Did you have a good time?"

His eyes lifted from her hands and met hers directly, then his face split into a shy half-smile that utterly transformed him. He looks like a boy, thought Toni with shock.

He Signed: "I stood on top of Beautiful Mountain."

It took a second for Toni to gather her stunned wits, then she held her little finger up near her chest and tapped her palm against her heart.

"I'm happy for you."

Behind them, a twig snapped. Toni instinctively turned to listen, then kicked herself. She had ruined a perfect chance to test his deafness. Blade pulled sharply away from her.

"Toni?"

Mary's voice. Damn, damn, damn! She'd been so close! And that response was so very unexpected! Reluctantly Toni answered.

"Over here."

A spot of light bounced among the trees, and Mary walked into the clearing.

"I thought you might be here," she said quietly.

"Did you tell Alberta?"

"She sent me to find out why you switched off your phone." Mary looked uneasily at Blade. "If I don't call in ten minutes she's following with a search party."

Damn it to hell! thought Toni savagely.

"I just wanted to get him away from the crowd," she said.

Mary gave her a piercing look, then lowered herself stiffly to the ground on Toni's left side, away from Blade.

"I thought you'd given up trying to talk to him."

"This is the best chance I ever had!" Toni snapped, more angrily than she intended.

Mary sighed.

"Love, I know I've said this before, but I'll repeat myself. I wish you would stay away from Blade. Of all the sadistic businessmen in this town, the one I would least want to make my enemy is Choi."

Toni looked away, struggling not to let her sudden sick sense of fear show. It was far worse than Mary knew. Toni was still a potentially hot item on the training market, even after ten years. The technology and methods hadn't changed much. She would make a very useful acquisition for someone like Choi, and she had no illusions about her own capacity to refuse. She knew all too well what torture and head twisting could accomplish. Years ago she'd made provision for quick suicide and she still carried it with her but she wasn't sure she'd still have the nerve and the speed if she needed it.

Mary's warm fingers touched Toni's left arm gently.

"I'm just worried, that's all."

Toni nodded, trying to calm her anger, and focused her attention on the distant bonfire. The crowd around it had fallen silent, then someone played a few chords on a minstrel and several strong voices sang the first words of "Amazing Grace." Others joined in. Beside Toni, Mary began singing in a husky contralto. Toni hesitated, then joined in self-consciously, all too aware of Blade's taut figure beside her. The last echoes died into the evening hush.

"Are you in love?" asked Mary suddenly.

It took Toni a startled second to answer.

"Of course not." She kept her voice brisk. "I enjoy Klale's company, that's all. And she definitely leans het. She's just lonely."

Mary was silent for a few seconds.

"I'm glad you've found a friend," she said at last, very softly, and her voice had that slight Tlingit lilt that it slid into sometimes when she was emotional. When she whispered in the dark she sounded like a young girl. Toni glanced over at Mary, saw the naked sadness on her lined face, and ducked her eyes away again.

That night Toni slept fitfully, kept awake by futile speculations about Blade. She'd stayed by his side all the way back to Vancouver but he remained completely remote, and when they disembarked at the Cardero Wharf he strode down the gangplank and vanished into the darkness. Toward morning she dozed and fell into a vivid dream.

Rain fell through the black night onto Toni's terror. She huddled on a rocking concrete slab. Waves slapped nearby, the float lurched, and salt blood ran down her face. She'd been beaten and raped, and she was distantly aware of a great storm of pain all through her body. She whimpered, her arms wrapped around a big, warm, piling. No, not a piling. It was Blade. She sat in his lap, clinging to him, his arms pulled tightly around her. And it wasn't the float that was rocking. They were rocking together. Back . . . Forth . . . Back . . . Forth . . .

Toni woke abruptly in the dimness of her room, heart pounding, and stomach knotted with fear. Was that a dream or a memory? She had arrived at the KlonDyke ten years ago with a concussion, broken teeth, broken ribs, and prod burns in her mouth and vagina.

Had Blade rescued her from that?

Or—an uglier possibility—had he done that to her?

11

Alberta marched over to the desk and leaned on it with both hands.

"What in hell is going on with Blade?"

Toni swiveled the office chair around, raising her eyebrows.

"Alberta. Good afternoon to you, too. Please don't bother with small talk. Just come right out and tell me what's on your mind."

Alberta met her gaze and sighed, but didn't smile. Uh oh, thought Toni. The security chief pulled a chair over to the side of the desk, while Toni pushed back and swung her boots up, appraising the other woman carefully. Alberta sat scowling with her arms folded tightly.

"Why the sudden interest?"

"The picnic. Blade isn't behaving like any tool I ever heard of," said Alberta bluntly. She took a breath, then looked Toni straight in the eyes. "And you know a lot about tools."

That was it. The unspoken word "trainer" stood between them. Alberta loathed trainers. But until now she'd chosen to ignore the rumors about Toni.

Keeping herself outwardly calm, Toni leaned back in her chair, distantly aware of a cool breeze from the open window, carrying traffic noise from Robson Street. She saw two options. She could claim to know nothing. That would simply make the security chief angry and suspicious. Or she could share her clinical observations about Blade, effectively confirming Alberta's suspicions.

There was a sick feeling in her stomach, and it wasn't just fear. In some ways it had been much easier when she hadn't let herself care whether other people hated her.

Finally she spoke, keeping her voice casual.

"What exactly was it you noticed about Blade's behavior?"

Alberta sat stiffly in her chair.

"You know what. I caught up to Klale on the trail and I saw what happened at the waterfall."

"Waterfall?" asked Toni, with new apprehension.

"Klale didn't tell you?"

"No."

Alberta grimaced. "Yeah, well, it was a stupid thing to do."

Toni felt her jaw clench. What now?! She should never have encouraged that girl to stay Downtown.

"What happened?" she asked.

Some anxiety must have leaked into her voice because Alberta gave her a sharp look before answering.

"I was worried about Klale so when we got Saph over the worst part of the trail I ran down and caught up with them at Swan Falls. Found a place higher up where I could see down on the pools—I wanted to get a really good look at Blade without him seeing me. He was at the top pool. Klale was down at the third—going for a swim."

Toni pictured it and sighed. Another stupid risk.

Alberta frowned down at her hands, then looked over.

"He stripped off his shirt. Did you know that there's heavy padding in it?"

"Padding?" asked Toni stupidly. Of all the things Alberta might have said, she wasn't prepared for that. "But what . . . ?"

"To make him look heavier and slower, I think. Most rough tools are over-muscled—makes 'em slow and short on endurance. But not Blade. He's built like a martial arts fighter—long, lean muscles, even development. Moves like it, too. I don't know how I missed it before. I listened behind me on the hike. He didn't miss his footing once, and he was barely breathing hard at the top. And with those enhanced reflexes . . ." She paused, staring distractedly at the opposite wall, then visibly forced herself back to the topic.

"He acted strange all day. Different."

"Different how?" asked Toni.

"In six years, I never seen an expression on his face. But yesterday on the hike he seemed . . . I don't know, more alive. And at the waterfall when he took off his shirt it was like he changed. I mean, he acted different. He looked . . ." She paused, groping for words, and her voice suddenly dropped. "He looked like a kid at his first Solstice ceremony. Stood there staring around with big eyes. Then he plunged in and out of the top pool and shook himself, and," she looked over at Toni, "he smiled."

Toni stared at her in real surprise.

"Terrawatt grin," said Alberta. "I didn't believe it. Then Klale screamed."

Toni clamped down on an irrational pulse of alarm. Obviously Klale hadn't been hurt.

"Screamed?"

"Yeah." Alberta shook her head with exasperation. "She jumped into one of the lower pools, little cret. They look shallow, but they're a brute to get out of." Then she fixed Toni with a challenging stare. "Did you know he's not deaf?"

Toni felt a cold sensation in the pit of her stomach, but met Alberta's gaze.

"No. I've wondered, but I've never been able to catch him out. I take it that you did."

Alberta held her gaze searchingly, then dropped her eyes, dissatisfied.

"He heard her, all right. Ran over and looked down at where she was. Then he helped her out of the pool."

"He touched her?" asked Toni sharply.

"Yeah. He took her hand and pulled her out. Then he made off like she'd bit him and lay down, peering over the edge, watching her while she dried off. He seemed very . . . intense—like he was heated."

Toni blinked. "Fascinating," she muttered.

"Fascinating?" said Alberta with annoyance. "I was goddamned terrified. Thought I might have to try jumping him if he went for Klale. However, lucky for me, he didn't. Just watched her, with his back to me. After three or four minutes he got up and went to get his shirt and he seemed—I don't know, confused. He sat down with his arms around his knees. I could see his face then."

She paused and swallowed uncomfortably. "Even through that ugly mask he looked sad, Toni. Like he understood what he was and it made him sick. I thought maybe he was going to cry."

"He can't," Toni heard herself saying in a clipped voice. "He's conditioned not to."

For a second Alberta looked disgusted, then she pulled herself straighter and focused angry blue eyes on Toni.

"So what's this with Klale? He acted almost like he had a pash for her, but that's impossible! Isn't it?"

"Well . . ." Toni hesitated. "His hormone levels should be regulated at close to normal, so in theory he might show interest in a woman, but it shouldn't happen. And he certainly shouldn't be aware of it."

"Well, he's not like any rough tool I ever heard of. So what is he? A chameleon?"

"No." Toni leaned back, staring at her boots. "At least, I don't think so. The whole point of a chameleon is to blend in. Blade couldn't be more conspicuous."

"An assassin?"

"Maybe. But again, he stands out too much, and besides I don't see why Choi would need his own assassin. Corpses don't pay blackmail."

Alberta nodded reluctantly and Toni paused. She didn't want to go further, but Alberta had asked, and she was right—as security chief she needed to know.

"I think he's a listening post, and what you've said tends to confirm that."

"You mean he fakes being deaf and listens to what's going on?" Alberta scowled. "He's damned good. Until yesterday I would have bet my net account he was deaf. I've seen loud noises go off behind him. He doesn't even blink."

"He wouldn't. He's not acting," said Toni.

"Huh?"

"My guess is that he's been conditioned to believe that he's deaf. If done properly, it's extremely effective—certainly nobody could pretend that well. There are ways to enhance memory, too, so he'd hear things subconsciously and then repeat them verbatim in response to a hypnotic command."

"Could that be the Boss's leak?"

"I thought of that. But he doesn't go near the private meeting rooms. He must pick up a lot in the bar for Choi's dossiers, though."

"Yeah." Alberta sighed, then looked at Toni again with wary eyes. "He smiled. You want to explain that?"

And demonstrate my expertise? she thought grimly. But she'd committed herself now.

"I'd say it's a personality relic. Have you heard of those?"

"No."

Toni recrossed her boots, not looking at Alberta. "Let's use an analogy. See this lovely wooden desk? Pretend that that's Blade before he was trained—say thirteen, fourteen years old."

"Yeah," responded Alberta cautiously.

"The process of training him was like breaking the desk apart with an ax, then pulverizing it. The trainer took the sawdust, put it through a digester, squeezed it into composite board, and built another entirely different desk."

"But," she continued, "if the trainer was just a bit sloppy, a piece of desk might have been left out. Human beings, even children, can be astonishingly inventive when they're desperate. So what the trainer ended up with was a new desk with a chunk of old desk embedded in it. Maybe a big chunk—even a whole corner with a leg. It's an original piece all right, but by itself it isn't a desk. It isn't anything. It can't stand, it's not functional, and it needs the new desk for support."

She glanced over. Alberta looked like she was swimming in dirty water and Toni didn't blame her.

"You think that's what Blade has?"

"Yes. Your observation about him being childlike would be exactly right. What you saw is a fragment of the child before he was altered. We took him away from his usual routine and familiar landmarks, and it came out. Anything could have triggered it—the woods, the picnic, the boat trip—no way to tell. There may even be something about Klale."

"You've seen that before, haven't you?"

"A little," admitted Toni. "But I had no idea he retained such a major relic. It sounds like he has some capacity for both enjoyment and spontaneity. That's very unusual. I wish like hell I'd been there." She looked up again and realized that she'd let some of her old professional enthusiasm creep into her voice. Alberta's eyes had a shadow of that familiar look that said "how can you be such a callous bitch?" Toni shifted her gaze back to her boots.

"Toni," said Alberta sharply. "I want to know what you do in the office with him on Thursday nights."

Toni let a sigh escape.

"I told you. I hold his hand."

The security chief blinked, then frowned incredulously.

"I thought you were joking."

"No."

She looked unconvinced.

"Why?"

"It's an . . . experiment."

Alberta's eyes were making her uncomfortable and she felt herself getting defensive.

"Look, when I first started at the 'Dyke, I worried a lot because it was Blade who brought me here." She fixed her eyes deliberately on the other woman. "I have no memory of it. Mary told me. And I have no idea why."

She looked away and paused for a moment, fighting back her own reluctance.

"For a long time I was afraid I'd been altered, by Choi or some-body else. I've got four missing months—more than enough time to be conditioned or given an implant. I checked myself over about a hundred times, and I got Mary and Doc to check, too. They couldn't find anything and Doc thought the memory loss was consistent with a mother of a binge."

"So I started watching Blade for clues, and after a while I realized that he was watching me, too. That's out of character for a rough tool unless he's under orders, or has a suppressed personality rem-nant. I wanted to know which. So I tried to communicate. I gradually got him used to having me within his defense radius, then I tried touching him. In chronically touch-deprived people, tactile stimulus can knock loose intense emotions."

"He could of killed you!"

Toni shrugged.

"I needed a response. And I got one that's consistent with extreme abuse. But it didn't really tell me anything. I tried again, and got him in the pattern of coming by the office late on Thursdays. He's been doing it now for close to nine years. He sometimes misses a week, but not often. He just kneels right there on the floor next to me," she pointed, "and holds my hand for as long as I let him. Then he leaves."

Alberta stared down at the floor, then looked away uncomfortably.

"Unfortunately, that's all he does. I've tried everything I can think of to get him to communicate, and there's nothing more I can do to him here without the risk of triggering violence, or attracting Choi's attention. I don't have the time or the equipment."

Toni's voice was rising in frustration and she stopped. There was a short silence in which she heard voices outside the window, the swish of bicycle tires, and then the quiet whine of a tong car passing.

"How smart is he?" asked Alberta suddenly.

"Hell I can't talk to him, never mind test him," she snapped, then reined herself in. That wasn't an answer. "You can assume he's got at least average intelligence."

Alberta paused, then said carefully:

"The Consortium meets Thursdays."

"Yeah, I've thought of that, but if he's tapping us, I can't figure out how."

Alberta nodded reluctantly. Toni hesitated, then volunteered more.

"There is one other thing you should know. Blade's behavior used to be consistent, but lately I've been seeing anomalies."

Alberta's gaze snapped up.

"That sounds bad."

"It is. Tools don't change routine. But something's destabilizing Blade. Choi could be tampering with him, or Blade's training might be disintegrating."

Alberta's jaw clenched.

"You mean he might go berserk?"

"Yes."

"Shit!" she said intensely.

"Mary says he's been coming around here twelve or fifteen years. That makes him at least thirty—probably older. Tools aren't designed to last past forty or forty-five at the outside. It's partly the physical damage caused by systemic tweaking, and partly training erosion. Negative reinforcement is not reliably permanent. Or, to go back to our analogy, the adhesive that holds the composite board together eventually deteriorates and then the whole desk crumbles. If there are personality relics, they push the process faster."

"When will he go?"

"No way to tell. It could happen tomorrow, next month, or years from now. It depends on too many variables that I don't know anything about."

"Surely Choi knows he's coming apart!"

Toni frowned.

"He should. Maybe he hasn't got a replacement ready. Or maybe he's screwing up. He's an amateur trainer. I hear his last tool went berserk, too."

Alberta sat in silence for a long moment, then rubbed her forehead wearily.

"So Blade might go berserk here—in a crowded bar. I've got a top team, but they're unarmed and they're not combat troops. Hell, it would take a cannon to stop a boosted tool, anyway." She looked over desperately. "Is there anything at all I can do?"

"Not that I know of. But, I'd appreciate it if you tell me anything you see or hear about him."

There was a pause in which Alberta looked at her tensely.

"Nothing will do any good, but you've kept doing it for nine years? You want to tell me why?"

Toni hesitated. Mary had asked the same question, and she'd never come up with a convincing answer. She made her voice brusque.

"It might buy me a second or two some day when it counts."

"I don't believe you."

Alberta's bluntness startled her for a second, then she shrugged and swung her legs off the desk.

"Believe what you want. I can tell you that I'm not Choi's operative, but I can't prove it. Maybe I'm trying to expiate old sins. Or maybe I'm a stubborn cret. Take your pick." She met Alberta's gaze coldly. "Was that everything you wanted?"

There was a long pause, then Alberta sighed and stood up. "Yeah."

Toni turned back to the netset, expecting to hear Alberta leave, but Alberta's footsteps moved around to the front of the desk and stopped. Toni looked up reluctantly.

"I checked on that new medic like you asked," Alberta said.

"Oh?" said Toni, surprised. "Find anything?"

Alberta shrugged.

"Dr. Lau's shiny. Everybody loves him, even his ex-wife. Worked the last fourteen years for Black Cross tong clinics in the Hong Kong slums but only doing legit medicine. Belongs to the International Anti-Poverty Alliance and the Hong Kong Renters League. And that's confirmed. Mary found two people who've known him in person for years."

This glowing report did nothing to lift Toni's unease about the new doctor.

"Thanks," she said gruffly.

To her surprise, the security chief leaned forward and extended her hand across the desk.

"So, we're on the same side, OK?"

Toni nodded slowly, then reached for the hand.

"OK."

Long after the door shut she sat staring blindly at the set, wondering if she should have told Alberta more. And should she have been more honest with Mary from the very beginning?

Finally she shrugged. It was senseless to worry about the past. And as for the present, perhaps it was time to get much more aggressive with Blade. Waiting for Choi to move against her, or for Blade to explode, was foolish.

She tried to get back to work but found that she couldn't concentrate on accounting, so she shut off the set and went out to the bar where Delilah's Quintet was playing a lazy Monday afternoon set to a small house. She was surprised to spot Ron McCaskill sitting alone on the second tier in the Guild section. He was wearing formals, too. She poured herself a coffee and walked over to his table.

"This seat taken?"

"Hello, Toni. Of course not. Please join me, dear."

She put down her cup and gave the elderly man a sidelong glance. His suit fitted hollowly, as if he'd shrunk in the years since he bought it, and with his shoulders slumped forward he looked frail and very old.

"Been to any good funerals lately?" she asked casually. It was an old joke between them, but this time his smile was forced and his eyes were sad.

"Just came from one. Good food, lots of scotch at the reception. Had too much of both."

"A close friend?" she asked gently.

"No. But I knew him for more than eighty years. Went to school with him." He looked at his untouched beer glass. "You know, most of the time when I overhear somebody talking about 'that old man' I'll look around, wondering where the old guy is. But sometimes, when I think about the friends I've lost, I do feel old. There aren't many of my generation alive, you know. I'm starting to feel like a museum piece. And it's been twenty years since Jean died. Hard to believe. I still dream about her most nights."

Toni reached for his hand, and they sat quietly for a moment, pretending to watch the musicians. Finally Ron wiped the tears off his cheeks.

"Guess I'm getting maudlin. Sorry, Toni."

She let go his hand and reached for her coffee.

"Ron, you are one of the most refreshingly sane people I've ever met."

Ron managed a chuckle.

"I'll take that as a bartender's professional compliment."

Toni smiled back, then it suddenly hit her. Ron had been around Downtown for decades, and he knew everyone.

"Ron?"

"Hmm?

"What do you know about Blade?"

She half expected him to put her off with one his usual jokes, but he hesitated, then answered grimly.

"Too much. I knew his folks."

"Folks? You mean parents?"

"Yeah."

She stared in astonishment. That was better than she could possibly have hoped for. Hell, she'd never dreamed of tracing a street kid.

"Please tell me about him," she said.

Ron looked at her sharply, frowning.

"You know it's not a good idea to talk about tools."

She leaned forward and spoke quietly. "Ron, it's important or I wouldn't ask."

She waited. McCaskill seemed troubled, but she was pretty sure he wanted to talk. She took a chance and poked him in the shoulder, smiling.

"You can trust your bartender."

He gave her an uncomfortably direct gaze for another long second, then relaxed, and his eyes started to crinkle.

"What's it worth to you?"

"A beer?" No response. "Two beers?"

"How about a double Colombian?"

"Done," she said firmly. "If you'll find a booth at the back, I'll get your fee and join you."

"Not quite yet," he told her, standing up. "Come with me first."

He led her through the tables toward the washroom, walking a little unsteadily without his cane, then turned into one of the pay phones. It was a squeeze, but with Ron on the stool and Toni standing behind him, she could just pull the privacy screen shut. She stood jammed up against his musty-smelling suit, looking down at pink, freckled skin under thinning white hair.

He unclipped his phone and mated it with the terminal, then called up his home account and rummaged around. Suddenly he grunted, and called up a file.

It was a holopic, slightly fuzzy on the cheap netset, or maybe a poor shot to start with. It looked like a home vid. A group of fire-

fighters milled around a shabby, concrete-floored room—a fire station, decided Toni, looking at the equipment racks on the walls. Two
men with inhalation equipment collared a third man and demonstrated the gear on him. There was a lot of self-conscious laughter.
Toni scanned the ring of people in the background and spotted a
somewhat younger Ron, standing with his helmet under his arm.

"That's him," said Ron, pointing to a figure beside him.

Toni leaned forward, staring at a boy, maybe twelve years old,
dressed in shabby clothes that were too small for him. Ron rotated
the pic, and familiar burn scars came into view on the left side of
his face. Blade, all right. But the rest of his face looked very different.
He had delicate features with beautiful long-lashed eyes, though his
expression as he watched the firefighters was typical of street kids—
sad and wary. Then Ron leaned down and squeezed the boy's shoulder. He looked up eagerly and Ron teased him until he smiled. Toni
felt a jolt of recognition. She'd seen that smile.

"I found this a few months back when I was going through my
albums. I'm putting together a history of the Downtown firefighters,
you know." He paused for a second, then said quietly. "His name
was Simon."

"Would you copy it to me?"

He hesitated, then nodded. "Sure."

He sent it to the address she gave him, then closed the file and
shut off the phone. Toni opened the booth door in silence.

At the bar she took care of a cash sale, then poured two cups of
coffee, making the motions automatically while she thought over
what she'd seen. She added hash oil, honey mix, a cinnamon stick,
and cream to one cup, but left her own coffee black.

Ron was waiting for her in a quiet booth, and she slid in across
from him. He started talking without prodding.

"Simon's parents were flots. His father was a refugee from Asia,
trying to be a performer, but I wouldn't have pinned much hope on
it. He was good at first aid, though. Volunteered with the unit sometimes and I was sorry to lose him."

"When was that?" asked Toni.

Ron used the cinnamon stick to stir his coffee, moving with

deliberation. He had an instinct for drama, thought Toni with amusement, and he was enjoying this.

"Hmm. It must have been all of twenty-five years ago. Let's see. We got the new inhalation gear in eighty-six or eighty-seven, and Simon was around eleven in that pic. His parents were gone by then—make it four, five years before that when I met him."

That fit. It put Blade in his early thirties, thought Toni.

"Simon was named after his mother, Simone." He smiled reminiscently. "What a pyro girl. Wanted to be a dancer. Very tall, beautiful, and full of vitality—like an explosion when she entered a room. Made sure everyone noticed her, too. Dressed like a hurricane that went through a wardrobe."

He smiled, then sighed a little.

"It was the usual story. They were very young, doing anything they could for money. I think she was from the American floats, but they lived on a decrepit old hulk on Lost Lagoon with Simon's grandfather. Apparently he sailed it across the Pacific. Miracle it didn't sink. I didn't like the old man. Well, he was about my own age, but he seemed older. Looked like he'd had a hard life."

Ron paused, frowning, and sipped his coffee. Then he spoke quietly.

"When I first met them, Simon was six or seven and real clever. He adored his mother—loved to dress up and imitate her. And he had a tremendous gift for music—played any instrument he could get his hands on. Of course, he ran wild a lot. They were putting in long hours with a theater troupe and that grandfather was no good. I took Simon fishing one morning when I found him out wandering on his own. He was a nice boy."

Ron stared off into space. Toni waited a while, then prodded.

"What happened?"

"Hmm? Oh, the parents went away on some acting tour and left Simon with his grandfather. Then they died in an accident—never came back. That's when things got bad for the boy. The grandfather sent the kid out begging and then spent the money on jolts. Simon was always hungry. He used to come by the station and I'd give him part of my lunch."

"How did he get the scars?"

"The old guy's cooker blew up and set the boat on fire. Simon was never the same after that. It can't have been long after his parents died, either. He lost most of his hearing and it seemed to take everything out of him. I imagine the damage to his ears could have been repaired, but they didn't have the money, and his grandfather didn't give a damn anyway."

Ron paused, and Toni saw the sudden tension around his jaw. When he spoke again, his voice was thick with fury.

"That bastard sold everything he could put his hands on to get jolts, then he sold his grandson. I wouldn't sell a dog I hated to Choi—I'd put it down myself. And to give a child to a trainer . . . I can't help thinking of my own grandkids . . ."

Ron's hands shook and coffee splashed on the table. He put his cup down.

"Toni, I've always regretted that I didn't do something—anything—but by the time I realized what had happened it was too late. Simon had been gone for days. When he turned up again, maybe four, five years later, I wouldn't have recognized him if it hadn't been for the burn scars." His hand clenched into a fist on the table. "I'm not usually a vengeful man, but sometimes I hope there's a hell just so that man's burning in it."

Toni had never seen Ron so angry. She sat in silence waiting until he was able to speak again.

"He doesn't recognize me at all so far as I can tell. Choi took out all his memories and most of everything else. What's left is a twisted mess." He looked over at her grimly. "He went into a rage a few years back, beat three men against a concrete wall until they were nothing but bloody meat. Doc had to use genetic sampling to make IDs."

Had something like that happened the other night? But why hadn't Toni heard anything? She said quietly: "Do you ever try to talk to him?"

Ron shook his head sadly.

"No. I don't take any chances. And don't you either, Toni. He's beyond your help and mine—the only one left who can do anything for him is the Good Lord."

He cleared his throat.

"But there's others I can help, and Simon's my reminder. Since I quit fire fighting, I've been working with the Vancouver Foundation to help children on the floats. They're sold to trainers all the time, you know—especially the smut trade. We do what we can, but there's far more than we have resources for."

Toni nodded grimly and waited a long moment, but he didn't seem to have anything more to add.

"Thank you for telling me, Ron."

He looked at her, blinking. The hash was taking effect. It took him a second to collect his thoughts, then he reached over and put his hand on hers.

"Toni—be careful. Choi is vicious. He wouldn't hesitate to have you killed. By Simon."

She nodded, keeping the chill she felt from showing in her face. Then she got up. Ron followed, slightly unsteady on his feet.

"I shouldn't have had the coffee," he told her ruefully. "But I didn't feel like going home quite yet. I think I'll just see if I can find somebody else to bore with old stories."

"Tell me when you're leaving, Ron. I'll call a cab, and have one of Alberta's people escort you to the ferry." He started to protest and she overrode him firmly. "I'm not going to lose our favorite customer."

As she walked through the tables toward the bar, she couldn't help glancing to the back corner of the tong section. Blade's seat was empty.

So your name is Simon, she thought to herself. Goddamn it, Simon, I want to know what goes on in your head!

12

There was nowhere to dance on the arm of the loading crane and Simon was bored. Blade sat in the control booth of the Pier B-C crane scanning east through night rain toward the entrance to Gastown Channel. The Kung Lok's Longshore traffickers found it convenient to have an irremediable radar glitch in between Pier B-C and the Viet Ching docks. It was a favorite rendezvous for smuggling and payoffs, but nothing moved there now.

Simon concentrated, visualizing the last dance he'd seen at the KlonDyke and trying to remember the music that had gone with it. Sometimes if he tried very hard he could retrieve music and listen to it, but tonight it eluded him. He could only hear snatches of tune, not the whole piece. It was frustrating. And he badly needed to dance. It seemed to be such a long time in between real body dances. Sometimes when Blade stood still he could dance on the streets or wharves. That helped, even if it wasn't as good as body dancing.

But Simon couldn't practice here. If he had to imagine a whole dance floor, Blade would have to take too much attention away from the water and Blade had surveillance orders. If he failed he would be punished. Simon could run away from much of Blade's pain, but he could not escape punishment.

He felt a familiar stab of terror at the thought of punishment, and crawled farther along the arm of the crane. The rain splattered in gusts against the beams and gradually his gnawing fear receded. It felt peaceful to be suspended in midair. Below him black water gurgled and slapped at the old pier's drowned cargo level. He looked back. He could barely see the outline of Blade sitting motionless in the cab.

Sometimes Simon wondered if Blade was invisible, too. If it wasn't that people moved around him on the street, he wouldn't be sure that Blade was real. Nobody looked at him or talked to him or touched him. Except Toni. Toni had even touched Simon!

He thought back, savoring the thrill of her warm hand against his skin. He remembered her sitting beside him at the picnic, her body pressed up against his. She had reached up and touched Simon with her brown eyes, and spoken to him. Simon knew that Toni sometimes tried to talk to him in the KlonDyke office, but only Blade was permitted there. He felt a distant needle of fear as he remembered what Blade had been doing to Toni. She would find out. And then she would never let him into the office again. She would never touch him with her soft hands or make those terrible delicious aches in his chest.

Abruptly Blade snapped alert. His night goggles registered a glow out at the end of Pier B-C. It was an approaching boat, probably a water taxi. The intercepted Viet Ching message had said two A.M., and it was on time. The boat turned, steering toward the radar shadow. Blade pressed the pad on the goggles to start recording.

He scanned the taxi, then continued east and caught the snout of a Patrol Boat edging around the end of the Viet Ching docks. As it moved to intercept the taxi, Blade switched his goggles to visible light. The PBoat had most of her running lamps off, but he could still see the number on the side. Seven. Dhillon's boat. Excellent. His master anticipated much profit from Captain Dhillon's activities.

He switched back to infrared. A figure stood near the bow and two others in the wheelhouse. Then he stiffened. There were also two people in the cabin. Patrol boats had a crew of four and they didn't carry Longshore inspectors at two A.M. He focused on the figures in the cabin, took a still, then enlarged and enhanced. On the left he identified Neil McCaskill, Dhillon's new first mate. Next to him stood

Linden Chan. Most interesting. The PBoat should not be carrying a civilian, much less a Viet Ching operative. What was so important that Chan would risk riding with them?

The taxi pulled alongside the PBoat, bow to bow, and cut her engine. The two boats were less than a hundred meters east of Blade now and drifting slowly in his direction, with the Patrol boat broadside to him. The Patrol appeared to be hailing the taxi. For a few seconds Blade saw no movement, then figures stepped out of the taxi cabin onto the deck. He scanned them closely. They looked like a typical taxi family—four shabbily dressed adults and three small children. Then a white-haired man in a tailored raincoat appeared in the doorway. Blade recognized him instantly. Mr. Kwong, Heung Chu of the Sun Yee On.

He pulled the zoom back and checked the larger view. Linden Chan crossed from the PBoat to the water taxi. She waved Mr. Kwong back into the cabin. Kwong leaned down slowly as if to put his briefcase down, then Blade saw a flash as he pulled a weapon. Chan fell. More shots flashed on the Patrol boat and the taxi. When they ceased, bodies lay strewn on the taxi deck.

The Patrol officers seemed frozen in place. The two boats spun very slowly with the incoming tide, bows turning toward the pier, and Blade made out stark horror on young McCaskill's face. On the taxi, two prone flots climbed to their knees and scuttled into the cabin. Chan staggered up, holding her arm, and checked Kwong's body, then stumbled back onto the Patrol boat where the officers surrounded her. They held a tense conference. After a minute, Captain Dhillon waved her crew back to their posts and jumped over to the water taxi herself. She stepped up to the first body and shot it through the head, then moved to Kwong and did the same. Then she went into the cabin.

The starboard side of the water taxi rotated into view and Blade glimpsed movement just above the water line. A child was scrambling out of a porthole. It got about halfway, then it was yanked back inside. A few seconds later Dhillon appeared at the porthole. She examined the hull and adjacent water, then disappeared.

For half a minute he saw no movement on either boat. Then Dhillon came out. She dragged the two bodies on deck into the cabin, fastened the door, and jumped back to the Patrol boat, casting off and signaling to the officer in the wheelhouse. Number Seven pulled away, using its quiet mooring engine and no running lights. The water taxi bobbed in its wake.

Blade was just zooming out from the scene when the taxi exploded in a blinding flash, hurling debris in the air. Flames shot through the remaining portholes and the boat listed. Blade saw a moving shadow and focused. A child squeezed through a porthole, hair and clothes on fire, and fell into the water. A gust of wind slapped Blade's face, carrying the harsh smell of smoke. . . .

Simon heard a crackling roar. He gasped and reached for the left side of his face. He felt flames on his clothes, flames in his hair, being thrown into icy water, screaming, crying, mouth and nose choking on brine. . . .

Something flashed in his eyes and he blinked in confusion, then clawed urgently at Blade's goggles. The Patrol boat hadn't left yet. He zoomed. Dhillon stood in the wheelhouse looking toward him. The flash had been her scope beam. He had leaned forward in the cab and she'd spotted him. On the bow an officer raised a long-barreled gun.

Blade!

Blade yanked the goggles down around his neck, pulled his armored serape tight around him and sucked in a breath, then kicked open the cab door and leaped into the buffeting wind. A long fall, then he slammed into the sea feet first. Just before the water swallowed him, he felt an impact and searing pain in his side. Then the shock of the icy water penetrated and he had to fight down the reflex to gasp.

His armored serape and equipment belts dragged downward and he stayed limp. He must sink quickly and play dead. Something, probably another bullet, grazed his head. Icy water soaked through his clothes and pressure clawed his ears. His lungs stretched taut. He thought carefully. Three minutes. He could last that long and the Patrol boat would have to leave quickly, before the fire was reported. Dhillon also had to get rid of Chan. She couldn't afford to be found with a Viet Ching agent on her boat. He began to count.

Ten. Eleven. It grew colder as he sank and the pressure on his ears increased. His mouth tasted of seawater. He must hit the bottom soon; surely there was no more than fifteen meters of water. He opened his eyes but could see nothing. Then his knee bumped a solid object, and he settled onto slimy rocks. He ignored the desire to flinch and stayed limp. He was well out of range of the Patrol's guns, but not a subsurface infrared scope. He had to remain motionless as long as possible.

Fifty-two. Fifty-three. He pictured each Chinese number carefully, ignoring the agony in his lungs, the blazing pain from his right thigh to shoulder, and the warm current of escaping blood. At one hundred twenty he expelled some air and considered the problem of getting back to the surface.

He reached for his serape clip, fingers clumsy with cold. Luckily his left arm was uninjured. He fumbled for long seconds before the clip popped loose. The records stored in the goggles around his neck were not expendable, but his tool pouch and shoes were. He kicked his shoes off and felt an answering increase in buoyancy. He wouldn't need to abandon his weapons. Good.

Time to surface. He tried to push off, but he'd already drifted above the bottom, so he kicked, sending a stab of pain down his right leg. Remembering the proximity of the pier, he stretched his left arm out in front of him.

He could feel himself gaining momentum, but the journey up seemed to take a long time. Suddenly his hand grazed something and before he could react, his head rammed painfully into seaweed covered concrete, forcing a choking spurt of salt water into his nose and mouth. He reached up and felt above him. He was trapped under the drowned lower level of the old pier. He couldn't be far from open water, but which way?

Blade had lost all sense of direction. He loosed a measure of air from his burning lungs and groped around, then tried opening his eyes again and saw a glow. The boat fire. He somersaulted, pushed against the concrete with his feet and swam toward the light. After a short distance his hand met no resistance. He shot upward, finally breaking surface.

He tried to be silent, but reflex made him gasp and cough. He accessed audio—acceptable in an emergency—then realized that the roar of the burning boat would mask any sound he made. It drifted no more than ten meters away, its glare temporarily blinding him. If the Patrol was still out there, they'd have a clear shot.

He squinted and looked around. A barnacle-encrusted pillar nearby had bent rungs stapled into it. He swam over awkwardly and hooked his good arm on a rung, then turned and began searching the area methodically as his eyes adjusted.

The flames rising from the foundering taxi illuminated his surroundings clearly. The PBoat was gone and nobody else had arrived yet, but he had to get away quickly. The blaze would be visible from the North Shore, and the Harbor Authority would call in fire and patrol boats, probably including PBoat 7. But he couldn't climb up onto Pier B-C. Hatches above the emergency ladders were kept sealed against refugees and smugglers, and the shore under the pier was also secured. To escape undetected he would have to swim. If he swam toward the fire, he risked being seen. Besides, the Viet Ching docks beyond it were busy all night. West then. Beyond Pier B-C lay Pier A and then a small drydock used by tramp freighters. The drydock was his best option—it had only one night watchman who would probably be distracted by the fire. But it would be a long swim and he could already feel the effects of blood loss and hypothermia.

Something splashed on the other side of the pillar. Blade swung around, gripping the vertical surface with his knees and grabbing for his knife, but his right arm was clumsy and his fingers slid past the holster. Then the other side of the pillar came into view, and he found himself looking into the terrified eyes of a child with burned skin and a charcoaled mat of hair. The child clung to the pillar, shuddering.

Simon froze. He could hear the fire burning; feel its heat radiate across the water. He could feel the burn on the child's head, too, and he knew that agonizing terror in his stomach and throat. The child's eyes kept him snared to the pillar. I'm afraid! It hurts! I'm cold! I'm going to drown!

He reached out his hand slowly. The child flinched back. Simon hesitated, then lunged forward and grabbed. It squealed in panic and tried to fight him, but it was very small. He pulled it away from its clawhold, then pinioned it against his chest while its struggles became feeble.

They had to get to shore! Simon fought back his own panic, trying to think. He must swim west!

He shook the child until it stopped struggling, then, working awkwardly, he opened the front of his shirt and shoved the child inside, face out. He held his wounded arm tight against the small body. Numbness was dulling the pain. He pushed off on his back, striking out with his good arm.

It was utterly black under the pier and he could feel the tide pulling against him. His progress was laborious and very slow. The child squirmed, spluttered, then stopped and clung tightly to him. A siren wailed in the distance. After a while Simon lost sight of the taxi's glow, and began to lose his bearings. He tried to swim straight, but feared slamming headfirst into a pillar in the fetid blackness. Then he glimpsed faint light and felt rain in his face. He was out. One more open stretch of water and one more pier to go.

Stroke, kick. Stroke, kick. Stroke, kick.

Simon was nearly exhausted. He triggered an adrenaline surge, then fled into Blade's remoteness. Don't think, don't feel, just do. Be wood. Be stone. Stroke, kick. Reach the destination.

The Coast Ferries drydock was deserted when Blade grounded. He felt vibration as his body scraped against barnacle-stuccoed concrete, but he couldn't feel any pain. He crawled up the ramp, his left side pulling his failing right side along. After the cold water the ground seemed warm. The little body hung limply against his chest, half spilling out of his shirt.

At the top of the ramp he sat panting, trying to think through a fog of exhaustion and confusion. He had no orders. No procedures. What should he do?

Simon?

Simon was scared. He knew he had to go somewhere quickly, but where? Bentall was near. But he couldn't take the child there.

A flicker of memory came to him. Toni had been cold and wet, too. Simon had picked her up. He had taken her to the KlonDyke. She was safe there. And it was close.

He triggered another burst of adrenaline in Blade, but even with the boost he had difficulty standing up and balancing on bare, numb feet. He walked stiffly around the drydock building to the wire fence, pulled out his knife, and slashed the thick strands with his molecular blade, ignoring the barbs that tore at his skin and clothes.

13

Toni shoved a tray of dirty glasses through into the kitchen. They clattered loudly, sending echoes across the empty bar. It was a quarter to four and she still had the cash reconciliation and night report to do. As she racked the last few glasses, Alberta walked over, tossed her coat on a table and pulled up a stool.

"Make it a pint."

Toni raised an eyebrow, but grabbed a clean glass and set up a pint of porter.

"Bad night?"

"Yeah." Alberta took a deep draught. "One fighting drunk, two pukers, and a diabetic coma. Banned the last one. She can kill herself someplace else."

Toni nodded and looked at Alberta's glass, then on impulse, reached back and poured herself a half of the same and leaned on the bar. Alberta was trying to be friendly and she could at least try to respond.

It was Alberta's turn to raise an eyebrow.

"Bad night here, too?"

"Not particularly." She took a mouthful, swirling the rich flavor around on her tongue. She didn't often drink beer—smelled too much of it all day long—but tonight it felt good on her stomach.

"Did Klale really complain about Dhillon?"

"I don't think so," said Toni.

The door alarm beeped and they both ignored it. Another late night drunk trying to get in.

"Good. Maybe she's learning," said Alberta. She drank more beer, then put her glass down and looked at Toni. "I heard some spin about that new medic, Lau . . ."

The door beeped insistently. Toni sighed and straightened up. "Just a minute."

She stepped over to the netset while Alberta watched.

"Back door," said Toni, surprised and suddenly tense. She flicked on the monitor. "Blade!"

Alberta braced her arms on the bar, jumped over it, and peered over Toni's shoulder. The pickup showed Blade standing at the double delivery doors. Blood dripped down his face, but he seemed calm.

"I'm letting him in," Toni said abruptly and started for the rear entrance at a jog. A little to her surprise, Alberta didn't argue. The security chief followed and positioned herself on the opposite side of the big loading area, beside a stack of delivery pallets. With a faintly defiant air, she pulled an automatic pistol out of her belt pouch, then stood with legs spread and arms braced, covering the door.

Toni lifted the left floor bolt out of its hole, drew back the heavy bar, and swung open the door. Blade staggered in a few steps, then stopped, swaying. He was barefoot, dripping wet, and shivering. And something bulged out of the front of his shirt. It was a child, Toni realized, then she felt a tightness in the pit of her stomach. This was the same door Blade had come to with her.

Toni stepped forward and he let her lift the cold, limp child out of his shirt. About six years old, she estimated, and badly burned. She had to hold her ear to the child's chest to tell that it was still breathing. She turned to Alberta.

"Hypothermia and burns. We'll need warm water in the sink. You know the treatment?"

Alberta hesitated a second, then nodded, lowered her gun, and went to the big utility sink. She placed her gun carefully on a shelf within reach and kept her body half rotated so she could watch Toni. Toni turned back to Blade and then realized that his knees were buckling. She reached out automatically, trying to break his fall, but even without the child in her arms it would have been futile, like stopping a landslide. He collapsed face forward on the tiled floor, and lay unmoving. Pink stained water dripped from a long bloody rip in the back of his shirt.

"I'll call Doc," said Alberta from behind her.

"No. You take the kid. I'll call," said Toni. She handed over the child, checked the temperature of the water gushing from the taps, then went for the loading bay console. Doc answered immediately, voice gravelly with sleep. She told him to bring two IVs and wet plasma, then cut the connection, thankful that he'd been in. Doc went anywhere any time, he took cash, and he kept his mouth shut.

Next, she fetched an emergency kit from the downroom and hurried toward Blade. Alberta's urgent voice stopped her.

"Toni!"

Alberta stood holding the child carefully in the bath. She twisted to look back over her shoulder, fixing intense eyes on Toni.

"Should you help him?"

Toni turned and stared at the long body on the white plastiche tiles. Blade's skin was unnaturally pale and his breathing sounded labored. She walked across the kitchen, knelt down, and pulled up his shirt. His skin felt cold and he had a deep, angled bullet wound, bleeding much too slowly. Serious blood loss and hypothermia, plus unknown other damage. He would die without treatment, but probably not in the next five minutes. If he survived until Doc arrived, Doc would certainly treat him.

She leaned back on her heels. Killing him would be a favor to the KlonDyke and Downtown. It would also be a favor to Blade. There had been dozens of nights she'd held his hand and wished that she could release him. And it wouldn't be difficult. There were sedatives in the first aid kit. She knew how much to administer and Doc wouldn't ask too many questions.

She pulled out an ampule, but found herself unable to go further. She was remembering his smile. This wasn't euthanasia or an assisted suicide. Blade was sentient and he hadn't asked to die. He might be horrifically altered, but some small part of him was still a boy named Simon.

More seconds ticked by. She stared at the ampule, then dropped it back in the kit. Maybe it was the wrong decision, but she couldn't do it.

She picked up a laser scalpel and started cutting his shirt away from the wound. The material was very tough—padded, too, as Alberta had noticed. The bullet had sliced through the muscles on the right side of his back, but it looked like a rib had deflected it away from the lung. She sponged the wound off, sprayed in disinfectant/congealant foam, and began slapping tape across.

A loud rap sounded. Toni jumped in alarm, realizing that she'd forgotten to lock up after Blade, but it was only Doc. She closed the door and rammed the bolt tight behind him.

Doc put down his shoulder bag and shrugged out of his rain-spattered jacket. Underneath were the rumpled blue pants and tunic that he wore in the day and evidently slept in at night. He opened his bag and took out plasma and oxygen. Toni grabbed them from his hands and gestured at Alberta.

"I can handle this. That one's more critical."

Doc gave her an inscrutable look, got another IV, and went to the sink. While he examined the child, Toni slipped an oxygen mask over Blade's face, triggered the cylinder, then unwrapped an IV needle. He was an easy stick despite the blood loss—the muscles in his arms pushed the veins to the surface. She was pumping a plasma bag to force the flow when Doc kneeled down beside her and wrapped a blood pressure cuff around Blade's arm. Doc's paunch bulged between his lower shirt buttons, and his gray hair and beard were unkempt, but his manner was completely professional.

"What happened?" he asked in a neutral voice.

"Don't know," said Toni shortly. "He just turned up here with a bullet wound. He's been in salt water."

"Is that the only injury?"

"There's lots of scratches and a shallow scalp wound. I haven't been able to turn him to check his other side. How's the child?"

"Shocky, but he'll pull through. Kids can survive a lot." He looked at the reading on the cuff, then pulled it off. "Do you have a mat to roll him onto?"

There were blankets in the first aid cupboard and Toni used them to make a long pad while Doc kept the plasma going. It took all three of them to roll Blade over without dislodging the IV tube. He didn't stir.

They stripped off the rest of his wet clothes and Toni toweled him down while Doc checked for injuries. Alberta had been right, thought Toni. Blade wasn't as heavily muscled as a standard tool, though he was otherwise typical. With his waxy, hairless skin he looked like an oversized mannequin except for the burn scars on his abdomen and arms which she recognized as self-inflicted injuries from obedience training. There was a different type of scar on the inside of his right wrist. Toni saw Doc glance at it, his expression unreadable.

"He's lost a lot of blood. Plasma won't be enough. He needs a unit of whole blood. And heat."

"There should be heating pads upstairs," said Toni. "What about the blood?"

"I have a source," said Doc. "They'll deliver, but it's faster and more discreet if you pick it up yourself. They charge fifty dollars plastic."

Toni hesitated, then Alberta said: "I'll go."

"Get the pads first," Doc told her. "I want Toni here."

Toni got up and took the child while Alberta left. When she turned back to look, Doc was taking a blood sample to run through his analyzer. He looked at the results, frowned, then pressed reset and ran the test again, this time staring at the readout intently. Suddenly he became aware of Toni's gaze. He made a show of clearing the analyzer's memory, then got up to use the netset.

What had he seen? Toni desperately wanted to look, but she was stuck at the sink with her hands full. Alberta came back at a jog with a stack of heating pads. Toni told her how to set up a fifty dollar unassigned credit on the office set, then Doc gave her the address and blood type, and she departed.

The next few minutes were a blur as they moved back and forth trying to get their two patients warm and stable. When the child was finally wrapped in a blanket with a heating pad, Toni sat down on the stack of pallets to rest for a minute. Doc was checking the dressing on Blade's head. She watched him absently, while giving grim consideration to what to say to Mr. Choi. She hated the idea of calling Blade's owner, but she didn't see any other choice.

Doc's stillness suddenly caught her attention. He was staring very intently down at his index finger, pressed against Blade's head. Abruptly he moved his hand away, but Toni hurried over and kneeled beside him, reaching for the same spot in the left posterior occipital region of the skull, Underneath the skin she felt the almost indiscernible round button of a plug.

Toni's eyes met Doc's for a few frozen seconds, then she started searching Blade's head with her fingertips. She worked methodically in slow sweeps from the thalamic plug at the back of the skull. She found five more plugs. When she looked up, Doc's face was ashen and she could feel that her own was, too. A rough tool should only have had one or two neural plugs. Blade had six. He was a weapon. And that piece of information could easily get them both killed.

They leaned back, studying each other warily. Toni kept her face blank, but her thoughts spun rapidly, and she felt her heart pounding. Blade's inconsistencies suddenly made a great deal of sense. But she'd made a terrible mistake. Tools might be partially salvageable, but weapons weren't. She should have killed him when she had the chance.

"He might still die . . ." she said, keeping her voice expressionless.

Doc hesitated, then shook his head.

"Choi will find out where he was and who was with him. And he'll be furious if he loses an investment this big."

"He's going to know we touched his tool. He may have us killed anyway."

"Yeah. But if Blade lives, and we keep quiet, we might survive this. Choi won't know we found anything and he might let it drop, rather than attract attention by killing us."

Especially Doc, thought Toni grimly. A bartender wouldn't be missed Downtown, but Doc would be. The tongs used him frequently. A thought occurred to her.

"Blade didn't see you. He may not have seen Alberta either, but we can't know that, so both of us have to admit we were here. . . ."

Doc looked at her, then pulled up one corner of his mouth in a faint, ironic smile.

"I appreciate the offer, Toni, but there's no point. All the tongs tap my ID so your call to me is known. I've never tried to secure my records and I don't lie. If they think I'm hiding anything, they'll kill me."

He was right of course. She nodded again, and stood up. It was nearly five A.M. She couldn't put off notifying Choi. She walked over to the netset.

She didn't expect a live answer; nonetheless when she reached a reception protocol she let out a relieved breath. She left a short, carefully worded message. Mr. Choi's package was at the KlonDyke, somewhat damaged but intact. It would be kept safe for him.

Doc got up stiffly and looked at the child, then at Toni. It must be an eerie experience for him, she realized suddenly. Ten years ago it had been Toni he'd treated right here under very similar circumstances.

"Blade brought the boy?" he asked her.

"Yes. I have no idea why. He collapsed before he could tell us anything, if he ever intended to. I doubt we'll ever know." She looked at the child and sighed. "We'd better hide the kid until we can find out who he is and what happened."

"I believe that's the usual procedure in these cases," said Doc, very dryly.

Toni looked at him, momentarily nonplussed, then gave a brief rueful smile. She gestured at Blade.

"I'll have to hide him, too. How long do you think he'll be out?"

Doc frowned. "I really can't tell you. I haven't treated many tools. With a normal person in that condition I'd say twenty-four to thirty-six hours, but with his accelerated metabolism he'll wake up a lot faster. I just don't know how much faster. For one thing, I don't know whether he has a depressed pain response."

"Rough tools usually do, but I doubt that Blade's blunted," said Toni shortly, avoiding the word "weapon."

Doc gave her a very sharp look before continuing.

"I'll give him pain patches, but I can only guess at the dosage and I'll have to make it a conservative guess. You can expect them to be of limited effectiveness and wear off fast. He's going to wake up feverish, disoriented and in a lot of pain. I wouldn't care to be around."

"I don't think I have a choice," said Toni grimly. "I certainly can't leave him alone anywhere in this building. No way to tell what he'll do when he wakes. What else do I need to know?"

"He needs liquids and calories. Other than that it's just a matter of warming him, watching for shock, and keeping him still, if possible, so that wound doesn't tear open."

There was a tap on the back door. They both jumped violently, then looked sheepish. Toni checked the monitor before opening up for Alberta. She stepped inside, pulling a unit of blood from under her coat, and Doc began hooking it up immediately, while Alberta walked over to check the small body lying near the sink. Toni followed her.

"Did you call Choi?"

"Left a message."

"Mention the kid?"

"No. I'm hoping Choi doesn't know, but that means we'll have to hide the boy."

"I'll take him," said Alberta. She'd clearly been thinking it over. "Rill will help. I'm more worried about Blade."

"I'm going to put him in one of the rental rooms and watch him."

Alberta nodded. "I'll stay with you."

"No," said Toni firmly. "He doesn't trust you, Alberta. But he might be all right with me."

The security chief gave her a worried frown.

"I'll lend you my gun."

Toni shook her head. "If he went for me, I'd never have time to use it."

Alberta looked unhappy, but she nodded reluctantly, then went into the store room and returned pulling a loading dolly. The three of them manhandled Blade onto it, then Doc and Alberta wheeled him to the elevator and hand-cranked their way to the third floor while Toni stayed behind to watch the child and clean up. She knew it would take several minutes just to raise the elevator, but it still seemed like a very long time before Alberta reappeared with the empty dolly. Toni had already run over the kitchen and loading bay with a commercial sterilizer and checked the alley for obvious traces of blood. The two women finished by using their joint security override to purge the records of Blade's arrival.

When they were done, Alberta slipped on her coat and gathered up the bandaged child. Toni let her out the back door, then went up to Number Twelve.

Doc was just removing the IV unit. His patient lay face down on the futon's furry pink coverlet, warmer and breathing better, but still unconscious. Four blue pain patches adhered to the inside of his left arm, and a small heap of replacements lay nearby. Blade would be all right alone for a while.

Toni took Doc downstairs, locking the room behind her. Two abandoned glasses of porter stood on the bar. She looked regretfully at her own glass before tossing it down the drain and then pouring a pint for Doc. He drained it in three long swallows while she started a pot of coffee.

"Cash, plastic, or barter?" she asked him.

He wiped his mouth and thought it over. "Twenty-five plastic for supplies, twenty-five barter on my drinking account."

Toni rang it through on the bar netset, then let him out. She grabbed supplies from the kitchen and office, left a message for Mary, and shut off the lights. Mary could reconcile the till in the morning.

In Number Twelve, the scented smell of sex oils and dim pink light brought back unwanted memories of fat sweaty men grunting on top of her. Toni put down her supplies and went to the window. The sky was graying outside. She left the thermal curtains open a crack, then checked Blade. He was still unconscious, lying on his stomach with the unscarred side of his face turned up. For a long moment she stared, trying to pierce the enigma. He was far more than a listening post, but what?

Finally she lowered the lights and settled on the far side of the big futon with her flask of coffee and a reader she'd grabbed from the office. But for a long time she didn't look at the screen. She was trying to figure out what to do when Blade woke up. Knowing that he was a weapon was little help. Toni had no experience with weapons—never even seen a live one. She'd only worked with rough tools, lovebirds, domestic jobs, and one wizard. Weapons were rare and they were all unique. She had no idea what to expect.

She mapped out some priorities, then found her thoughts circling anxiously and decided to quit. Head twisting was an art, not a science, she reminded herself. Instinct and intuition counted, and she'd been an expert. She was simply going to have to wing it.

At eight A.M. Mary tapped on the door and they held a whispered conference. At ten o'clock Mary returned with food and the largest clothes she'd been able to find. Toni placed them on the bureau, then checked Blade again and found that he'd slipped into a feverish sleep. She changed the patches, but there was nothing else she could do, so she settled back with a meal and the reader.

The food made her drowsy and the book bored her. She put the reader down for a moment to rub her eyes, and dozed off. When she started awake Blade was thrashing in the throes of a nightmare.

She sat up, fighting off grogginess and wondering what the hell to do. The nightmare was no surprise—he would normally sleep under induction and dream suppression—but it was certainly a problem. He might tear his wound open. Or he might wake up fighting. Suddenly he stopped thrashing and lay still, his breathing fast and very shallow. Toni automatically moved a little closer, trying to get a better look at his face in the slice of light from the window. He rolled very fast, grabbed her wrist with a steely hand, and clamped the other on the back of her neck.

Toni gasped, fighting back terror. Shit! She should have realized how far he could reach! She took a slow breath, forcing calm. Blade's face was masklike in the dimness, eyes flat and cold. His fingers tightened painfully on her neck. She had to act fast. On impulse, she spoke loudly in a tone of command:

"Simon! Let go!"

His eyes widened and the grip on her neck released. Bingo! she thought, with a brief flash of exultation. But she had tipped her hand, and she was still in trouble.

He reached for her again and sat up, shoving her roughly so the light from the window fell on her face. She could sense his alarm and confusion.

"It's all right, Simon," she said, with all the reassurance she could manage. "There's nothing to be afraid of. It's just Toni. You know me. Toni. I won't hurt you."

He blinked, then abruptly his hand twitched and let go as the pain caught up with him. He sank back on the bed, gasping.

Toni kept her eyes on him and used her most soothing tone.

"It's all right, Simon. Lie still. You're hurt and you're feverish."

His breathing betrayed intense pain, but he made no sound and his face had gone blank. Trained to endure pain, but not blunted, Toni decided. He closed his eyes for ten or fifteen seconds, then opened them and looked around.

"You're at Sisters'," she lied. He undoubtedly had specific restrictions on what he could do at the KlonDyke.

His breaths came faster. Panic. He knows he's given himself away, thought Toni, and he's terrified of punishment from Choi. He'll do anything to avoid that. She was in intense danger, but she couldn't afford to be frightened. Better to picture him as Simon, the child who used to eat lunch with Ron at the fire station. And she must stay in command. Simon would see people only as masters and servants and it was imperative he treat her as a master.

Keeping her movements slow, she sat cross-legged on the futon, picking her position so that the window lit her face from the side. She relaxed her body, then put a calming hand on top of Simon's. His face was rigid and he stared directly at her. Bad. Tools were trained never to make eye contact except when challenging people. She kept a gentle pressure on his hand, looked back, and spoke softly.

"I know you can hear me, my friend. I've been watching you for years and I've always suspected you weren't any deafer than I am. And if you're not deaf, I'll bet you can talk, too."

There was no response.

"Simon, I think you need someone to talk to. I know that you do. I've seen it in your eyes. All that silence is very, very empty. Holding hands isn't enough."

Still no response. Toni held his gaze for a few more seconds, then reached slowly to her right. His goggles and knife holster were where she'd left them, near his pillow. She grasped the holster and pulled it over, then placed it in the palm of his left hand.

"Simon, I'm ordering you to talk to me. You must talk to me, or kill me. You choose."

As soon as the words were out of her mouth she nearly choked in horror. Christ, did I say that? Tools don't know how to make choices! She had to battle not to let it show on her face, but she could feel her stomach churning and her hands and feet turning cold with fear. That had been crazy. She used to ride hunches before, but her subjects had been restrained. Simon could kill her.

Simon's hand closed around the knife. He looked down at it for several seconds, then began to tremble and Toni felt her own fear ebb a little as she realized that he was utterly terrified. He pushed the holster across the bed, then lay rigid with tension, not meeting her eyes. His skin was pale and sweaty, and he was shaking. Toni took his hand again and spoke very softly.

"We're all alone here, Simon. Nobody else can hear us and I won't tell anyone. I won't tell Him. Talk to me."

Then she waited. There was nothing more that she could say. If he had a direct, clearly worded order never to talk to her, he wouldn't be able to break it.

Long seconds passed before he answered in a little boy voice, wildly incongruous with the deathmask face.

"You can't die."

Toni let out her breath and tried to still her stomach. Finally! Now she had to maintain control and keep him distracted. She squeezed his hand and put all the warmth she could into her voice.

"I know you won't hurt me, Simon. You're my friend. Are you thirsty?"

He wouldn't meet her eyes, but his fingers curled around her hand and he answered in a tiny voice.

"Yes."

"OK. I have to let go of your hand for a minute to get you a drink. I'll be right back."

She moved across the bed onto the tatami-mat floor, fighting an urge to rush, and got a tall glass of water and the fruit shake Mary had brought. Then she helped prop Simon up on his left side and held the cup while he drank through a straw. When he was finished she put the cups aside, and very cautiously leaned over to view his bandages. There were signs of renewed bleeding, but it wasn't severe. She pushed him gently back and pulled up the blanket, then took a cool, damp washcloth, and wiped it across his face. He closed his eyes, but a throbbing pulse at his temples betrayed the intense emotion that her touch pulled to the surface. When she put the washcloth down and took his hand again, he opened his eyes immediately, though he wouldn't meet her gaze.

"Simon, do you remember the picnic?"

He started to nod, but movement obviously hurt and he stopped. "Yes."

"Do you remember sitting by the lake holding hands?"

"Yes."

"Let's go back to that night. We sat under the trees, hand in hand. Close your eyes and remember how it felt. There was wind, there was the sound of the picnic, and the smell of trees..." She went through the routine of inducing hypnosis and he slid under easily, as she'd expected. Undoubtedly he was put in a hypnotic state regularly. The tension around his jaw and temples relaxed as he moved away from the pain.

"What did you do today?" she asked, finally.

Immediately his voice shifted to a flat, mechanical tone and he began giving her a report, in detail, starting with the boat trip to the picnic. Toni listened for a couple of minutes, fascinated but chilled, as he listed the people who had been present. He knew a lot of names. She wondered grimly if he had already given this report once.

"Stop, Simon. I'm not asking you for a report. I just wanted you to tell me about things that happened at the KlonDyke picnic, things that you enjoyed."

That was obviously an unfamiliar request, but he tried to obey. He still sounded like he was giving a report, but as Toni kept encouraging him to remember his own reactions, she started to get a better response. His impressions of the people were flat. But when he described the hike, his voice gained warmth and excitement. His altered face was very hard to read, but she knew from experience to look for subtle signs of animation around his eyes and mouth, and she saw them.

She listened with fascination. He had taken a keen interest in everything around him, and he described plants and birds in vivid detail. Toni kept drawing him out, amazed at his depth of emotional response. It was almost like talking to a normal child. When he got to the mountaintop, she asked him directly how he felt, and he broke into a radiant smile that made her catch her breath.

She moved quickly to reinforce it. She stroked his hand, then cupped his cheek and spoke to him affectionately, watching his bewildered, desperately eager response. She had wished earlier that she had some chocolate to help link his positive reactions to her, but it didn't look as if it would be necessary. Simon was starved for human contact. Whatever Choi was using to motivate him, it wasn't love of his master. That was a serious mistake on Choi's part, but consistent with his phobic profile. And it left her an opening—a crack in Simon's training that she could use to manipulate him. She drew back.

"How old are you, Simon?"

The smile had faded, but he was still at ease. He thought a little, then said: "I don't know."

"Have you ever lived on a boat?"

"No."

That was what she expected—his memories had been suppressed or removed. Then he spoke again.

"I live inside Blade."

Toni blinked. Inside Blade? Did he believe Blade and Simon were separate? She thought quickly.

"What do you look like, Simon?"

"I'm invisible," he told her, matter-of-factly.

A common distancing technique, and it made sense. Simon must have an urgent need to separate himself from the violence and degradation of being a tool. But why had Choi retained Simon's identity at all? He couldn't have made an error that big. She had to assume it was deliberate.

"What does Blade look like?" she tried.

"Ugly."

Simon's voice was even, but his hand clenched hers painfully. She carefully disentangled herself from his grip and rested her hand on top of his.

"How is he ugly, Simon?"

"He's . . ." Simon paused, searching for words, then continued. "He's mutilated. His face, his body, his brain, his blood . . . He's an ugly tool." Simon's voice was expressionless but his fist squeezed so tight that it shook and the tendons in his arm bulged.

"Enough, Simon," she said quickly. She needed a more neutral topic. On impulse she tried: "What does Klale look like?"

He blinked, and his muscles began to relax. Finally he said: "Klale's beautiful."

"Why?"

He hesitated, then spoke haltingly.

"Klale is . . . whole. She's not broken inside. When she dances . . . she soars. Not on the stage. Inside. In her eyes. And she laughs with her whole body."

Toni stared at him, astounded. Most normal people she knew wouldn't have been capable of making that assessment, never mind a tool. But she had to keep remembering that he was a weapon. Don't assume anything. And don't underestimate him. Ron had said he was a clever child, and nobody spent money making stupid weapons. Damn, she wished she knew more!

"Simon, do you watch me?"

His eyes shifted nervously, then flicked for an instant past Toni's. "Yes."

"Why?"

"Because you can see me."

"Can anybody else see you?"

"No," he said with sudden emptiness in his voice. She felt a rush of sympathy and had to push it back. Then she felt the muscles in his hand tighten again and saw fear in his eyes. He whispered.

"Yes. *He* can."

"He can't see you now, Simon," she said quickly. "You're with me at the picnic, remember? Look at the water for a little while. Watch the way the light from the bonfire ripples across it . . ." She was able to calm him again, but she could sense his unease. He wasn't going to stay under much longer.

She reviewed her priorities urgently. She didn't dare question him directly about what Choi used him for, and he wasn't likely to know much about how he'd been trained. The distinction he made between Blade and Simon was interesting, though. It could be an induced psychosis. "Multiple personalities" were easy to create under hypnosis and could be maintained under controlled conditions. Theoretically he could have dozens, but she doubted he had more than a few.

"Simon, how many people live inside Blade?"

"Three," he said, then caught his breath and his hand clenched again. "Two!"

He was very frightened now. She was losing him. Toni bit her lip. What the hell, she thought. I might never get another chance. I'll try a big one.

"Simon, what happened that night you came to see me?" He froze, muscles taut. She kept her voice level and quiet. "There was blood on your hands and you were afraid. Remember?"

He turned his head and stared directly at her for a second, eyes wide with panic, then he visibly retreated. It was like a door slamming. She'd seen the same sort of thing many times, but it was always disturbing. The personality faded from his eyes and face, then she was looking at Blade again.

Damn. She had expected that, but damn anyway. And she was in trouble. Simon's last panicked adrenaline surge was now pulsing through Blade.

He pulled away from her sharply, and sat up, reaching for his shoulder harness. It wasn't there. She heard his sharp intake of breath, then his eyes focused on the knife sheath lying on the tatami behind her. Toni turned to glance at it, and instantly realized her mistake. She saw his lunging shadow just before his hand slammed into the side of her head.

14

Klale stood on stage, naked and sweat-slick under hot lights, reveling in the tumult of applause from the audience. The house lights came up. She bowed again, dribbling sweat on the stage, and scanned the audience. Toni had promised to watch tonight, but Klale couldn't see her. She saw Cedar de Groot, though, on his feet clapping loudly.

She picked up her coveralls and slipped them on, then scooped up the rest of her clothes and went backstage to shower. A few minutes later she emerged, picked up her pad and tray and made a round of her section. The KlonDyke was quiet tonight, she realized. There were fewer Guild customers than usual, although several big tables of Guildless sat pressed together, talking in low voices and nursing their beers. The tips would be tox. Of course, Cedar de Groot always left a big tip, but Klale found his attention and his tips embarrassing.

She was standing at the bar watching the act on stage and keeping her eyes well away from de Groot's table, when Alberta strolled up. She leaned back against the bar, looking idle, but her eyes kept scanning the room.

"Why so quiet?" Klale asked.

"The game," said Alberta. Then at Klale's blank look, she added: "Soccer. Vancouver United Guild verses Seattle Allstars."

"All that sweat without a single climax, but there's no accounting for taste," came Bracken's voice from behind them.

Today Bracken was blonde. She wore a filmy pink tank top and matching briefs that clung to her scrotum. Pink-lumed nail polish, lipstick, and eyeliner, and mirrored pink contact lenses completed the ensemble. She posed against the polished bar and Klale caught her own reflection in Bracken's pink eyes. She looked away uncomfortably and turned to Alberta.

"What did you think of my new dance?"

"It was funny," said Alberta, unexpectedly. "The Guild crowd liked it."

Bracken sniffed. "Needs work."

"Needs work?" Despite herself, Klale was annoyed. She turned to look at Bracken and pink mirrors flashed back at her.

"You don't know where the vid pickups are, do you sweets?"

"No," said Klale, with a sudden sinking feeling.

"You need to give them good feed because those lazy bitches don't edit. Especially facials. You pout for the close-ups," Bracken said, demonstrating. "Tits, hips, and wiggles, that's for midfeed and front live. Big movements," she threw both arms up, "that's for the back rows. You need all of them. And for gods' sakes, brush that hair! One hundred strokes every time before you step on stage."

Klale looked at her in astonishment.

"That's pyro advice! Thanks!"

"I'm not just another pretty face, you know," Bracken told her archly. Alberta snorted.

Klale had an inspiration.

"Bracken, would you be my choreographer? I really need some help. And I wouldn't expect it for nothing. We could arrange a barter or a fee exchange."

Bracken hesitated, with an odd look on her face. Embarrassment, Klale recognized abruptly, then the realization hit her that Bracken was unused to being taken seriously. For just a second she had an image of Bracken as a lonely, frightened child, alternately ignored and ridiculed, and she felt a rush of sympathy.

"Well . . . I shall demand a cut!" said Bracken.

Alberta had turned around to watch with interest. Bracken puckered her pink lips and fluttered long, ludicrous eyelashes. "Still scared, pussy puss?" she asked, wiggling her middle finger. "You wanna try it, you'll like it."

"I don't do prongs," snapped Alberta. "Or dickheads."

She looked annoyed, and Bracken was clearly winding up for more, so Klale interrupted.

"Why don't you make passes at me?" she asked teasingly. "Not a long enough acquaintance?"

Bracken smirked.

"Darling, I don't tread on Toni's back porch."

Klale was caught off balance.

"Uh . . ."

"But, now you mention it, we all *do* want to hear how you wriggled between Toni's legs!"

"Look, we're just friends," said Klale, annoyed to feel herself blushing.

Bracken pouted.

"Don't be such a bore! You Zit clits are always coming down here for a little R&S. That's what they teach you in school, isn't it? 'Rub and Suck, never fuck.' Gotta save that hymen for Mister Clean Genes." She waggled a pink tongue. "Never mind, sugarbush. I don't care if you spread your legs for Toni. But better watch out for the Boss. . . ."

"Mary?" said Klale blankly. "Why?"

"In case she's jealous, darling. After all, Toni jilted her and rumor says she's still clasping to the pash."

This was news to Klale. She looked rather desperately at Alberta, who was smirking.

"Is that true?"

Alberta shrugged.

"That's what I hear. But I wouldn't worry, kid. Mary's not the jealous type."

"Thanks," muttered Klale. She tried thinking back on conversations she'd had with the Boss, then shook herself. If there was a problem, Toni would have mentioned it. Which reminded her . . .

"Have you seen Toni? She said she was going to watch my act."

Alberta's grin faded.

"She's off tonight," she said shortly, then strode away leaving Klale staring after her in puzzlement.

Trade picked up around ten with a rush of disgruntled sports fans trading loud opinions about what had gone wrong and why it was just a fluke. For a little while things reminded Klale of Prince Rupert, then Captain Dhillon walked in with a big group of Free Vancouver League supporters. They joined Cedar de Groot, so Klale pasted a smile on her face and went over to take orders. Tommy Yip greeted her with his perpetual oily smile. Captain Dhillon glowered and ordered a fru-fru. Three other Patrol officers sat with her, including her first officer, Neil McCaskill. Klale remembered that Neil was old Ron McCaskill's grandson and she studied him surreptitiously. He was blonde-haired and blue-eyed, but his sullen expression bore little resemblance to Ron's.

Klale had to wait at the bar while Bracken mixed the fru-fru, and she watched with fascination as Bracken delicately layered chilled fruit juices in a tall glass, moving from deep orange at the bottom to green at the top, and topping it off with a strawberry speared on the rim. It was quite beautiful, and Klale carried it very carefully over to Captain Dhillon.

She had just turned away when she caught a motion in the corner of her eye and looked back. Dhillon had picked up the fru-fru and was holding it over the floor. As Klale's eyes met hers, she let go. Glass and juice sprayed in all directions.

Klale leaped back automatically, then stared down at the mess in disbelief.

"You did that deliberately!" said Dhillon coldly.

"*I* did it?" sputtered Klale. "*You* dropped it!"

"You knocked my arm. Clean up that mess and get me another one."

"The hell I will . . . !" started Klale.

Cedar bobbed to his feet, looking alarmed.

"Now, now, I'm sure it was just a glitch," he said, his hands waving anxiously at the spill.

Then Tommy Yip turned in his chair, light glinting from the gold chains around his chubby brown neck. He gave Klale a jovial smile.

"I'm sure you didn't mean to hit her arm," Yip said. "But I saw it clearly. If you apologize, I'm sure the captain will forget all about it."

For a second Klale's mouth hung open. Yip's back had been turned the whole time. She was just winding up to tell him what she thought when Pum grabbed her roughly by the arm. The big bouncer dragged her out of earshot, then swung around and cut off Klale's explanations.

"Servers don't talk back to patrons. Never."

"But she dropped it! On purpose!"

"Yeah, and she's a citizen and you're a server. So you apologize and you clean it up and you apologize some more. Now!"

She strode away, leaving Klale stunned and red-faced with fury.

"Little oopsie?" caroled Bracken, as Klale went back for a mop.

"Just make another drink!" snarled Klale.

"Temper, temper! Remember, broken knees will not improve your dance style!"

Klale bit back another angry retort, then stood with her eyes closed and took a series of long, deep breaths. When she felt somewhat calmer, she put a fierce smile on her face and went back to the Freevie table where she spent a full three minutes cleaning up every last drop, polishing the floor and the table, and delivering a salvo of over-solicitous apologies under Dhillon's smoldering gaze. She served the Captain's second fru-fru without a backward glance.

She was standing at the bar a few minutes later watching Bracken pour a pitcher when Alberta walked over. Klale braced for another lecture on patrons, but instead Alberta nodded toward Dhillon.

"You've made an enemy. Be careful."

"Thanks, I noticed."

"Yeah, well watch the others, too. That's a tox group traveling with Yip—couple of Longshore thugs and some former Ghost Shadows."

Klale looked back, taking note for the first time of the square-faced young men beside the chubby restaurateur.

"What do you think of Yip?" she asked.

"Tommy Yip would beat his grandmother to death for her reusable prostheses and cry at the funeral."

Klale found herself grinning.

"I guess you don't like him."

"I guess. Look, why don't you and your temper take a dinner break."

That struck Klale as a good idea, so she carried a bowl of rabbit stew into the back to get away from the crowd and calm down. The downroom reminded her of Guild rec rooms back home, with battered old furniture and staff hanging around watching vids or playing poker. Tonight it was quiet—just one server lay sprawled asleep on a couch. Klale sat in an old chair while she ate, then checked the time and looked at the netset in the corner.

She didn't want to call her older brother, but he'd been leaving more and more irate messages for her. And if she called this late, she'd almost certainly be shunted to triage. Hans worked an early shift, so he didn't answer his phone after ten. She could leave a message saying she was fine and be done with it.

She went over to the grubby old set, wiped the screen with her sleeve, and then entered Hans's ID. To her annoyance, a sleepy growl answered immediately.

"Klale?"

"Klahowya, kahpo."

"Hang on."

She sighed and waited. After half a minute the screen blinked to life and she saw her big brother settling into an armchair in his toy-strewn living room. He wore an old plaid bathrobe and his red hair stood up in tufts. Klale had worn her hair short, too, when she was little, and she'd told everybody she was his twin sister.

"I'm fine," she announced before he could say anything.

"Yeah, I could tell from your dance. You're looking real healthy."

Shit, thought Klale sinkingly. Why hadn't it occurred to her that people back home would see her strip?

"Hope you liked it," she said weakly.

"Lots of people sure didn't. Enough so the Guild's going to revoke your citizenship."

Klale snorted.

"The Prince Rupert Fishers haven't revoked anybody in years. They didn't even revoke Dad. I'd have to murder someone or rape the president or sink all the boats and then probably they'd just hold a lot of meetings and yell."

"Klale, I'm serious! It's on next week's agenda."

Klale stared at him, stunned.

"I thought you were fogging. . . ."

"Not this time."

"They won't pass it!"

"The hell they won't!"

Hans glared at her. The dim light in his living room cast shadowed lines on his face and she suddenly realized how much he was starting to resemble their father.

"It was just a dance!" Klale told him. "I did one like it at the benefit. You saw it!"

"Yeah, that was a little act at some armpit Guild thing, but this is a Fisher flaming her own people on CoastNet! What the hell did you think you were proving?"

"You're a logger now, what do you care?" retorted Klale before she could stop herself.

She expected Hans to yell at her, but he sighed instead and gave her a long silent gaze from Dad's blue eyes. It made her want to squirm.

"Klale, what the hell's wrong with you?" he said at last. "Dad never had any sense, but I always figured you'd run level."

"So I didn't need any help, huh?"

"Help? Like when?"

"Like where were you when Dad was dying?"

"Standing on your fucking doorstep with the door slammed in my fucking face!" he yelled, then shot a guilty glance toward the dark bedrooms.

"Oh," said Klale weakly. She'd forgotten that. Hans had come around several times when she hadn't wanted to see him. She changed tacks, trying to sound more conciliatory.

"Look, you don't think they'll really revoke me, do you?"

He ran his hand through his wiry hair and sighed.

"You know how much Klassen had it in for Dad, and it's still his friends running the exec. I think they might spill you, especially if you're not here to stand up for yourself. You've got to come back for that meeting."

"Can't afford it," muttered Klale.

"I'll pay for the ferry."

She looked away, tugging her fingers through her hair, and tried to think. If she lost her citizenship, she'd lose her university slot. She didn't want that. But she'd sworn never to go back to Rupert.

"Sis," said Hans softly. Reluctantly Klale looked at him, seeing the worry in his eyes. "Would you think it over, please, and call me back. OK?"

"Yeah," she said. "OK."

The rest of the night seemed very long. The bar stayed open until almost five and Klale wasn't busy, so she had plenty of time to stand around while her thoughts spun in anxious circles. How could anybody in Rupert hate her enough to revoke her? And what if they did? Maybe she could enroll at UBC as an independent. But there weren't many independent slots and competition was fierce. Should she go back?

When the bar finally closed and Klale started her trek up the stairwell she was so drowsy she could barely walk straight. At eighteen she opened the door, then stopped in confusion. In the faint pre-dawn light she saw her sleeping roll spilled carelessly on the floor and beyond it her clothes strewn around. A horrible suspicion seized her and she hurried forward. She'd left her phone and her tips from last night in her sleeping roll. They were gone.

For a long moment, she stood paralyzed with shock, then furious indignation hit. Someone had sacked her! She turned and headed up to Toni's.

When she let herself through the security door into Toni's hallway she was surprised to see light coming from Toni's partly open apartment door. Surely nobody could have sacked Toni's place, she thought in alarm, and approached quietly to peek in. Everything looked normal, except Alberta stood beside Toni's couch, unfolding blankets. She heard Klale pushing the door wide and whirled, pulling out a gun. Then recognition dawned on her face and she lowered the weapon.

"Don't you knock?"

It took Klale a second to breathe again and her thoughts whirled in confusion. The bouncers were supposed to be unarmed except for knockout spray! Why was Alberta carrying a gun? And in Toni's apartment?

"What are you doing here?" she managed.

"Sleeping," said Alberta, putting the pistol back in the pouch at her waist.

"Where's Toni? What's wrong?"

"She's fine," said Alberta then looked more closely at Klale's face. "What's wrong with you?"

"I've been sacked!"

"Oh." She sighed, but didn't look surprised. "We try to keep this building secure, but there's too many people coming and going, and some of the servers . . . Well, places get sacked all the time."

Robbed all the time? Klale tried not to show her dismay. Somehow she'd expected poor people Downtown to cooperate, not hurt each other.

"You know the only real answer is what Toni's done?—block off the whole floor with proper security doors. That's thick sweat and expensive."

Klale didn't want to hear that and she certainly didn't want to think about how easily anybody could get at her while she slept. She felt her face crumple.

Alberta gave her a gruffly sympathetic look. "Why don't you stay here tonight. You can take the couch."

Klale looked her in the eyes.

"Tell me what happened to Toni. No fogging."

"She tripped and fell in the stairwell and hit her head. Got a concussion, but Doc says she'll be OK. I'm just watching for tonight."

"Oh," said Klale, deflating. But as she walked back down to get her sleeping roll, she reviewed Alberta's words with growing unease. Toni might have had an accident. But why hadn't Alberta told her that earlier? And why was Alberta sleeping in Toni's apartment with a gun?

15

Toni awoke in her own bed with an aching head, a groggy awareness that she'd made a fool of herself, and an uneasy sense of danger. She started to sit up and then groaned as pain stabbed through her neck muscles and her head throbbed. Well, she deserved it, she told herself bitterly, for making such a stupid amateurish mistake. She was lucky to be alive.

"Toni?"

She started in alarm and looked up to see Alberta's concerned face peering in her door.

"Where's Blade?" Toni snapped.

"Huh?" said Alberta, looking blank for a second. "Oh. No idea. He was gone when we found you."

In her current state Toni wasn't sure whether to be pleased or disappointed, but at least it seemed he hadn't gone berserk.

"What are you doing here?" she asked Alberta, trying unsuccessfully not to snarl.

"I'm watching you."

"I don't need to be watched! I'm fine," snapped Toni. She started to rise, then sank back dizzily, pressing her hand against the stabs of pain in her forehead.

"Yeah, you look just lume," said Alberta, crossing her arms. "You gonna jump up and throw me out the door?"

Toni choked down a wave of nausea, unable to answer. Alberta watched for a few seconds, then walked over and kneeled down beside the bed to check the readouts on an old portable med unit, and Toni realized abruptly that she was hooked up to the unit by optic cable. It was those damned KlonDyke jammers again—even this bedside med unit had to be hard-wired to an adhesive sensor patch. Alberta took Toni's left arm and applied a pain pad with surprisingly gentle hands.

"You have a concussion, so take it easy. It'll be a few minutes before that kicks in."

"I know how long it takes!" Toni growled, then felt ashamed as Alberta stiffened and pulled back. She clutched at Alberta's arm, wincing at the resulting throb in her temples.

"I'm sorry. I'm angry at myself and I'm taking it out on you."

Alberta settled back down on her knees, face relaxing.

"Yeah, I'm a bad patient, too. Good thing I don't get sick much, or Rill would divorce me."

Toni managed a faint smile.

"Look, Toni, just stay put. I'll get you some breakfast if you like."

"Uh . . . what time is it?"

"About nine-thirty." She hesitated, then added: "It's Thursday morning."

Thursday? Toni stared at Alberta in confusion. The last thing she recalled it had been Tuesday afternoon. Then she glanced at the med unit. Doc must have put her on a thirty-six-hour monitored sleep. She felt another surge of annoyance but stifled it with an effort.

"Coffee, please. No food."

Alberta looked doubtful.

"Is coffee OK on a concussion?"

"Beats caffeine withdrawal on a concussion."

"Mmmm . . ."

Toni let Alberta arrange her pillows, then waited, fighting back the desire to go out and supervise. The bangs and muttered curses from the kitchen were not reassuring, but eventually Alberta returned with two steaming mugs. Toni wrapped both hands around hers and inhaled deeply, then sipped. Weak, but not bad. Alberta sat down beside her on the futon.

"How's the child?" Toni asked.

"OK, but the burns are pretty bad. Rill stayed home with him today, but she can't keep calling in sick. She's going to ask her folks in Chilliwack to take him."

"Then you haven't identified him?"

"Oh, we got a good guess. There was a water taxi fire near Pier B-C just before Blade got here. Five dead including the passenger—Mr. Kwong of the Sun Yee On."

"Shit," said Toni, feeling a resurgence of fear in her stomach.

"Yeah. It gets worse," said Alberta grimly. "Patrol divers found Kwong with four bullets in him. The Sun are offering a reward for information, and there's spin of tong war all over Downtown. They've called a special Consortium meeting here tonight. I'm putting on extra staff, but I'm worried."

"Has the boy said anything?"

Alberta shook her head.

"Won't say a word. Just cries. Kid is terrified. We think he was a witness. We'll have to keep him hidden. No point looking for his family—if any survived they'll be hiding, too." She frowned for a moment, then looked over at Toni. "We told everyone you slipped on the stairs, banged your head. They seem to be credding it."

Toni started to nod, then winced. She felt frail and trembly. Like an old woman.

"Have you heard from Choi?" she asked, trying to keep her voice calm.

"No," said Alberta, scowling. "And Mary checked your mail this morning. Nothing."

Toni had been afraid there would be a message, but the prospect of waiting for something to happen felt even more ominous.

"Alberta?" she started tentatively.

"Look, when I'm away from the bar I have a real name. It's Pat."

"Right, sorry. Pat. While you're here . . ." Toni paused awkwardly, feeling foolish, but made herself continue. "Would you mind checking over my apartment security?"

Alberta grinned.

"Already did. Checked this whole floor and the stairwell all the way to the roof. Nobody's been up there except to work on the cisterns. Your security's good, Toni. Not impossible to sack your place, but damn hard."

Toni thanked Alberta as warmly as she could manage, then began trying to persuade her to leave. Alberta stayed two more hours until Toni drank some soup and demonstrated that she could get up and stagger around. Then she agreed reluctantly to go. At the door she paused and looked back.

"You do all this work yourself?"

"Yeah."

Alberta gave a brusque nod of approval.

"Good job."

With Alberta gone, Toni collapsed back onto her bed and started reviewing her session with Simon, worried that the concussion might have confused her memories. Fortunately, it all seemed to come back. She spent a long time trying to figure out what Choi could be using Simon for. And what was Simon's third personality? An assassin? Had it been Simon who killed Mr. Kwong?

And why did he have a fragmented persona? Had Choi intended that from the start, or had he changed his mind during the course of training? That was an interesting possibility. If Choi had changed Simon's training once, perhaps he was tampering with it again, causing the instability she'd seen.

But all of this was guesswork and she had no way to get more data. She cursed herself again. The worst mistake she'd made in that bungled interview had been failing to set up another opportunity to talk to Simon. She needed to get him alone some place other than the KlonDyke and she had no way of doing that.

Suddenly she pulled herself up short, appalled. Was she actually contemplating more interference with Choi's weapon? That was both dangerous and futile, she reminded herself savagely. She was entirely alone, with no equipment and no resources. Her personal ID had been suspended years ago, and the KlonDyke's account wasn't subscribed to any research libraries. She had allowed curiosity and pity to cloud her judgment.

She tried diverting herself by reading, but she couldn't concentrate, and the thought of using a headset was unbearable. Finally she put on some music and dozed, trying to keep her thoughts away from Choi. The sudden buzz of a call made her jump, and she answered on audio, assuming it was Mary or Alberta.

"Toni here."

"Good afternoon."

Fear prodded her into alertness at those cool, measured tones.

"Good afternoon, Mr. Choi."

"I understand that you've been injured. Most unfortunate. I trust you are recovering."

"Yes, thank you." Toni hesitated, then continued: "I hope your servant is recovering, also." She thought there was a very slight pause before he responded to that.

"Satisfactorily, thank you. And since you have raised the subject, perhaps you would allow me to move with discourteous haste to the point of my call. I wish to know exactly what happened on Tuesday morning."

Toni was prepared for this request and recounted carefully how Blade had arrived, the extent of his injuries, and their treatment. Mr. Choi listened silently until she got to the point where they put him in the upstairs room.

"You stayed with him yourself?"

"Yes."

"Alone?"

"Yes."

"Why?"

"The doctor said he would wake up disoriented, and I thought it would be too risky to leave him alone. Other people use that floor all the time. Blade knows me from the bar, so I was hoping he wouldn't hurt me.

"Very well. Continue."

"There isn't much more. He woke up in the afternoon, just the way Doc predicted. My injury was my own fault. I went too near him. He hit out and knocked me unconscious."

"I see." There was a pause, in which Toni wished urgently that she could see Choi's face. "Given your experience with him, I'm surprised that you were not more cautious or that my servant was not more . . . tractable."

She sensed menace behind his words and spoke very carefully.

"I'm not sure he recognized me, Mr. Choi. And I would not describe Blade as tractable."

"Indeed. How would you describe him, then?"

Bad choice of words. Toni kept her voice calm with effort.

"I wasn't able to get a good look before he hit me."

"That wasn't what I meant, as you are well aware, Dr. Almiramez. I was interested in your clinical assessment of his condition."

The sound of her old name hit Toni in the stomach and throat. Her heart thudded in her ears, sending spikes of agony into her head, and beneath the warm blankets her hands and feet turned cold.

"Mr. Choi, I no longer go by that name, and I no longer pursue my former profession."

"So I understand. But perhaps, given the uncertain future of your current job and the increasing hazardousness of the situation Downtown, you will consider taking it up again."

"No," she said flatly.

"I would venture to suggest that you are making a hasty decision, Doctor. Even a small consultative sideline in your former profession would bring in considerably more than your current salary. I, for example, would be willing to pay a generous fee for a consultation."

"No," she said again, sharply. There was an ominous pause. He won't accept that answer, she realized sickly.

"I am going to let you reconsider this offer, Doctor, but I am not infinitely patient. And I think that you will find the tongs, if they should happen to discover your background, would not bother with the formality of asking you. Under the circumstances, you may find the protection afforded by working for someone such as myself to be very appealing."

That was a direct threat. But Toni had been expecting it for a long time and she knew how to answer. She made her voice as hard as she could.

"Mr. Choi, you won't find me a good blackmail victim. If you or anyone else tries to force me into training, I will commit suicide. Without hesitation. As you have already pointed out, I have very little to lose."

Was it a stalemate? Toni wondered later as she lay in her bed, shaken and afraid. Suddenly she regretted sending Alberta away. Her apartment no longer felt private—it felt empty—and she couldn't keep her thoughts from Choi. Would he sell her dossier? If so, she'd have to make good on her threat. There was little point trying to run again. The tongs would be ready this time, and they had connections around the globe. And she couldn't put off suicide until the last moment. As Blade had just demonstrated, she could be incapacitated very, very quickly. Was she a fool not to kill herself immediately?

How long had Choi known? she wondered suddenly. It was possible he'd done a trace in the last two days, but that would be extraordinarily fast work. More likely he'd known for years and hadn't played his hand. But why? He could have turned a profit selling her to a tong.

He must be waiting for something. Or using her somehow. Her mind went to Blade's Thursday night visits. She'd assumed that there was little he could do in the office, but she hadn't known then that he was a weapon. He probably had a neural interface chip, which meant he could easily infiltrate their netset without triggering security. That had to be Mary's leak.

But how was he doing it? She wanted to know. And there was a Consortium meeting tonight. Choi had tipped his hand, but he was arrogant and he wouldn't want to miss an opportunity to check his tap after a meeting this vital. Blade should be ambulatory enough to make a short trip. She had to be ready, too.

She managed to eat a light lunch and get herself dressed by three o'clock, then started the long trip downstairs, taking flights very slowly and pausing every few floors to rest. No point credding Alberta's story by taking a real fall. The stolen lights had all been replaced, she noticed, and then she realized with wry amusement that somebody had cleaned the garbage out of the entire stairwell. Even the broken chair that had been on the sixth floor landing for months was gone.

Downstairs Toni fought off Alberta's insistence that she was too sick to work. It wasn't as hard as she'd expected. Everyone in the bar seemed distracted and jumpy. Kwong's assassination was being discussed at every table. And Lincoln had released an unprecedented public announcement deploring the murder and denying Screaming Eagles involvement. No one was sure if he could be believed, but there was no doubt that the situation was explosive.

Other rumors were flying, as well. The most interesting was that Kwong had been negotiating with the city behind the backs of the Consortium—arranging a special deal for the Sun Yee On only. That struck Toni as a real possibility, and certainly a strong motive for assassination by one of the other tongs.

She worked the bar very slowly. A combination of analgesics and caffeine kept the headache to a manageable level but she found herself making mistakes and dropping things. The worst part was being forced to listen to a lot of well-meaning advice about the inadvisability of living so high up "at her age." She retaliated by complaining about the condition of the stairwells and managed to elicit several guilty looks.

Just before four o'clock, tong execs started arriving in tight, hard-faced groups. According to Alberta's reports they came in cars, which they left blocking the street out front. Around five they re-emerged and left through the lobby, staring straight ahead. None of them stayed for drinks. Tension in the bar increased. Mary arrived, tried futilely to send Toni to bed, and then did her usual rounds with a serene smile.

Around dinner time Alberta bullied Toni into taking a nap and, to her surprise, she actually fell asleep on the office couch. It was after nine when she walked back into the bar, rubbing bleary eyes. Klale was there and gave her a warm hug which Toni returned with tight self-consciousness, though she could feel herself yearning for comfort. The place had filled up, but patrons were clumped in uneasy groups and orders were light. There was no sign of Blade.

"Cedar's here," Klale told her unhappily. "Alone. And he's dripped."

Toni looked around and spotted de Groot a few tables away from his usual place, staring miserably into a pint. Interesting, she thought. She hadn't seen him alone in weeks. Evidently the Freevies had other problems tonight.

"Is he pestering you?"

"Mother, yes! If he stops me one more time, I'm going to try the chili technique."

"Don't worry," she told Klale dryly. "In another minute or two he'll see me."

It actually took almost three minutes before de Groot noticed Toni, picked up his pint and hurried over to the bar. Klale Slanged the exact time from across the room with a wide grin. Toni watched from the corner of her eye, suppressing her own amusement, then gravely asked Cedar how he was. She had uncorked a geyser.

For forty-five minutes he followed her back and forth in front of the bar delivering a long diatribe on his burden of responsibility as president of the Free Vancouver League, his worries about the Maglev, and even the sad state of his boat. He showed an astonishing disregard for his audience, thought Toni, even considering he was drunk. Complaining to Toni about Mary's D.R.A. campaign and then his yacht troubles showed all the sensitivity and astuteness of a carp. But one thing was clear. It was finally penetrating his skull that he'd taken on far more with the Freevies than he'd anticipated. As he finished another pint, he treated her to an increasingly frantic monologue about what wonderful people his executive members were and how much he trusted them.

Toni barely listened, waiting for him to work his way around to the point. Finally he trailed off into a series of nervous pauses, and then blurted out the news that he'd just been taken to a restaurant for dinner. Toni kept her face bland.

"Oh?"

"Fine Citizens. Javinder Dhaliwal and his cousin Harpreet. They recognized me from a Free Vancouver League ad, they said, and they're friends of Baljeet's family. Merchants. Mr. Jav Dhaliwal did most of the talking. Had some good points to make about the Maglev, too."

"Then you had a nice dinner?" prodded Toni.

"Yes. Well, I think so.... It's just..." He peered at Toni anxiously.

"What happened, Cedar?"

"He, uh... He started talking about marriage. Me and Baljeet." Toni lifted an eyebrow.

"He's a marriage broker?"

Cedar flinched.

"No! I mean, he didn't say so! After all, I really don't think . . . You don't think he was, do you?"

"I don't know, Cedar. What did he say?"

"Well, he wanted to know what I think of Baljeet, and of course I told him what a pyro vice president she is. And then he asked if we were planning to marry. Well, I had to explain that he had the wrong idea. She's a fine woman, a very fine woman, but I don't feel exactly . . ."

Interesting, thought Toni. It sounded as if Baljeet's family was progging de Groot out. Surely that wasn't Baljeet's idea! She was too shrewd to scare Cedar off. Another year of careful work and she might have had him, but this was too fast. Or maybe something had pushed her to take a risk—the pending tong war?

"I think he was worried, you know. About me, not being Sikh. So I told him not to worry, I absolutely wasn't interested in marriage and Baljeet's not my type anyway—too beefy. Well, maybe I shouldn't have said that, but he was joking, too, and it wasn't like they were her family."

No, thought Toni. If Dhaliwal was a marriage broker it was much worse than that. De Groot had rejected and then insulted Baljeet publicly. Her family would be furious.

Something finally seemed to trickle through Cedar's brain.

"Toni, what you said, you don't think that Baljeet sent this man, do you?—that it was her idea?"

"I don't think it's traditional for a woman to do that," said Toni cautiously, but Cedar wasn't really listening.

"I didn't think about that, you know, and if she did, well, then she'll be taxed. Especially after that water taxi thing. It upset her, I could tell. Her Patrol Boat got there first, you know."

No I didn't, thought Toni. Interesting.

"This could be difficult. With both of us on the executive, I mean. We've been seeing a lot of each other. For League affairs. That is, I thought it was League . . . But I guess she's been coming over to my rez pretty often, and the boat, too, and Tommy was kidding me about what a great wife she'd make. He thinks a lot of her. I don't know, maybe I made a mistake . . ."

Cedar stared at his beer miserably. Getting to the maudlin stage, noted Toni, repressing a sigh, and rubbing her temples. She needed another pain patch.

"But there isn't any romance with Baljeet! I'd still like to meet the right woman, you know?" He looked up anxiously, so Toni nodded. "Then again, she's a good friend and I'll be forty-three next year. I guess it's stupid to hold out for romance at my age."

He was waiting for her to protest and reassure him, but Toni wasn't in the mood. She simply fixed him with a calm look.

"You seem to manage very well on your own."

Cedar pouted.

"That's all right for you to say. You have Klale. But I'm all alone." His slurred voice was beginning to whine, then he looked over and focused on her intently. "Toni . . . Uh, is Klale really lez? I mean, does she hate men or is she just, you know, experimenting?"

Several retorts rose to her mind, but Toni bit them back with an effort. She reached over and pulled away de Groot's half empty glass with a menacing smile.

"I think you've had enough beer, Cedar. Why don't you go home while you still can?"

Cedar opened his mouth, then looked at her more closely and shut it again. Toni turned to Bracken and made a chopping motion—she was cutting him off. Bracken beamed. When Toni turned back, Cedar was walking unsteadily toward his table.

She glanced at the till. Ten o'clock and still no Blade. Maybe he wasn't coming. She started keeping a sharp watch on the door. She had almost given up when he arrived. He walked more stiffly than usual and favored his right side slightly but she doubted anybody else would notice. She found herself unaccustomedly nervous as he approached the bar, but it was easy to fall into their usual routine. His eyes didn't meet hers.

By midnight the crowd had thinned. People were afraid of being in the streets tonight, Toni guessed. She felt grateful, though. Despite the nap she felt so weary she could hardly stand. At twelve-thirty she dismissed Klale and one other server and at one she gave the last call. Alberta was visibly relieved to be closing, and went through her nighttime security check even more thoroughly than usual.

Toni didn't even try counting the cash or running the night report. She just wiped down the bar, went into the office and sank into the chair to wait for Blade. She was tensed for something unusual when he came through the door, but he repeated their routine mechanically. Toni tried calling his name once, got no response, and didn't try again.

She paid acute attention to how he touched her and how she felt after holding his hand. More relaxed, definitely. She often felt that way, she noted with grim suspicion. When he was gone she locked the office door, then went back to the desk and took out the med unit she'd carried down from her apartment. It was an old model, but comprehensive.

She splashed some water on her hand, rubbed it against her skin, then transferred several drops into the analyzer intake and let it run. When the readout stabilized, it showed what she'd been looking for: traces of a short-life sedative, a mild euphoric, and a skin penetration matrix, already breaking down. Another hour and they'd be undetectable.

Simple and very elegant, she thought, gritting her teeth. Simon was more than twice her mass, with an accelerated metabolism. All he had to do was smear his palm with the drug and hold her hand. The dose wouldn't affect him, but it would knock her out for a short time—two to five minutes, she guessed. That compound was very subtle. She'd been completely unaware of it, attributing any sleepiness to the time of night. Probably he didn't do it every week, either.

Choi had been using her. He'd known her background all along and used her predictable fascination with Simon to siphon the KlonDyke's netnode. The bastard had used her like a tool! Like a smut!

She slammed the desk drawer shut, wincing at the pain in her head, then sat looking at her shaking hands. The hell with waiting for Choi to make a move. And the hell with committing suicide. As she'd told him, she had nothing to lose. She wanted revenge.

16

"I'm not leaving," said Klale the instant she saw the KlonDyke's security chief walk out of the stairwell door onto the eighteenth floor. She straightened up from where she'd been nailing hempboard partitions and crossed her arms. "Look, I'm sinking bolts into the concrete and I'll rig bars across the stairwell doors. It'll work OK—at least at night when I'm here, I'll feel safe."

Alberta looked annoyed.

"Why not move in with Toni?

"Because I'm not letting any smogging sackers drive me out of here! And anyway, Toni likes her privacy."

Alberta sighed and ran a hand through her short blonde hair.

"You don't sink those bolts right, they'll rip right out." She looked at Klale and sighed again. "I can throw you out of this building, but you'll probably go and pick someplace worse. When you get done, tell me and I'll check it over."

"Thanks!" said Klale.

She watched Alberta leave, then got back to work. She'd borrowed tools from Sisters Co-op and was banging together crude partitions to make an apartment. Next she planned to install pipes and wiring, but that would have to wait until she had more money. She'd had to borrow from Toni for the hempboard and she felt guilty about it, even though she knew she could pay her back as soon as the Fisher Bank released her savings.

When she finished, she stood looking at her handiwork. Crude, but having walls made her feel safer and protected her from gusting drizzle and prying eyes. She took the tools up to Toni's apartment for safekeeping, then went down to the bar to use the backstage showers and cadge dinner before she helped set up for the Downtown Residents Association Annual General Meeting.

When she pushed through the double doors into the KlonDyke's biggest meeting room, Klale expected to see everyone working, but the staff stood clustered by the tall, narrow windows, staring out into the street. Alberta glanced over her shoulder as Klale approached, then moved aside so she could see.

Robson Street seemed very empty, Klale thought. She stared through the gray drizzle, then saw a line of leather-clad figures standing across the road.

"They've cordoned off the 'Dyke," said Alberta. "Ghost Shadows and Tigers.

Those were the Kung Lok and Viet Ching gangs, Klale remembered.

"What about the Sun Yee On's gang?" she asked.

"The Lotus Family?" Alberta snorted. "Buncha rich kids, look like a Junior Commodities League. Hire henches to do their dirty work. But yeah, they're not there." She gestured out the window. "Gonna be one small meeting. Robson's blocked above and below us, and the alley behind is closed, too. They aren't stopping anyone, but they're recording names and faces and that does the same thing."

The staff watched in grim fascination for another minute, then Alberta herded them away and they started setting up chairs in strained silence. Klale felt her good mood evaporating as she lined up rows on the worn carpeting, and her thoughts strayed to Toni, who still looked worried and ill. Klale had confronted her and asked if it was true she'd been bludged by Mary's tong enemies. Toni denied it, but she wouldn't say anything more. Eventually Klale gave up trying to penetrate the stone wall, marched downstairs to a pay phone, and took out her frustrations by calling the Harbor Patrol. She had to locate a live supervisor and argue the woman into logging her unwitnessed complaint, but it was filed now and Klale was scheduled to testify before an internal tribunal. Next, while she had her momentum up, she'd phoned Hans and promised to attend Saturday's Fisher Guild meeting by remote. Finally she'd tracked down Mary and bought a D.R.A. membership. None of it would help Toni, of course, but it gave her the feeling that she was doing *something*.

At seven-thirty they opened the ballroom doors and a trickle of people walked in, collected their voting cards and then stood talking in hushed voices or sat in lonely clumps in the sea of chairs. Klale recognized many faces from the picnic. Mary and several of her executive members arrived at 7:45. Mary walked around the echoing room, shaking hands and chatting with her usual serene confidence, but the other execs looked uncomfortable.

"Alberta!"

Klale turned. Pum was beckoning urgently from a window. Klale followed Alberta over and peered out. On the far side of the cordon a dense crowd had gathered. At the front of it were a dozen unmistakable sets of gray overalls. The Bloods.

"Whole crowd just came around the corner," said Pum.

As Klale watched, Bloods strode toward the cordon. Although their assault rifles were slung on their backs, there was no mistaking their menace. Klale saw Tigers and Ghost Shadows looking at one another. This was clearly more than they'd been prepared for. Then several of them looked up and Klale followed their gaze. Four Bloods stood on a low rooftop with rifles trained on the cordon.

The Americans continued to move forward. Klale heard several distant shouts, then the cordon broke in the middle and the gangs stepped aside.

She half expected a cheer, but the street remained eerily quiet except for a swelling rumble of footsteps as the crowd swept toward the KlonDyke. The lead Bloods were followed by a group that looked mostly American, then a mixed crowd of other flots and squats. There were hundreds. Many held coats or scarves over their faces as they went past the cordon, but others openly stared at the gang members, and a few yelled at them or spat.

Alberta pulled back from the window, gave brisk orders to her staff, then moved to the main doors. Klale got a stack of voting cards and followed.

In half a minute the crowd began streaming into the room. Almost all of them were Guildless—thin people in shabby, wet clothes. At one point the flow from the stairs ceased and Klale looked over to see the hall blocked by a group of beggars, led by tiny crippled Violet, lurching laboriously on her crutches. They approached the door with an air of nervous defiance, but Alberta seemed to be expecting them. She stepped forward and escorted them to a row of empty seats near the front.

As more and more faces went past, Klale found herself trying to figure out what else it was about the crowd that seemed odd. There were no tong execs, of course, and very few merchants. Then she realized that most of the people passing her were gray-haired and stooped from years of hard work. When she got a chance she moved close to Pum and asked about it.

"Expendable," said the bouncer bluntly.

"What?"

Pum gave her an exasperated look.

"Young people earn more money. And old people gonna die anyway."

Klale tried not to show how much that viewpoint chilled her.

"Where are the Bloods?" she asked.

"Outside. Guarding the KlonDyke."

Klale caught something in her tone.

"Doesn't sound like that makes you feel safe."

"No smog," the bouncer told her sourly.

The meeting started late. After the ballroom filled, people were routed to overflow rooms and screens patched in so they could participate. Klale helped carry folding chairs into the overflow rooms, then rushed back to the main ballroom in time to see Mary greet the crowd and test the meeting system to make sure she could be seen and heard in all the rooms. Klale found a place to stand at the edge of the crowd, beside Alberta. Mary finished her system test, then stepped back to let Lincoln up to the podium and Klale was suddenly struck by how small and dumpy Mary looked beside Lincoln's towering elegance. His dark skin emphasized his white eyes and teeth and the elegant gold band gleaming on his arm.

"I have no affiliation with the Downtown Residents Association," he announced in his powerful, resonant voice. "The Screaming Eagles are only here today because we defend the right of our people to go where they choose and to speak freely!"

Someone cheered, then cheers swept the crowd, and Klale heard a distant tumult echoing down the hallway from the other rooms. Lincoln waited patiently for the noise to die, then added:

"All of us living in Vancouver have the right to freedom, peace, and prosperity—rights which cannot be denied. By ourselves, each of us is only one drop, but many drops make an ocean, and oceans shape the world."

As he walked off stage to thunderous cheers, Alberta's expression caught Klale's notice. She sidled over and spoke near Alberta's ear.

"He worries you?"

"Damn right. Mary figures he's the only guy who might be able to stop a war Downtown, not just start it. But I don't see him stopping nothing."

The grim tone of Alberta's voice alarmed her.

"You don't think there's really going to be a war, do you?"

"Bet on it. The flots and squats will fight because they got no place else to go. Tongs will arm them and we'll have a full scale guerrilla war. The Guilds aren't gonna win it either, not unless they bomb us to rubble, and that's what I figure they'll end up doing. I've got our suitcases packed. If war starts, Rill and I are out of here. Screw the rez. It's just a building."

Mary's presence at the podium seemed anticlimactic at first, but she quickly took command. She opened the meeting, announced the executive elections, and explained nomination and voting procedures in simple language. Then she paused and surveyed the audience. The room fell very silent.

"I'm going to speak freely with you," she said quietly. "We've been warned that anyone running for the executive tonight risks retribution from the Kung Lok and the Viet Ching." There was a collective intake of breath in the room as she named the tongs. "That's why we didn't take nominations in advance and also why I'm asking all of you to consider very carefully before putting your name in."

She let a pause hang, then continued.

"But we won't succeed by giving in to threats. I've had my own doubts and fears, but seeing all of you here tonight gives me new courage. It is with very great pride that I open the floor for nominations."

There was a tumult of applause and Klale joined in enthusiastically. Mary turned over the podium to a neutral convenor during the election. It was very brief. Mary and five other officers stood for re-election, and the new medic, Dr. Lau, ran for member at large. The slate was acclaimed.

After a very brief annual report, Mary got right to what the audience was there for—the Maglev.

"The railroad proposal has been endorsed so far by Sacramento, Eugene, Salem, Portland, Olympia, and Bellingham," she told the attentive crowd. "Seattle is likely to follow. But the situation here is uncertain. The Vancouver Council of Guilds is deadlocked. Many key Guilds are either undecided or unwilling to take a stand until they see which way other Guilds go. The Merchants Guild is so divided over the issue that they have members publicly committed to both sides."

Klale listened intently, fanning her damp neck. The ceiling fans were having little impact on the rising heat in the overcrowded room.

"The D.R.A. has been given a seat at negotiations and related Council sessions, but so far we have not succeeded in getting housing and employment commitments for the Guildless. I have spoken with all sixty-three councilors, and only received public backing from twelve."

There was an unhappy murmur in the crowd that confused the room's ancient automike system and it quit in a burst of static. Mary had to override from the podium to continue.

"But we haven't lost yet!" She looked around, her eyes moving from one face to another. "What we've learned is that our tactics aren't working. So it's time to change our tactics. Many councilors have told me that they're personally sympathetic, but they don't believe their Guild members care about Downtown. Then we have to *make* them care! We must go out to the citizens and speak to them face-to-face!"

She paused, scanning the audience.

"It's an enormous job. We want to send D.R.A. reps to at least two hundred Guild meetings in the next two months. So we need your help. We need volunteers to go to meetings and talk to citizens about Downtown."

Mary's voice rose with urgency.

"Our opponents want to keep us quiet, so we can be 'relocated' without publicity. That's what we have to avoid at all costs. We have to make noise—as much noise as we can. We have to make Downtown real to those people sitting comfortably over there in their rezzes. They can ignore a problem they never see. They can't ignore a Guildless person staring them right in the eyes."

She paused, face serious but determined.

"The tongs are going to pressure us. We'll have to protect each other. But we must act now. We must defend our lives and create real hope for the future."

Mary stood still for a moment, letting her words sink in, then opened the floor to questions. The first person to stand was a frail Afroid woman with deeply wrinkled skin.

"That council, all them Guilds—they won't do nothing," she said angrily. "And that railroad don't matter neither. The tongs our problem. So long as they here, nothin' change. We gotta smash the tongs, then we make it better." She turned and looked at the people around her. "I done worked a Ching factory fourteen-hour days, got that booster in my head so I'm smiling while I breathe their shit, eat their shit, live in their shit rooms. Work till my feet gone bad, hands gone bad, then I'm garbage in the street. Thirty years and I got nothing! Like a slave just like on them fucking plantations! Well, I wanna fight. I don't care if I die so long as I kill some of them!"

The woman's face was livid with hatred, but the fist she held up shook with palsy. There was an uneasy stir in the room.

"Screaming Eagle plant," whispered Alberta cynically.

Mary banged the gavel.

"The D.R.A. is not going to organize a rebellion against the tongs."

"The Americans will help us," called someone from the audience. "They got weapons."

"Crap!" yelled another voice. "If the Bloods could smear the other tongs, they'd of done it by now!"

Klale saw some nods in the crowd. Mary whacked her gavel again.

"This is a *peaceful* campaign. We don't need more violence Downtown. We need safe, clean homes. We need jobs and education and medical care and housing. That's what we're working for!"

She looked around, then pointed to someone near the front.

"Chair recognizes Violet."

A man stood, then turned and lifted the little red-haired beggar onto a chair. Violet's head barely cleared the seated people around her, but her voice was strident.

"I just want to say I volunteer to go to them meetings. Me and my friends here. We can show them Zits what Downtown's about."

There was a silence. The man helped her down again and the audience realized she was finished. A scattered round of applause started, then grew in volume and enthusiasm. Alberta gave a sardonic snort.

"Mary's plant."

Klale grinned.

Mary went on for a while answering questions from all the rooms, then she called a vote on the new campaign. Klale was poised to assist with manual card counting in the unwired rooms, but it proved unnecessary. Support was close to unanimous.

"Thank you," said Mary, looking around with a warm smile. Then she spread her arms wide. "Come and help! Bring your family, bring your neighbors, bring your friends! Tell them who you are, how you live, and what kind of a future you want for yourselves and your children. Nobody goes to a meeting alone—we'll assign at least four in each group. You can stay now to sign up, or phone us, or come back to the KlonDyke any time this week."

"Now, before we close I'd like to call a seated Circle." She beckoned her executive to stand and join her at the front of the room.

"Our success depends on courage and faith and trust. It depends on the help we give each other." Mary paused, looking around. "Please take the hand of the person next to you."

The executive team formed a chain on either side of Mary, stretching their arms out to join up at either end with the audience.

There was a rustle as people stood and reached awkwardly to their neighbors.

"For the next minute I'd like everyone to pray in silence. We must create the future first inside ourselves."

The room was utterly silent except for a baby wailing in the back. Klale bowed her head and began a prayer, but a disturbance out in the hallway distracted her. Alberta dropped her hand and strode toward the nearest door, but just as she did so a young man burst into the other end of the room.

"Fire! Pendrell and Nicola!" he yelled.

Immediately several people rose and ran for the door. The rest sat for a second in frozen silence, then others followed and the room became pandemonium. Klale tried to maneuver her way out of the stampeding mob, then shrugged and joined the flow.

She had second thoughts when she got outside where it was dark and drizzling, but the excited crowd pulled her along. She crossed her arms tightly over her cheap shirt and trotted along the street amid the throng. It seemed that half of Downtown was rushing to get a glimpse of the fire.

As they left the KlonDyke's jammer radius, Klale reached for her phone to call Toni. Her hand found no phone; then she remembered for the hundredth time that it had been stolen.

"Damn," she muttered, starting to feel nervous.

After several blocks the crowd slowed to a shuffle, then stopped. Klale could smell smoke, but she couldn't see anything. She shoved her way to the side of the street and climbed onto a rickety vendor's stand along with four or five others. From that height she could see a cordon of yellow-coated firefighters across the street, but not much else. And she wasn't going to get any closer.

She jumped down from the stand, and tried to make her way back through the press of bodies but progress was almost impossible. She looked around in frustration and caught sight of an alley not far away. She didn't trust the alleys at night, but she was getting wet and she wanted to go home. She'd taken this alley before and knew it went through to the next street, where she could walk back to the KlonDyke. She shoved her way across the street to the mouth of the alley, hesitated a few seconds, and then plunged into inky blackness.

Trying to ignore the dank stink, Klale walked as fast as she dared. She stumbled in an invisible pothole, then somebody brushed past her and she jumped violently, taken by surprise. The distant roar of the crowd had muffled their footsteps. She walked farther, straining to hear. Was someone following her?

Don't panic! she told herself. It's not much farther.

Gravel crunched close behind, and before Klale could turn, something slammed into the back of her knees, knocking her facefirst into slimy dirt. An immense weight landed on her back, crushing the air out of her lungs. Klale flailed desperately and tried to gasp. Rough fingers dug into the back of her neck, she heard the hiss of a med-spray, and then she blacked out.

17

Simon watched the movement on the wall mirrorscreen three times, then stood and arranged himself carefully in the starting position. The tracking system chimed softly. He corrected a slight deviation in his stance, and his silhouette in the mirrorscreen flashed green. He took two fast steps forward, then jumped up in a twisting backflip, tucked, and exited into a slow roll. He hit the floor awkwardly amid a flurry of chimes, overshooting the patch of friction floor and careening across glide surface to the next friction strip where he scraped to a clumsy stop, pain flaring along his taped left side. He took a deep breath, then rolled to his feet and replayed his attempt against the mirrorscreen template, noting his inaccuracies. It had been a very poor attempt.

He tried the new move six more times, but he felt weak and uncoordinated despite healing accelerants. And his concentration was bad. Even during tai ji he'd found his mind wandering back to the dim, perfumed room where Toni touched him. She'd leaned so close he could smell her hair and see the tiny flecks in her brown irises. He remembered the smooth warmth of her fingers stroking his cheek.

He shivered with sudden, sick fear. He shouldn't think about that. Only dancing mattered. Only dancing was beautiful and safe. He forced his attention back to the gym and started the music for his Morning Dance. That always made him happy. It began still and quiet like glassy water before dawn, then grew with the breeze and sunrise. The soft opening bars were Yun Shou—Moving Hands Like Clouds. Then woodwinds entered, spilling like raindrops with the sun behind them, spinning into circles inside each other, pulling in and out.

The joyous sound usually propelled him into spins, and then up into the air until his jumps felt like flight. But today his legs felt wooden and joy eluded him. As his happiness began to rise, he had a sudden vivid memory of the taste of chocolate, and he lost his timing, then tripped. The music still soared, but he sat on the floor, jumbled and hurting inside. He couldn't seem to stop thinking about Toni.

No! He paused the music, and sat with wrapped-around arms in the emptiness trying to figure out what to do. There must be a way to use music to make these thoughts release their grip. Dancing about Simon's fear or Blade's anger often eased his pain. He stood up and concentrated, this time letting himself go back to the tatami room and trying to visualize motions that would match his feelings. He mapped out a tentative series of steps, then found himself kneeling with his hands outstretched, reaching to her. Toni smiled at him, then turned, and Simon saw Klale dancing behind her—spinning and laughing in a cloud of red hair and a blur of smooth pink skin.

He started to rise, then stopped in horror. He couldn't dance with Klale! Simon wasn't real. She couldn't see him. She only looked at Blade. But she had seen Simon. Like Toni had. Toni always saw Simon. And when she talked to him her warm breath brushed his face . . .

No!

The room spun wildly. Simon curled into a ball, trying to push the reeling, crazy thoughts away. He had to stop them. They were tearing him apart, tearing apart his music! They must be wrong. And wrong thoughts were punishable!

He sought desperately for something safe to focus on. Seagulls. They never changed, and they ignored him. He could just watch. He put himself onto the waterfront and concentrated on a pack of screaming, bickering gulls. They took off, circling. Round and round, up and up, into the sky.

Finally he reached out for the gym again. It didn't spin anymore, but he still felt frightened. He had to dance!

He could do the Tiger Dance. It was simple, calming. Simon had always known the Tiger Dance.

He walked over and started the music manually, entering the library designation, the play sequence, and then, unconsciously, "record."

18

Toni crawled stiffly out of bed at noon, determined to get her next moves over with. She made coffee, then took it into the study, slipped on her headset, and entered Scott's ID from memory. It was still active, and still based in Seattle.

She expected a triage screen, but Scott answered himself, materializing a few feet in front of her. For a second she saw no reaction, then his eyes widened in shock.

"Ann?"

"Hello, Scott."

She met his incredulous gaze stoically, suddenly aware of how much she'd changed. Her hair had been much longer back then, and she'd always worn expensive hand-tailored clothes with bright head scarves, jewelry and makeup. This morning she wore a cheap blue sweatshirt and faded brown hempens. A hard life and lack of juvving treatments had aged her a great deal, too. Ten years ago she'd looked younger than her age; now she looked older. Her hair had grayed, lines were worn into her face, and this morning she had black smudges of exhaustion under her eyes. She looked like hell.

Scott, on the other hand, showed very little sign of his forty-five years except for more pronounced laugh lines around his eyes and mouth and a hint of silver in his blonde hair—something most academics wore when promoted to a full professorship. The office behind him looked unfamiliar, but she recognized some of the book spines on the shelves.

"Oh my God. I was sure you were dead . . ."

"Not yet," she said harshly. "Look, Scott, before we say anything else, I'm going to tell you why I've called, then you can ask me to climb back into the grave if you want to." She took a deep breath, feeling the tautness in her neck and shoulders and the dull ache in her head. "I'm asking a favor. That should be rather predictable. I always did take advantage."

She'd been trying to speak unemotionally, but she could hear the bitter self-deprecation in her voice. Scott interrupted, his voice husky.

"What happened, Ann?"

"I need library access."

He stared for several long seconds, then sighed and sat back in his chair.

"I'm sorry," she added more apologetically, "but it's urgent and I couldn't find any other way to do it. I'll reimburse you for costs."

"You could get your ID reactivated."

"There are . . . difficulties."

He frowned.

"Are you in trouble?"

"It doesn't matter," she said curtly, then sighed and tried to be less defensive. "I suppose I am."

Scott looked away unhappily, tugging his hair the way he always used to when he was frustrated. She waited. Letting Toni use his personal key was a serious violation of university code, not to mention net regs. He could even lose his post. He had broken rules for her before, but that was years ago, and she had no right to expect it now.

"What access do you need?" he asked finally.

"Research library. SciNet professional forums. Labnotes."

He paused another long moment, then nodded.

"All right. I know I'm cleared on the first two. I'll check about Labnotes. But you'll have to work through my site when I'm off."

"Fine. I'll try not to be conspicuous," said Toni. "Uh . . . and I'll have to keep some files there."

He just nodded. "All right. And no, I won't read any of it."

Toni felt her cheeks burn. She had never learned to trust Scott and she'd been much too obvious about it.

He accessed a code and it flashed up as a gold key. She logged it, then looked at him awkwardly.

"Thank you."

Scott smiled slightly, then fixed her with penetrating eyes.

"How are you?"

"Fine," she said automatically, then remembered how he always used to ask: which kind of fine? "The good kind of fine," she added.

He flashed a sudden smile, then it faded and all the hurt came into his face.

"We looked for you every place we could think of and we kept net searches running for two years. What happened, Ann?"

Toni had expected that question, but answering it was still difficult. She shrugged uncomfortably.

"Exactly what it looked like, I imagine. I was a wreck and it was only a matter of time before I was forced into review. So I ran away and went on a binge." She grimaced a little. "It must have been an Earthmother. I don't remember much. About the time it was becoming fatal, a good Samaritan took me in. Don't know why I decided to clean up."

"Because you're a survivor."

"Damn if I see the point. I just keep making more mistakes. I have to survive." She heard the bitterness in her voice and changed tacks. "How about you?"

Scott smiled, widely this time, and she had a sudden vivid memory of the sweet, vulnerable young man he'd been.

"Oh, I did exactly what you predicted. Took covenant with Mica. We've got two children. And I'm doing well at the U. I'll probably get my turn at the section crown next year."

Toni made herself smile back. "You look happy."

"I am," he said, looking at her steadily. "Are you?"

Toni hesitated. Eleven years ago she would have lied, but surely she could do better now. She owed him that, at least.

"More than I was," she said finally. "Maybe it's just age, but I'm slowing down. Less angry. Less pushy."

"Doing any of your old work?" he asked carefully.

"No," she said, a little too sharply. "I don't twist people's heads anymore."

"Then why the library access?"

She grimaced. He had a point.

"All right. I've come across something . . . unusual. And I need to know more about it."

"That certainly sounds like old times."

"No. It isn't. And Scott—please don't tell anyone else about this."

He looked unhappy.

"There are people who would like to know that you're alive."

She shrugged, keeping her face hard.

"Then you're not coming back?"

"No."

He looked at her searchingly, with that sad, puzzled expression she remembered so well. But he didn't seem so wounded—there was a new resilience in him.

"All right," he said finally. "But I hope you change your mind." Then he added with a gentle warmth that brought tightness to her throat. "I'm happy to know you're alive. Please stay in touch this time, OK? Good luck."

Afterward, Toni sat for a long time staring at the wall, caught in a cascade of memories. It felt as if a decade had vanished; as if she'd just walked out of her old office, desperate, angry, and half-tripped, looking for some place to run. That had been the third time she'd tried running away from herself. How ironic that when she finally found a place she didn't want to run from, she would be forced to leave.

She shook herself sharply. Brooding was pointless. She had access; now she needed equipment.

She placed two more calls, ate a meal, packed Doc's med monitor in her carryall, and then went out, still taking the stairs slowly. It was a patchwork fall day; streaks of sunlight beaming between fluffy clouds, and a few gray patches that threatened rain. She walked along Broughton Street to Barclay, then searched for the address. Thirteen forty-eight was an algae-stained concrete high rise with the number hand-painted across the front doors. A small sign pointed to DOC-TOR'S OFFICE. She walked around the back.

Toni had never been to Doc's place before. It was on the ground floor with a separate entrance. It must cost a lot, she thought, or more likely one of the tongs gifted it in return for his services. When she walked into the hallway she realized that it had originally been two small apartments. One was now an office; the other must be Doc's home. A hand-lettered sign announced that office hours were two to eight P.M. and it wasn't yet one o'clock, but when she peeked in the door there were patients waiting—an old man slumped in a chair, a young woman crying silently while she breast fed a thin baby, and a bloodied boy lying on the floor. She backed out of the waiting room and phoned. Doc answered, then opened his apartment door, hustled her in, and closed it quickly behind her.

The stench of cats hit Toni and she had to stifle the urge to cover her nose as she peered into curtained dimness. Doc's place was a jumble of old books, data cubes, flimsies, and dirty dishes. The basket of laundry beside the door looked like it had been there for a long time. A cat lay in the laundry, and more pairs of feline eyes peered suspiciously at her from behind furniture. She counted six . . . no, seven. Doc scooped a mangy animal off a chair and cleared some junk away, then waved at her to sit. She sat gingerly.

"Tea?" he asked. His voice was strong, but he was bleary and red-eyed, with a slight tremor in his hands.

"Thank you," she said.

"I'll just put on the kettle," he told her, and disappeared into the kitchen, leaving Toni in the suffocating little room exchanging hostile stares with the cats and wondering why he didn't just use his steam tap. Surely the apartment must have a water supply. In a minute he reappeared and stood leaning in the doorway.

"I wasn't aware that you were such a cat lover."

"Well, I don't know that I'd call it that," he said ruefully. "It's just that I've never been able to get used to seeing them killed by children in the streets. I started feeding one and the next thing I knew . . ." He gestured around the apartment futilely, then snorted with grim amusement. "I believe the neighbors think I practice surgery on them. Actually, they're a hell of a nuisance, but I can't quite bring myself to throw them out."

Toni nodded. She pulled the med unit from her carryall and handed it to him, then Slanged: "Can we talk?"

He shook his head, then wiggled his upturned fingers in the sign for "wait" and pointed behind him toward the kitchen.

"You can't make a proper cup of tea without boiling the water two minutes, you know," he said aloud. "Now, let me take a look at that head of yours."

While Doc checked her over, Toni examined him in turn. His beer paunch, baggy clothes, and stained teeth contrasted as always with his polished Oxford accent. Toni had heard the rumors that he was an unqualified butcher, but in her estimation he probably had top credentials, and his alcoholism had remarkably little effect on his competence.

He dragged out the exam and she was wondering why when the kettle in the kitchen began to hum, then climbed to a piercing shriek. Doc kneeled down next to her chair, and spoke close to her ear with warm, freshly whiskeyed breath.

"It makes a fine audio jammer and there aren't any eyes."

Toni tried to ignore the pain knifing into her fragile head.

"Have you heard from Choi?" she asked.

He nodded. "Since we're not dead yet, we must have told him a consistent story."

Toni would have preferred to lead up to the next question, but she couldn't take much more of the kettle, so she simply asked: "What did you find in Blade's blood?"

"Mmm." Doc was wary, but after a short hesitation he shrugged. "It looked to me as if he has tailored immune protections."

Toni raised her eyebrows. That was usually an assassin's alteration. Doc continued.

"Other than that, I can't tell you much. He looked pretty standard except for the custom neural work."

Toni was frowning. "If you had to make a guess, what would you say he's being used for?"

"Data infiltration, maybe. Listening post. I don't know, Toni. The immune protections might be Choi's attempt to shield himself from disease—after all, Blade goes in and out of that bunker. Only a paranoid would resort to such an extreme measure, but Choi lived through the pandemics and he's apparently quite insane." He paused again then looked at her. "Now I have a question for you."

Toni returned his gaze cautiously.

"That scar on his wrist. It looked to me like a dog mauling, but you seemed to find it interesting."

Toni nodded, choosing her words carefully. "I saw a very similar scar once on a man who'd tried to chew his way through his own wrist. It might have been a truly desperate suicide attempt, or even part of training—self inflicted on orders."

"Seems excessive."

"As you already remarked, Choi is very twisted," said Toni, hearing the acid shadow of rage in her voice.

Doc nodded, looking unexpectedly angry himself.

"I'll add it to my personal horror hall of fame along with the chap who was trying to saw off his own foot, and the used lovebird who set herself on fire." He grunted as he started to rise to his feet, but Toni put a hand on his shoulder.

"I have another favor to ask," she mouthed.

He sank down and leaned closer and she whispered near his ear.

"Can you get a training collar through your suppliers?"

"Jesus Christ!" he exploded between clenched teeth, then whispered: "Woman, you truly are planning to get yourself killed, aren't you?"

"I need a junction with six interactive sockets, and a neural analysis chip with software. The rest I can patch together myself."

"And if I don't help?"

"I'll go elsewhere."

He glowered at her.

"It'll be expensive."

"I'll find the plastic if you can find the chip," she told him grimly.

Doc grunted, then got heavily to his feet and went into the kitchen. The whistle died to a whine, then stopped, and she heard him pouring water. She massaged her temples with relief. In a minute he came back out carrying a tray with a brown Betty and two china teacups with saucers scoured so vigorously that most of the pattern was gone. He put the tray on a table next to what was obviously his favorite chair, then sat down with a gusty sigh. A tabby streaked across the room and climbed onto his lap. Doc patted it absently.

"Getting too old for this," he said. Toni looked at him, wondering if he meant medicine or drinking. Or both.

"Had you thought of quitting?" she asked in an equally casual tone.

She expected one of his usual acerbic jokes, but instead he looked around pensively. There was a framed print on the wall behind him— an English landscape in pen and ink.

"If the Maglev comes, I'm sure the city won't offer me a choice. And I've Scrooged enough lucre to keep body and soul together. But then what? I can't malpractice anywhere else and I can't imagine what I'd do instead."

"Find a hobby?" suggested Toni dryly.

He gave a snort of humorless laughter.

"Haven't got any, unless you count drinking. I tried going on vacation once—got bored in two days. I suppose I'll stay put until the Maglev runs me over or I drop in harness." He looked over. "What about you?"

She shrugged.

"The same, I imagine. One way or another I don't think the KlonDyke can survive much longer."

"A great shame," he told her regretfully. "Good bars are hard to find." He gave her an abrupt, piercing look. "Good bartenders, too."

Then he leaned forward to pour tea and began chatting. Toni hadn't intended to stay a minute longer than necessary, but she didn't want to refuse the tea and she found herself enjoying Doc's clever conversation. Her nose had adjusted somewhat to the smell. She stayed for half an hour, listening, rebutting, sipping milky tea, and swatting cats away. Then she walked out into the sunshine, brushing cat hair from her pants, and headed for her next priority—Mary.

At Sisters' rez she passed the security check, then walked through a shady tunnel in the toxin-filtering hedge that circled the complex. Only eight years old, the hedge already towered fifteen meters, almost completely screening the buildings from view. Inside she took a cir-

cuitous route through the inner courtyard garden, enjoying its lush-
ness. It was wonderfully quiet except for birdcalls and occasional
shrieks from toddlers in the play yard. She breathed in the smell of
warm, damp earth and studied terraced rows of vegetables. Twenty
years before she never would have believed that she could get interested in gardening, but now she grew vegetables and herbs on her
own balcony.

Yet again she found herself admiring the garden's clever meld of
beauty and efficiency. Enhanced breeds of fruit tree lined her path,
and an irrigation stream tumbled through the vegetable garden end-
ing in a lily-paved fish pond by the shrine. The co-op even produced
its own honey from hives up in the roof garden, near the chicken
runs.

Mary's apartment was on the second floor, north side. The door
stood open, so Toni rapped and walked in. The apartment looked
much like Mary's office—homey, cheerful, and neat. Green-spattered
light poured through the windows and flickered across Mary, working
at the kitchen table. She looked up at Toni with concern.

"You're supposed to be resting!"

"Doc just gave me a check-up," Toni told her. "He says I'm fine."

"He told me you were a reckless, pig-headed fool."

"Well, rest won't change that," Toni told her, then as Mary gave
her an exasperated smile, she Signed quickly: "Is it safe to talk?"

"Alberta's been through here every week," replied Mary aloud.
"It's as safe as we can make it. Would you like tea?"

Toni was sloshing, but she nodded anyway and followed Mary
into the kitchen, noticing the slight sag in Mary's steps and the tension in her hands. She wore a beautiful iridescent copper chemise
and pants, which was also a bad sign. Mary always made a point of
dressing especially well when she felt low. As always, her embrace was
large and soft, smelling very faintly of the cedar sachets she kept in
her dresser drawers. But her hands were uncharacteristically cool.

"Bad news from the Consortium?" Toni asked.

"Not yet, but there will be," said Mary, grimly. "Kwong was the
Sun's incense master, you know, and that's a key position. They
haven't directly accused another tong of assassination, but they want
revenge. Soon."

She measured out jasmine tea, then adjusted her tap to boiling and filled a blue-patterned china teapot. She carried it to the table, shoved her work aside and straightened the yellow flax cloth.

"Any reprisals from the meeting?" asked Toni as she carried over a plate of scones and sat down.

Mary shook her head. "I think we caught them by surprise. We had close to two thousand attendees, you know. And four hundred more have joined in the last two days."

She sighed ruefully.

"I'm paying the taxes, too. We set the membership fee low to encourage the Guildless, and now every new member actually costs us money. I just spent a full day soliciting donations to cover our expenses instead of working on real issues. And to make things worse, I was counting on Ron's help with the Guild meetings."

"He isn't going?" asked Toni, unable to believe that the kind old man wouldn't be in the thick of activities.

"You didn't hear? He went to help with first aid at that fire last night, tripped over a hose and broke his leg. It couldn't be worse timing. He can attend remote, of course, but what we need is real presence."

She sighed and lifted the teapot.

"Pass your cup."

Toni obediently held out a blue-laced porcelain cup. Mary poured pale tea and gave her a shrewd glance.

"But this isn't what you came to talk about."

"No." Toni took a deep breath, sat straighter, and told her what she'd learned about Blade tapping the KlonDyke. Then she described Choi's call.

"I'm not going to be blackmailed," she concluded as calmly as she could, although she felt the sharp edge of her own renewed anger. "I think I may be able to get at Choi through Blade, so I'm going to try it. It's dangerous, though. And Choi may try to involve the KlonDyke. If you think I should leave, I will."

Mary's face had grown somber as Toni talked. She reached out and wrapped her wide, brown hand around Toni's, studying her with a penetrating, worried gaze.

"Toni, love, I've never questioned you about your past because I knew you didn't want to tell me. But now is the time for truth."

Toni dropped her eyes and nodded.

"You're right," she said quietly. "And . . . thank you for not having me traced when I came here."

She paused uncomfortably, then something about Mary's stillness caught her attention and she looked up sharply.

"Mary?" Was there a shadow of guilt in the other woman's eyes? Then it hit her. "You did trace me!"

"Yes. You were listed on missing persons. I was going to report you, but Doc talked me out of it."

Through her sudden anger, Toni remembered Doc's shrewd gaze and all the questions he hadn't asked. A fellow fugitive. He'd understood.

"He called me an 'interfering biddy,' " added Mary, quietly. "And he said we had no idea what trouble you might be in. I let him talk me out of it and then I spent years wondering if I'd done the right thing. I'm still not sure in my heart, love. If you'd had children or parents, I would have called. . . ."

"I see," Toni heard herself say caustically. "There I thought you'd accepted me on my own merits when you had my curriculum vitae all along."

There was a tense pause.

"Toni, I'm not going to apologize. I did my best."

Mary's voice was dignified, but she sounded hurt. Toni sighed and tried to collect herself.

"I know, Mary. I'm just an old street dog. You can take me in and feed me, but I still bite." She remembered her tea and busied herself sipping at it while she calmed herself. "Look, why don't I just start from the beginning?"

Mary nodded and refilled their cups. Toni leaned back in her chair.

"I grew up in Chicago Relocation Camp B, better known as 'the Zone,' " she began, and saw Mary blink in recognition. The Zone was one of the most notorious of the "temporary" relocation camps established in Old America during the redevelopment of the inner cities. Some of them still existed. The Zone had burned a few years after Toni left. Six thousand people died in the inferno.

"I was unauthorized and unregistered—my mother was fifteen and didn't get an abortion. She had another baby before she was fixed, and by that time she was a juice junkie and a hooker. She died on the wire."

Unexpectedly, Toni found she had to pause.

Mary asked quietly: "But you went to school?"

"The UN schools didn't check ID and they fed us. We all went. I liked it, too. I was smart and the teachers encouraged me. One year they took us on a field trip to the University of Chicago. When I saw the giant trees and clean buildings full of rich, fat, safe people I knew right away what I wanted. But I needed money."

She looked out the window, unseeingly.

"I was twelve years old and pretty. Persuasive, too. And lucky. I found a small-time uptown pimp and convinced him that a real "school girl" would get him lots of wealthy Zit clients. He plugged me, broke me in, got me a false ID, and enrolled me in an uptown high school as his cousin. That's where I got the name 'Almiramez.' I fucked the men he sold me to and spent every hour I could studying."

"It must have been hard to keep up your grades."

"Yeah, and a lot harder in university, but I was lucky again. My pimp screwed the wrong dealer and got himself slagged. I pimped for myself after that until I was nearly beaten to death. My seminar advisor found out, but lucky for me she wanted a girlfriend. She moved me into her place and got my neural plug removed without any med records.

"I enrolled in general medicine, but failed some courses and switched to behavioral therapy. It turned out to be more interesting. I did my thesis on the long-term effects of behavioral and personality modification by direct cortical stimulation. Thirty years ago that was a pioneering field. After my senior apprenticeship I left Chicago and got a position at the behavioral institute in Seattle."

"Then you studied tools?" asked Mary.

"Tried to. There weren't many live examples available. We spent most of our time with routine cases and teaching. Compared to the trainers, we were years behind, underfunded, and ill-equipped. And our methods were . . . crude. Behind the jargon and the sentiment, we were just using the same methods as trainers. When we couldn't salvage an original personality, we'd create a new one—very functional and socially attuned, but just as artificial.

"And I couldn't be objective—it was too close to me. I got into bitter disputes with the hospital and my colleagues. I got far too involved with patients, and I'd be torn to pieces when they died."

She sighed ruefully.

"I was hell to work with. Hated my colleagues and stepped on faces all the way up. Arrogant, too. I was the only researcher who knew anything because those Zits were spoiled fools. I wasn't entirely wrong, either. The staff tried but they didn't understand what it was like to be desperate, or what kind of damage neural twisting does to your soul. I knew. Which makes it additionally stupid that I wouldn't see what it had done to me. But no, I didn't have a problem."

She paused again, staring at the uneaten scone on her plate.

"I was soul sick, but I kept pushing to get the next thing that would make it all come right. Finally I made the biggest mistake. . . ."

She risked a glance across the table. Mary's gentle brown eyes made her look down again.

"I married 'Mr. Made It'—a blond human studies apprentice five years younger than me. I figured I could handle a thousand johns, I could handle one naive boy. Give him sex, dress well, go to socials with him, push his career—that's all I had to do.

"Of course it didn't work. Scott figured out soon enough that he was seeing a façade. He kept trying to break through it."

She looked down at the table, remembering Scott's gentle, stricken face, and feeling deeply ashamed.

"I guess he must have loved me. I treated him like waste and he took it and kept coming back, trying to help. He treated me better than I deserved."

Toni paused again, choosing her words carefully while Mary waited in patient silence. She couldn't bring herself to tell all of it. Not even to Mary.

"After the divorce, the old nightmares started catching up to me. I did drips in the evenings, trips in the day, trying to hold it together. I tried suicide, but I couldn't do it, so I ran instead. I shaved my head, changed my clothes, went to the worst waterfront bar I could find, and hitched a ride on a tramp. If I'd been younger somebody would have grabbed me for a smut and probably traced me. But . . ."

She was interrupted by knocking. Mary glanced uncertainly from Toni to the door. Toni sat back, took a steadying breath and waved at her to answer.

"Door's open," called Mary.

Alberta strode in.

"Found the son of a bitch," she announced, and looked at Toni. "You tell Mary about Blade's tap?"

Toni nodded.

"Good morning, Pat," said Mary. "Tea?"

Alberta shook her head impatiently and refused a chair. She planted herself in Mary's cheerful yellow kitchen, arms crossed on her chest, looking out of place in front of cupboards papered with scrawled pictures from the apparently endless supply of small children who wanted to impress "Aunt Mary." Mary's bedroom had an entire wall covered in pix of friends and relatives. Despite her protests, Toni was among them.

"Found a hidden sequence in a basement level subfile that changed size between Thursday and Friday for no reason. It's not even on our node system; just on the office set and the one in the board room. I figure it gleans data from meetings, compresses it, moves it downstairs, and then stores it there until Blade dumps it. It didn't trigger our watchdog because it's accessed direct from the box without interface."

"You didn't touch it?" Mary asked, with a hint of urgency.

Alberta shook her head.

"No point setting off an alarm before we decide what to do." She paused, then looked at Mary and Toni very pointedly. "What *are* we going to do?"

There was a long silence, in which Toni kept her attention firmly on her tea cup, leaving a response up to Mary. As the adrenaline from her emotional confession ebbed, she felt bone tired and every bit her age. Even ten years ago she'd had more stamina, and those long ago student years when she'd survived on four or five hours of sleep a night seemed almost unimaginable.

"I don't think there's anything we can do now," said Mary finally.

"I'm certainly not going to tell the Consortium that Choi's been spying—it would just push things further toward war. And I don't want to provoke Choi by telling him that we've found his tap."

Alberta frowned.

"Why not use it as a bargaining chip?"

Mary shook her head adamantly, carefully not looking at Toni.

"If he feels threatened he'll try to get revenge. And in some ways he's more dangerous to us than the tongs. We're just going to have to live with it and hope the tongs don't find out," she said firmly.

Alberta sighed and folded her arms.

"Yeah, I guess. Mary, I know you don't like it, but some of the security team want to start packing firearms. I'm already doing that," she tapped her equipment pouch, "because of Blade. My guess is knockout spray wouldn't even slow him down."

She glanced over at Toni for confirmation and Toni nodded, feeling slightly sick. Alberta clearly wished that Toni had killed Blade when she'd had the chance. She was right.

Mary shook her head slowly.

"Pat, if we arm now, it will scare the Guild customers and start an escalation with the rest. We have to look confident—keep face." She sighed, eyes worried. "But I'm not wearing a yellow shirt. If you feel your team is in serious danger . . ."

Alberta grimaced.

"Bottom line, eh? OK, we'd feel better with guns, but, shit . . . We can't handle a tong hit, armed or not. I have a good team, but they're bouncers, not soldiers. And the bar area is indefensible." She paused and bit her lip while Mary waited. "So we'll hold off on guns. But if there's serious smog, we got to close the bar."

Mary simply nodded without comment and Toni kept still, fighting an unexpected surge of distress as she thought of her apartment. If things got bad enough to close the bar, they'd likely abandon the building altogether and concentrate on defending Sisters' Residence. She focused out Mary's window, noticing that the sun had vanished behind overcast. It made the garden seem suddenly less friendly.

They talked a while longer, but came up with nothing further they could do. Alberta left, shutting the door behind her. Mary poured more tea for both of them, then looked over at Toni.

"What do you plan to do about Simon?"

Toni put down her cup.

"I won't be sure until I do some research."

"Research takes time," said Mary. "Surely Choi knows you've talked to Simon."

"Actually, there's a good chance that he doesn't know."

Mary looked skeptical. Toni leaned forward.

"Mary, tools have to be asked exactly the right question to elicit information. Simon must know he'd be punished for talking to me, so he'll try to hide it. He can't lie if he's asked directly, of course, but he's capable of some intricate deviousness." She grimaced. "Of course, the flip side of that coin is that it's difficult for me to get information out of him and I don't know if I can trust the answers I get. He could be lying. He could be following Choi's orders. And he's delusional."

"But," she automatically shifted to her "hopeful prognosis" voice, "I think I can manipulate him. He's emotionally vulnerable and close to cracking. I may be able to find a trigger that will turn Simon's rage back on Choi."

Mary frowned. Abruptly she asked: "Why did he save that child?"

Toni shrugged.

"The fire might have caused a flashback to his childhood. Ron said he'd been in a boat fire. His memories are deeply suppressed, but intense sensory stimuli can trigger vivid recall and strong emotion."

Mary stared at her, mouth tightening.

"You mean he remembered being burned and felt empathy for the child?"

"Possibly," said Toni, uncomfortable.

"And why did he bring you here?"

"Either he had orders or it was another anomalous behavior."

"Anomalous behavior?" Mary's voice vibrated with sudden anger. "You mean kindness, don't you? Listen to yourself! You're talking about him like a tool! But he's a human being who's reaching out to you for help!"

"I'm being realistic," Toni snapped. "I don't know that this isn't some elaborate hoax of Choi's. And even if it isn't—I can't 'fix'

Simon! The hard truth is he's hopeless, Mary. He's burned in—permanently altered. Feeling sorry for him won't do anything except put me at a disadvantage to Choi."

"*You* weren't hopeless."

Toni blinked, feeling a sense of foreboding even as she replied.

"What do you mean?"

"Ten years ago Doc told me not to waste my time on you. I think that's why I took you in, really. I got so mad, I was determined to prove him wrong. You remember withdrawal? I sat up all those nights with you screaming abuse because I knew that you wanted help. You were just too frightened to reach for it."

Mary leaned forward, staring into Toni's eyes.

"And what about when Bracken ran away? It was your idea to go in and haul him out of that smut shop. I doubted that time, Toni, but you had faith and you were right."

She reached across the table and grabbed Toni's hand. Toni flinched, but Mary didn't release her.

"Ever since you told me about Blade years ago—about how he comes and holds your hand, I haven't been able to get it out of my mind. You know what that is?" She shook Toni's hand roughly. "That's love. The Goddess only knows how he's still got any, but when you touched him you woke that up."

"He holds my hand because he was ordered to!"

"And because he loves you! Damn it, Toni, you're all he's got! I believe he brought you here himself, the way he brought the boy. You are debted to him!"

Mary's voice was thick with urgency and her grip hurt Toni's hand.

"Please, dear, don't let your own fear of being loved make you turn away from him. Do everything you can. If it's hopeless, it won't make any difference. But you must try or you're as wicked as Choi!"

Toni felt a hot rush of shame and found she couldn't trust her voice to answer. Her eyes burned with unshed tears and she felt horribly fragile, like she'd be smashed into shards by her emotions if she gave in to them. She struggled for control, clinging to Mary's warm, broad hand.

Just like Simon, God help her.

———————

When she returned to the KlonDyke, Toni discovered that Klale was two hours late for work. She felt a stab of worry. That wasn't like the girl. She walked into the lobby and hesitated, not wanting to hike up all those stairs to check the apartments, but she had been fretting about Klale ever since the sacking, feeling guilty that she hadn't made her more welcome. She never should have let Klale move back to eighteen. Finally, she trudged upstairs,

She found no sign of trouble on eighteen, but no Klale either. She continued up to her apartment and checked it. Empty, except for a stack of tools that Klale had intended to return to Sisters that morning. With a sudden feeling of dread she began making phone calls. Nobody had seen Klale since the D.R.A. meeting. Finally Toni called Alberta, feeling the twist of fear in her stomach. If Klale had tripped her emergency transmitter, Alberta would already know.

Outside, the day had turned gray and rain drummed against her tall apartment windows.

19

Klale woke slowly to the awareness that she felt very cold. Her right arm stretched heavy and dead beyond her head, and her mouth was dry and gluey. Must have kicked off the blankets, she thought groggily. She dragged her arm toward her and fumbled for covers. Instead, she dug into some kind of coarse sand. She coughed and woke up, opening her eyes to utter blackness.

A stab of pain in her head triggered the memory of being ambushed and Klale sat up with a surge of terror, clutching her numb arm and stifling more coughs against her shoulder. The cold air was thick with dust and her movements sent rivulets of prickly granules trickling into her clothes. She blinked, but couldn't see any difference. The blackness was dizzying. Could she be blind? At least her arm wasn't seriously injured. She could already feel painful twinges of returning circulation.

She groped for her phone. Gone. No, it had been stolen when her apartment was sacked and she hadn't replaced it yet. She felt another sick stab of fear, then remembered her emergency beacon. She reached inside her shirt and slid her fingers along the inside of her left arm, feeling a wave of relief when she realized the subdermal tab was still there. It flexed soundlessly, and Klale wondered for a panicked second if it was working, but of course it wouldn't be audible to her. It would take time for Alberta to respond, though. She'd better do something now.

It was hard to force herself to move in the black void, and Klale found herself irrationally afraid of getting lost. Stupid, she muttered to herself. I'm already lost. She started by reaching as far as she could in all directions. It was even difficult to distinguish up and down in the dark, but she seemed to be partway up a big pile of pellets. When she tried to stand she started sinking, so she threw herself forward in a swimming motion. She stopped to button her shirt up over her nose and mouth, but still she found she had to move in short bursts and then wait for her own panic and the choking dust to subside. In a very short time she found the top of the pile, but there was nothing there, so she turned and moved down again, this time on her back, half sliding, half creeping with her arms and feet outstretched.

It seemed to take an eternity. More grit leaked into her clothes, and Klale found herself flinching constantly from the instinctive conviction that her head was about to hit something. She had to close her eyes against the dust and when she tried to open them she found that her eyelids were getting glued shut. Finally her outstretched foot bumped something solid. She explored it gingerly with her shoe, then with her hands. It was a smooth metal wall stretching as far as she could reach. She could feel dents and scores in its surface, but nothing that resembled the outlines of a door or hatch.

She fought down another spell of vertigo, then realized with sudden clarity that it wasn't internal. The surface under her had moved slightly. She put her ear against the metal and faint sounds became clearer. Waves. Slopping against a hull.

Abruptly everything clicked into place. She was in a ship's cargo hold. And the musty smelling granules were grain—probably wheat. Had the ship left port already? she wondered fearfully, then forced herself to reason the situation out. She couldn't hear or feel engine vibration and anyway the hold wasn't full. They hadn't finished loading.

Then she caught her breath in horror. She knew how bulk vessels were loaded. A gigantic, flexing feeder snout swung into position over the hatch and poured grain inside. It was all done automatically—people rarely ever looked down into the hold, and with all the noise they would never hear a scream.

20

When Blade left the KlonDyke in the early hours of Sunday morning, he was followed. It was a small person and clumsy—easily avoided—but he had standing orders to find out who tried to follow him and why. Four blocks from the bar he turned down a side street into Kung Lok territory, then slipped in between some stalls and waited, silencing his breath. When uncertain footsteps passed his position he moved swiftly, pinioning his pursuer and shining a dazzling hand-light.

It was the bartender. Her lips moved and he read the words on them.

"Simon? I need to talk to you."

Blade felt Simon stirring inside, wanting to respond, but they were in the street. It was forbidden. He pushed Simon away, flicked off the light, and released the woman. She was no threat, and he wasn't to harm the KlonDyke staff without specific instructions. He turned to go, but she grabbed his arm and hung on. She was making more words at him and Simon wanted to listen.

"It's important, Simon. I must talk to you."

Simon could feel her fingers on Blade's arm, surprisingly strong for such small hands. She pulled at him, tugging with her words. He became suddenly aware of the sound of rain against his serape and the smell of damp salt air.

"Simon, take me somewhere safe where we can talk."

There were no safe places. Didn't she know that? He hesitated a long moment, wondering what she meant. Humans were often confusing. Drops of rain beaded on Toni's dark hair and splashed her face. She had looked like that on the float under the wharf when she'd touched him. Maybe she wanted to go there. He felt a sudden ache in his stomach. Maybe if he took her there she would put her arms around him again.

Even now she was reaching for his hand, wrapping it in hers. He closed his eyes for a second, savoring the feel of her skin against his, then gave Blade instructions. Blade dropped her hand and began walking. She followed.

It was over an hour since the last ferry sailing to the North Shore, and Cardero Wharf stood empty. The security gate at its foot was reinforced, locked, and wired, but Blade knew the protocols and could enter them in the dark.

Partway along the wharf a ramp led down to floats where private taxis and emergency vehicles moored. People rarely came here so late at night. One of the floats extended beneath the shadow of the wharf, and there was a place under the ramp behind a set of pilings that was well hidden.

Blade walked to that spot and sat exactly the way he had before. It was very dark. He hesitated, then pulled out his light and thumbed it to a low glow. Toni stopped for a moment, looking around the float with a puzzled frown, then she walked over and crouched in front of him on the wet concrete, her knees almost touching his. Simon felt a pang in his chest. She was not going to sit on him the way she had before. He must have failed to please her. But he didn't know what she wanted him to do.

Toni was looking at him intently, trying to snare him with her deep brown eyes and Simon felt suddenly afraid. If she could see Simon, maybe she could hurt him. He tried to pull back behind Blade, but she reached out, stroking his hands and wrists. Her fingers felt cold and tiny. He remembered how smoothly they'd brushed his face.

"Simon, I brought something for you."

She reached back with one hand into a pocket and pulled out a small package. Simon recognized the scent instantly. Chocolate. It had the most astonishing, powerful flavor—like a tango in his mouth. When she placed a brown lump in his hand he took it right away, closing his eyes and letting the sweet richness glide against his tongue. He waited a long moment then sucked and the intensity of taste exploded. When he finally swallowed, it lit a glow in his stomach that melted his fear. He could listen easily when Toni spoke again in her soft voice.

"Simon, Klale is missing. We think she went missing Friday after the D.R.A. meeting. Do you know where she is?"

He shook his head.

"Do you know who might have taken her?"

That was a complicated question. He considered it uneasily, then gave a strictly accurate answer. He dared not speculate.

"No."

Toni looked away and he studied her cautiously. She seemed afraid. She had been frightened before when she'd held him. Maybe she would decide to hold him again. But she merely tightened her grip on his hand and asked urgently: "Can you find her?"

It wasn't possible to know that. Not knowing was sometimes punishable, but wrong answers were always punishable. He spoke quickly.

"I don't know."

She was frowning. Was she angry? He felt another surge of fear. Then she took a deep breath and moved closer to him, trying to trap his eyes again. Her voice sounded stern now.

"Simon, I need your help. Find her for me. Tell me where she is and what condition she's in. Then, if possible, bring her back to the KlonDyke."

That was an order. Simon drew Blade around him and started to rise, but Toni pulled him back.

"Wait. Let me give you the information I've got."

He waited while she detailed Alberta's search and then added everything else she could think of that might be relevant. Toni's voice was tight with anxiety, and he realized suddenly that she was afraid because of Klale. If he found Klale, she might be pleased with him. He vividly remembered the feeling of Toni's arms around his chest and the warm weight of her body against his legs. He wanted to find Klale.

Simon closed his eyes for a minute, reaching inside and sharpening his focus, then he asked Toni for Klale's subdermal transmitter code. She passed him her phone, staring sharply, but he kept his eyes well away from hers. He needed to concentrate. He mated her phone to his, then entered a tracking query. It took over a minute to get an answer, during which he handed Toni's phone back and waited. She sat silently.

The tracking response from Cascadia Search and Rescue was negative, as he'd expected. KlonDyke security would have checked that already. The Kung Lok's highly sensitive smuggling network also showed nothing. But a history search of marine navigation satellites had turned up an interesting result from The Gulf of Alaska Fisheries. One navsat was recording a weak intermittent signal on Klale's frequency beyond the edge of its service area, about seven kilometers east of Downtown, near the old wheat pool. The satellite only picked it up for brief intervals every ninety minutes as it orbited overhead, as if the sending beacon were at the bottom of a well. He couldn't get a pinpoint location, but he might be able to pick up the signal if he got near enough. He made another call, then flicked off the readout and dropped his phone.

Simon closed his eyes again and sat for a moment formulating instructions, then he had Blade lead Toni up the ramp. She seemed to understand, and didn't try to make him talk. At the gate she passed him a small oblong box, then walked away up the street. He paused to examine the box. It contained a first aid kit. He scanned to make sure it was clean, then slipped it into his equipment pouch.

The floats in between the dilapidated noahs in Lost Inlet were very dark. Blade strode swiftly with one hand on a weapon, keeping a watch all around him. He knew how to walk with little noise, but his movements here were betrayed by the swaying of the old floats underfoot. He could not disguise his weight.

The phantom waited for him at the end of an outer walkway. From the outside it looked like an ancient plywood junker, but it had a fast, quiet engine and was signal-transparent. Blade stepped aboard and the pilot immediately pulled away from the float, moving slowly to minimize wash, running lights off.

Blade could smell the pilot's fear. The man turned long enough to watch Blade's Slanged directions then slipped on his headset, leaning nervously away from Blade as he navigated through the shallow channel into Coal Harbor. Once in open water he hit the throttle and Blade felt a tug of acceleration, then the jerky bang of waves against the rising hull.

It was difficult to see in the rain and the wheelhouse was too low for Blade to stand in, so he sat on a bench seat at the back and waited. They changed course abruptly several times and stopped once to wait for something to pass, but they still made good time. Eventually the man turned and signed that they were close. Blade pulled out an extra headset and studied a detailed shore map, then pointed to where he wanted to be dropped. The flot nodded, keeping as much distance as he could in the cramped cabin, then cut the engines back for their approach to the wheat pool.

At one hundred meters Blade used his phone to send a smuggling code so the ghost boat would not set off proximity alarms. Official Longshore access codes were logged and tracked, but the Guild also maintained special smuggling codes that allowed workers to get in and out of areas without record. Those codes were very useful.

The boat pulled alongside a maintenance ladder. Blade Signed at the skipper to wait offshore, then he waited for a swell and jumped to the slippery ladder, not bothering to look back. He knew the flot would obey him.

Once up on the wharf, he put on his night goggles, attached them to his phone, then scanned the area carefully, matching what he could see with Harbor Authority data. Blade had rarely been outside of Downtown and this place was unfamiliar. His map showed a long floating platform serving as berthage for up to four ships. Beyond lay the old wheat pool complex, heavily diked and retrofitted.

He tried to pick up Klale's transmitter signal and caught it, but very weak and fuzzy. Water would not account for this distortion, but a steel grain elevator or a ship's hull might, he decided. He folded out the panels on his phone and used an abbreviated keypad to call up berthage records and manifests. Two of the four ships currently tied up had been there since Friday. One, an old bulk carrier of Hawaiian independent registry, had been delayed by a dispute over money owed for chandlery and wharfage fees. The unpaid crew, confined aboard ship, had started a drunken fracas early Saturday morning which had been attended by the Harbor Patrol. The debt was now resolved and loading would resume this morning at eight A.M. That ship seemed most promising.

Blade hesitated, then took more time to work his way through the wheat pool's local netnode. It was slow and laborious work on his tiny phone via several transmission bounces, but he eventually accessed the watchman's log. The wheat pool had only two live watchmen who made hourly rounds. He had thirty-five minutes until the next round.

Taking a circuitous route to avoid pools of light, Blade trotted over to the Hawaiian freighter, then checked the transmitter signal again. Stronger. He scanned the ship carefully. The bowline was rigged with vermin traps and alarms. The only other access was via a narrow steel gangplank at the ship's stern. The first three meters of the gangplank was electrified to repel rats and alarmed against intruders, but the rest was unguarded.

Blade secured his phone, then examined his target carefully. It was permissible to access audio when stealth was necessary and he did so now. Sounds around him were muffled by wind and rain. Good. He backed off, ran at the gangplank, and jumped. He cleared the three meters easily, but his serape caught on a rough piece of railing, jerking him sideways. He grabbed for the rain slick metal railing, feeling a stab of pain along the healing wound in his back as he fell heavily onto his side. His hip hit the edge of the gangplank, knocking his handlight off his equipment belt. He grabbed, but it slid off the side and vanished into the inky gap between ship and wharf.

That was an error. Even through Blade, Simon felt a piercing needle of fear. There had been too many errors recently.

He got to his knees and crawled to the end of the gangplank, peering cautiously forward past the ship's rail. Movement. He froze.

A burly woman paced restlessly just a few meters to his left. Her posture suggested boredom and discontent. Watch duty in port would be unpopular.

Blade drew back and checked Klale's signal again. Stronger now, and coming from near the bow. A double-hulled hold would certainly explain the signal quality, but the hold would be difficult to reach. Beyond the peeling superstructure, a flat expanse of deck stretched for two-thirds the length of the ship, brightly lit by amber floodlights. A large black tentlike structure near the bow puzzled him at first; then he realized that the two foreward grain hatches had been left open and temporarily covered with tarpaulins.

For fifteen minutes he waited and watched, ignoring the steady beat of cold rain on his head. Then the crewman's footsteps picked up speed. Blade ducked back and braced for a fast retreat, but her steps turned and then a door slammed. She'd gone inside.

Blade reacted instantly, running down the deck toward the bow, then ducking behind the bulging tent. He checked behind him, then turned his attention to the hatches. Each hatch was about four by four meters, completely covered with a heavy bioplast loading tube which cinched tightly around the lip of the hatch. He could not find any way to unfasten the material—it was designed to be attached and removed by loading crane.

He checked Klale's signal again—starboard hatch—then unsheathed his knife. Its molecular edge could cut almost anything, given sufficient force behind it. He grasped the handle with both hands, braced, and stabbed.

The knife sank in a few centimeters, then stuck. Blade adjusted his position, triggered a small adrenaline surge, then shoved downward. The knife sliced down in slow motion, opening a vertical slit about half his height. He cut a horizontal stroke at the bottom allowing him to fold open the bioplast like a tent flap. Then he adjusted his goggles and leaned inside. A bright infrared body glowed beneath him. Klale. Alive.

Blade pulled back, lay down behind the hatch, unrolled his deaf interface pad and called Toni.

"*Klale alive, Oahu Star hold, Prairie Wheat Pool.*"

"Is she injured?"

"*Unknown.*"

"Can you get her out?"

He thought about it. He could enter the hold unseen, but getting out was a different matter, particularly with Klale. Further, the crewman could easily trap him, so it would be necessary to incapacitate her first, without being seen, and that would be very difficult. He was not permitted to kill without orders. The time factor was a problem, also. The next docker shift would not arrive until seven-thirty, but it would be daylight before that, even with the rain. He was still considering all the factors of the problem when a further message from Toni scrolled across his set.

"Simon, find out whether she's injured. I'll help you get her out. I can also bring Alberta and her team."

Those were orders, with an option.

"*Not Alberta. You come, bring rope. Data follows.*"

He marked his location on the map, then downloaded it to Toni's ID, along with the security codes and watchman's log. He was reconsidering the problem of the crewman when he remembered the 'Dyke's spray guns. They were silent, and it wouldn't matter if Toni was seen, so long as she knocked out the crewman. He composed a explanation slowly on the tiny pad, and received an acknowledgment.

"I can do that. I'll be there as fast as I can. How long have we got?"

"*3 hrs.*"

Next he checked safety data in the local node. Grain dust was extremely explosive and in high concentrations could cause asphyxiation. He checked his equipment carefully for anything that might produce a static charge. After some hesitation he took off the powered goggles. His phone was also risky and would be unreliable in the hold, so he programmed it to transmit a homing signal at random intervals to Toni's frequency and laid it on the deck.

He would need air filtration. He took a length of gauze from the first aid kit and tied it over his face, then looked around the deck. Small vessels usually had ropes on them, but he couldn't see anything like that on the bare, rust-eaten decks of this ship. It was inadvisable to enter the hold without one, but Toni's orders had been explicit and he could not determine Klale's injuries without examining her.

He peered in again. The drop was about six meters, but the grain would muffle the sound of his fall and cushion the impact. He checked for the watchman one final time, then kneeled and pushed inside the tarp, groping in darkness for the edge of the hatch. Finding it, he lowered himself until he hung by his hands from the metal rim. Then he let go and dropped into blackness.

21

Metal screeched against metal as the Ghost Shadows tore the hinges from the stairwell door. They were coming and Klale was trapped alone in her apartment! She huddled in terror against the wall, cold and horribly thirsty, straining to hear their footsteps. She heard a whump . . .

She woke, heart pounding in terror, realizing that she was still in the cargo hold and she'd dozed off again in the bad air. She was sweating despite the cold, and her throat felt raw from useless bouts of yelling for help. Had she dreamed those sounds or were they real? Suddenly she heard a rustle as something moved in the grain. She strained futilely to see in the dark, then noticed a tiny slice of yellow light far above her head. A hatch?

Klale tensed to scream, then stopped, suddenly afraid. Who was in the hold with her? If it was Alberta, she would have called out. Her imagination conjured up nightmare images: crazed Americans, mutant squats, gigantic rabid rats. They were the horror stories that the kids in Prince Rupert had frightened each other with on service trips, and now they'd taken on life.

Little landslides of wheat came closer. Klale stifled a cough and froze against the bulkhead, seized by incoherent fear. Something warm brushed her face. Instinctively, she screamed, and a hand slapped across her mouth, choking off her noise. She fought futilely against an iron grip. Then the grip on her mouth shifted and a big hand grabbed one of hers, forcing it upward. She redoubled her struggles, but her hand was pressed against a smooth neck and then an ear. She stiffened her fingers to jab but they were gripped and her palm shoved against the earlobe. It felt wrong somehow, chewed. Then, abruptly, she understood. It was a scarred ear. And there was no hair on the skull behind it. Blade!

She stopped fighting. Blade let go of her wrist, then slowly pulled his hand away from her mouth. Klale lunged out and hugged him. She felt him flinch and try to pull away, but she clung with desperate relief. He felt warm and familiar and she was irrationally terrified of losing him in the dark. She wasn't letting go. She felt tears start trickling down her face.

"Am I ever . . ."

Her attempt to speak triggered a coughing fit that racked her whole body,. Blade stood stiffly, then shifted around and sat down with his back against the bulkhead. Klale slid down beside him, coughing helplessly, and felt him rummaging, then a large hand gripped the back of her jerking head and a cool triangular cup slid over her nose and mouth. It hissed quietly. An inhalation unit. Between coughs she breathed as deeply as she could. In a few seconds the urgency began to fade from her burning lungs and her breathing eased.

She lay against Blade's warm bulk, letting the wonderful oxygen soak in. It left her weak and dazed, but much calmer. After a moment he removed the mask and pressed a flask into her hand. She found it an effort to move, but she made herself unscrew the cap and drink, enjoying the flavor of rehydration mix for the first time in her life, and nearly draining the container before it occurred to her that he might want some.

She recapped the flask and pressed it against Blade's chest, but he didn't take it. Instead, he groped her thigh with long fingers and she felt a distant sense of startlement until it occurred to her that he was checking for injuries. When he got to her left knee she said "Ouch," then belatedly realized that it wouldn't do any good. He couldn't hear.

Then it hit her. Blade couldn't hear and they couldn't Sign in the dark. She had no way of communicating! She grabbed his hand

and moved it back to her left knee, talking anyway just to hear the sound of her own voice.

"It hurts there." She swallowed and suppressed another cough. "It's not broken, but there's a bad bruise or maybe a sprain. I was lying on it crooked when I woke up. In fact, it feels like I'm going to have a hell of a set of bruises all down my left side when I get out . . ."

Then she remembered the *whump* noise. That must have been Blade dropping into the grain. Was he trapped, too?

"I hope you know a way out!" she said. She tried to make it sound like a joke, but she could hear new terror in her voice. She moved in front of him, putting her knees on either side of his legs and grabbing at his hand. "Did they throw you in here? Talk to me! Please, talk to me!"

She tried to think of Signs she could make against his fingers, but in her panicked state she couldn't remember anything. She shook his hand desperately. Then she heard a soft voice, so unexpected that she was shocked into stillness.

"I jumped in."

She sat, stunned, staring toward him as if she could somehow pierce the blackness with sheer willpower.

"You jumped?" she heard herself echo.

"Yes."

"Uh . . . why?"

"Toni told me to determine if you were injured."

"Toni knows I'm here?"

"Yes."

"She *is* coming to get us out?" Klale asked shakily.

"Yes."

Klale felt a rush of relief, even as she started coughing again. Blade put the mask back on her face and this time she sat for a long time, breathing in the gas and trying to think. Toni had sent Blade? And he wasn't deaf? Toni had told Klale that she didn't know much about him, but obviously that wasn't true.

She'd lied.

That chain of logic disturbed her and Klale found herself thinking back to the rumors that Toni had been a trainer. She hadn't believed them then, but now . . . ? What else would explain Blade? What if Toni worked for Mr. Choi?

She tried to puzzle out the implications of that, but it was getting much too difficult. There must be muscle relaxant in the oxy mix, she thought muzzily. She felt like she was melting—lungs first, then muscles, then her brain. She pushed the inhaler away and tried to focus on the immediate situation. Picturing Blade's strange face above her she felt a distant stir of fear. Make him talk again, she thought. She wanted to hear that astonishingly normal voice. She groped for something to say.

"I'm Klale Renhardt," she tried, feeling absurd. But they'd never been introduced, exactly. He didn't respond, so she prodded. "What's your name?"

"Simon."

His voice ought to be deep and rough, but it was a medium timbre, soft and hesitant. Almost shy. All her questions came pouring to the surface.

"Where are we? What time is it? How long have I been in here? And when will Toni get here?"

Simon answered methodically. "This is the forward hold of the *Oahu Star*. It is approximately four-twenty A.M. I don't know how long you've been here. It's likely to take over an hour for Toni to arrive." He hesitated, then added: "It is important to be quiet. There's a watchman on deck."

"What day is it?" she asked, lowering her voice.

"Sunday."

"God, I thought I'd been in here forever." Then a thought struck her. "Who threw me in?"

"I don't know." There was a pause, then he asked carefully: "Do you have any other injuries?"

She shook her head, then sighed at her own stupidity.

"I don't think so. I feel woozy and sick and I have a headache, but I don't know whether that's dehydration, concussion, or just the air."

He didn't reply and the silence between them stretched out. The blackness of the hold felt oppressive, and nightmarish thoughts began closing in on Klale again. What if Toni didn't come? What if there really were rats? There was no point telling herself that the odds against it were astronomical; she was seized by a horrid feeling of unreality where anything could happen. *Kwass.* That was Chinook for fear—an ominous, hissing word.

She tried to converse with Simon again, but his repertoire seemed to consist entirely of "yes," "no," and "I don't know." Well that was hardly surprising. She didn't imagine he got a lot of opportunity to practice small talk.

Abruptly she found herself giggling at that thought and told him the joke. She heard no response and she couldn't see him. Maybe he had managed to make that face smile or frown, but she couldn't tell. He was as enigmatic as he'd ever been—more so. Sometimes in the bar he looked like a totem; carved from wood. But here he felt warmly human.

Klale was shivering again.

"C-c-cold," she told him. "Let me sit on your lap."

He didn't protest, so she climbed on top of him, sitting sideways and curling her legs up. She felt nervous, but Simon didn't seem threatening. And Toni had sent him here to help, she reminded herself. Underneath her, Simon shifted a little and she tensed, then felt him drape the heavy, rough folds of his serape over on top of her.

Klale gradually relaxed, resting her head against Simon's chest and basking against his warmth. He was so large that she felt like a child snuggled up in a parent's lap. His shirt was damp and she could smell his sweat. A little to her surprise she realized that she was getting aroused. A reaction to fear, she guessed. In the dark it was easy to forget how he looked.

Klale's thoughts jumped around and she found herself having wild emotional surges—frightened one minute, happy the next, then sad. Earlier she'd been thinking about Hans, wondering how he would feel about her dying. Of course her brother wasn't close. But he'd be mad at her for missing the Guild meeting . . .

The meeting! she realized in sudden horror. She'd promised Hans to attend remote, but now she had missed the motion on her own expulsion. What if they had . . .

No! She wasn't going to think about that. She couldn't do anything about it, so worrying was pointless. What she needed was a distraction. *Mamook cultus wawa*, she told herself. Talk about nothing. Anything. Babble. Maybe Simon was afraid in the dark, too. Maybe her voice would help.

She started by joking about how she'd found half-forgotten specters from her childhood creeping up on her in the hold, but that seemed like a poor avenue to pursue, so she moved onto better memories, such as the wonderful summer that she and some of the Gitksan kids had repaired an old boat and taken it to the hot springs down the coast. She hadn't intended to start talking about Prince Rupert but somehow she found herself explaining what she'd loved best about it as a child.

"Every town on the coast has a public wharf," she told her silent audience. "It's not for mooring, just for day use, and it's always busy. People load and unload, or work on their boats, or come in on a beer-and-grub run from one of the villages, or just stand around gossiping. And there are always little kids fishing off the floats, breaking open mussels to use as bait for shiners and rock cod."

There was a catch in her voice and she paused, feeling foolish and more than a little dizzy and not quite sure how long she'd been talking. But Simon didn't seem to mind.

"Some very tilted characters used to wander around the waterfront in Rupert," she told him. She described a few she remembered, then decided to try again for conversation. "What do you see on the wharves Downtown?"

As she half expected, she got no answer. She shifted against him a little. Well, it hadn't been a brilliant question. And the answer might have been very unpleasant. What she'd noticed most on Downtown docks was the jarring disparities—Guild shoppers in neat felt coats waiting for ferries next to AIV-infected beggars with sticklike limbs.

Klale became so lost in her own thoughts that when Simon spoke up hesitantly she started.

"A tiny old Chinese woman comes to Pier A in the morning around dawn. She hobbles, wearing a sweater over her night dress and bedroom slippers and sometimes a coat when it's raining. Sometimes not. Sometimes a younger woman follows and scolds her and takes her away but I think that hasn't happened for a long time. Her clothes have stains and holes in them and her wrists are thin so her veins stand out like blue worms.

"She brings food to the gulls. Little bags of food, like she scraped it off her plate. She throws it in the air and they swoop down, screeching and fighting, and then she talks to them."

His voice dropped to a whisper.

"On windy mornings she dances. She hops on one slipper with her arms stretched out and her nightgown flapping in the wind. She wants to be a seagull, too. She wants the wind to pick her up and carry her away."

Klale listened in astonishment. She could picture the old woman vividly. And she could picture Simon as she'd seen him before, standing in the rain, with the water beading and dripping off him. People around the bar said he often stayed in the same place for hours, waiting for orders.

Simon's voice had been calm, but underlying it she heard a gulf of desolation. Impulsively she wrapped her arms around his chest and hugged him tight, then, with sudden curiosity, reached up to find his face. She needed to touch it—to see if it felt as alien as it looked.

When her fingers found his chin she heard a sudden intake of breath, but he didn't try to stop her. She continued her exploration, pulling down the cloth wrapped around his nose. Simon's hairless skin was taut but extraordinarily smooth. Like a child's. She stroked her fingers across his cheeks and nose, and along the smooth ridge over his eyes, avoiding the brand on his forehead. She didn't want to feel that. He held very still. On sudden impulse she stretched up his chest, and kissed his lips.

Simon gasped and she felt his body go rigid. His breathing didn't resume. Klale pulled back a little.

"Simon?" she asked anxiously.

No answer. She found his hand and squeezed it reassuringly in both of hers. Simon didn't resist, but he didn't respond either. She lifted the hand and placed it against the side of her head so his palm pressed against her hair.

"Simon?"

He still didn't answer and she was growing frightened when his fingers started to bend ever so slowly, shaping to the contours of her head. She demonstrated a stroking motion, then let go. His hand stayed there, then began stroking her hair. It felt large and warm against her head—immensely comforting. And he'd started breathing again. Eventually, with great gingerliness, he moved his fingers to her face and ran them across her skin, exactly the way she'd done to him.

His touch released a flood of emotion in Klale. She could feel his yearning and imagine how horrifically lonely he must be. And she felt very heated. She reached for his other hand and turned it so she could kiss his dusty palm, then, reckless with sudden want, she leaned upward and kissed him again, this time sliding her tongue along his lips until they began to part. At first he remained passive, then he began to respond, copying her movements.

The hold spun around her, but Klale didn't care. The inside of Simon's mouth felt soft and hot and slippery. She pressed tightly against his body, flooded with sudden urgency, wanting to lose her terror in hot excitement.

Something scraped at the hatchway.

"Klale?"

Toni's voice. Klale pulled back and managed to call: "Here!"

Beneath Klale Simon moved, then he lifted her off his lap.

"Here comes a light." Toni's voice sounded brusque, but Klale thought she heard an undertone of relief. Then light exploded and Klale had to shield her blinded eyes.

"I've got to find something to tie the rope to. Back in a minute."

Klale blinked painfully, then tried to stand up and felt a wave of vertigo. She fell back, feeling like a stunned moth. As her eyes adjusted she made out Simon wading waist deep through the golden brown wheat. The grain pile was big, but not nearly as vast as it had seemed in the dark. And the sight of Simon jarred her. It was hard to reconcile the skull-like profile of Blade with the man she had kissed in the dark. She willed him to turn around and look at her. Surely she'd be able to see something in his face that she hadn't seen before.

But he didn't look back. He picked up the light and waited under the hatch until a rope spilled down from above, then he took it and waded down the pile. When he reached Klale, he started tying knots to make a loop, still not meeting her gaze. She grabbed his hands and stared up.

"Simon!"

His eyes met hers for just an instant and she thought she saw something. Longing? Fear? Then he pushed her hands away and retreated behind stony blankness.

She might never talk to him again, Klale realized suddenly. She grabbed his hand again.

"Simon! Come and talk to me again! Please! I live on the eighteenth floor, OK?"

He shook off her hand again without replying or looking at her and she pulled back, alarmed at his blankness, then angry at her own stupidity. Why hadn't she asked more questions? Found out more about him?

Simon passed her the rope and she put the loop over her head, then under her shoulders. Usually she could climb a rope easily, but right now she was having trouble breathing, never mind climbing. Simon checked the knots, staying at arm's length. He passed her the handlight, then swarmed up the rope with easy agility and squeezed through a hole slashed in the black tarpaulin. There was a short pause, then the slack was drawn up. Klale braced as the taut rope grabbed her, dragged her through the grain and jerked her up into the air, spinning like a net full of fish—undignified, not to mention nauseating. At the rim of the hatch, Toni reached down and Klale took her arm gratefully, needing help to struggle out and flop onto the wet deck.

Klale gulped clean, wet air. Rain felt wonderful against her face. She heard Simon cough. Toni had brought Klale's Cowichan sweater and helped her into it.

"Are you all right?"

She moved Klale to arm's-length and peered.

Klale didn't want to contemplate what she looked like. She felt exhausted, filthy and hungry. Wheat filled every crevice of her body. And she was barely holding back a storm of tears. She turned away slightly on the excuse of running her hand through her tangled hair, and said: "Fine."

A shower of grains pattered onto the metal deck.

"I sprayed the sentry," said Toni. "She may not have known any-thing about this, but I couldn't take the chance. However, she won't be down long and it's close to dawn. We have to move fast." Behind her Simon coiled the rope with swift, efficient motions. "Can you walk?"

"Of course," muttered Klale. She started out across the deck, limping on her bad knee and keeping the other one from buckling only with difficulty. A hand grabbed her shoulder.

"The hell you can!" hissed Toni. She turned back and Signed at Simon. "Carry her."

Klale thought she saw him hesitate a split second, but his face remained expressionless. He stepped forward and picked her up with stiff, impersonal hands.

22

When they reached her apartment Toni finally had enough light to study Simon closely, and what she saw alarmed her. His posture was rigid with tension and he had a slight tremor around his eyes. On Toni's orders he put Klale down, and the girl limped toward the bathroom. Simon turned to leave, but Toni had positioned herself between him and the door.

"Simon," she ordered sharply. "Stay here and wait for me." She reinforced the message by Signing and thought she saw a flash of uneasiness, but he stayed where he was. She'd been counting on that. He was almost incapable of refusing a direct command. But she didn't dare leave him long.

Klale was in the bathroom trying to strip off her dirty clothes with shaking hands. Toni helped her, then made her sit while she checked for abrasions and treated them. While Klale fumbled with hot water and soap, Toni heated soup and placed a fast call, canceling Alberta's search with a few quick words and cutting the security chief off before she could ask any questions. She helped Klale into bed and gave her the soup, relieved to see color coming back into the girl's white face. Feeling slightly guilty, she put a skin patch on Klale's forearm, telling her it was a stress formula. It was actually a fast-acting sedative. She couldn't afford any interruptions while working with Simon. Klale tried to ask questions, but she started dozing off before she finished the soup.

In the hallway, Simon stood motionless exactly where Toni had left him. She walked up cautiously, then held out her hand and led him over to her couch, speaking in a soothing tone. She sat him down, stroking his hand and reassuring him that he was safe. It was a relief just to have him seated. Standing, he towered over her and she found it difficult to avoid being intimidated. She tried thanking him for bringing Klale back, but got what she expected—mute incomprehension.

After five minutes he was still too tense for hypnosis, so she chanced a direct question.

"Simon? What happened with Klale in the hold?"

She wasn't sure he'd respond, but Simon's eyes shifted around the room and he began twisting his fingers together. He blurted out in the little boy voice: "I talked to her."

Toni kept her face calm only with effort. He shouldn't have been able to do that, but he'd already overcome the barrier once. It must be getting easier as his training eroded.

"Why?" she asked softly.

"She told me to."

He was getting more agitated and Toni studied him, trying to puzzle it out.

"What else did Klale do, Simon?"

There was a long pause in which his hands froze, then he answered in a harsh whisper.

"She touched me. . . . She kissed me." His voice was thick with fear and bewilderment, almost inaudible. "Like people do."

Jesus God, Klale! Toni stared at Simon, dumbfounded. Simon could just as easily have killed that idiot girl as kissed her! Any sensation that powerful was more than enough to push him over the edge. As it was, he seemed close to panic. She had to calm him down before he slid into his Blade persona again.

"Simon! Don't go away, Simon! I want you to stay here with me." She took a deep breath and made her voice warm and slow. "It's safe here. Nobody can see you. I'm not going to hurt you. I won't make you do anything. Just sit quietly and relax."

There was grain dust caked into the sweat on his neck and face. She started to reach over, then stopped. Intense touching might be unwise after what Klale had done. Instead she took his hand again.

"Just sit here quietly for a few minutes. All right?"

He managed a nod and she saw a quiver of tension along his jaw. Bad. She put his hand down, and got up, casting urgently around her apartment for ways to calm him. Hypnosis was out. And she doubted he would let her administer drugs, even if she knew what dosage to use. What about music?

She went over to her netset, called up a soothing instrumental piece and then entered some quick pad commands to record her session with Simon. Then she turned back to look at him and realized she was in trouble. Simon was frozen halfway to his feet, face openly terrified. Damn! Had he seen her set up to record? But he wasn't looking at her hands, he was looking at the speakers. . . . It was the music! And he was sliding back into Blade!

"Simon!" she yelled. "Simon, don't go!"

His head swiveled toward her, eyes wide, breathing fast. She put her hand out to turn the music off, then it hit her. Blade was deaf. Simon could only consciously hear the music if he was in one of his two other personas. She hesitated a split second, then gambled.

"Listen to the music," she instructed firmly. She turned the volume up and waited, heart pounding. Conflicting emotions tugged at his strange face. This was an unfamiliar place and Toni wasn't his master.

"That's a command, Simon. Listen to the music," she said again, more sharply. Another long, frozen second stretched out, then he closed his eyes and his shoulders slumped. He sat down on the floor against the couch, tension draining.

A hypnotic cue? Toni studied him for long moments as he sat motionless. The music she'd chosen was very slow, with little tune. How would he react to something faster? She called up one of her favorite reggrags and faded the other out. This piece opened fast and happy, with a series of cascading saxophone riffs. For the first few seconds, he showed no reaction, then his whole face lit up, and, as the riffs grew louder, he broke into a delighted smile.

It was the transformation she'd seen before. Simon drew up his legs, and wrapped his arms around them, swaying to the rhythm like a child. Suddenly his eyelids rose and he smiled directly at her with glowing joy. Then his eyes closed again and he sat rapt, lost in the sound.

The carrot, Toni thought. My God, I've stumbled on his motivator.

It was an incredible piece of luck. When the music finished he'd be receptive and she could work with him. But she was finding it hard to focus, despite her excitement. It had already been a long, exhausting night. She needed a cup of coffee. And Simon would be hungry. Well, the music gave her time to prepare.

She programmed the netset for two more short selections, then went to her kitchen and put on coffee, scones, and some of Klale's ginseng tea, finding it easier to think while her hands carried out the automatic motions.

Music was certainly the oddest motivator she'd ever run across, but it would be very effective if one didn't want to entirely destroy a personality. There was a famous case in the literature of an artist who'd been trained as an adult by making his art the carrot—pushing him into such an obsession with it that he literally didn't care about anything else he did. Choi might easily have heard of that, and it fit with the blackmailer's manipulative style. Also, Ron had described Simon as musically gifted. Choi must have repaired the boy's damaged hearing and then enhanced the pleasure Simon received from music, while ensuring he was unable to receive enjoyment from any other source. It also explained why Blade remained deaf—so he couldn't be distracted.

And it further confirmed that Choi was using Simon for tasks requiring intelligence and initiative. Toni was sure she'd heard a trace of that third persona earlier in the night. When Simon had asked her for the transmitter code the pitch of his voice had been distinctly different—more adult. She wished he'd said more than a few words.

Could he be a data shark? Very possibly. He was wired for direct interface. That tap in the 'Dyke's system was set up by an expert, and Simon had located Klale's transmitter signal with impressive speed.

She looked over at him, trying to puzzle out the personality behind that altered face. Outside her apartment windows, gray dawn light seeped from under heavy clouds, sucking the warmth from her lamps. How much time did she have? She pushed that thought away.

Hurrying could be fatal, as she'd already learned. She studied Simon's posture. He looked relaxed, but he didn't seem to like this song as much as the first. She needed him as receptive as she could manage.

On a hunch, she waited until the tune ended, then asked him to name his favorite piece of music.

"*Inversion* by Cloudburst," he said, with cautious hopefulness. Toni was surprised. It was a powerful composition but somehow she hadn't expected him to be so current.

"While you listen to it, I'd like you to relax and enjoy it as much as you can. Let your whole body feel the music. Can you do that?"

He nodded eagerly. She called it up from the net and started it, then sat at the table a few meters away, watching his reactions while she waited for her coffee to drip.

As the music soared, Simon's enjoyment visibly intensified. His breathing grew deeper, his head rolled back, and the notes sent vibrations rippling through him. He looks like a juice addict, she thought, studying his beatific face with sudden recognition, then she realized that he was rising toward an orgasm. At a crescendo in the music he began to shudder.

Abruptly she got up and went to the netset to check the length of the piece. Nine minutes, with six yet to go. Well, she'd wanted to relax him, she told herself dryly. She had her eyes focused intently on the readout when she realized what she'd just done. She had turned away from observing her patient at a critical moment.

She forced herself to turn back and look. Simon's back arched and he gasped raggedly as the waves of sound passed through him. It was a classic filament-conditioned response, she noted. He wasn't touching himself at all.

But watching him created an intense conflict in her—a dismaying heat coupled with an urgent desire to flee. She took a deep breath, closed her eyes for a few seconds, and forced herself to examine her own feelings. The problem was immediately clear. Simon's reactions reminded her far too vividly of her own plug.

It had been nearly thirty years, but watching him flooded her with the old raw yearning. The sexual arousal induced by her plug hadn't just made her hot—it had slammed her into a state of overwhelming need, beyond all semblance of control or rationality. It had been terrifying and intoxicating—an intensity of abandonment impossible to experience any other way—and it hadn't taken long for her to become addicted. No matter how repulsive or painful her tricks had been, once a few days had passed her desire had escalated into desperation. Even after her pimp's death she'd kept hooking month after month. If she hadn't been forced to get the plug out, she would never have quit.

The price of freedom was rigid repression. Without the filament, men repulsed her and normal arousals left her with such a frantic sense of frustration and loss that she'd walled off her responses entirely. Even her recent cautious experiments with Klale had been tolerable but achingly empty.

The oven chimed and Toni shook herself harshly. That was her problem, not Simon's. She went to the kitchen and pulled out the hot scones, splitting three open for Simon and drenching them in butter and honey. Then she carried the food to the living room and sat cross-legged beside him, waiting for the music to end. He trembled with small aftershocks as the notes died away, and she let him sit for a minute in silence while his breathing slowed.

Toni called softly. Simon opened his eyes and looked at her with dreamy, naked happiness. Then he blinked in confusion, disoriented by the strange place. She immediately took his hand to reassure him. He accepted her touch with childlike trust and his anxiety melted. He was completely pliant.

"Are you hungry?"

Simon was staring around her apartment as if he had found himself in a grotto of the Arabian Nights, but food grabbed his attention. He nodded, with a stretched caricature of the shy smile she'd seen in Ron's picture. She passed him the plate of scones and saw his eyes light up as he smelled the honey.

When they had both finished eating she put the dishes aside and induced hypnosis, placing him on top of Mount Beautiful on the day of the picnic. She was very thorough this time, telling him that the mountain was far away from all his fears and problems. He responded to her profoundly, more deeply relaxed than she'd ever seen him.

This time she started with a simple, open question.

"What does Simon do?"

He answered matter-of-factly.

"Simon dances."

She blinked in startled revelation. That explained Simon's physique and gracefulness, and also his interest in Klale. But he hadn't tried to dance a few minutes before, or when Alberta had seen him at the waterfall.

"I would like to see you dance, Simon. Are you permitted to dance here?"

"No," he said definitely.

There must be a designated place. Too bad, thought Toni. It would be interesting. A man with no normal outlets for his emotions was likely to be an extraordinary dancer. But that was irrelevant. What she needed was information.

Proceeding with extreme caution, she tried to find out whether Choi knew that Simon had talked to her. She'd phrased her questions beforehand to avoid direct conflicts with Simon's instructions, but she still had little success. He was profoundly terrified of Choi. Even under hypnosis the mention of his master's name got him too agitated to give her a useful response, and the answers he did give were muddled. He confirmed that Choi didn't interrogate him every day or even every other day, but she was unable to establish a frequency.

Abandoning that line of questioning, she tried to find out something about Simon's third persona, but his fear and resistance there were also extremely high. Finally she backed off, careful to keep the frustration out of her voice.

Damn, she wanted that training collar! With direct neural feed she could calm Simon and keep him immobilized. But the collar would be useless without access codes, and breaking the codes was a long, painstaking process. How could she get that much time?

On an impulse she asked Simon if he knew his access codes. No. Well, it had been worth a try.

She sighed and shifted her position on the wood floor, trying to get more comfortable. If she couldn't get any answers about the present, maybe she could learn something about the past.

"Simon, do you remember when you first saw me?"

"I don't know," he said, uncertainly.

Bad phrasing, she reminded herself. Tools had no real concept of past or future, so their time sense was very distorted.

"Did you ever see me when I was tripped?" she tried.

He nodded.

"Where was I?"

"In the alley behind Dick's. You were sitting on the ground talking, but you were alone. Blade saw you. Then you saw Blade and looked through him and saw Simon. You talked to me."

"What did I say?"

"I don't know. I was frightened. I ran away."

"Can you describe another time I talked to Simon?"

"Yes. On the float under Cardero Wharf. Blade went there to vomit. He had been punished."

A shadow of that old terror was creeping into his voice. Toni leaned forward quickly and reminded him that he was on the mountain—far away from pain. When he calmed she had him continue.

"You came there. You were sick, too, and you had to hold onto the ramp railing. When you saw Blade you weren't afraid. You came close and looked in his eyes until you could see Simon. You said: 'Poor fucker. You've been punished.' Then you screamed 'Curfucking trainers!' "

Toni winced. That sounded accurate enough. Then she realized that Simon's anguished eyes kept flicking near her face and away again.

"Then you touched me. Like I was real. You kneeled and reached out your hand and touched me." He demonstrated, reaching his hand up to his face and cupping it along his jawline. His voice dropped to a whisper. "Then you put your arms around me."

Oh my God! thought Toni, jolted. I was insane! But it explained why Klale had survived her exploit. Simon would view Klale as Toni's property—an extension of Toni.

She studied Simon's face, noting the longing in his eyes. All these years he'd been hoping that she'd do it again, she realized. He didn't know that she'd forgotten. And he had no way of asking.

But Toni wasn't drunk now or suicidal, and Klale had already shaken Simon badly. Toni reached out and touched his cheek, but didn't go any further. It was far too easy to get enticed by Simon's childlike behavior and forget how dangerous he was.

"Was I injured?" she asked.

He shook his head mutely. She frowned.

"I thought I remembered you holding me when I was bleeding. Did you ever do that?"

He nodded.

"What happened?"

He obviously had to think back. She waited patiently.

"They beat you," he told her finally. "Three pimps. In the alley. They kicked you and shoved a prod in your mouth."

Pimps. That wasn't surprising. She had a dim memory of picking a fight with one, and he'd probably had friends. What had he looked like? She closed her eyes to concentrate and got a fleeting glimpse of a face. Now, put it in an alley. At night. With a prod.

The memory came suddenly: cold, wet pavement under her naked back, her arms being crushed under booted feet, the pain of dry, tearing force between her legs. Her jaw was grabbed and cold metal rammed into her mouth crushing her tongue, choking her. A bolt of searing pain ripped through her head.

Toni flinched involuntarily, and had to fight to keep her voice steady.

"What happened next?"

"Blade got angry."

"What did he do?"

"I don't know. I went away."

Rage-induced blackout? Deliberate suppression? Maybe both. Ron had mentioned an incident where Blade killed three men; this might have been it. He'd probably saved her life, but his extreme violence appalled her.

And this didn't answer one vital question. Why had Simon looked at her in the first place? Why had he allowed her to touch him? He shouldn't have done that, especially ten years ago. He would only have been about twenty then, recently trained. Or had Choi orchestrated the incident?

She tried asking, but her questions confused and then alarmed him. And it was getting late. She had to finish.

Toni deepened Simon's calm again and told him not to remember their conversation. She would have liked to try blanking Klale's rescue, too, but he hadn't been under hypnosis then and it was very doubtful she'd succeed. She would have to hope that Choi's procedures were lax. Then she took the big chance. She instructed Simon to return to her apartment after his next Thursday night visit to the KlonDyke. With some misgivings she gave him the passcode for the stairwell door in the lobby and told him to wait on the twenty-first floor landing.

Her last action was to get a wet cloth and wipe the honey off his hands, feeling absurdly like a mother with a small child, although his hands were enormously bigger than hers.

After he left, she looked into the bedroom. Klale lay asleep, breathing deeply and quietly, her red hair in a tangled riot around her head. Toni watched her for a long moment, trying to be angry at the girl's recklessness, but merely feeling afraid. She had taken a gamble to find Klale. By using Simon, she had involved Klale in her private war with Choi. Then she shook herself. If she hadn't used Simon, Klale would be dead by now. Toni was a little surprised by the amount of grief she felt at that thought.

She closed the door quietly and walked back into the living room, too tripped on adrenaline and caffeine to settle down yet. It was suddenly hard to believe that Simon had really been there, but she could see an imprint of grain dust on her couch, like a gigantic shadow. She looked at it, letting her face settle into worried lines.

Stumbling on Simon's motivator had been a tremendous piece of luck, but if Choi found out, he would have her killed immediately. And he was certain to discover her tampering sooner or later.

She found herself pacing the apartment and forced herself to stop, then decided to try and get some research done, despite her weariness. She had already scanned the little literature available on multiplug patients but she hadn't read up on access code decryption. She doubted she'd learn anything useful, but she'd be foolish not to try.

She went into the study, closed the door softly behind her and then sat down and adjusted her headset with cold hands. She automatically scanned her mail list. Two urgent messages shunted from Klale's mailbox, both from Klale's brother. Well, let Klale deal with it. Then Toni froze, staring at an anonymous holo file in her mailbox.

Sender names were not supposed to be erasable, but the tongs could no doubt manage it. Or Choi.

Had the old blackmailer missed Blade? Toni felt a surge of panic and fought it down with logic. Blade had only just left and this mail had arrived hours ago. She took a long steadying breath and told the computer to open the file.

"Please state your name for voice-verification."

"Toni," she said.

"Access denied."

What? She tried again with the same result, then hesitated a long moment and tried "Dr. Almiramez."

The file opened. Toni's stomach lurched.

She was braced to see Choi's office again, but after a second of blackness she found herself looking down into a vast, empty room. A man stood below and in front of her with his back turned, and from the unfamiliar perspective it took her half a second to recognize Simon. But there was something odd about his posture—he seemed stooped. She froze the playback quickly and checked the file data. It was a high quality image recorded from two perspectives. She switched to the other track for a front view.

Simon wore a signal reflective body suit, the sort used for martial arts training. The room behind him looked like an old level under one of the office buildings, with pipes protruding from rough con-crete walls. It had been fitted out as a gym. Full length mirrorscreens ran along one wall and gym mats were stacked in one corner. A large section of floor had been painted as a square bull's-eye, with alter-nating wide stripes of light green and dark green. The bright colors somewhat alleviated the starkness of the surroundings, but it still felt bare and cold.

This was where Simon danced, she realized. Maybe he'd sent her the vid.

With a surge of excitement, she restarted the playback. Simon walked a few steps across the room and she studied him curiously. For a moment she thought that his injuries were troubling him, but he moved with the stiff, shuffling gait of an old man. He stopped, turned, stretched a little, and dropped his hands to his sides. Mime, she realized. And he was good at it.

He raised his arms slowly to waist height and lifted one foot. Toni watched in puzzlement, then recognized the glacially elegant movements of tai ji. She used to pass a group practicing on campus in the early morning. Simon's movements had the smooth fluidity of years of practice. His arms reached, pushed, circled, then he began gliding from stance to stance like a skater. Abruptly Toni realized that the light green stripes on the practice floor were frictionless strips and his body suit also had frictionless areas. She'd seen the effect before in vids, but the floor colors were always edited out so the dancers seemed to change the rules of physics at will. As she watched, Simon's motions gathered speed. The old man was becoming young, and Simon was turning his tai ji routine into a dance.

She became aware of soft music, also growing stronger and faster—a neotraditional Asian piece with bamboo flute, sitar, and drums. With it, Simon took on a sinuous feline grace. She tried to remember: wasn't one of the tai ji positions named after a tiger? His suppleness amazed her as he mimicked the movements of a big cat with eerie accuracy.

She watched in fascination, occasionally switching perspectives, and then gave up and stayed in one place. Clearly he'd arranged the dance without any thought of an audience. A few times he almost froze in a particular position and she was struck by the feeling that his pose had some meaning. But he wasn't Signing, and even by stopping, reversing, and changing tracks she couldn't make any sense of it.

Eventually she just sat back and let the dance unfold. She had expected Simon to be good, but when he exploded into a series of powerful spins and leaps, she found herself gaping. The extraordinary gracefulness of his body contrasted bizarrely with his blank brutal face, but what really gave the dance impact was the controlled hurricane of emotions in his movements.

And those emotions were so unexpected. There was grieving and futility in the old man, and an ominous undercurrent of rage in the tiger's stalk, but Simon predominantly radiated delight. And it wasn't the mindless euphoria of a juice addict, or even the oblivious transport she'd seen before. He was clearly in a state of creative, passionate concentration. He was doing what he loved and it was uniquely, incredibly beautiful.

The dance peaked at a near frenzy, then the movements slowed again until the old man re-emerged, finishing his tai ji. When he dropped his arms into silence and walked away with a shadow of youth in his stiff steps, Toni found tears pooling in her headset. She tugged the apparatus off her face, and wiped at her eyes with her sleeve. Her stomach and chest ached with old grief, as if Simon had somehow stabbed her with his own agonizing vulnerability.

She sat in silence, trying to gather some semblance of detachment and failing. Had Simon sent this or Choi? If it was Simon, she had no doubt what he was doing. He was reaching out to her for help. And if it was Choi . . .

Well, it didn't matter, she realized. The result was the same. Mary was right. She couldn't turn away. Simon had asked for help and as hopeless as it might seem, she had to try.

She sat for a very long time with tears still burning in her eyes, considering the astonishing, exquisite beauty she'd just seen, and knowing that she couldn't save it.

23

Klale woke from nightmares of suffocating in grain while Simon whispered in her ear. She lay for a long moment letting her racing heart slow and reassuring herself that she really lay safe in Toni's bedroom. Beside her, Toni let out a gentle snore and Klale propped herself up on one elbow, grinning.

She licked her dry lips. They tasted of grain dust and she could still feel the gluey stuff in her eyes. She felt tired but she couldn't sleep anymore, so she got up quietly and checked the time on Toni's netset. 1:06 P.M. Under the time display, Toni had left a flashing note for Klale. She had mail. With a sinking feeling, Klale checked. Her brother, of course. She hoped Hans didn't know that she'd gone missing. He'd be frantic.

She grabbed Toni's too small bathrobe from the closet, then went in the study and closed the door before calling Hans. He took his time answering and when he did she saw that he was sitting in the cab of a log picker in his shirtsleeves, holding a sandwich.

"Hans, I'm sorry . . ."

"I called you on emergency priority half a dozen times Saturday night and you couldn't be bothered to answer until now?"

Oh gods, the Guild meeting! Klale felt a sick stab of dread in her stomach.

"I'm so sorry. I couldn't call . . ." she said, then trailed off. How could she explain? If Hans didn't already know she'd been abducted, she wasn't about to tell him.

Hans kept his eyes fixed on his lunch, not meeting her gaze, and she had a sudden vivid memory of the day he'd packed his clothes in two big laundry bags and walked out of the house. Neither he nor Dad had looked at each other, but Klale remembered how their father had sat down afterward at the kitchen table and cried. She'd wrapped her arms around his big shoulders feeling helpless and terrified. The only other time she'd seen him cry was when her mother died.

"Hans, what happened?" she asked finally.

"Oh, you care?" Hans slammed his lunchbox closed. "Well, it's too late. You're out."

Klale gasped. The floor lurched underneath her, like being hit by a rogue wave, and she found herself clutching Toni's desk. She opened her mouth but no words came. She'd never expected this—never dreamed that the friends and neighbors she'd grown up with could discard her so casually.

Hans finally glanced over and saw her face. He sighed.

"Look, it was what I figured. They saved the motion for a long boring meeting packed with Klassen's neps, and put it to an in-person vote. You got anally scutted, but you asked for it. You weren't here standing up for yourself."

"Yeah, well what's the point?" snapped Klale. "They would have done it anyway!"

"Grow up!" growled Hans, then cut the call, leaving Klale staring at the screen with her arms wrapped tightly around her chest.

She wanted to cry, but for once tears wouldn't come. She showered, dressed, ate some scones she found in Toni's kitchen, and then paced the living room restlessly. After all those hours in the grain hold she felt a desperate need to see the sky, and *move*. But the thought of risking Downtown streets again terrified her. Somehow, she'd never before *really* believed that she might die, not even in bad storms out in the boat. But now she knew, with visceral certainty, just how easily she could die.

She paced into Toni's balcony garden, catching a glimpse of whitecaps in English Bay under a blustery sky. A westerly gale of about forty-five knots, she guessed. There'd be real *solleks chuck* out in the gulf. It was a good day not to be fishing, but the thought gave her a pang and she felt suddenly empty, as if part of her identity had been extinguished. Who was she? Abruptly she realized that she'd always seen herself in the reflection of her Guild, for good or ill. Without a Guild she felt faceless.

Hans was right—she should go back and fight. But she couldn't leave now. Ever since waking she'd been haunted by Simon's lonely whispers in the ship's hold. He must have taken a terrible risk for her, and she felt ashamed that she couldn't remember thanking him. Klale had pitied Simon before, but now that she had touched him and spoken to him, she felt outraged. How could Toni ever have claimed that he wasn't a person? And how could she refuse to help him? Had she been lying all along? Did she really work as a trainer . . . ?

No! Klale wouldn't believe that of Toni. There must be an explanation, and Klale would demand it. Then they would get Simon out of the hell he lived in. His troubles were more important than Klale's Guild citizenship. Toni said there were always more options than you thought, so Klale would find them.

Finally she decided that she might as well work, and she went down to the bar. To her surprise, it was packed, mostly with flots and squats. And for once, the projection setup was running, flashing news coverage to an intent audience. Klale walked up near the front and watched scenes of rescue workers peeling back twisted, scorched rubble. Hundreds of blissers had burned to death in a factory fire near Seattle, she learned. The factory had been hidden under a sanctioned Bellevue warehouse and nobody knew how many Guildless workers had been inside, jacked into their workstations.

Pum came by and provided details that weren't in the official news. The factory was one of the Viet Ching's largest, she said, and spin said it had been bombed by the Sun Yee On.

Klale didn't have time to digest that because she was called over to the bar where Su and the Boss were swamped by the unexpected crowd. Klale grabbed a tray, then Mary beckoned her to the till and gestured to a short, middle-aged Afram woman dressed in a neat but threadbare wool suit. The woman held her head high, but clutched her rough, scabbed hands nervously in front of her. Obviously Guildless.

"Miz Johnson and her family are at table twenty-six, Klale. Please give them table service if they need anything more. I've put in their order and I'll have it ready for you in five minutes."

Klale nodded politely. The woman looked grateful, then broke into a smile as the Boss reached over the bar and shook her hand.

Klale waited on tables, then returned to the till and discovered that Mary had brought out an embossed thermal flask, spiral glasses, and a silver tray for a cheap order of mulled wine and moon cakes. Mary lit the candle and passed her the tray.

"I'd take it myself but I can't leave the till. Thank you, dear. I know you're busy. Please wish Jubilee a very happy sixteenth birthday for me."

Klale found herself wishing uncharitably that Jubilee had been born on a less busy day, but she picked up the tray, praying that nobody jostled her. The crystal glasses were fragile and very expensive.

Her irritation faded when she reached the crowded table and saw the smiles. Jubilee was being feted by all of her female relatives, old and young. They must have spent hours braiding the girl's hair into a spiral sculpt, and hand-sewing her patchwork robe. Klale delivered everything with as much flourish as she could manage, reminding herself that these women had probably saved for months to afford an evening at the KlonDyke. Other nearby patrons caught sight of the candle and offered congratulations. The girl glowed, radiant despite her crooked teeth and sallow, pox-scarred skin.

Jubilee had a right to be happy, thought Klale suddenly. She had survived her childhood Downtown.

Orders piled fast and Klale quickly discovered that the 'Dyke's cheapest drinks were also the heaviest—pitchers of beer and steaming ceramic dragonpots of tea. She was even called to help at the tong tables—work she quickly found exasperating. The tonglords got special food, drinks, dishes, and cutlery. They demanded fresh glasses for every drink and new bottles for each toast. Since Kwong's assassination the senior tong execs were staying in their secured rezzes, and without their restraining influence the young tonglords were rowdy and arrogant, seeming oblivious to the swell of surreptitious hostility in the crowd around them. They kept Klale running.

It was several hours before she was able to stop for a meal. She ate quickly at a stool at the bar, watching footage of the burned factory split-screened with a group of lume-coifed newsers and officials tut-tutting over the "accident." She wondered cynically if any real people were patched into this commentary, or if they were just running personal replicas in a simmed studio.

"I'm beginning to sympathize with your brother," came Toni's dry voice from behind her. "You might have left a message saying where you were going. Or called."

"Oh, I'm sorry!" said Klale, turning in dismay to find Toni, weary and annoyed, sipping coffee from a KlonDyke cup.

"Mary needed help," Klale said, gesturing at the crowd, "and . . . I got busy."

"Don't do it again," snapped Toni. She started toward the till and Klale jumped off her stool to follow.

"Toni, I need to talk with you. About . . . Simon." She dropped her voice low. Bracken stood some distance away but she seemed to have very sharp hearing.

"Klale," Toni spoke over her shoulder in a hard, clipped voice, "I know you want to start a rescue mission, but you can't help. Stay out of it."

"I can't stay out!"

"Yes, you can."

"Then I'll find a way to help him by myself!"

"Damn it!" Toni whirled, looking furious. "You are a naive Zitkid who's lucky to be alive, but you won't stay that way if you keep on like this!"

"And you've given up!" retorted Klale, hearing her voice rise. "You've given up on yourself so you've given up on Simon, too! You don't care anymore!"

For a second she thought Toni was going to explode, but the older woman simply took a deep breath and then spoke between clenched teeth.

"You're off. I don't want to see you back here tonight."

"But . . . !" Klale found herself puffing with indignation, despite the fact that she'd been longing to quit only minutes before. Alberta walked up to the bar just in time to catch Toni's words and she nodded at Klale.

"You heard it. Off. But I want to talk to you. In the back. Fifteen minutes."

Klale glanced from Alberta's stony face to Toni's angry one, then shut her mouth and started to lift off her apron. A movement caught her eye and she turned her head to see Miz Johnson waving from her table.

"Just this one, then I'm leaving," she told Toni, and strode into the tables before Toni could reply.

As she walked over, she tried to wipe the annoyance off her face. She expected another order, but instead Miz Johnson simply thanked her with stiff dignity, and then pressed two coins into Klale's hand. Klale started to refuse, then looked in the woman's proud eyes and thanked her. As the rest of the group rose to leave, she wished the girl happy birthday again. Then she glanced down at the coins in her hand. Two five dollar pieces.

She stood for a long moment, turning the coins over in her fingers, thinking about how much that had cost them and feeling very, very small.

Klale waited almost an hour in the downroom for Alberta, growing more miserable as the minutes passed and her thoughts kept flashing back to the grain hold, or to her Guild expulsion. Each time someone came into the downroom Klale jumped, and when Alberta finally arrived she rushed over anxiously.

"Sorry I took so long," the bouncer said. "Had to exit those tong bastards."

"Bounce them?" asked Klale incredulously. "Why?"

"They started grabbing Lily, wouldn't lay off. They know it's against the rules to touch staff, so I had to kick them out."

"And they left?" asked Klale, wondering for the first time what usually happened when a tong exec wanted a dancer or server. How far could Mary really protect her staff? And with things getting worse Downtown, how long would any of them be safe at the KlonDyke?

"Yeah, they left," said Alberta, but Klale thought she looked worried. "Told them we'd complain to their Dragon Head, tell him they dishonored their tong's oath of conduct."

She glanced around the downroom, then led Klale to a quiet corner and interrogated her about the abduction. Klale told her everything she could, but it wasn't much. Finally she asked, a little hesitantly: "Do you think it was Captain Dhillon?"

Alberta shook her head.

"She's a bent bitch, but I can't see her risking her hitch. Tommy Yip, he's another case. You step on his foot lately?"

"No," said Klale. "At least I don't think so. But I, uh . . . I did file a complaint about Dhillon."

"*What?*" Alberta stared at her, aghast. "Are you tilted? No, forget I asked."

"So now do you think she did it?"

"No! Look, Dhillon's a captain. She's up for maybe a slap on the wrist *if* the brass even looks at an unwitnessed complaint by a Guild runaway. I'm not saying she wouldn't bludge you. And I'm not saying she wouldn't maybe kill somebody if she had a hot reason, but she's not stupid. Shit!" She fixed Klale with a glower.

"You scared the hell out of Toni, you know. And Toni's one of the best, OK? Don't you spill on her."

Klale looked at Alberta, a little surprised.

"I won't. Really. She's my friend."

As the words left her mouth she remembered their argument and felt a flood of shame. Toni had saved Klale's life last night, at what cost Klale had no idea. And Klale hadn't thanked her, she'd just started yelling about Simon.

"Yeah, well I know it doesn't come natural, but try to be careful."

The security chief insisted on escorting Klale up to the eighteenth floor and checking the entire floor. Klale didn't argue. She thanked Alberta, rammed her homemade bolt across the door, then stood alone in her apartment in the light of one flickering candle. A gust of wind buffeted her makeshift walls, making the hempboard creak. She looked around miserably at the cold, damp room and fought down a desperate urge to flee downstairs. She dreaded another night alone. She longed for a shoulder to cry on and a warm, comforting human body to curl up against, but she could hardly invite herself up to Toni's apartment after that fight. Not until she had a chance to apologize properly.

Well, then she'd have to get on with it, wouldn't she? Klale pushed back lurking tears, and kneeled by the little camp stove Rill had loaned her. She really should go to bed, but she felt so tense that she didn't think she could fall asleep despite her exhaustion. What she really wanted was a very large, very hot, very alcoholic drink.

Fortunately, she'd bought a cube of hard cider from the bar. She poured some in a pan, added spice mix, and put it on the burner. While it heated she rummaged around in a box for more candles and lit them. She used to think candles were romantic; now she just longed for electricity.

She carefully picked up two burning candles, stood and turned around, then jolted to a heart-stopping halt, splashing hot wax on her hand. Blade stood behind her in the center of the apartment, gigantic in his slate-gray serape. Looking at his stony, immobile face, Klale found it suddenly impossible to believe that she'd ever touched him or heard his voice.

All of Toni's hard-faced warnings came pouring back, then she made a desperate grab at self-control. His name was Simon, she reminded herself. He hadn't hurt her when they'd been alone in the hold. And she had asked him to visit. He probably just wasn't used to knocking.

"Hello," she tried. Her voice squeaked, so she cleared her throat and tried again. "I was just making myself a nightcap—I'll add some for you, too."

She didn't wait for a reply, but turned back to her little stove and added more cider to the pan, trying to keep her hands from shaking. She started chattering, saying anything that came into her head. When the cider steamed vigorously she turned off the flame and poured two mugs. When she handed him a mug, he reached from under the rough folds of the serape and took it, then held it awkwardly without tasting, so she drank from hers. He sipped cautiously. Then she sat down on her sleeping roll and invited Simon to sit, too. For a few seconds she didn't think he would, but he lowered himself to the concrete floor a few feet away.

"I'm glad you came," she said. "I wanted to talk to you again."
She waited, but he didn't look up at her or reply.

"Are you going to talk to me?" she tried gently. There was a long
pause, then he nodded, still looking away. She felt a mild flare of
exasperation. "That wasn't talking," she told him, hoping that the
amusement in her voice covered her anxiety.

In the silence that followed he seemed to hunch his shoulders
slightly. Then finally he answered in a low voice.

"I don't know what to say."

She felt a rush of relief. Of course he didn't know how to make
conversation. She considered it a little.

"Often the best thing to do is to ask the other person a question
and get them to do the talking," she told him. "And that works pretty
well with me—once I'm going the trouble is getting me to stop."

She still couldn't read any expression on his face. What was he
thinking? How did he feel? She was intensely curious about him, but
asking "what is it like to be you?" was pointless.

"Ask me a question," she told him. He sat in silence for a long
time, his eyes sliding nervously around the room, but she held her
tongue and waited him out. Finally he spoke tentatively.

"I wondered why you live here."

She smothered a sigh. It was a good question.

"Because I'm too cretting stubborn for my own good. I should
ask Toni if I can move upstairs with her, but I don't think she really
wants me there, and anyway, I guess I was trying to prove my in-
dependence. I've never lived by myself before, you know."

She glanced his way again, wondering how much of what she'd
said made any sense to him. She sipped some cider, then looked over
at him. Simon was drinking, too; then it hit her that he'd been copying her all along, drinking every time she did. It was too eerie to be
funny.

"How did you get in here, Simon?"

He gestured to the other side of the floor.

"From the balcony."

She lifted her eyebrows in astonishment, thinking of the tiny
ledges, no more than thirty-five centimeters wide, edged with rotting
concrete rails. She was afraid to step on them.

"You climbed up the outside of the building?"

"Down," he said.

He must have swung down from the floor above. As she pictured it, her incredulity faded into fear. So much for her ideas about security. It was time to swallow her pride, apologize humbly to Toni and then ask to roll out in her study. The thought made her wince, remembering how she'd yelled at Toni. And the twenty-first floor had balconies, too.

Her fear brought back memories of the grain hold, and then of the risks that Simon had taken to find her. She glanced over to where he sat looking at his mug in silence.

"Thank you for coming to find me, Simon," she told him softly. "I could have died."

He showed no response at all, and she studied him uneasily.

"You do understand why I'm thanking you?"

A pause, then, "No."

She frowned, trying to figure out what it was that he didn't understand. Talking to a space alien would be like this, she thought, glancing at his smooth, eerie face. Finally, she tried: "Why did you come looking for me?"

"Toni told me to," he answered immediately.

"That was the only reason?" she asked, trying to keep the sudden hurt out of her voice.

"Yes."

His voice was flat, completely factual. She stared at him unhappily for a few seconds, then looked away, unsure what to think. He sounded cold, but then he had helped her those other times—when he'd walked her home, and when he'd lifted her out of the pool. Toni couldn't have given him all those orders. Could he be afraid to admit how he felt?

"Why did you come tonight?" she asked.

"You said to come."

"No other reason?"

This time there was a long pause, then, hesitantly: "I . . . thought about you."

This time she heard the shame and longing in his voice.

"I've been thinking about you, too, Simon," she told him warmly, leaning forward and trying to reach out with her voice, but he wouldn't meet her gaze. "Why won't you look at me?"

His voice was so low she could barely hear him.

"You don't like to look at Blade. He's ugly."

Klale felt a twinge of guilt as she realized that she had indeed been avoiding his face. Its stretched blankness always disturbed her and the grooves burned into his forehead were so appalling that she kept moving her eyes to his hands or looking around the room. It must have felt much safer for him in the dark, she realized. She thought for a few seconds, then got up and blew out the candles, leaving only one burning by her bed. She walked back to where he sat and kneeled, wanting to reach out, but still uncertain.

"Is that better?"

His eyes flicked past hers, seeming surprised, then he gave a tiny, tense nod.

"Simon, I won't tell anybody you talked to me. I don't want to cause you smog. I just wanted to talk to you because . . . well, I felt drawn to you."

She drew in a nervous breath, but forced herself to continue, realizing that her fear was ebbing. She urgently wanted to reach out and comfort him—and to take comfort herself. She had felt marvelously safe with his arms wrapped around her.

"When we touched in the dark you were so different than I expected, so gentle." She moved forward very slowly and put her hand on his arm. "You didn't feel ugly or hard or frightening, and I realized that there was a very wonderful person in there. You're not ugly inside, Simon. I think you're beautiful."

Even seated his size was intimidating, but she focused on how he'd been in the hold and summoned up the nerve to lean forward and kiss him lightly on the lips.

She pulled back. Simon hadn't moved. But the feel and smell of him sent heat surging through her own body. She remembered how his hands had stroked her hair in the cargo hold. How would he feel between her legs, pushing inside of her? The shocking thought gave her such a rush of excitement that she felt almost dizzy. She wanted to make love with him, she realized—and do it properly. Simon wouldn't know or care about Guild morality. And she didn't need to care anymore either. Ironically, she now had a freedom she'd never had before.

But there was still no response from Simon, and she pulled back doubtfully. It was a tilted idea. Hell, maybe he didn't even want her. But, then why had he kissed her? And why had he come here to talk to her again?

Well, if she wanted to know she would have to ask. Certainly dropping hints wouldn't do her any good. Grinning a little at that thought, she reached for his hand and then tried to catch his eye.

"Simon? When we were in the cargo hold, I wanted to make love with you. Did you want that, too?"

He looked straight at her with a flash of unmistakable shock, then dropped his eyes and shook his head. She felt a stab of dismay.

"Why not?"

He glanced past her again, and she actually saw the faint furrow of a frown above the bridge of his nose.

"Why?" she repeated.

He answered flatly.

"Tools don't make love. Only people."

Klale stared at him in dawning horror as his meaning sank in. Toni had told her that tools didn't know they were human, and it was literally true. The man sitting in front of her really thought he was something different—some sort of object. All the people he'd seen around the 'Dyke, the whores, the strips, the sex acts on stage, must have meant nothing to him. It was something humans did. Not tools. Never Simon.

She sat back, sickened by his degradation. How would it feel never to be touched? The misery in his voice ignited a responding ache inside her. She wanted to reach into him, to pour herself into that loneliness.

Damn it, he must be able to make love! She reached over and squeezed his hand.

"Simon, that night we were in the hold, what did we do?"

His breathing quickened.

"You touched me." His voice dropped to a whisper. "You kissed me."

"Would you like me to do that again?"

His eyes widened slightly and flicked past hers, then she heard a barely audible: "Yes."

She moved forward again and kissed him gently. He winced and closed his eyes with an abrupt intake of breath. He wanted her, all right, but he couldn't ask. She looked at him for long seconds, then came to a decision. She sat back on her heels, then stood up and began unbuttoning her shirt before she could entertain second thoughts.

"Take your clothes off," she ordered.

His gaze snapped up to hers and he froze fearfully for long seconds. She saw a struggle in his eyes. Then he rose very slowly, removed his serape, and began to unfasten his own shirt. When hers dropped to the floor, his followed.

Underneath the shirt was his knife holster, and he fingered the straps uncertainly. She felt a catch of fear in her throat but made her voice firm.

"Everything."

He hesitated an instant, then began pulling it off. Equipment belts followed with a heavy thud. Klale sat down to take off her shoes and socks. She still had Toni's phone, she realized, so she called up some favorite soft music and set it on the floor by her bed. The tiny speakers gave poor sound, but it was the best she could do. Simon's pants hit the floor, and she glanced up self consciously, then froze, aghast. There was nothing between his legs. Nothing at all. His crotch was as smoothly naked as the rest of his body.

She looked away in sick horror. He was castrated. That explained the nipples—they'd been removed, too. Suddenly some of Bracken's acid jokes made horrible sense. And Simon's words. Tools didn't make love. They couldn't.

She was shivering in the raw air, and she made herself straighten up, hoping that he hadn't seen the horror on her face. Simon stood naked, eyes downcast. He seemed ashamed.

Klale wondered frantically what to do. This was a hell of a time to be in a jammed building—she couldn't even fall back on grabbing the phone for a fast research call. Were castrated men capable of . . . anything? Well, orgasm was a brain function. And it seemed as if he could be aroused. But wouldn't he need neural stimulus to reach a climax? And what if touching her just made him more and more frustrated until he became violent?

When he moved forward, she flinched back, but he only took one step then kneeled down and sat back on his heels so that he was lower than she was. He bowed his head.

The gesture reassured her. He didn't hurt you before, she reminded herself. She swallowed hard, then stepped toward him and lifted one of his hands, trying to concentrate on what she knew. He wanted to be touched. She could certainly do that much for him. And maybe it would be enough.

There were goose-bumps on her pale arms and breasts, but heat radiated from Simon's skin. She cupped his hand around her face, holding it until he began to move it of his own accord, just like before. Then she caressed his muscular back. His hairless skin felt like warm, toffee-colored silk, except for pale, rubbery splashes of old scar tissue and a recent scar, still red and scabbed over. Her hands traveled over his shoulders to the back of his neck.

Simon jerked violently, and sprang backward. She jumped, too, then cursed silently over her pounding heart. Damn!

"Simon?" she asked anxiously, as soon as she could manage her voice.

He was huddled against the wall, breathing in gasps, with one arm wrapped tightly across his chest and the other clutched protectively around the back of his head. The hempboard bowed backward, shaking where he leaned against it. She stood very still.

"Simon, I'm sorry! I didn't know that I shouldn't touch you there. I won't do it again."

She watched a few seconds, feeling her own fear dissolve into pity as he struggled with stark terror. That must have been near the fishhook or the plug that was used for torture—no wonder he was afraid. And how desperately he must need her touch to take such risks. She was probably tilted to be doing it, but she couldn't stop now.

"Simon?" His breathing was easing a little, so she moved forward very cautiously, then kneeled in front him and rested her hand on top of his knee. "I'm so sorry. But I'll remember. I won't do it again."

He didn't answer, but he seemed to be calming down, so after a little while she reached for his face. Using both hands this time, she pressed her fingers along the ridges above his eyes, stroking across and down along his nose and cheeks. She hesitated at his forehead, unwilling to touch the grotesque brand, then stroked the skin on either side of it. Finally she put her hands on his cheeks, leaned forward, and kissed him very softly on his eyelids. When she drew back, he opened his eyes and stared directly at her in astonishment.

"Are you better now?"

He nodded. He seemed dazed.

"All right. We're going to touch each other, Simon. I'll show you how." She reached out with her index finger and brushed his lips. "It's important to touch everywhere. With our fingers, our hands, our lips, our tongues, with our whole bodies. It's like . . ." She groped for words to express it, then whispered: "It's like dancing."

She took his hand and led him to the bed, then told him to lie on his side and joined him, pulling the cover over on top of them. She had turned on the heating panels earlier and it felt deliciously warm against her skin.

This time Klale showed Simon how to caress her, guiding his hands until he moved of his own accord. The skin on his palms was rough, but he touched her with wonderful gentleness. And she could see his mouth moving. He was beginning to smile. She watched in delight, then impulsively leaned forward, touched his cheek and grinned at him. He looked at her, then ducked his eyes away, but his face opened into a wide, astonishing smile that took her breath away.

It was her turn to feel dazed. He was stroking her in time to the music she realized, and she reached back to turn it up. For a little while she lay basking in delicious surges of arousal and watching his motions in the dim light, then she reached out and began touching him.

With her first stroke Simon dropped his hands in complete distraction. When she ran her hand lightly over his chest he gasped in almost comical amazement, then he started to whimper. His muscular body felt delightfully sensuous. She kept her hand moving slowly downward and, forcing back her revulsion, caressed even the sexless space between his legs. He had a normal anus and a tiny bump with a plastic valve inserted in it that must be his urethra, but other than that his crotch felt smooth. Not even a scar.

He closed his eyes occasionally, then opened them to watch her hands with astonished wonder, as if he had never imagined anything like her touch. She hadn't intended to arouse either of them so much, but the intensity of his response intoxicated her. When she ran her hands over his ribcage, she felt as if she was reaching right into his heart, and she found herself responding to this utter defenselessness by opening herself up. She had intended to give her love to him, but as they began kissing again she realized that she was also more naked that she had ever been before.

A favorite movement of Bach began and she hummed along. She licked Simon's undamaged earlobe and he shuddered. On impulse she pushed him onto his back and climbed on top, lying full length against him and sucking on his lips. His head jerked back, he moaned, and she felt spasms begin. She slid against his sweat-slippery chest, clinging to him in a tumult of kissing and whispering and crying, suddenly awash with her own need and loneliness. When his urgency eased she grabbed his fingers and guided them inside of her, riding frenziedly against them and then collapsing in waves of release.

Much later she rolled off drowsily and showed him how to spoon around her. She fell asleep hugging his arm against her breasts.

24

Simon lay on his side in the dark, Toni's Klale asleep against him. Her soft skin pressed against his legs and stomach and chest. He could feel the slow swell of her lungs and warm gusts of breath against his arm. She smelled of salt and sweat—hers and his.

He inhaled very gently so as not to disturb her, amazed at the feel of her body and the sensations in himself. Klale had said it was like dancing, but this aching joy felt different. He had never imagined anything like it. That Klale had slid her moist, hot tongue across his skin astounded him; that she would whisper "I love you, Simon" went beyond comprehension. Somehow she'd reached into Blade and pulled out Simon; made him visible, tangible, audible. He felt as supple and alive as he did when he danced, but his stomach glowed with a deep wonderful pain that he didn't want to stop.

He felt astonishingly aware, too. Each sound and sensation seemed magnified, and his thoughts had an unnatural clarity. Despite the warmth under the thick cover, he wasn't drowsy, so it was easy to keep from falling asleep. That was forbidden.

He pushed that thought away quickly and concentrated on Klale. For a long time he simply lay still, feeling her sleep, smelling her, listening to her—trying to absorb every detail. She was so beautiful. And she was Toni's. He was touching Toni.

He had a sudden memory of Toni's limp, bleeding weight in his arms, then an image of Klale being beaten—her flesh ripped open, and the life in her eyes stamped out. And he felt a searing flash of Blade's wrath that nearly engulfed him.

Klale whimpered in her sleep and wriggled. He had clenched his arm against her ribs. He relaxed it, then closed his eyes and concentrated on pushing the anger away. It didn't belong to Simon. Simon didn't get angry. Simon didn't hurt people.

But he might.

The thought hit him with sudden certainty, and he examined it with alarm. Was Klale in danger from him? If he hurt Klale, that would upset Toni. And if Simon was dangerous . . . He also might harm Toni.

He moved away from Klale, untangling himself very carefully until she lay alone in the bed. He pulled the cover up to her shoulders, then kneeled, studying her in the flickering candlelight. Her hair lay tangled and her mouth had fallen partly open. At last he turned and stepped silently to his clothes, then began to put them on. They seemed strangely rough against his skin.

When he was dressed he looked around for a place to think. There wasn't much room. He seated himself, lotus style, near the balcony and concentrated on centering himself as if he were ready to begin tai ji. The intense pleasure had faded, but lingering chords still echoed through his body. He slowed his breathing and began to clear his mind. In this dance he kept still and let the universe weave around him. A cool draft lapped against his skin. It carried distant, muffled sounds from outside—traffic, shouting, a ship's horn in the harbor. He drew air into his nose and let it swirl through his lungs, becoming part of him.

When he floated deep in the pool of stillness he focused on the problem. How could he be sure not to hurt Toni? Immediately the outline of the answer appeared. Simon couldn't look at it, and even through the trance he felt a strong tremor of refusal. It wasn't possible for him to do this. Blade would have to do it. Blade could act without emotion or understanding, and once set in motion he was unstoppable.

Simon focused on the candlelight fluttering against the wall and deepened his hypnotic state. Then, very carefully and deliberately, he moved outside of his body and began to take each piece of the answer and strip the meaning from it.

"Blade does not think. Blade is stone. Blade will walk across the room. Blade will go out the door. Blade will walk up the stairway . . ."

He rehearsed the choreography from start to finish several times. When it was drawn inside of him like a many-stroked character, he closed his eyes and called Blade.

25

Klale reached sleepily behind her for Simon's warm presence, but the bed was cold and empty. Her blooming delight crashed into disappointment and she forced open her eyes, then realized with a rush of relief that he was still there, sitting lotus near the window with his eyes closed.

She studied him with a fascination that faded into unease. He didn't seem threatening—in fact, in the shadowy half light he reminded her of the Buddhist monk who sat at the corner of Davie and Nicola. But he had become remote again. She wanted to go over and put her arms around him, to reassure herself that he felt warm and human, but she lay where she was, unwilling to disturb his meditation. Then, without warning, Simon rose.

Klale smiled and held out her hand, but his eyes grazed right over her, and he walked toward the door. She froze, suddenly frightened by his heavy, stiff movements. He moved like Blade in the bar, not like the man who'd just made love with her. Had he received an order from Choi? But that shouldn't be possible here—the jamming field was too strong inside the building.

She lay still as he walked past, then turned to watch. His serape lay in a heap near her bed and he didn't stop for it. That was wrong! He never went anywhere without it. With a sudden sense of dread, she rolled out of her bed, threw on her shirt, and followed him, scooping up the serape on impulse and then staggering under its unexpected weight.

Out in the hall, a slice of light from the east stairwell narrowed, then vanished as the door thumped shut. Klale ran across the rough concrete in her bare feet, pulled the door open, then stood on her toes on the cold landing and eased it silently closed. She turned to start down the staircase but the sound of Simon's footsteps echoed from above. He was going up to Toni's!

Klale ran up the stairs, grabbing the railing to help her speed around corners and praying she wouldn't step on anything sharp. On the twentieth floor landing she slowed, wondering what Simon would do at Toni's security door, then she heard the familiar click of the latch sliding back. He'd opened it! Two seconds later it shut.

She waited at that door for a count of fifteen before entering her passcode, then she opened it a crack to peer through. The hall was empty, and Toni's inner door stood open. Klale slipped inside and padded down the hallway hugging her shirt tighter around her and trying to quiet her uneven breathing. The apartment was dark and silent. She hesitated, straining to see. A shadow moved against the window and she glimpsed Simon walking away from Toni's bedroom. Several seconds later the study door closed, and a crack of light appeared along the floor.

Klale looked uncertainly toward the study, then hurried to Toni's bedroom and peered inside. A familiar mound lay in the bed, snoring gently. With a last check over her shoulder, Klale pulled the door shut behind her and kneeled down to shake Toni awake.

Toni came awake with a jolt and struck out, and Klale ducked backward, barely escaping the blow.

"It's me!" she whispered urgently, scrambling to her knees again.

"Klale? What . . . ?"

"Shhh! Simon's in your study."

"What?" Klale had been wondering if Toni expected this visit, but her voice sounded shocked. "How did he get in?"

"Through the door. I think he had the code."

"Shit!"

Toni sounded frightened and Klale felt her own fear intensify. Toni grabbed her bathrobe and rose quickly. She was halfway to the bedroom door when a horrific scream ripped from the study. Klale froze in sudden terror, but Toni ran forward. The scream didn't end. Klale ran after her.

Simon writhed in the office chair, face contorted with agony. Veins bulged on his neck and face, and his high-pitched screams tore at Klale's ears. As she reached the doorway, the chair slid out from under his convulsing body and he spilled heavily onto the parquet floor. His arm slammed into a bookcase, then one flailing leg sent the chair splintering against a wall. Toni shouted in Klale's ear.

"We have to turn him onto his stomach. When I signal, grab his left arm and drag it over as hard as you can."

Simon's chest heaved as he started to vomit. Klale stepped forward fearfully and focused on Toni's instructions. On the third try they managed to catch Simon's arm and used his own flailing strength to start the roll, then Toni switched sides quickly and heaved at his back. He went over. She grabbed his other arm with swift expertise and pulled it out from underneath him. Then she ran for the kitchen.

Klale stood paralyzed, Simon's screams tearing at every nerve. Her instincts shrieked at her to do something—anything—to make it stop, but she didn't know what to do. Where was Toni? She clenched her hands and bounced on her feet as agonizing seconds stretched out, then Toni ran back in clutching a medkit and her phone. She checked the readout.

"About twenty seconds so far, I think," she said. Klale grabbed her arm frantically.

"Do something!"

"If I do something, it might kill him," Toni told her harshly. "If we wait, the signal may shut off automatically." She shoved at Klale's shoulder. "Get out of here. Put your hands over your ears."

"No!"

Klale wanted to flee, but Simon's torment kept her rooted there, half crazed. She turned her back on him, her muscles clenched with frantic tension, and fixed her eyes on Toni. Toni muttered, and Klale strained to make out the words—anything for a distraction.

"Punishment is usually set in increments of five seconds. There should be an automatic cut-off . . . Thirty. *Goddamn!* If it doesn't stop in one minute, it won't."

Simon's limbs pounded with mindless force against the parquet floor. It was everything Klale could do not to hit Toni and scream at her to help him. Toni kneeled and opened the medkit. Klale dropped down beside her.

"Narc him!"

"Useless." Toni fumbled in the box, then dumped it on the floor and started pawing through the contents. "Where in hell is that thing I took off Bracken? There!" She pulled out a short metal tube which looked oddly familiar, then glanced back at the readout.

"Forty-six . . ."

Klale rocked from side to side, then darted a glance backward. Blood splattered against the floor and wall.

"Fifty-eight . . . Fifty-nine . . . Sixty. *Mierda!* Cur-fucking bastard!"

Toni shoved her phone aside, took several swift steps and jumped astride Simon's thrashing back. She grabbed his neck, probed with sure fingers, then moved the tube into position and pressed it hard against the base of his skull.

Nothing happened.

She yelled at Klale without looking up.

"Pass me the phone!"

Klale dived for it clumsily, barely able to grasp the small device and shove it at Toni.

Toni gripped Simon's rib cage with her knees to keep her balance and clamped the metal tube between her teeth to free her hands. She flipped the phone over and tore off the back panel, then clawed at the power supply recess with mounting frustration. Finally she leaned sideways and smashed the phone hard against the floor. Metal and plastiche fragments skidded across the polished wood and the power pack bounced loose. She grabbed it.

She pulled the cylinder out of her mouth, twisted it, then snapped it into position against the power pack. Klale finally remembered where she'd seen that cylinder before—in the smut shop. It was a booster. Toni leaned over Simon again and pressed the new assembly against his skull.

This time Klale saw a galvanic jolt travel through Simon's body and his voice cut off abruptly in mid scream. In the sudden silence

Klale realized that she was wailing herself, and stuffed a hand against her mouth. Toni pulled the booster away but Simon didn't move. Was he dead? There was a ringing silence of several seconds, then he shuddered and began to choke out horrible scraping sobs. Toni pressed her fingers against his neck, checking his pulse, and Klale saw her let out a deep breath.

"Got it," she muttered, and stood up, staggering a little as she moved away from him. The whole length of Simon's body still jerked with aftershocks and retching. Klale smelled feces and urine. Toni tossed the booster on the desk and put out a reassuring hand, which abruptly became a grab when Klale started toward Simon.

"Don't go near him," she warned sharply. "I don't know what he'll do next."

Klale was about to argue when she realized that the room was swaying. She was going to throw up, too. Toni saw it in her face and shoved her toward the bathroom. Klale ran unsteadily, getting there just in time to expel the little that was in her stomach. For several long moments she just knelt, hanging onto the toilet and shaking, with one horrible thought spinning through her head again and again. "This was my fault."

She didn't want to go back into that room. She didn't want to face what had happened to Simon. But she forced herself to get up, wash her face, and then walk, watery-kneed, to the study.

Toni stood in the doorway, her face very hard. On the floor, Simon had stopped thrashing. He raised himself up on one elbow, then struggled painfully to his knees. His breath still came in gasps and blood gouted from his nose.

Klale stepped forward, but Toni pushed her back, then placed a warning finger across her mouth. Simon's face was changing. The twisted muscles were slackening. An occasional twitch, like a reflex, made them clench, but his expression was becoming horribly, utterly blank.

"He's turning off all reactions," Toni whispered tensely. "It gets him back under control fast and prevents him from going catatonic. It also makes him extremely dangerous." She pulled her hand cautiously away from Klale. Klale stayed still.

Remembering how hard Simon had pounded the floor, Klale was

surprised he could stand, but he clambered to his feet. Toni pulled back into the living room and he followed, swaying as if his knees might buckle, then stopped and clutched the door frame, staring about in confusion. Toni Slanged and pointed to the bathroom. After several long seconds he limped in that direction.

"Stay here," said Toni, shoving Klale onto the couch. Klale stayed while Toni followed. A minute crawled by, then another, then she heard running water and a whispered curse from Toni, who was watching through the bathroom door. Toni turned and went to the kitchen, rummaged in a cupboard, then went back to the bathroom with a pail and a sponge. There was another endless wait. Klale pulled her icy feet up underneath her, and wrapped her arms around her knees to muffle her own shivering. She was too upset to think straight or to do anything—even to cry. Finally Toni backed into the room, and Simon came out after her, his shirt and pants hanging wet against him. He walked toward the study carrying the bowl and sponge. Toni watched him, then joined Klale at the couch.

"He's been taught to clean up after himself," she told Klale, in a low voice that cracked with anger. "How very sensible."

Klale reached up and grasped her hand. Toni took it, but her attention was riveted on the study door. Finally she sat, poised uncomfortably on the arm of the couch.

"No point staring at him. I'm just one more unfamiliar distraction. But if he doesn't come out in ten minutes . . ."

"What happened?" asked Klale in a low voice.

"I would guess that he disobeyed a primary instruction. That was punishment—direct full strength stimulus to the pain center."

"But . . . what about the jammer? How . . . ?"

"It's an automatic function."

"You mean the neural plug monitors everything he does?" Klale asked in dawning horror.

"Oh no," said Toni, her voice savage. "It's much simpler than that. If you train a person extensively enough, especially if you start them young, you can make punishment triggers work like a guilt reflex. He's probably trained to start the punishment himself, subconsciously, if he disobeys certain orders. It's very effective."

She paused, and, for a second, weariness and grief showed through her anger.

"He wouldn't know that, Klale. He may have taken a risk, thinking that the jamming field here would prevent him from being punished. Unfortunately, what it did prevent was the cut-off signal; either that or the automatic one malfunctioned. I tried knocking it out with a power surge and got lucky, but I had to use a big jolt. I may have burned out the chip and caused neural damage—I don't know how much." Her fingernails dug into Klale's hand. "I wish I knew what the hell he did to cause this."

Klale made herself force out the words: "It was me."

"You?" Toni looked at her, seeming for the first time to notice her appearance. Klale felt tears welling in her eyes and Toni put a reassuring hand on her shoulder, taking on an air of controlled calm.

"What happened?"

"I asked him to talk to me. He came to my apartment. We made love."

"You . . . !" Toni gaped in astonishment, then collected herself. "Was that just now?"

"I don't know," Klale said, fighting to keep her thoughts in some sort of rational order. "I fell asleep afterward. When I woke up he was coming here. I followed him."

"But he was all right before that?"

She nodded.

"Then you didn't trigger the punishment, Klale. It would start instantly when he broke a command."

"But I didn't know!" she told Toni urgently. "I didn't think . . . Oh God . . ."

"Shhh," said Toni, reaching out, and Klale pressed her face against Toni's dressing gown, trying to find refuge from her sick horror. She'd heard of torture, of course, but she'd never seen it—never even seriously imagined it. The reality was devastating. And she couldn't shake the certainty that she'd somehow caused it.

Toni stiffened and pushed her away as Simon emerged, heading back to the bathroom. Klale heard Simon empty the pail, then he came back out and walked to the center of the room. His feet dragged, and his face looked appallingly empty. Klale could see no trace of intelligence or personality—nothing of the man who had smiled when she caressed him. He looked broken. He stopped in the middle of the room, clasping his hands behind his back, then kneeled heavily and bent forward until his forehead touched the floor. On his skull, near the back of his neck, Klale saw a circular red burn, like a coin.

She stared at his abasement, remembering how he had kneeled before her only a few hours before. At the time she'd been touched. Now, thinking about it made her sick.

There was a long silence. Finally Klale looked over at Toni and discovered her staring at Simon, tight-faced. She doesn't know what to do, realized Klale with a stab of terror.

"Toni?" she whispered.

"I'm thinking!" hissed Toni, then clenched her hands and closed her eyes for a second. "I've got to get him out of here fast, but I don't know how to give him orders when he's in this state, or even if I can! But I have to try something."

She took a long, deep breath, then moved directly in front of the prostrated man.

"Get up!" she said loudly. Klale flinched, but Simon gave no response. Toni waited a few seconds, then shouted the order. Still no result.

She nudged Simon's shoulder roughly with her foot. Klale caught her breath, but Simon didn't move. Toni leaned over and grabbed the back of his shirt, then scooped her hand under his chin and yanked his head up until she could see his eyes.

"*Sit*"

Klale vibrated with fresh terror for a long second, then Simon raised himself slowly to his knees.

"*Stand!*" ordered Toni. She stood in front of him with crossed arms, showing no sign of impatience or fear. God, she has iron self-control, thought Klale.

Simon staggered up, towering over Toni.

She signed: "Leave."

He turned very slowly and limped heavily toward the door with Toni following a few paces behind. Klale watched, then her eyes fell on Simon's serape lying at the door to Toni's bedroom, where she'd dropped it.

"Toni!" she whispered urgently. Toni looked around and Klale pointed. Toni lunged over and scooped up the serape, then shoved it at Simon who clutched it automatically. Klale closed her eyes in dizzy relief. She hated the thought of Simon leaving when he was injured, but she couldn't face him either. It was as if he wasn't really Simon anymore—as if he had become something monstrous.

Toni came back in, shut the door behind her, and leaned against it, then spoke in a flat voice.

"If our luck holds, nobody will see him come out of the building, and Choi won't be able to trace him back here." Abruptly she straightened. "I wonder if he left anything."

She went to the study and Klale forced herself up off the couch to follow. The floor was clean, but the room still smelled acridly of vomit and human waste, and Simon had gouged savage scars and dents in the shiny parquet finish. Toni looked down at the floor, her eyes bright with anger, then crossed the room and rammed open the sliding window.

Simon had picked up everything, though he hadn't remembered where it went. The bookcase stood in the wrong place. The broken chair was piled neatly in front of the desk, which had been pushed askew from its usual position. The netset on it, fortunately, looked undamaged. Toni waved it awake and the display lit up with a line of type. They both leaned forward. It looked like a math formula, thought Klale.

"I think it's some kind of fluctuating signal," said Toni, frowning. She asked the set to graph it and a complex wave pattern flashed up. "Could be a passcode of some kind, but I don't know what. I was never any good at telcomm stuff. Do you know?"

Klale shook her head.

"Sorry, no."

"Damn!" said Toni tightly. "It's got to be important." She stared at it a few seconds longer then shook her head and began digging around in the desk. She found a piece of paper and painstakingly wrote down the equation, proofreading it twice and having Klale check it, too. Then she wiped the screen.

"You didn't save it!" said Klale anxiously.

"Of course I did," said Toni, waving the paper. "But nobody looks for data in hard copy—or at least they don't look there first." She paused with her hand on the netset, then looked up at Klale and asked her to go to the kitchen and make tea. When Klale left, she was placing a call.

Make tea, Klale told herself. She stood in the kitchen staring blankly at the counter. She couldn't remember what to do. Her hands and feet felt like ice and she was shivering so hard that her teeth chattered. Toni came back out, looking distracted, then abruptly took a close look at her, moved her aside and began heating water. Klale tried to apologize, then gave up and simply stood watching until Toni towed her into the bedroom, sat her down under the blankets with a warming pad, and handed her a drink. She was still shaking so much that Toni had to help her hold the cup. Hot tea flowed into her mouth. It tasted of liquor. Klale's muscles slowly began to relax as the warmth from the bed and the drink penetrated. Toni left her alone and finished in the kitchen, then climbed in beside her with a steaming mug of her own.

"Toni?" One painful question kept circling in Klale's head and she had to know the answer. She forced the words out. "You were never a trainer . . . were you?

"I was a behavioral therapist, Klale. I did my doctorate at the University of Chicago. I'll tell you about it . . . another time."

"Oh." Klale felt a great rush of relief, with an undercurrent of embarrassment. She should have trusted Toni more. "How . . . how badly is he hurt?"

Toni took a long sip before answering.

"Neural scarring and extensive memory loss, at the least. Of course, that's not all bad. Choi may never piece together what happened."

Klale tried to digest that with a brain that felt like it was wrapped in wet towels, then remembered something she'd wondered during their love-making. It seemed like years ago now.

"Could his plug be removed?"

"For all the difference it makes," said Toni shortly, then looked at Klale and visibly summoned up more patience. "Plugs are just surface junctions, Klale. Here." She took Klale's finger in her hand, and pressed it up against the skin-art on the back of her skull. At first Klale noticed nothing, then she felt a round dent in the bone, like a tiny, shallow meteor crater.

"That's all?"

"They're small. What you're feeling is the recessed microchip seat, and a slight calcium buildup around the edge which is typical in people who have plugs implanted before they stop growing." She dropped Klale's hand.

"The plug connects a controller chip to radiating filaments that penetrate the brain tissue. Complex data transfer is done via an infrared Davidson sensor placed on the skin over the plug site. Simple signals can be broadcast. Plugs and filaments can be removed, but the real problem, Klale, is the behaviors they were used to create. They become so imprinted in the brain chemistry that they're virtually unchangeable."

"Oh," said Klale weakly, then her tears finally broke through. Toni took her cup and put it down, then held her with unexpected fierceness.

"Did you . . . Did you know that he's castrated?" whispered Klale after a while.

"It's standard practice, Klale."

"That's horrible! I just can't believe . . . He was so sweet and gentle, Toni. So vulnerable."

"Yeah." Toni's voice was savage. "Vulnerability is what it's all about. You rip them open and then rearrange their minds and souls to your specifications." Toni's fingers dug painfully into Klale's shoulder, then her grip loosened.

"Klale, could you describe exactly what happened in your apartment?"

Klale swallowed the trailing edges of her tears and recounted every detail she could remember. When she finished, Toni sat staring unseeingly across the room.

"What happened?" Klale prodded finally.

Toni pulled her thoughts back.

"It sounds like he used self-hypnosis to make himself break a command. In a sense it's not surprising—he's an expert at it. Nobody

is hypnotized by another person, you know—you do it to yourself."
She glanced over at Klale, who nodded. She knew the basics from
school.

"What Simon did—it's like jumping off a cliff," continued Toni.
"I couldn't jump if I thought about it, but if I could convince myself
that I was just going to take a little walk ahead and not look under
my feet, it would be quite simple." Then she looked away and added
in a very quiet voice: "I'm amazed he managed it, though. For someone who's undergone torture, it took astonishing courage."

Klale felt another stab of remorse.

"I ordered him to touch me," she confessed. "I treated him like
a tool, didn't I?"

"No, Klale," said Toni softly. "You made a mistake, that's all. And
it's partly my fault. I should have told you more about him, but I
was hoping you'd stay away." She let out a small sigh. "I should have
known better."

Klale focused on her pleadingly.

"Toni, we have to help him!"

Toni stiffened.

"I'm doing what I can, Klale, but it's extremely dangerous. I don't
want you involved."

"I have to be part of this," she said simply. Then: "I love him."

Toni closed her eyes, then spoke with deep weariness.

"Klale, please believe me—I do understand how you feel. Simon
has a deep childlike neediness that brings out all your protective
instincts. But you must understand that it's futile. Everything you
could possibly give him wouldn't be enough. Simon can't be healed.
You're going to have to learn detachment or he'll crawl inside you
and tear your heart out, and it won't change anything."

Klale lay still, letting the tears leak out of her eyes, then whispered: "Yes it will. It has to."

26

Toni couldn't sleep. The sounds and smells of Simon's punishment had unleashed a flood of bitter memories from the wards. Simon's was the worst punishment she'd ever seen. Automatic sequences were almost always less than thirty seconds. Longer punishments didn't accomplish more and they greatly increased the risk of permanent neural damage or heart failure.

She turned over again. Klale lay asleep beside her, and Toni listened to her breathing for a while, envying her resilience. The girl had an astonishing ability to bounce back, but her earlier recklessness was nothing short of dumbfounding. Toni wasn't sure what was more incredible—that Klale had even contemplated making love to a tool, or that Simon had been able to tolerate it. It was yet one more wild incongruity in his behavior—and one more sign, she admitted to herself, that he might be salvageable.

She shifted restlessly, then afraid she would wake Klale, she got up quietly, put on her robe, and went into the lighted living room. Neither of them had felt like leaving the apartment dark. She made herself another cup of tea, then on impulse, sat down at the table, logged into her set, and reran Simon's dance sequence.

This was the fourth time she'd reviewed it in detail, and she felt certain now that a few of his complex positions had some significance, but she had no idea what. She had cross-referenced his stances to tai ji and other martial arts, but she couldn't find an exact match.

And she knew so little about dance that she couldn't even start research in that direction. It was frustrating. If he had deliberately or subconsciously included a message in his dance, she had no way of reading it.

A sudden vivid memory of Simon writhing on her floor hit her, and she ended the replay abruptly, pulling off the headset. Thank God she'd remembered that old junkie trick. Simon could have suffered in agony for hours until his heart gave out. As it was, the punishment would throw him deeply back into his conditioned responses and might even erase all the progress she'd made. And in the meantime, Choi's suspicion would logically fall on Toni.

The netset chimed and Toni flinched so violently that she knocked over her empty mug. She closed her eyes, took a deep breath, then checked the call source. When she saw Doc's name, she felt a wave of relief. She slipped on her headset.

"Can't get there for fifteen minutes," he said. His voice sounded gravelly and he looked haggard. There was a dirty concrete wall behind him—could be anywhere.

"It wasn't a medical call," she told him. "I just had a question."

He stared at her incredulously, then his face darkened with outrage.

"You called my emergency number at five in the morning to ask me a question?"

"Yeah. Call me back, silent channel."

Toni cut her signal and waited, picturing Doc's face as he swore at his phone. It would take him some time to find a quiet place and then get an untraced connect. Of course, no calls Downtown were completely safe, but it improved the odds.

In fact, it only took him about two minutes. This time he called voice-only.

"What in Hades do you want?"

"What would somebody use a complex fluctuating signal for?"

There was a very long pause in which he must have debated cutting her off. Finally he responded in an acerbic tone.

"Even without a medical license, I'm reluctant to offer my opinion on a telcomm problem."

"Humor me."

His sigh crackled from her speakers.

"Very well. Could you describe the symptoms in more detail?"

Toni had taken the paper out from its hiding place. She read off the formula, changing several digits. There was another short pause.

"Hmm. I believe that could easily be broadcast on any standard phone, so in this cozy neighborhood it could have a plethora of uses. A security lock override, perhaps. Or silent access for a custom set."

Toni frowned. That didn't seem right. Of course she didn't know what she was looking for, but she had the feeling that she'd recognize it when she heard it. Finally she gave a frustrated sigh and began to apologize, but he interrupted abruptly: "Fishhook code."

That was it!—the signal that triggered Simon's explosive implant. Toni closed her eyes, and swore under her breath.

She hadn't intended the words to carry, but Doc must have heard.

"Toni. If this involves what I think it does . . ." He hesitated, then said harshly: "My advice is to use it fast—while you still can."

The channel went dead.

Toni stared blindly toward the windows, remembering the last tool she'd worked on. He'd been utterly unresponsive to treatment and every time they released him from restraints he'd started smashing his head against the nearest wall. They'd had to keep him strapped down on intravenous for months waiting for euthanasia approval to come through. Toni had administered the dosage herself and held onto him while he died, then she had gone back home and kicked a hole in her bedroom wall.

Ten years ago she'd left all that behind, but now Simon had dumped her right back into it.

She found herself cursing in a furious whisper.

"Damn you! Damn you, Simon! I don't want your fucking life in my hands!"

But it was already much too late.

27

When Bracken clattered toward her, Toni took a very deep breath. Today he looked like some demented collision between a flamenco dancer and a toreador in tight black pants, a top with plunging flounced neckline and clackety shoes. He flicked a bar cloth perilously close to the glassware and yelled: "*Olé!*"

"Bracken . . ." she began, then pulled back from the sharp warning she'd intended to deliver, looked at him for a long second, and said simply: "I'm very tired."

"Ah . . ."

That had caught Bracken off guard. Toni used his uncertain pause to drop her grocery bags and shrug off her wet coat, but he rallied and continued in a conspiratorial stage whisper.

"Señorita is the center of intrigue and mystery!"

He ducked below the bar, thumbed open a locked cupboard under the till, and pulled out a cloth bag that had been shoved to the back.

"This came a couple of hours ago, very anonymously. I issued them a breathtaking sum, so I certainly hope it's yours."

Toni kneeled, and glanced inside at a code-sealed, unmarked box. Probably the training collar components. She should be glad to have them, but right now she felt too discouraged. In the two and a half weeks since Simon's punishment he hadn't come near the KlonDyke.

The cost of the collar was another worry. She'd have to beg a loan from Mary.

Bracken stared down at her, eyes avid with curiosity. Toni pushed her groceries and the bag into the cupboard, locked it, and stood up. She didn't feel like walking up to her apartment and she had work to do.

"And then that very lume, well-garbed medico came by again looking for you . . ."

"Not interested," said Toni shortly, trying not to show her unease as she walked over to the till and logged on. Dr. Lau had come to the bar several times to visit Mary, and he persisted in trying to talk to Toni. It was getting harder to avoid him.

"Which is precisely what I told him," said Bracken breathily behind her. "I said, why look for that old dragon when *I'm* available . . ." He paused an instant but Toni showed no reaction. ". . . but he wouldn't stay, though he does flirt *very* well."

"Bracken, if you don't have enough work, you can count coins. The sorter broke down again last night."

"I have fruit to juice," said Bracken quickly, and retreated, jingling. His vest was trimmed with bells, noted Toni with irritation.

She rang up a few sales, then spent half an hour at the tedious job of sorting and counting last night's cash. They'd done average trade last night, but today it was very quiet. The whole of Downtown had been poised for over two weeks now, expecting shooting to start, and people's nerves were worn raw. On her shopping trip, Toni had noticed a large gang presence and tong security patrols.

She threw a worried glance toward the tong section where two groups of natty mid-level execs sat at opposite sides of an old conference table, exchanging wary, insincere smiles, and pretending to get drunk. Viet Ching and Kung Lok only, and they had armored cars and gang escorts waiting outside. How long could this go on?

She looked toward the main doors and was surprised to see a wheelchair rolling in. Then she relaxed into a smile as she recognized Ron McCaskill, one cast-encased leg stuck stiffly out in front of him. A pretty young blonde followed his whirring chair up to the bar.

Ron smiled up at Toni and introduced his granddaughter.

"You look very well for a man who was attacked by a fire hose," Toni told him.

"I've had the whole family fussing over me," he told her, a little smugly.

"And you ran out of beer?"

He twinkled up at her.

"Never. I'm here to meet Mary. I wouldn't miss today for the world. We're taking some water taxi families to meet the Royal Vancouver Yacht Club."

Toni raised an eyebrow. She wouldn't mind seeing that herself. Then she noticed another familiar face approaching and felt herself tense. Dr. Lau stepped up beside McCaskill. Today the medic wore an expensive gray wool suit that flattered the silver highlights in his hair. She greeted him shortly.

"Good afternoon, Dr. Lau."

Ron looked up, smiling. "Ah! The D.R.A.'s newest executive member. We haven't had a chance . . ."

Abruptly his smile faded into a frown.

"I have looked forward to talking to you," said Lau, holding out his hand. "Perhaps you remember me. We met many years ago."

Toni caught a flash of shocked recognition on Ron's face, followed by unhappiness and then something else. Anger.

He knows something about the medic he doesn't like, thought Toni, alarmed.

"Ah, yes . . ." said Ron stiffly, then reached back and tapped his granddaughter's arm. "Let's take a table, dear."

Toni watched worriedly as Lau followed Ron to a table. She'd better warn Mary.

Unfortunately, she didn't get the chance. Mary arrived in a rush, rounded up her group and hustled them out. Toni recorded a message, but she knew Mary wasn't likely to check her mail for hours.

Finally, unable to concentrate on bartending, she took her groceries and the package upstairs where the presence of Klale's belongings strewn about her apartment still felt odd. After putting everything away and testing the training collar components, she found herself pacing, obsessively checking her new phone to make sure it had Simon's fishhook code. Of course there was only one way to find out if it really was Simon's code, she thought grimly: Use it. If it worked, Simon would die. And maybe that's what she should do. If she waited for an emergency and it didn't work, other people would die.

Back at work, afternoon dragged into interminable evening. Toni spent a long time polishing the top of the bar. The gleaming wood didn't really need her attention, but there was something comforting and timeless in the long sweeping strokes. She'd noticed that customers found it reassuring, and after years of doing it she had grown to feel the same way. And all of them, she felt, were in need of reassurance.

She found herself staring anxiously at Blade's usual table, then botched three drink orders in a row. She gave up in frustration, got an order of chili, and took it to the office where she could eat alone. After a few bites she shoved the bowl aside and leaned back on the couch, exchanging a baleful stare with Pauline Johnson, who lay in a boneless feline sprawl across Mary's desk.

"I hate goddamned waiting!" Toni muttered, then groaned to herself. Talking to a cat! Well, if she was that jagged, perhaps she'd better quit waiting and act. She had the training hardware now—all she needed was Simon. And if he wasn't going to show up on his own, she'd have to lure him.

Not allowing herself to entertain second thoughts, Toni got up, went to the netset and called Mr. Choi. She intended to leave a message but, to her shock, Choi took her call in person.

"Good afternoon, Miz Toni."

"Good afternoon, Mr. Choi. Ah . . ." Toni floundered a second, realizing she was unprepared. "I'd like to discuss a matter of mutual interest."

"Very well. Will my office be convenient?"

"Certainly."

Toni used the few seconds as the netset scanned in an image update to urgently collect her thoughts, then Choi's office sprang into view around her. Once again she sat on a chair several paces back from Choi's big mahogany desk. It looked exactly the same as she remembered and so did Choi. A replica? Or did he always wear identical black clothes? It was certainly possible.

Looking at his stoic, parchment-skinned face, she wondered again how old he was. The best data Alberta had been able to come up with was that he had moved to Downtown from China about sixty years ago, and he'd been a businessman there, too. He must be eighty-five at least, but he could be much older. A good enhancement program would disguise the appearance of his features and hands, but his movements would be copied accurately. Mary said she'd never seen him stand up in the sim; maybe he couldn't, or maybe he didn't want to betray a doddering walk.

On sudden impulse she asked: "Shall we have tea?"

Choi hesitated, then gave a stiff nod.

"By all means." He swiveled around and reached for something out of sight behind the desk, and Toni suppressed a surge of disappointment. He wasn't going to stand up. She watched a few seconds more, then slid off her headset and ran to fetch coffee from the bar. Damn, she hadn't thought this out, she told herself grimly, as she hurried back across the lobby, trying not to spill hot coffee. She'd never dreamed that Choi would take her call immediately.

Choi waited impassively for her, hands folded on the desk before him. By custom they couldn't deal until they both finished at least one cup, so they embarked on a stilted discussion of the weather, health, and current events. Aware that Choi was always fishing, Toni had to concentrate on keeping her responses devoid of information, but with the other part of her brain she watched him with growing unease. His conversation seemed excessively stiff, almost disjointed. And when he poured tea his hand trembled.

Choi was failing. Under other circumstances that would have been good news, but not now. He could easily have a stroke before she could get to Simon.

When Choi put down his teacup, Toni took the initiative.

"I've been reconsidering your offer."

Choi blinked, and she had a fleeting impression of confusion. Had he actually forgotten? Nonetheless he recovered fast.

"Indeed? And for what reason?"

Toni had that answer ready.

"Things Downtown are getting worse," she said, making no effort to hide her bitterness. She should seem angry and desperate. "The

KlonDyke will probably close soon and I'll have no job. I need money. I want to know more about this consulting project of yours."

"I will not, of course, discuss details by phone."

"What's the fee?"

Choi viewed her rudeness frigidly.

"We shall negotiate."

"We settle it now, or I won't do it." she said. "Four hundred dollars. Plastic."

"I will pay you two hundred and fifty dollars for an initial consultation. If your work is satisfactory, we will discuss additional payments."

Too much, thought Toni. He must want me very badly. She sat, gripping her hands tightly against one another as if struggling with a dilemma.

"In advance," she said finally.

"Half now. Half at the conclusion of our appointment."

"Where do we meet?"

"At my office."

"You'll let me leave again?"

"Of course," he said smoothly.

Choi was a very good liar. Toni saw no betraying movements in his face and hands and heard no nuances in his voice. But she knew that he'd never let her leave his bunker. He'd keep her as his permanent trainer, or sell her to one of the tongs. Even thinking about that made her sick.

She sat back in her chair, letting her shoulders droop.

"It doesn't look like I have any choice," she said finally. "When do you want me to come?"

"At your earliest convenience, naturally. Tonight?"

Tonight? She wasn't ready!

"I'm working," she said coldly. "Monday night?"

"Tomorrow afternoon."

Still too soon, but she must seem desperate.

"All right. You'll send your servant for me?"

His eyes clamped on her.

"For what reason?"

"Escort. There are gangs outside the KlonDyke and all through the streets. I won't go alone and I can't use our security staff. They'd ask questions." She got the words out evenly, then fought down the urge to hold her breath. It was a thin excuse. She could feel the piercing calculation in Choi's stare, then he bowed his head slightly.

"Very well. He will meet you in the alley. Four o'clock."

"I'll be there. I'll expect your first payment within an hour," she said, then snapped off the set with deliberate rudeness.

She pulled the goggles off, and leaned on the office desk, thoughts whirling. Damn! This was much too soon and, worse, she'd intended to meet Simon inside, not in the alley. She'd have to figure out a way to lure Simon out of the alley and then tranq him. Then she'd need help to hide and transport him. They'd have to get away from the KlonDyke as soon as possible, and four o'clock was a terrible time— broad daylight. She'd been hoping to move him late at night. Gods, and she had less than twenty-four hours to set this up!

Choi was another alarming factor. The old man had all the symptoms of having suffered a minor stroke. It would certainly explain his failure to spot her tampering with Simon, but it would also make his behavior erratic. She could only hope he wouldn't change his mind about the meeting or forget it, or even die before he sent Simon.

The netset chimed. Toni tensed again, wondering if Choi had already changed his mind, but Pum was paging her from the bar.

"I need you *now*. Bracken's got smog."

Toni didn't wait for details. She ran out of the office and across the lobby, then slowed to a walk at the door and made what she hoped was a casual entrance. She looked toward the bar. Bracken wasn't there. She scanned the room and spotted Bracken beside Cedar de Groot's usual table, hands defiantly on his hips. Several Freevie henches loomed over him, and three yellow-shirted bouncers were closing in. Toni Slanged at the bouncers to hold back and strode over, keeping her walk and face confident. She cleared her throat as she came up behind Bracken, but he jumped anyway when she touched his shoulder.

"Is there a problem here?"

To her surprise, it wasn't Cedar at the center of the disturbance.

Tommy Yip sat at the table, his round, usually jovial face creased in a scowl. Next to Tommy, with her hand on his arm, sat a strikingly beautiful Oriental woman in a creamy velvet dress. She looked close to tears.

"Your bartender insulted my wife," said Tommy sharply. "I demand an immediate apology!"

"I just reminded him that we don't allow blissers," hissed Bracken.

Shit, thought Toni, feeling her stomach clench. Yip had brought in his Fine Wife just to see how far he could push Mary's rules. He'd left his shirt unbuttoned, too, so his "wedding loop" was visible hanging from a gold chain around his neck.

"Bracken, let me handle this," she said.

Bracken looked at her, then turned and stomped away with an attempt at haughtiness that didn't mask his fear. The henches exchanged derisive looks, then caught Toni's eye and, after an uncertain pause, sat down. Beyond them, Toni saw yellow shirts backing off.

"Thank you," said Toni. "Mr. Yip, perhaps you and I could discuss this privately."

Tommy shook his head, feigning angry indignation, but his dark eyes were like chunks of hematite. "Anything you can say to me, you can say in front of my wife."

You mean that you're going to make me humiliate your victim in public, thought Toni, feeling her anxiety turn to cold fury.

"Very well," she said, then focused the most sincere smile she could manage on the woman sitting next to him. "I don't believe we've been introduced."

Tommy tensed at that, but he couldn't argue.

"This is my wife, Candace. We call her Candy."

"I'm honored."

Toni leaned forward and shook her hand, and the woman brightened, tears already forgotten. Over thirty, thought Toni; maybe even over forty, but she had the unlined face and mannerisms of a shy teenager, clinging to Tommy's plump arm with puppyish devotion. It reminded Toni sickeningly of the way she'd been taught to behave for johns.

"Have you been married a long time, Miz Yip?" she asked carefully. The woman's eyes widened slightly in a cued pleasurable response.

"Nineteen years."

"May I ask if you have a family?"

"Four children," she said, breaking into a radiant smile. Toni reflected it warmly back at her.

"That's wonderful, Miz Yip." Then, quickly and in an admiring tone, she added: "You must be a Fine Wife."

The woman nodded with immense pride, and Toni saw Tommy's jaw clench. Typical wife owner, she thought with a stab of grim satisfaction. He was so used to thinking of his wife as a sort of house pet that it had never occurred to him that Toni would question her directly. She kept her focus on Candy and made her voice gentle.

"What the bartender was telling your husband is that we have a house rule excluding people with neural plugs. It's really intended to keep out certain types of prostitutes and addicts, but it just says 'No plugs.'" She gave Tommy a hard smile. "It doesn't come up very often, Miz Yip. I'm sure your husband just forgot."

The woman's smile crumpled into bewilderment, and she looked back and forth from Toni to her husband in obvious disbelief that anybody would want to ban her. Tommy patted her arm automatically, but kept his attention on Toni and smiled coldly.

"Clearly the rule doesn't apply to staff." Toni felt her face tighten.

"It certainly does," she said evenly.

"Or to Choi's tool."

Toni's smile vanished.

"You know why he's allowed in here, Mr. Yip."

"Perhaps. But I'm very surprised that you would think of evicting a harmless and beautiful girl like Candy." He glanced over at his wife, then reached up and casually stroked the gold transmitter resting against his plump brown chest. Toni saw his wife's very slight shudder and intake of breath as the pleasure/arousal response hit her. Candy leaned forward and smiled at him eagerly. Yip turned his attention back to Toni. He's goading me, she thought distantly, but she could feel her rage mounting.

"She even dances beautifully," continued Tommy. "She's very . . .

pliable. I'm sure she could teach the dancers here a few things."

Toni's temper snapped. She put her hands on the table and leaned toward him.

"Your wife is most welcome to stay. As you pointed out, we do make exceptions to our rules. However, I'm afraid *you* will have to leave. We do not under any circumstances tolerate bloated, shit-licking *pimps.*"

She spat the last word out deliberately and her spittle hit him in the cheek. His face reddened and twisted with rage.

"You diseased smut!"

Chairs scraped backward and Toni was suddenly aware of being surrounded by large, hostile men. In the distance, yellow shirts rushed forward. She stood very still, clutching for control. She wanted to kick Yip in the balls so badly that her foot was almost cramping.

"I suggest you leave before you're exited," she said finally, in a low voice that shook with rage.

In the long frozen pause which followed, she heard anticipatory breathing all around her. The henches wanted a fight. Tommy's wife cowered behind him, wide-eyed with terror.

Finally Yip gathered his self-control. He reached back and put a protective arm around Candy.

"I'm taking my wife out of here immediately, but this isn't the last you'll hear about this. You've insulted my honor . . . and my wife's honor." He turned to leave.

Toni felt hostile, disappointed eyes on her, but the henches followed, taking out their frustrated bloodlust by kicking chairs in their path. One aimed a kick at Toni, but she anticipated it and stepped aside.

She was lucky that Tommy hadn't wanted a real fight, she thought, then shook herself angrily. What he'd wanted was an incident, and she had provided it. She'd played right into his game. She dug her nails into her palms.

Yip had just reached the main door when Mary walked in. Toni swore under her breath and tensed even further. The bouncers moved closer, but Tommy simply stopped and started talking.

Abruptly it was too much. Toni whirled and headed for the office, keeping her steps steady with tremendous effort. Her hands shook so hard she could barely open the door. When it closed she walked over to the couch and let loose a blow with all her force. The couch skidded backward on the carpet, and the cat leaped away from her chili bowl with a yowl. Toni kept kicking, then picked up a pillow and beat the furniture as hard as she could, keeping up a steady stream of curses until she ran out of breath.

When Mary arrived, she was sitting with her head in her hands, gradually calming down. Mary said nothing, but walked over and sat down next to her. Toni waited until she was sure she could trust her voice.

"Mary, I'm so sorry."

"What happened?"

"Yip baited me until I lost my temper. Hell, I should have left Bracken to handle it—he couldn't have spilled it any worse than I did." She raised her eyes and risked a look at Mary. "What did he say to you?"

Mary shrugged with almost convincing indifference. "He made some threats. Nothing I haven't heard already." Toni started to apologize again and Mary put a hand on her shoulder. "Dear, he wanted trouble. He would have succeeded eventually."

Toni shook her head. "I should have handled it better, but..." She drew in another shaky breath, then forced the words out. "I used to do training."

"I didn't know," said Mary, very quietly.

"In Seattle. After the divorce. I never was good with money and I spent a lot. Drips and trips, mostly. A man approached me, very discreetly, and asked me to take some private consultation work. Very well paid. I knew what it was, of course."

It had been over ten years, but Toni still found it astonishingly difficult to admit. She'd never told anyone before.

"I was hurting so bad I didn't care. So I did ma and pa jobs on the weekend—mostly parents who wanted their kids to behave, do better in school, or people with caregiving problems. With a plug and a bit of adjustment, you can keep your sick grandmother happy and manageable. It's not difficult, and there's immense demand. Hell, licensed therapists are so damned focused on client consent..."

Toni realized she was getting defensive and lowered her voice.

"And I guess it was a revenge for me. I blamed all those Zits for creating the Zone where I grew up. Why should I consider their dignity or consent? They never considered ours when they walled us into hell."

She shrugged uncomfortably.

"Of course, once you've done a job, you're trapped. There are heavy penalties for involuntary alterations. So the jobs got nastier . . . You know how they train Fine Wives like Tommy's?"

"I've heard that they start before puberty," said Mary. "But I don't know how it's done."

"It's treated as a big honor, only for the prettiest daughters. The girl is introduced to her Teacher, and given a pretty collar that gives her a nice jolt when she puts it on, so she likes lessons. The Teacher uses a combination of hypnosis and reward to reinforce submissive behaviors. Obeying male relatives gives the girl a thrill of happiness. Disobedience triggers intense sorrow and guilt. That kind of positive reinforcement, started early and maintained, is unshakable. You produce obedient, devoted, uncomplaining wives—just like Yip's."

They were sexually patterned, too, but Toni didn't feel like going into that.

"I guess I should be grateful in a way," she continued. "It was much too much like pimping. Turned my stomach. So I quit. And then I had to run before I was prosecuted by the institute or caught by the training brokers."

She couldn't look at Mary, but she felt Mary's comforting hand on her shoulder. Abruptly she found herself saying:

"I want to take Simon to the institute in Seattle."

She looked up. Mary didn't seem surprised. She nodded gravely. "What can I do to help?"

"Damn, I'm sorry, Mary. I don't want you involved in this! Or Klale. But . . ." She took a deep breath and steadied herself. "I've set up a meeting for four tomorrow afternoon. I'm going to try to drug Blade—keep him unconscious—but I can't manage him myself. He must weigh close to a hundred and fifty kilos. Also, I've got to move him without being seen and I need transport to Seattle. Probably a boat," she added miserably. She hated boats.

"Ask Ron."

Toni shook her head vigorously.

"Even if he didn't have a broken leg . . ."

Mary interrupted, tapping her knee.

"No, listen. Ron belongs to that group that rescues flot kids from the meat market. They take risks all the time. I'm sure they'll help."

Toni felt a surge of hope.

"You have a point . . ."

She sat for a moment, thinking about it.

Mary spoke just a little too quietly.

"Will you stay in Seattle with Simon?"

"I can't go that far and abandon him," said Toni brusquely, avoiding Mary's eyes. "Having one person he recognizes might give him something to hang onto. As for the institute . . . So long as I don't ask for my license back, I can hope they'll let me stay and not prosecute."

"And the training brokers?"

"Keep my mouth shut and hope they have short memories," she said grimly. "It's been ten years."

She felt Mary shift on the couch, then a warm arm went around her shoulders.

"Toni, I don't want to lose you, but I think this is your true path. I'll give you all the help I can."

Her words were interrupted by a tap at the door, then it opened to loud jingling. An outrageously curled dark wig poked through.

"I was sent to remind you that your taxi awaits," Bracken told Mary.

Mary made an apologetic noise and pulled her arm away.

"Sorry, love, but I'm late for that meeting. I just rushed back for something I forgot."

"I didn't realize I was keeping you," Toni told her, biting back another apology.

Mary squeezed her hand, then got up, rummaged in the desk, and hurried out. Toni waited until she was gone, then got up stiffly and turned to the door. Bracken still stood there.

"Are we in trouble?" he inquired.

It took Toni a second to remember Tommy Yip.

"No," said Toni shortly. "At least not with the Boss." She ran a hand through her hair, then realized that Bracken was watching her with anxious eyes.

"Are *you* in trouble?" he asked.

Toni held back her impulse to deny it and studied his face. It had taken a lot of nerve for him to be so direct. Finally she grunted.

"Yeah."

"Can I help?"

Despite herself she raised her eyebrows, then shook her head.

"No . . . Thank you."

She moved to leave, but Bracken closed the door behind him and stood blocking it, arms crossed.

"Why not?"

Toni shrugged impatiently.

"I'm in a . . . complicated spill. I don't think there's anything you could do."

"Bullshit!" he yelled suddenly, and glared at her, trembling with passion. "You never trust me! You treat me like some smegging little prick who would run out on you!"

Listening to his reedy voice Toni had a sudden vivid memory of the last time he'd run away. When she'd finally located him in a grimy smut shop on Granville Street, the pupils of his eyes had been black dishes ringed by a tiny corona of brown. She'd sat down on his bony chest to pull out his booster, and he was too weak to move her off. He had cried and pleaded, but she'd told him that she had paid for an hour and by all the gods she'd have it. Within minutes he'd been clinging to her, choking out sordid pieces of his life.

Somehow it had become much too easy for her to forget how far he had come since then, and how hard he tried.

"Bracken," she started in a gentler voice, then stopped, as an idea hit her. "There is one thing. If anything happens to me, would you take care of Klale?" Bracken looked startled and she hurried on.

"I may have to leave suddenly, and if she's not with me, she'll be in danger. She'll have to get out of Downtown fast, without using ID or tong travel brokers. You know how. Would you help her?"

Bracken pulled himself up straighter, jingling.

"I can do that. I promise." Then his certainty faded and she saw a surge of vulnerability in his eyes that made him look suddenly like a child playing dress-up. "Toni . . . are you leaving?"

"It looks like it. Might as well, before the building falls down." She tried to make her tone light, but her throat was very tight. She turned toward the couch, put one boot up on it, and started fiddling with the snaps to hide her expression. "I'm afraid you'll be stuck supervising the bar," she said over her shoulder.

"Then I guess they'll have to get somebody else," said Bracken harshly. His voice was suddenly low and ashamed. "I'm sorry, Toni. I tried learning that reporting stuff on the tills, but it's too confusing." He hesitated, then pushed on. "Well, that's not really the problem. It's that I'm too stupid. I never could learn things at school, either."

Stupid? thought Toni incredulously, then the obvious finally thudded into place. How could she have missed it? She put her boot down and turned to look at Bracken, who was staring across the room with a flushed face.

"Can you read?" she asked bluntly.

"Sure!" he retorted, then his eyes met hers and his shoulders drooped. "Well, I can make out words if they're by themselves and nobody's pushing me. But that jumbled mess on the set . . ."

Of course. Summaries could be done by voice interface, but the detailed reports were spreadsheets or charts. Toni wanted to kick herself and the frustration leaked into her voice.

"Why didn't you tell me? No, never mind, I should have had the intelligence to ask. It's just that you're so damned articulate, Bracken. I didn't think of it."

He shrugged miserably.

"There's not a lot to do in Fort Chipewyan in winter. I used to watch old vids and I memorized hours of dialogue. Costumes, too," he added, with a flash of his usual style. "I fake it beautifully, you know."

"You do extremely well," Toni told him seriously, and saw the jolt of surprise in his eyes. She sat back on the edge of the couch and regarded him gravely.

"Bracken, there's nothing stupid about you. If you haven't

learned to read, you probably have some minor neurological disorder. Have you ever been assessed?"

"They did some sort of test at school. Then they told me that I needed to be fixed."

"And you didn't get that done?"

He crossed his arms.

"Darling, when two big techs in smocks came at me pointing machines at my head and saying that they wanted to correct me, I ran like hell and hid out until they left town."

"They didn't call your parents or the Métis Council?"

"My mother didn't care, and neither did anyone else," said Bracken with venom, then he looked at Toni and asked suddenly: "Did your mother beat you?"

Toni's mother's hand had made a sharp cracking sound when it slapped the side of her face. Toni remembered a bewildering storm of pain and betrayal, then arms hugging her and a girlish voice sobbing "I'm sorry, baby, I'm sorry." The intensity of grief that came with the memory was shocking.

"No," she said shortly. "My mother was too wired most of the time." Bracken was staring. She took a quelling breath, hating to think what might be visible in her face.

"Bracken, I would guess that you have a mild astigmatism or a neural pathing disorder such as dyslexia. They're both easily treated. It's not expensive. With the right help you could be reading well in six months."

"Oh . . ."

Toni watched the confused emotions crossing Bracken's face, then rose.

"And I owe you an apology. You're right that I don't trust you, but it's not just you, Bracken. I have a hard time trusting anybody. I'll try to do better."

She looked at the badly shielded neediness in his eyes and held out her arms. He took an uncertain half step forward and she closed the rest of the distance, reaching up around his bony shoulders, and resolutely ignoring the sticky cloud of perfume that cascaded from his wig.

Hard to believe, but she would miss him, too.

28

Simon's head had been hurting a long time. Blade's rage swelled against his temples, sending shooting pains across his eyes. The schedule was all wrong and it kept getting more mixed up. It was the wrong time to dance, but he had permission. It was confusing. But he needed to dance! If he didn't dance soon it felt as if his head would explode.

He hurried along the gleaming white corridor toward the stairs, turning his head away from the sealed door on his right. Something terrible lurked in that room, something that Simon wasn't permitted to know.

Climbing the stairs his legs felt oddly numb and leaden, as if he were a long way away from his body. He heard a humming noise in his ears. It sounded like the air recirculation system, but it followed him.

It had been with him in the KlonDyke, too. He'd walked up the tower stairs, following a confused scrap of memory that told him he must go to the twenty-first floor and wait. The stairs had looked familiar. He recognized small details—scuffs on the wall, broken treads. On eighteen he'd stopped, aware of an incongruity. The stairwell door stood ajar. He scanned with his phone, then went inside and searched with his handlight. The only apartment on the floor was empty. That wasn't right. There should be things in it, he was sure. And it smelled wrong. It should smell sweet, like apples, and salty, like sweat.

A sudden vivid image hit him. He saw the dancer lying on the floor with her eyes closed and a cover over her body. Toni's Klale. Was she dead?

Perhaps. The tongs had marked the KlonDyke and Mary Smarch for vengeance, and the dancers who'd joined the D.R.A. were promised as gifts to the gangs. They'd be raped and bludged. And Toni. Toni would be killed.

No!

The wave of panic that hit Simon then had left him trembling on the floor. He'd had to summon Blade to get to the twenty-first floor, where he'd waited outside the security door. Hours passed. A security patrol came up the stairs and Blade had to hide. But Toni didn't come.

Maybe she was already dead . . .

No!

Simon stood just inside the gym, clutching at his head with shaking hands, trying to make all the wrong thoughts go away. Think about dancing! Dancing always made things better. And Blade liked the Dance of Knives—it was an angry dance.

Simon stripped off his clothes and changed into his training suit. Then he took his two best knives, put on headphones, and turned the music up very loud.

Harsh chords broke the silence and he gasped in pain and relief as the wave of resonance traveled through his body. A burst of staccato notes thrust his limbs into familiar motions. Knives flashed in his hands. He leaped and spun, fighting the air, slicing and stabbing invisible opponents, wounding them, killing them again and again.

The music changed rhythm and he tossed the knives high. They twirled almost too fast to see and Simon concentrated hard, aware that he had to be very careful. Serious wounds were not permitted and the blades were sharp. If he did not time his moves with absolute precision the knives would fall into him, slicing through flesh and bone. The blades had grazed him before. Once they'd sheared his finger off, leaving a smooth-ended, bleeding lump of meat that his master had reattached and transformed into a finger again. Then he'd been punished.

He caught the left knife while flinging the right. Then his feet slipped very slightly and he realized that the right knife was dropping past his hand to the floor.

He felt nothing, but when he looked down, there was a long perfect cut along his suited right leg, its edges just pulling open. For an instant it was clean, then crimson seeped out and trickled in tiny streams down his leg. He stared at it, aware of a faint sense of disappointment. He would have liked the blood to gush out, pooling on the floor until all the pain was outside of him.

He retrieved the knife, and started from the beginning, but his control this time was even worse. He only managed to get a minute into the dance before he lost his balance on a spin and brushed the wall. His left knife fell to the floor.

Stupid! That was a stupid mistake! A voice agreed, echoing in his head—an implacable, emotionless voice that said "You are too stupid and repellent a creature to be worthy of my contempt."

Automatically Simon dropped to his knees and began to intone the servant's gratefulness words, but his tongue stumbled, choking in his mouth. He stopped and looked down, swaying in confusion. Blood smeared his hand. There was a knife in it.

Blade's rage exploded inside him. Simon opened his mouth and screamed.

29

When the D.R.A. execs finally arrived at the KlonDyke just after two o'clock, Klale rushed over with her pad, released at last from her agonizing wait. She was surprised to see Ron McCaskill in a wheelchair with one leg propped up in a plastiche cast, so she greeted the old gentleman first. He looked tired, but when he saw Klale his faded blue eyes lit up in a smile and he reached out a hand.

"Hello, beautiful dancer."

Klale glowed as she took his old, knobby hand in hers. He had a strong, warm grip.

"Hello, Mr. McCaskill. What happened to your leg?"

Ron beckoned until she leaned down and put her ear next to his mouth.

"Nothing," he whispered. "I just wanted some attention."

Klale laughed, then took the opportunity to lean down and whisper back: "He's coming at four. Toni asks: will the boat be ready by five?"

"Of course, dear," said Ron, his voice still perfectly casual. He gave her a wink. "You're in good hands. And," he nodded at the person sitting next to him, "We have more help. Dr. Lau has volunteered to assist with that little project."

"Strat!" said Klale, beaming a smile at the handsome Chinese medic. She liked Dr. Lau. She'd served him several times, enjoying his clever, flirtatious conversation and large tips. Then she looked at

Lau more closely, abruptly worried. All the exec members seemed tired and tense, but he looked haggard. He slumped in his chair, barely returning Klale's smile. Even his tailored suit seemed limp. What was wrong?

"How are your meetings going?" she asked McCaskill.

Mary answered.

"We're making quite an impression," she said obliquely. "Dear, I'm sorry to hurry you but we're running late. Could you ask the kitchen to rush our lunch?"

"Sure," said Klale. She took their orders, then retreated. Behind her, she heard Mary begin a short executive meeting.

The bar was in its mid-afternoon doldrums, so once she'd downloaded the orders and served a round of drinks Klale had nothing to do. She walked casually up to the till and made a fast call to Toni's apartment. Toni answered, voice-only.

"Yeah?"

"They're here," Klale told her. "Everything's fine." Then she caught sight of a scowling Pum, striding across the room to the bar, with her eyes fixed on Klale. "Hold on."

"You seen Toni?" asked Pum as soon as she got into earshot.

"She's off today."

Pum halted in front of the bar and crossed her arms, her scowl growing blacker.

"You got smog?" Klale asked.

"Blade. Damn ghoul's in the alley out back, just standing there. Making me nervous."

Simon! He was two hours early! Alberta and the borrowed delivery van wouldn't be here for another hour.

Pum echoed her next thought.

"I'm calling Alberta," she said.

"Good idea," agreed Klale.

She waited until Pum strode away, then returned to Toni.

"Did you hear . . . ?" she started, then heard thumps and distant cursing.

". . . knew Choi was fucking erratic, I should have been ready . . ."

"Can I do anything?"

"No. Be right down. Shit!"

Klale cut the call and stood for a moment, taut with the need to *do* something. Then she heard the kitchen chime and hurried to the pass-through for the first exec orders.

By the time Klale finished serving all the meals, Toni had arrived at the side door. She wore a loose gray hempen jacket and had a carryall slung over her shoulder. Klale had seen her packing earlier and knew it contained neural equipment, a medkit, and a change of clothes. Despite Alberta's urgings, it didn't contain a weapon. Toni said she hadn't fired a gun in years. Klale had never fired anything more than a flare gun.

Klale hastily pulled her apron over her head, hung it up behind the bar, and then followed Toni through the side door. Toni led her across the lobby and into the back hall.

"We've got to get him inside. Quietly," she said over her shoulder.

"Where are we going to put him?" asked Klale, hurrying to get abreast of Toni. "There's servers in the downroom and musicians backstage setting up. The office?"

"Too risky." Toni continued at a normal pace down the hall into the loading bay and halted just inside, waiting until the door shut behind Klale. Then she pointed to a battered metal door across the room, behind a pile of pallets.

"That door leads to the old parking garage. I'm going down there. Klale, you go out to the loading bay and wave Blade inside. Make sure nobody sees you. Tell him that I'm down here . . . damn!"

"What?"

"Just thought of something. Once he's unconscious, we'll never carry him back up these stairs. I'll have to get Alberta to park the van beside the garage exit down on Nicola Street . . ."

"Oh, I forgot to tell you!" interrupted Klale eagerly. "Mr. Mc-Caskill brought help."

Toni frowned at her.

"Help? Who?"

"Dr. Lau."

"No!"

Klale jumped backward, startled at Toni's vehemence. Toni took a deep breath and pressed her palm against her forehead.

"I don't trust him. But one problem at a time. First we've got to get Blade inside. Now, repeat what you're going to tell Blade in Slang."

"Simon," corrected Klale.

"No! Right now he's Blade," said Toni sharply. "Treat him like a tool, Klale. Keep your distance and don't try to talk to him out loud. Now, run through the Signs."

Klale did her best, but her eyes keep straying to the lump under Toni's shirt where her phone hung. Simon's fishhook code was on that phone. If they failed, they might have to use it to kill him. She gritted her teeth and forced herself to concentrate. After a second rehearsal, Toni nodded.

"OK. Give me two minutes, then go."

"Right," said Klale. Then, on impulse, she caught at Toni's arm. "Toni . . . what if Choi sent him early because he suspects a trap?"

"Then we're caught," said Toni. She frowned at Klale. "Look, I'm committed to this, but you're not. You can back out now."

"No!"

Toni studied her face closely, then nodded and crossed the room. She keyed a password in the old door lock, wedged the door open, and disappeared into the stairwell, leaving Klale alone in the loading bay.

Klale paced, trying to focus on the task at hand but worrying instead about what would happen to Simon when he reached Seattle. Toni said that Simon might respond to treatment, but he would never be a functional person. Klale didn't believe that and she knew she had to help him prove Toni wrong. That morning while Toni slept, Klale had packed her own duffel bag and stashed it in the downroom. When Toni and Simon left, Klale intended to be with them. She had already put off going back to Prince Rupert until she was sure Simon was safe. Her Guild troubles could wait a while longer.

Two minutes. Klale hurried out through the loading bay, down the steps beside the van dock and into the alley. Simon stood a few paces up the alley with his back to the wall, and when Klale got close to him her breath caught in her throat. He looked terrible. There were dark bruises around his eyes and his skin had an unhealthy gray sheen. He didn't make eye contact. Not Simon, she reminded herself—Blade.

She glanced around the alley, then beckoned. Blade didn't look at her, but when she started back to the door, he followed. On the stairs by the van dock she repeated Toni's message. He watched with a flat deadness that alarmed her and when she turned her back to lead him inside, she had to fight back fear. Toni said that he would do anything Choi ordered rather than risk another punishment. For the first time Klale believed her.

The parking garage smelled dank. Dim lights revealed rows of concrete pillars stretching into darkness under a low ceiling. Cracks and heaves in the sloping concrete floor betrayed earthquake damage. The place felt eerie and oppressive, as if it might collapse at any moment. Blade, she noticed, had to duck his head under the beams.

Toni stood waiting, hands shoved casually into her pockets, where Klale knew she had two loaded injection guns. The original plan had been for Toni to distract Blade while Alberta sprayed him with riot glue—a fast-acting cement that would hopefully immobilize him before he could hurt anyone. But Alberta and the borrowed riot gun weren't here yet. What did Toni plan to do?

Klale never found out. A rapid series of explosions sent echoes cascading through the garage. Klale flinched and looked wildly around.

"Gunfire," said Toni. "In the bar."

She pointed up, then pantomimed firing an automatic rifle. Klale strained to see Blade's face, but it was just a gray blur. He turned and ran farther into the garage, footsteps slapping the concrete. The two women looked at each other, then bolted after him.

Klale nearly plowed into Toni when Blade swerved suddenly into a shadowy corner beside a pillar. He shoved aside some empty kegs, then pulled open a rusty access panel set in the wall. He shone a handlight into the opening and then, as Klale watched incredulously, reached in backward with both arms and pulled himself inside. His shoulders just barely squeezed through. For a second his feet remained behind, then he lifted them in.

Toni dropped her carryall, and shook her head. "Old garbage chute," she said softly. "Kitchen used to be right up there. Shit, he knows this place better than I do." She flashed a regretful look at her carryall, then pulled her phone out from under her jacket and thumbed on a small light. "Better follow him."

Amazing, thought Klale absently, that someone had built a whole shaft just for garbage. But garbage in those days would have included compost and bio scraps . . . She stared more closely at the black-crusted metal chute.

"I could take the stairs."

"He didn't, and he probably has a reason," said Toni, fastening her sleeves tight around her wrists. "Besides, if I'm going to fall I'd like something soft under me."

"Thanks," muttered Klale.

Toni bent awkwardly backward, reaching into the hatch, then pulled herself inside. Klale thumbed on her own phone light and waited until Toni's feet disappeared, then followed, grimacing. In the light from her phone she could see Toni's buttocks braced against one side of the chute and her feet pressed against the other side. As Klale watched, Toni slid her back upward, then walked her feet up the opposite wall. Judging by her muffled grunts, it wasn't easy.

Klale, much larger than Toni, found the climb even more awkward. She finally resorted to squeezing her elbows and hands against the sides of the chute while she raised her legs, then bracing her knees while she lifted her torso. Fortunately the grime-caked metal wasn't slippery. Unfortunately it was rough, with jagged edges that tore at her clothes and skin. She tried not to think about staph or tetanus. A shaft of light shone down past Toni, then dimmed, and Klale realized that Simon had left the chute.

The sound of gunfire burst out around them and Klale lost her balance, sliding down the chute before jamming her legs and hands out. One knee caught painfully on something sharp, and she sucked in her breath. It occurred to her with sick fear that those bullets might be killing people she knew.

Please no!

She braced her aching muscles and redoubled her efforts, trying not to think what they might find at the top. Above her, Toni panted and struggled. One of Toni's boots whacked Klale's head, then Toni vanished into a rectangle of light. Klale shoved herself up until her head came level with the opening, then she maneuvered her head and torso out of the hatch, gave a big push with her legs and spilled backward into a heap on the floor. Toni caught at her, trying to break her fall and whispering "Shhh!"

For an instant Klale felt completely disoriented, then she sat up and realized that she was backstage. She turned around, and felt a heart-stopping surge of panic as she looked straight out into the bar.

Klale gasped, then let her breath out as she realized that she was looking through the one-way, mirrored backstage screen that she'd seen dozens of times. Blade stood at the backdrop, staring intently into the room. Toni edged forward, keeping her body low to the floor, and Klale followed.

For a second Klale thought the KlonDyke was empty, then she saw a foot and realized that patrons had either fallen or dived under tables. With a kind of horrified disbelief she found herself searching for traces of blood.

A loud male voice from her right startled her.

"Traitors! Stand with your hands behind your heads."

Klale strained to see, then cursed her own stupidity and shifted her focus to the mirrors at the back of the room which reflected a clear view. Three figures stood in front of the bar, pointing automatic weapons at the tables. All were entirely encased in black clothes, including gloves and baglike hoods that covered their heads.

Toni's head moved near Klale's ear and she breathed: "Tong death squad."

Klale glanced at her in horror, then a movement drew her attention and she saw another assassin throwing the bolts across the main doors. He turned and walked back toward the bar. Were there more? Klale scanned the room and spotted an assassin on her left at the rear emergency exit. Covering the death squad's retreat? She glanced back up at Blade who stood watching without expression.

When she looked back, she saw Mary and two other members of the D.R.A. execs standing beside the table where she'd served them lunch. Klale's first reaction was relief that they seemed unharmed, then sick fear as she realized that they were the "traitors." As she watched, Ron McCaskill levered himself awkwardly up into his wheelchair. Dr. Lau helped him.

"You—old man. Not you!"

Ron shook his head. The assassin repeated the order. Again, Ron shook his head, and when Mary stepped forward, he rolled his chair right behind her.

"Too well known," whispered Toni by Klale's ear. "They don't want to kill a City Services elder."

The assassins ordered the D.R.A. members to walk to the bar, one at a time. Mary went first, striding proudly, ignoring orders to put her hands on her head. She came straight toward backstage, heading through the tables to the aisle at the front of the room. Six others followed.

Klale clenched her hands in helpless fury as she realized that they were going to be lined up against the bar and shot. She looked at Toni, then turned desperately to Simon.

"Simon?" she whispered urgently. "Simon! Please! Can you help us? Help Mary!"

He stared straight out at the bar, seeming oblivious. Klale looked back. An assassin stepped forward, herding the execs with his gun barrel. Mary turned at the front aisle and walked slowly toward the bar with Ron rolling a few paces behind. Dr. Lau came last. Klale caught a glimpse of his face, taut with fear.

"Simon!" whispered Klale again.

The assassin waved his gun at Lau and snarled, "Move!"

Something flickered in Simon's face, then in a blur of sudden motion he drew a pistol, raised both arms, and fired. Klale expected deafening explosions, but instead the bullets burped as they blasted little holes in the quivering backdrop. Klale had a blurred impression of shocked faces turning toward the stage as she dropped to her knees, shielding her eyes from flying shards. She heard her name and looked over to see Toni rolling behind a pillar to stage left. Klale followed. Simon finished his round and dove after them, loading another clip as he rolled.

A roar of gunfire responded. Bullets smashed the screen to tatters and slammed into the concrete pillar in front of them. Klale braced for Simon to shoot back, but instead she saw Toni reach out and grab his gun. For a second they both held onto it, eyes locked.

"Secure it to Klale!" hissed Toni.

Simon grabbed Klale's hand and wrapped it around his gun,

pressing her finger against the security pad next to his finger. The safety scanned their prints, then buzzed quietly, clearing her to fire. Simon let go, dropping some clips on the floor. Toni waved him toward the back hall and turned to Klale.

"We need covering fire," she whispered, next to Klale's ear. "Hold both hands together, like this, and brace or you'll sprain your wrist."

She patted Klale's shoulder, then started after Simon.

"Where are you going?" called Klale in a panicked whisper.

"To get help. Shoot!"

The gun felt warm and very heavy. Klale raised herself on both elbows, edged out from behind the pillar, and squeezed the trigger, aiming high across the bar and praying she didn't hurt anyone. The gun popped rapidly, and recoil slammed against her hands, then she heard clicks. She pulled back, barely ahead of return fire, feeling dizzy and stupid with adrenaline.

Think! she told herself. What next? Well, the clip was empty. OK, then reload. How?

She fumbled with the gun for long seconds before a button depressed and the empty clip ejected. Loading a new one took only another second. Then she looked around and realized that return fire had stopped.

She inched forward and ventured a quick peek, but it didn't tell her anything. The bar was a sea of empty tables. She didn't even know whether Simon had shot any of the assassins or if they'd just taken cover. She hoped he hadn't hit any of the D.R.A. execs.

She raised herself on both elbows again and fired, this time aiming in a broad sweep toward the main doors. She wasn't trying to hit anything, just create a diversion. Return fire slammed into the wall in front of her, but fewer shots this time. She listened and decided they were all coming from her right, the direction of the bar. Maybe the assassin by the rear exit was down. Or perhaps he was edging around, working his way backstage.

Klale suppressed a surge of panic and busied herself reloading the gun. Where had Toni gone? How long would she be? Klale took a breath, then risked another look, checking in the mirrors at the back. The assassins were crouched in a row along the front of the bar, sheltered from Klale's line of fire, with the D.R.A. execs strung out beside them. All were temporarily pinned down—they'd have to cross three meters of open space to gain cover among the tables. Suddenly Klale caught a flash of yellow from near the main door. A bouncer was circling around, trying to get behind the assassins while their attention was diverted. But she would have to sneak up through the tables and get very close. The 'Dyke's spray guns were only effective at short range.

Klale braced again and squeezed off several more bullets. A light fixture in the ceiling exploded, spraying glass. She grimaced. This wasn't a convincing imitation of a threat. Well, maybe she'd confuse them. But there was no return fire this time. In the relative quiet she heard a moan of pain.

She rose cautiously to her knees for a better look in the mirrors at the back, then saw that the side door into the lobby stood ajar. She didn't remember that. As she watched, it eased open farther. Klale stared, then suddenly remembering her role, she braced her arms again and depressed the trigger, aiming high over the bar. As the gun bucked against her hands, she saw Alberta sprint from the side door, skid to her knees and fire her riot gun straight at the bar.

At almost the same instant, Simon erupted feetfirst through the kitchen serving window. He started to vault the bar, then seeing the spray of glue arcing toward him, he spun and hit the floor running toward Klale.

For a horrible second, Klale thought Simon was coming after her, then she heard shots directly in front of her and realized that one of the assassins had edged around to the other side of the concrete pillar.

She scrambled to her feet, adrenaline pounding in her veins, holding the gun ready. The assassin stood only a couple of meters from Klale with his back turned to her, firing wildly at Simon with shaking hands. Klale bit her lip, aimed for his thigh and pulled her trigger, but the gun clicked. Empty again! Before she could do anything Simon launched himself forward with breathtaking speed, pouncing on the assassin like a tiger on a lapdog. The man gave a high-pitched scream.

Somewhere in the background Klale heard Alberta yell for everyone to freeze, but Simon paid no attention. He draped the assassin in a lock over his thigh, bending the man slowly backward. He was going to break the man's spine, Klale realized in sick horror. Simon's deathmask face held no expression, but he stared fixedly at a stream of blood trickling down the side of the man's face, and she could see the rage blooming in his eyes.

Then a figure darted forward and grabbed Simon's arm.

"*Stop!*"

Simon's head swiveled and he glared at the gray-haired doctor who tugged his arm. Through the assassin's screams, Klale heard Dr. Lau's voice.

"Simon! Don't kill him!"

Simon's eyes widened and he flinched violently from Lau's touch, dropping the assassin. He backed up against the scarred concrete, then lunged forward again and grabbed Lau by the throat.

Someone rushed from backstage and ducked through the shattered backdrop beside Klale. Toni! Klale felt an immense rush of relief, then she realized that Toni had her phone gripped tightly in both hands. The fishhook code! Toni was ready to kill Simon!

"No!" yelled Klale. Toni glanced at Klale, saw the gun, grabbed it, and stepped forward. Klale froze, not knowing what to do. Toni didn't know the clip was empty!

Simon stood holding the doctor by the throat with one shaking hand while his wide eyes flicked erratically around the room. At first he didn't seem to notice as Toni took several slow steps forward, then he focused on her and his gaze dropped to the gun in her hand.

As Klale felt a fresh stab of alarm, Toni flipped the gun around and held it out, butt toward him.

There was a long, stomach churning pause in which time and motion seemed suspended. Despite Simon's fingers pressing against his throat, Lau held still and made no noise. Then Klale heard a loud thump and looked over in time to see the assassin Simon had attacked pulling the bolt on the KlonDyke's rear exit. He pushed the door open and fled into the alley.

Simon's head swiveled from the exit to the gun in Toni's hand. Then, abruptly, he shoved Lau to the floor and grabbed the gun. He spun it around and assumed a firing stance, pointing the barrel directly at Toni.

Toni held both her hands out very slowly, letting her phone rest loose in her palm.

"Go!" she said.

She pointed at the exit.

Simon's harsh breathing echoed across the stage. He took one sideways step toward the rear door, eyes scanning frantically. Nobody moved. Klale didn't breathe. He retreated several more steps, then reached the door and plunged through it into the alley. Klale drew in a deep breath and at the same instant saw Toni's shoulders sag. Then Alberta shouted for everyone to stay put and jogged across the room to the rear exit. She opened the door cautiously and looked through.

"Gone," she announced, turning back into the room. "All right, my team secure this area! Anybody with first aid, check for casualties! Su, you all right? OK, phone Doc, then get medkits from the back! Pum, we're going to need more riot glue solvent. Lots more." She hesitated an instant, then said tensely, "Mary?"

"OK," came a shaky voice. "Stuck, but OK."

Klale saw Alberta's sigh of relief. Toni had closed her eyes and was rubbing her forehead. Dr. Lau pulled himself up on shaky knees, then walked back across the stage toward the bar. Toni joined him, and Klale followed them both.

A bizarre scene greeted her. Alberta's burst of riot glue had sprayed three assassins and, to a lesser degree, four of the D.R.A. execs, pinning them face forward against the polished wood bar and its brass foot rail. One of the assassins was flopping like a bug squashed against a windshield. Toni and Dr. Lau grabbed a can of aerosol solvent from Alberta and began working on him.

Klale thought it funny until she realized that the struggling assassin, glued facefirst to the bar, was suffocating. Lau and Toni, alternately spraying and prying, freed his head from the bar and then peeled the glue-soaked black hood away from his face. The man hung limp. Lau tried resuscitation but glue had clotted in the assassin's nose and mouth. Toni and Lau held a quick whispered conference, then Lau draped the hood back over the man's head and they moved on to the next person, leaving the corpse pinned to the bar. Klale swallowed and steadied herself against a table, then went to see what she could do to help.

The next hour or two became a blur as Klale ran errands and talked to the glued D.R.A. execs, trying to keep up their spirits until more solvent arrived. Mary, closest to the assassins, was trapped in a half-kneeling position with her arms raised, and her hair plastered against the bar. Toni chopped through her hair, leaving big tufts of it behind the bar, but it was still over an hour before they could free her.

Of six assassins, one had been shot by Simon, one had suffocated, three were wounded, and one had escaped. One customer, hit by a stray bullet, was also dead. Klale desperately hoped it hadn't been one of the bullets from Simon's gun, but she didn't ask. The rest of the injuries were miraculously minor. Alberta offered first aid, but most customers just wanted to leave.

Eventually Klale found herself sitting in an almost empty room, staring at the ruins of the bar. Bullet holes cratered the beautiful polished wood. Mirror shards lay everywhere. The shelves that had held rows of antique glass bottles now dripped wreckage. Beside her, Dr. Lau peeled off his gloves and sank heavily into a chair. It was only four-thirty, Klale realized suddenly. It seemed much, much later. She studied Lau as he stared distractedly at the bar, a few loose strands of hair clinging to his damp forehead. For the last hour he'd been briskly competent, but now his poise was crumbling.

"Dr. Lau?" she said softly. He turned to look up at her, seeming dazed. "That was very brave—what you did."

"I had to try something. I thought he might recognize me." His voice sank to a murmur. "But he didn't."

"Recognize you?" asked Klale blankly.

Lau's eyes filled with pain.

"Simon. He's my son."

30

Simon's father? Toni's thoughts whirled as she trudged up the stairs to her apartment. But it fit. Simon had fired when the assassin threatened Lau. And Ron knew him, of course—recognized him. He must be Simon's father, all right, but Toni still had no proof that she could trust him.

I've got to plan what to do next, she thought, but she felt dazed from the assassination attempt and exhausted from climbing up that damned garbage chute. Alberta was evacuating the building and had tried to prevent Toni from returning to her apartment, but Toni refused to be budged. Eventually Alberta gave in, but the mulish expression on her face told Toni that she'd be back. Well, she'd worry about that when it happened.

Behind her, Lau and Klale stopped on a landing for a breather. Klale hadn't explained why she was carrying her fully packed duffel-bag, but Toni could guess.

When they arrived, Toni hustled Klale into the bathroom for a full decontam. Both women stripped naked, showered, and then checked each other from head to foot for cuts and abrasions, smearing any they found with cream from Toni's medkit. Other than scrapes from the garbage chute, Klale seemed fine. Toni, however, ached all over and had a dark premonition about how much she would hurt tomorrow. She dosed herself with oxygenated antitoxins to prevent muscle stiffness, knowing that she was going to need her concentration.

In the living room they found Dr. Lau brushing his tailored gray jacket, which he'd draped over the back of a chair. He'd removed it downstairs while he worked, Toni remembered and it looked unscathed to her, but his high-collared cream shirt was wrinkled and stained. He saw Toni's look and patted his jacket with an ironic shrug.

"I hope it will come clean. It was so very expensive and I look so very good in it."

True, thought Toni sourly. Lau might once have been a flot, but he'd picked up all the mannerisms she'd disliked most in her Guild colleagues. Such as arrogance. He was already taking charge in Toni's apartment, opening the cube of cider Klale had lugged upstairs and pouring it into glasses. He turned, and surveyed Toni's table and two chairs. Toni sat down in one and watched to see what he would do, but Klale rescued him from the social dilemma. She trotted into the study and returned towing the creaky office chair Simon had damaged.

Lau served drinks, sat, then leaned forward across the table, fixing Toni with a confident, persuasive gaze.

"Miz Toni. Mr. McCaskill has told me how you were trying to help Simon and I want to thank you very much. I will certainly arrange treatment for him, but I still have to get him away from Choi. Will you help me?"

"No," said Toni coldly and saw his startlement.

"But. . . ."

"You don't know Downtown, you don't know Choi, and you don't know Simon. I do. I'll get him out."

"He's my son!"

"I don't give a smogging goddamn!"

"My son is *my* responsibility!"

"The hell he is!" Toni yelled, abruptly losing self-control. "Simon held *my* hand for ten goddamned years! He chose to make himself *my* responsibility and you're not walking into my apartment at the last goddamned second and taking over!"

"Hold it, hold it, hold it!" Klale was waving her arms across the table between them. "Hit pause!" She looked from one angry face to the other and shook her head. "The school mediator always used to say, if you can't get it right, start again. So, let's do that. Both of you stand up!" She met Toni's glower directly with a determined stare. Toni hesitated, but when Lau stood she reluctantly followed suit. "Good, now, shake hands, and introduce yourselves. 'Hello, I'm Dr. Lau.' Try it!"

Lau's lips were twitching. He pulled himself straight, then bowed and held out his hand.

"Hello, I'm Dr. Amerigo Lau, Simon's father."

Klale shot Toni an anxious look. Toni sighed, thinking dark thoughts about Guild communal morality, but she took Lau's hand.

"Good evening, I'm Dr. Antonia Almiramez."

She savored Lau's stunned expression.

"From the Seattle Institute?"

"That's right."

"I was reading your papers last night. But I thought . . ."

"I'm only dead officially. You're welcome to check my DNA so long as you respect my privacy."

She had rendered Lau speechless. Klale was grinning ear to ear. Damn the girl for doing the right thing. But now it was time to take charge.

Toni sat and gestured to Lau. He dropped into his chair. Then she looked at Klale, who stood watching with avid attention.

"Klale, I appreciate your intervention, but perhaps you could do something else for half an hour. Check my mail, for instance, to see if there's anything from Choi. And you could answer your own, while you're at it. You had several messages, including one from the Fisher Bank."

"Finally!" said Klale. "All right. I know when I'm not wanted. But I expect to hear the details later!" She gave them a cheeky grin and retreated to the study, towing her chair after her.

"Let's start with a case history," said Toni. "Tell me about Simon."

She saw a flash of pain in Lau's eyes, then he swiveled and reached into his coat pocket for his phone. He unfolded the screen and keypad, accessed a file, then passed it over. The screen showed a grainy narrow-band net call. It took Toni a second to recognize the pretty, curly-haired child as Simon, aged nine or ten. He spoke in Chinese, then switched into English and Toni felt an eerie stab of recognition at his soft, childish voice.

"The first thing Mr. McCaskill asked me was why I never came back for Simon," said Lau. "Please believe me, I didn't know he was alive. . . ." He stopped to collect himself, then started at the beginning.

The story he related was substantially the same as the one Ron McCaskill had told Toni. Simon had been eight when his parents left to join a travelling revue.

"Of course, the tour was a farce," said Lau. "The bookings had never been made, the manager ran away, and we were stranded in Singapore. We couldn't make enough money to come back. We called Simon and I saw he was unhappy, but I thought he would be safe with my father. I didn't know . . ."

Lau clutched his glass.

"My father was not an evil man, Miz Toni. He was a factory worker in China and I believe he was exposed to slow-manifesting neurotoxins. After we left, he deteriorated very much. Then there was a fire on the boat. . . . I think my father was demented by that time. He told us Simon had died in the fire, then he stopped calling."

He looked urgently at her.

"I never thought he would lie . . ."

She nodded, watching his face closely.

"The next year my father tried to take that old junk out of Vancouver and drowned when it sank. Simone and I divorced. I married a Hong Kong woman, and her tong sent me to medical school. But I couldn't forget. I still kept these pictures on my phone. Finally, after I divorced again, I decided to come back."

Lau stopped and stared out the north window for long seconds, then turned back to Toni. She was ready, and she outlined what little she knew of Simon's recent history, painting him as a rough tool with personality remnants. Lau listened in grim silence, but he didn't seem surprised by anything she said. Undoubtedly he'd seen tools in Hong Kong.

"The only thing I've never understood," she finished, "is why he allowed me near him in the first place."

Lau looked up from pouring more cider, and flashed her a wry smile.

"I can tell you that. He recognized you."

"What?" she said stupidly.

"You look like Simone. It was the first thing I noticed when I met you."

Toni stared at him, aware of a cascade of confused emotions. She looked like Simon's mother? But it made sense. It was even appallingly obvious once Lau said it, but she'd been too busy looking for more obscure reasons for Simon's attachment.

"Am I that much like her?" she managed finally, irritated by his amusement.

"In the face, yes, especially in dim light. Simone's skin is darker and she's much taller—my height. But when we lived here she cut her hair very short, like you do. It's long now. Here," He picked up his phone and located a file. "I called her last night. She's . . . well, she didn't believe me. She thinks I am obsessive."

The screen blanked, then showed a strikingly beautiful Afroid woman with lumed skin-art and long flashy earrings. She resembled Toni all right, but not recently, thought Toni with a flash of sourness. Simone must be close to Toni's age, but she'd clearly had juvving treatments. She looked twenty-five. Lau had muted the sound, but as Toni watched the phone call she got a strong impression of polished charm, underlain by aggressive self-interest.

"She's an actress?"

"A dancer."

Of course, thought Toni. Of course.

"She finally qualified for the Entertainer's Guild, then refused to join," said Lau, his tone ironic. "She runs a small independent dance company in Eugene."

A tough woman, thought Toni. Few independents survived. Then it finally struck her. Two parents. Simon was a custom-designed weapon with two living parents and a strong personality fragment. She had stumbled onto a researcher's dream.

And she had a decision to make. She might not like Lau, but if she was going to work closely with him, she would have to trust him with all of the details about Simon. For a long moment she hesitated, worrying. Lau was tong debted. And he might still be a chameleon. On the other hand, Mary trusted him, and so did Ron McCaskill. Toni would just have to chance it.

"Let me show you something," she said finally.

She found her headset and passed it to Lau, who adjusted the goggles. Then she cued the dance sequence that Simon had sent her and leaned back to watch Lau's reaction.

Within seconds she saw shocked recognition hit him. He watched the entire sequence with rapt attention, then pulled off the goggles, looking deeply shaken. Toni passed him a handkerchief and he mopped his eyes. Finally he spoke in an uneven voice.

"My father and I taught him tai ji and those character positions. He used to copy us—that was my father he mimicked."

"Character positions?" asked Toni sharply.

"We were teaching him Cantonese. Imitating the characters was a way to help memorize them." His face crumpled. "Excuse me."

He stood, but Toni grabbed at the sleeve of his shirt.

"The characters he chose—do they mean anything?"

Lau focused on her.

"Mean anything? Oh, as a message? No. It's like English children singing the alphabet song."

Damn, thought Toni. Of course, a message would have been too much to hope for.

Lau was standing on Toni's patio, collecting himself, and Toni was trying to figure out what to do next when the study door burst open and Klale rushed into the room, tears dribbling down her cheeks.

"Toni . . . !"

"Klale, what's wrong?"

"They closed my net account! Took all my money, all my personal libraries, the family album, the boat logs, everything! They say it belongs to the Guild, but it was *mine!* They had no right to do that . . ."

In fact they did, and Toni wasn't surprised, but there was no point in saying so.

"I'm very sorry," she said gently.

"Those bent bastards!" Klale yelled. She yelled for another two minutes, then burst into tears again. Lau had quietly come back to the table and he passed her Toni's handkerchief with a sympathetic smile. Klale grabbed it and gulped back tears.

"Sorry, I interrupted you, didn't I?"

Toni looked at Lau.

"No, I think it's time we took a break anyway. I'll make tea."

She started for the kitchen, turning up lights, since the rain had brought an early twilight. Then she listened and realized that for some time she'd been hearing bursts of distant gunfire from the streets. The tong war was underway.

Klale was speaking to Lau.

". . . didn't mean to come in here and wail at you. But I got so upset . . . Oh, Toni, I checked your messages. Nothing from Choi, but there's one with no sender name."

Toni froze, teapot in hand, then turned and sprinted for her netset. She grabbed up the goggles and slipped them on, her fingers clumsy with tension.

Simon had sent her another dance. Toni opened it with excitement. Perhaps this time she'd learn something important. This file had no timeprint, but she froze Simon's face and magnified it, spotting telltale bruises around his eyes. A recent session, then. And when she started the playback she saw a distinct tremor at his temples. She restarted the sequence and watched carefully.

This dance was a form of anger catharsis, she decided. As the music took hold, fury lit up Simon's eyes and fired his movements. From a distance he looked magnificent and almost unbelievably agile, but as he started throwing knives in the air, Toni tensed. The shock from punishment and his recent injury must both have taken a toll on his reflexes. What if he missed? she wondered. Then he did.

For a moment she thought the knife had cleared him, then she switched angles and saw a cut on his leg. Simon looked down at it for a long moment as the music continued, then walked slowly back to the center of the room and started again, pausing to rub his hand across his forehead. In pain, she noted, and probably right on the edge of losing control.

Nonetheless when he screamed, she jolted and gasped. Damn! It had happened so fast! One second Simon's face was blank; the next second it contorted with rage. He fell to his knees, stabbing the floor with insane fury. The matting shredded, then shards of concrete spurted up.

Toni tried to keep her clinical calm; nonetheless she felt a sinking sense of futility. Had it happened this afternoon? Then he might be beyond her help.

She sped up the recording, skimming. Simon stabbed the floor for several more minutes, then the music finished and the file blanked. Damn, damn, damn!

What had happened? Had venting the rage allowed him to pull back under control for a little while longer, or was he too far gone?

She felt someone tap her shoulder, but ignored it and reran the file, studying Simon's behavior. As she watched his collapse again, something struck her. His empty hand stabbed too, as if he held a knife in it, and there was something about the way he moved . . . What did he see? His eyes were fixed beneath him, face livid with hatred, as if he was looking at some loathed object—Choi perhaps? Was he imagining killing Choi?

Then it hit her and she backed up the recording a third time, trembling with excitement. When he'd come to see her weeks ago he'd been covered in blood, especially his hands. Could he be reliving a memory of killing Choi?

She blanked the picture and sat thinking furiously. It was immensely tilted, but consistent. What if Choi was already dead? And what if the old man had trained Simon as his alter ego for net business? That would be the missing third piece of personality—the one that terrified Simon. He *was* Choi.

That explained the need to preserve Simon's intelligence and initiative, and it certainly explained Simon's deterioration in recent weeks. Simon couldn't let himself know that he'd done the unthinkable—killed his master. But he also couldn't function without the real Choi to reinforce and stabilize his psychosis, so his personality was naturally starting to reintegrate. In some confused way he must have sensed that he needed help. He'd come to Toni, but had been unable to tell her, or even himself, what the problem was. And since then he'd been making repeated, clumsy attempts to reach her.

Those calls from Choi might have been Simon! She thought back, trying to recapture every detail. The first call to Mary had occurred before Simon killed Choi, but if the old man had been sick at that time—a strong possibility—Simon might have made the call. He'd tried to buy the KlonDyke. And suddenly it made sense. The 'Dyke must be a sort of haven for Simon. He would want to protect it. Maybe he'd even wanted to protect Toni. Then he'd made a direct attempt get Toni to go to Bentall and assess him and she'd refused, saying she'd rather die than work for Choi!

She winced. No wonder she'd never heard back from Choi. Simon didn't know what else to do, and he was swiftly losing the ability to act.

Damn! She had to try again, fast!

She reached for her set and placed a call to Choi. It was shunted to reception, but she hadn't expected a live answer, so she recorded a message. Then she called three more times and repeated it: She was still interested in the contract and would come for a meeting as soon as possible. In Simon's disoriented state it was vital to keep pounding her message home.

Finally, she pulled off her goggles and turned to Klale and Lau who were sitting side by side at the table watching her.

"As you no doubt heard, I'm trying to set up another meeting with Simon. If that fails I'll go to Choi's bunker and try to get in," said Toni.

"I'll come!" volunteered Klale.

"And I," said Lau.

"No. It's too dangerous." She gave Lau a forceful look. "I especially can't take you. Simon reacted strongly to seeing you—it triggered a crisis. I can't risk that."

"But you can take me!" argued Klale. "Simon knows me and he trusts me!"

"He's extremely unstable, Klale."

"But what if you can't use your phone in that bunker and you have to call for help? What if Simon's unconscious and you have to drag him out? You can't go alone!"

Toni bit her lip. The hell of it was, Klale had a point. There was nobody else Simon might tolerate near him.

"All right," she said finally.

Klale grinned and jumped to her feet and Toni stared up at her, fascinated by Klale's irrepressible spirits. A few minutes ago the girl had been sobbing. Now she bounced on her toes and said: "Strat! So what do we do now?"

"We wait," Toni told her. "We can't go anywhere tonight, so we hope that Choi calls."

"Oh." Klale deflated and plopped herself down in the rickety chair. "Well, I can wait. Just watch me."

31

When the netset buzzed, Klale leaped for it and checked the call ID with a thudding heart. But it wasn't Simon. It was Mary calling for Toni. She sat back with a sigh, feeling her spirits sink.

They were gathered around Toni's big worktable, picking at the remains of a late lunch scavenged from the 'Dyke's kitchen. Lau had volunteered to cook and prepared the leftovers with gourmet flair, but no one had much appetite. Simon still hadn't called.

Toni took Mary's call and switched it to the wall screen. Mary glanced curiously at Dr. Lau but carried on as smoothly as if visitors at Toni's were an everyday occurrence. Did Mary know he was Simon's father? Klale wondered.

"I'm expecting a priority call," Toni warned her.

Mary nodded.

"This won't take long. I just need to talk to you. And Dr. Lau, too. We've been invited to City Hall tomorrow morning for an emergency council debate on sending the City Watch in to end the tong war. That, of course, would put Downtown under City control, so it's vital the D.R.A. be there. My problem right now is rounding up enough members to form a solid delegation."

"Is it safe to travel?" asked Toni.

"The City will provide escort. I'm bringing a group from Sisters and all the neighbors I can grab, and I'd like you and Klale and Rigo to come as well. It shouldn't take long. The meeting's at eleven. We'll leave from Sisters at ten and we should be back by one-thirty."

"I'd like to go," said Lau.

Toni frowned, then looked at Mary.

"We'll come if we can," she said.

Mary had to be burning with curiosity, but all she said was: "Thanks. Oh, and one more thing, love. Would you make sure that Pauline Johnson is fed?"

Toni grimaced.

"Didn't you take that damned animal with you?"

"Like someone else I know, she was too stubborn to leave," said Mary cheerfully, and logged off.

"It's a predator," muttered Toni at the blank screen. "Can't it go kill something?"

Klale laughed. The netset buzzed again. Mary must have forgotten something, thought Klale, but Toni checked the ID and tensed.

"Simon."

Klale sprang up and moved out of range of the optical pickup, towing Lau with her. Toni activated the big screen.

At first "Choi's" cold calm impressed Klale, then she noticed his hands trembling on the desk in front of him. And when he spoke, she felt a surge of alarm. His speech sounded slurred and confused.

But Toni must have been expecting that. She steered the conversation firmly, maintaining an appearance of reluctance to work for Choi, but giving clear orders for Simon to meet her at the KlonDyke's rear door. "Choi" seemed more coherent when they signed off.

They waited half an hour before setting out, Klale trying to act calm while she felt adrenaline pulse through her veins. Venturing into the bunker frightened her far more than she wanted Toni to know. She still couldn't forget the way Simon had looked after his punishment—blank and brutal, with all the humanity drained out of him. It wasn't difficult to imagine him killing someone.

But she loved Simon, she reminded herself again. She was debted to him for her life. She must have faith in him. If she believed in him rather than fearing him, surely he wouldn't harm her.

In the empty loading bay behind the KlonDyke, the silence was unnerving. No traffic sounds drifted in from the city's unnaturally empty streets. Klale hadn't even heard shots for a couple of hours, but it occurred to her for the first time that whichever tong had sent the death squad after Mary would be looking for Blade now, too.

"This is one way to get my mind off my bank account," Klale tried joking, then Simon appeared soundlessly behind them.

In spite of herself, Klale jumped. Simon held the familiar pistol in his hand, and she felt another jolt of apprehension as he pointed it at them and jerked his head toward the alley. Toni reached cautiously for Klale's arm and they walked uphill. Simon followed a dozen paces behind.

At each intersection they looked back and Simon gestured directions. Twice he checked his phone. Klale had expected to be led toward the old Bentall buildings near the harbor, but Simon angled east instead, through a maze of back alleys and rubble trails. After a number of blocks he directed them into a stinking blind alley and Klale felt a fresh rush of nerves. Why here?

But Simon paused partway down the alley at a rusted metal door set flush in a concrete wall. He dug in his pocket and, to Klale's surprise, pulled out a metal key. It fit in the lock and the door swung smoothly open.

Inside, Simon switched on a handlight and walked ahead of them through a maze of connected buildings, up and down stairs, through disused maintenance corridors and across abandoned mall and office levels. Klale caught occasional glimpses of daylight through cracks in boarded-up windows, but she quickly lost all sense of direction. Some of the rooms were empty, with thick, stifling air; others were partitioned into rough living quarters. Lights flicked off hurriedly as they approached, and people turned their faces away from Blade. The clammy darkness, fetid smells, and distant wails of children made Klale feel claustrophobic, and she kept a tight grip on Toni.

Eventually another battered maintenance door opened onto a brand new security entrance. Klale stared. It had a code pad, thumbprint glass and even a blood prick set for DNA scans. Simon stopped in the passage, holstered his gun, and searched both of them with impersonal thoroughness, then checked Toni's carryall. Klale caught her breath and felt Toni beside her tense, but he examined the neural gear expressionlessly, then replaced it.

The security door thudded shut behind them with sickening finality. Beyond was another long passage of pitted concrete, stained with leaks. It led to a staircase. They dropped three more flights and passed through a second air-sealed security door which opened this time on a new-looking passage.

What a monument to paranoia! thought Klale, as their footsteps echoed in a shiny, white-tiled corridor that smelled harshly of disinfectants. They were inside the bunker now, but all the inner doors also had air-tight seals, as in a submarine. Of course the bunker had probably been built back when nobody knew how far the sea level would rise. The oppressive silence was broken only by a faint hum of air recirculation.

Near the end of the corridor Simon stopped and signed at them to wait, then he opened a door and went through it. Klale stood silently next to Toni, fighting down the sudden fear that Mr. Choi would appear. When she heard Choi's cold voice with a faint Chinese accent, her heart pounded hard in her chest.

"Please come in, Dr. Almiramez."

Toni beckoned Klale and whispered close to her ear.

"Stay by the door. If there's trouble, run."

Yeah? Where? thought Klale. But she nodded.

The heavy door swung open under Toni's hand. Beyond it was the traditional Chinese room. And facing them, sitting ramrod straight behind a wide mahogany desk, sat Simon.

In front of the desk a harsh spotlight illuminated a circle of polished floor. Klale scanned the room but there were no chairs. Toni walked in with a confident stride, put down her carryall and stood slightly to one side of the light, arms crossed. She looked entirely at ease, Klale thought with admiration.

"Good afternoon, Mr. Choi," said Toni coolly.

"Good afternoon," returned Simon in Choi's voice. His face was blank, but his posture and movements were a bizarre parody of Choi's, and his eyes stared forward with piercing intelligence. He seemed much more coherent than he had earlier, thought Klale, but then Toni said he'd probably been planning this for some time.

Toni opened with a rude directness that made Klale flinch.

"I'm here. Now, what's your contract?"

"I require an assessment of my tool," Simon told her emotionlessly.

"Why?"

"It has become unstable."

"You could replace the tool," Toni told him in a hard voice. Klale caught her breath, but saw no flicker of reaction in Simon.

"It is inconvenient to do so at present," he replied. "I require you to diagnose the causes of the instability, and recommend corrective measures."

"I could do that," said Toni slowly, "but I'll need information. I assume that you kept training records?"

"Of course."

"Good," she said. "We can start by reviewing them."

Simon stared at her for just an instant too long, then he pushed his chair back and looked down at the desk, focusing on something near the floor. Without warning he raised his leg and kicked violently downward. Wood splintered. Simon leaned down and when he sat up again he held a handful of datacubes. He dropped them on the shiny desktop, selected one, then swiveled to his right and flipped up a screen on the arm of the desk.

Klale caught a flicker of dismay on Toni's face. Hadn't she expected him to have records? Or maybe this steely self-control was more than she'd counted on. Toni frowned at Simon, then stepped forward, as if to look over his shoulder. Simon whirled instantly, eyes icy.

"Stay where you are!"

Toni met his gaze for a second, then moved back. Simon wasn't going to let her near him, Klale realized. What was she going to do?

Toni cleared her throat and spoke in a clinical tone.

"How old was the subject when you acquired him?"

Simon turned back and his eyes flicked across the screen. There was a pause.

"Twelve and a half years."

"Do you have records of his appearance before alterations?"

"Certainly."

Another pause.

"May I see them?" Toni prodded.

Simon hesitated, then reached under the desk and nodded toward the side of the room directly opposite Klale. The sunlit courtyard vanished from the wall to be replaced by a twice life-sized image of a child with curly black hair and a familiar burn scar. He stared forward with terrified eyes. Klale felt a surge of pity and looked at Simon. He was looking toward the picture, but his eyes seemed unfocused.

"What physical alterations were made?" asked Toni sharply.

Simon looked back at his desk screen.

"Growth, strength, neutering, emergency response, immune protections, and multiple filament intrusions."

"And psychological changes?"

"Memory suppression and modification, emotional dissociation, behavioral conditioning, psychotic patterning."

Toni pushed harder, asking him to describe the training procedures and Klale listened with growing horror, wondering how Simon could describe the details with such detachment. He was reciting conditioning techniques, when Toni interrupted suddenly.

"What was his name?"

"Simon Lau," he answered, then a jolt ran through him and he gripped the edge of the desk. He turned to stare at Toni, eyes wide.

Toni leaned forward urgently.

"Simon! What did you do to Mr. Choi?"

Simon gasped.

"Simon . . . I . . ." He started rising slowly to his feet. "I . . . killed . . . him . . ." Abruptly Simon's arms whipped above his head, fingers linking into a two-handed fist, and he smashed down into the desk, screaming.

Klale jumped violently. Toni grabbed her bag, and backed toward Klale, waving her out into the hall. Behind them, Simon's fists crashed into the desk again.

"I didn't want to break his self-control like that, but I had to knock him out of the Choi persona," Toni said grimly. "I just hope that he wears off his adrenaline boost wrecking the furniture."

"We're not leaving him?" asked Klale anxiously.

"No. We're going to search the bunker," said Toni. She shrugged off her coat and wedged it under the office door so it wouldn't swing shut. "Try the next door."

Klale obeyed, trying to ignore the horribly familiar screams behind her.

"What are we looking for?"

"Training equipment. And Choi."

Klale stopped and turned back, staring at Toni with horror.

"But you said he's dead!"

"I *think* he's dead. I want to be sure."

"Wonderful. Now you tell me."

After the second door, Toni started cursing. They were all locked, including the entrance Simon had brought them through, and the locks were fingerprint activated. There was no way to search the place and, worse, no way out without Simon.

Klale looked back toward the office fearfully, then realized that the crashes and screams had stopped. That was quick, she thought uneasily.

"He wouldn't kill himself, would he?" she asked, with sudden fear.

"Can't," said Toni shortly, but she frowned. "Stay back," she ordered, then stepped quietly to the open door.

She paused in the doorway for a minute while Klale stood a few paces back, burning with curiosity. Finally Toni stepped into the room and Klale hurried forward to peer inside. Simon sat behind the wrecked antique desk, working on the netset. The top of the desk was broken in half, and the force of his blows had collapsed its legs, but the run-off arm under the netset stood intact. Toni approached him very cautiously.

"Simon?"

No answer. She leaned over the desk and reached toward him, then pulled back, apparently having second thoughts.

"Simon?"

He still didn't answer. His hands were moving swiftly over a keypad. Toni watched him for a minute, then went around behind the desk.

There was something trailing from Simon's skull, Klale noticed, and she moved farther into the room to get a better look, keeping what she hoped was a safe distance. Optic cables. They were attached by little suction cups, sticking to his hairless scalp. So that's what a fully wired data shark looked like, thought Klale. He didn't wear a headset and his eyes were closed, although the screen scrolled in front of him. He was experiencing the net with all his senses and might not even hear Toni.

Toni looked up frowning, then beckoned Klale forward. She came, trying to walk silently on the hard floor, and peered over Simon's shoulder at the screen. Graphics bloomed and vanished and a cryptic jumble of Roman and Chinese characters scrolled past.

Toni spoke in a low voice.

"Do you have any idea what he's doing?"

"No." Klale watched intently, trying to pick up a pattern. She saw what looked like a command chain. "Wait a minute . . . ! That was an address . . . I think these Chinese characters are local data files. That would make sense, wouldn't it, for Choi to keep records in Chinese? Could they be training records?"

Toni shook her head emphatically.

"No. Choi was careful to store them on cubes off the system, where Simon couldn't stumble across them. Which reminds me . . ." She looked around. "I counted six cubes. Here's one."

They searched around the desk and floor and retrieved the rest. Toni stuffed them in her carryall. Klale watched Simon again. More file addresses, and then delete codes . . .

"He's setting up a purge!"

"Of course." Toni smiled humorlessly. "He's killing Choi again— this time Choi's sim and his hoard of blackmail data."

Choi's data, Klale thought suddenly. He would know all about the tongs. He might know who had sent the death squad after Mary. He might even have something concrete on Captain Dhillon that would back up Klale's complaint.

"Simon!" she yelled.

Toni whirled, startled. Klale ducked past her and grabbed Simon's arm. Simon jumped violently, shoved his chair backward and opened his eyes. There were black bruises of exhaustion underneath them.

"Simon, don't wipe Choi's data!" Klale told him urgently. "Spill it!"

Simon sat motionless, his gaze fixed unwaveringly on Klale, but she wasn't sure he had even heard her.

"Just think!" she urged. "What would Choi hate more? For all his files to be destroyed? Or for them to be *given* away. *Free.* Send them to the KlonDyke."

"*No!*" Toni grabbed Klale's arm. "Simon, no! Klale, you cret! If Simon sends the data to us, the tongs will trace it and blame us!"

"Oh." Klale hadn't thought of that. Then Simon whispered hoarsely.

"Given away . . . *Free* . . ."

His face twisted with hatred. Klale backed up a step, alarmed. Toni moved past her and kneeled by the chair.

"Simon, please listen. Don't send the data to the KlonDyke. The tongs will trace it and kill us."

"A spill to one location is easily contained," said Simon suddenly. "Many locations are optimal."

He closed his eyes again, then spoke sharply in Chinese, making Klale jump. But it was just a voice command. The netset screen began scrolling again. Toni let go of Simon's hand.

"I didn't think that through," apologized Klale.

"No, you didn't," said Toni angrily, but her attention was focused on the screen. "He's reading in a whole netnode directory."

Klale stared in awe.

"That's immense! Do you think he can do it?"

Toni nodded.

"Choi did some notorious spills. He had the best stealthware. The nodes won't be able to inoculate fast enough."

It took a long time for Simon to finish, even though he worked swiftly with voice interface and a modified keypad. Eventually Toni leaned against the listing desk. Klale found herself fidgeting uncontrollably and paced the hallway. When that became intolerable, she went back into the room and paced.

"Klale!" said Toni with sudden urgency.

Klale looked up. The screen was white and Simon sat motionless in front of it.

"Back off a bit, please," Toni told her. Then she stepped beside Simon and put her hand gently over his.

"Simon? Simon, it's Toni. Take my hand."

For long seconds Simon did nothing. Toni repeated herself twice. Then Simon shuddered, and turned his hand over to grasp Toni's.

"Good!" Toni told him warmly, putting both her hands around his. "I'm here to help you. As long as you hold onto my hand you'll be safe, Simon," she told him. "Do you understand?"

There was a very long pause, then he nodded. He seemed dazed. Toni squeezed his hand and spoke encouragingly, as if to a child.

"That's right. You're safe with me. Now, when did you last sleep, Simon?"

He stared around vaguely, then spoke in a voice so small that Klale could barely hear.

"I don't know . . ."

"Are you hungry?"

There was a pause, then Simon nodded.

Toni spoke quietly to Klale, keeping her eyes on him.

"There's a flask in my bag. Take it out and pass it to me slowly, then move back again."

Klale did as she was instructed. Toni unscrewed the flask and poured some of the contents into the lid.

"OK, Simon. I brought this for you. It's an energy shake. Chocolate flavor. Unplug yourself first, then you can drink it."

Simon obediently peeled off the receptors, wound the cables up neatly, then drank what Toni gave him. Klale waited impatiently, shifting from foot to foot as Toni gave him some more and then recapped the flask with slow, careful motions. Simon's eyelids drooped.

"Simon!" called Toni sharply. "Remember you're with me. You're safe. But I need your help."

She tugged at his hand and he lurched to his feet, then towered over her, swaying with exhaustion. Toni shoved his optic cables into her pocket, then led Simon out of the room by the hand, looking absurdly like a child towing a reluctant parent. Klale followed. In the hall Toni had Simon open the door they'd arrived through and Klale looked at it with intense relief, then ran back and grabbed a piece of the broken desk to wedge it open. She wasn't taking any chances.

Simon opened five more doors. Three led into densely packed

DONNA McMAHON

storerooms. Choi could have stayed underground for decades, Klale decided. One door opened onto a second staircase, and another revealed the water tanks and air recirc systems. Toni was careful to make sure Simon left the doors unlocked, although that was clearly against his instincts. At the next door, Simon froze.

"Open it," Toni repeated.

"It is not permitted," he said flatly. His face was expressionless but his hands trembled violently. Toni hesitated, then moved on. At the next room he stopped, again without touching the lock. This time Toni used a different tactic.

"What's in this room, Simon?"

"It's . . . it's . . ." Simon backed away violently, pulling out of Toni's grasp. "I don't know!"

"All right, Simon," started Toni soothingly, but Simon turned and bolted down the hall into the second staircase. The door thumped shut behind him.

"Damn!" exclaimed Toni. "I pushed too hard!"

"What now?" asked Klale, fighting back her own fear. The door they'd come through was still wedged open, but she felt the bunker closing in around her like an antiseptic tomb.

Toni turned and focused on her, then put a reassuring hand on Klale's shoulder.

"Klale, he left the netset on. Would you please try to call my apartment? Tell Dr. Lau what's happening. And then look for internal security. I'll bet Choi put surveillance cameras in all these rooms. You can search for Simon that way. I'll look on foot."

Trying to keep me busy, Klale thought, but it wasn't such a bad idea. While Toni shouldered the carryall and headed for the stairwell, she went back to the office.

It took several minutes to patch in translation so she could read the Cantonese screens. Then she discovered that external communications were secured and she couldn't call out. However, Simon had left internal systems open and Toni was right—the rooms all had cameras. Klale began checking the vid feeds one by one.

Storeroom. Hallway. More hallway. Stairs. Herself sitting behind the broken desk. Interesting, but not helpful. She switched to the next camera.

This one looked down on a diagnostic couch. Klale maneuvered the lens. The room looked like a medlab, with imaging scanners and automated surgical lasers. Everything was very neat.

She made a note of the camera number, in case Toni was interested, then switched to the next room. Another storeroom. Then a room containing a single canopied bed with ornately carved bedposts. In stark contrast with the rest of the bunker, this room was a mess. A heap of clothes lay on the floor, a bag had been tossed carelessly on the end of the bed, and it looked like somebody had thrown food everywhere—on the bed and the floor and even the walls. Not food, Klale realized with a sudden sick feeling. Dried blood. And the heap on the floor was Choi.

Klale zoomed in, stifling her squeamishness. Choi had worn a robe of some sort, and one skinny naked foot poked out from underneath it, pathetically human. Well preserved, too, she noted, trying to keep a detached attitude. Almost mummified. Of course, this was a sterile environment. Probably the air scrubbers even removed the smell.

She swiveled the lens back toward the bed. There was something odd about the object on it, too, like wisps of gray hair . . .

Then she understood. Simon had torn off Choi's head.

32

Toni tried the pressure door on the second landing. Locked. She jogged up the stairwell, scowling. If Simon had locked a door behind him, she might never reach him. Choi's bunker was a fortress—air and water tight, and biologically filtered. And so was Simon, she thought suddenly—immunologically tailored to ensure he couldn't bring contagions from outside. She had wanted to work on him in Choi's medlab, but she was sure now that Simon wouldn't go near it. Well, he was extraordinarily tenacious to have held himself together so long after Choi's death. Surely he could make it another few hours.

On the fourth landing she found an unlocked door. She clutched her phone tighter and pushed it open.

An animal-like keening told her instantly that she'd found Simon. She opened the door wider and looked in. Her own reflection stared back, making her jump. Full length mirrorscreens covered one wall, and there was padded matting on the floor. This was the gym she'd seen in Simon's recording. It was a vast chilly room—probably an old parking garage with an intermediate floor knocked out to give a high roof. After the bleached sterility of the rest of the bunker, the blue-painted ceiling and even the irregular protrusions of old piping were a relief. There were speakers placed around the room, a netset in one corner, and a pile of training equipment. It was the first room she'd seen that had the faintest air of being lived in.

Toni followed the eerie wails and found Simon curled in a recess behind a support pillar, with his back tightly against the wall and his arms wrapped around his knees. His face was blank, despite the misery escaping from his mouth. Probably unaware of the noise, Toni thought, with a stab of pity. It reminded her grimly of the wards.

She called to him softly several times, then louder. He took no notice. Bad, she thought, debating what to do. Finally she dropped her phone, opened the carryall and got a tranq gun. She adjusted the dosage conservatively, guessing at what he could take, and pressed the gun against Simon's upper arm. It hissed. Simon didn't move or blink.

"Simon?"

She put the tranq gun back and kneeled in front of him, stroking his fingers where they were locked around his legs, and waiting for the drug to take effect. Within half a minute his rigid muscles began to relax slightly. She rested her hand on top of his and then reached out to touch his cheek. He flinched and the wailing abruptly stopped.

"Simon?"

Still he didn't look at her. Damn, she didn't want to risk any more tranq. She and Klale couldn't drag him up all those stairs unconscious.

"Simon! Get up," she ordered firmly. She repeated the order again, then yelled. Finally his eyes flicked past hers. They were terrible; sick with fear. He was paralyzed with vertigo, she realized—pressed into the corner trying to make the room stop spinning.

Abruptly she remembered another room with a ceiling much like this. She concentrated, trying to place the image, then it slid into place with a sickening jolt. She'd been twelve or thirteen years old. The pimp had taken her in a cab at night to the back of an old house somewhere in Chicago. They'd gone through a basement door into a room with piping between the ceiling beams and cement walls painted white. A fat woman with stiff gray hair had offered her a seat in a leather chair, then before Toni realized what was happening, the woman and the pimp had strapped her into it. So she wouldn't panic and run off, they told her. She'd retorted that she was braver than that, and they'd laughed contemptuously.

The woman had shaved part of Toni's head, wheeled over a brace, and immobilized her skull. Then the two of them walked out of the room, leaving Toni alone minute after minute after minute. Her bravado had dissolved into terrified tears as she realized that she was utterly helpless. They could do anything to her. Anything at all. No one would know or care. Nobody would help.

Toni had been far luckier than Simon. But she knew that vulnerability. That terror. She reached out again.

"Simon! Simon, let me sit with you!"

She tugged at his fingers until they unlocked, then pushed his knees down. He didn't resist. She moved forward and sat on his legs, then pulled his arms around her and wrapped hers around his chest. After a while she felt his arms tighten against her, then his chest started to shudder with the force of suppressed sobs. He gulped air, struggling to make no noise.

"It's all right to cry, Simon," she told him urgently. "You're allowed to cry!" Then she realized that she was giving herself permission as well. Her face was streaked with tears. She'd been so afraid. And Simon needed her tears. For the first time in years she let go and allowed sobs to rip out of her, pressing against Simon's warm bulk and wondering distantly as they rocked together who was comforting whom.

Finally she untangled her fingers from his shirt and pulled back a little, wiping her eyes. There were wet streaks on Simon's face. Good. That was a start.

"Simon?"

Her voice had come out shockingly small. He looked down at her, meeting her eyes for just a second before flinching away. She reached up gently and stroked his cheek, then looked inside herself, trying to find the right words.

She never found them. Instead she heard a door open and then Klale's urgent voice.

"Toni?"

"Here," replied Toni, hastily brushing at her face. Klale's footsteps thudded across the matting at a run, and Toni turned to look as Klale rounded the pillar. The girl's face was panicky.

"Toni, I was in the surveillance routine, when the set started some sort of countdown. There's less than ten minutes!"

Shit! A security trap. Either triggered by Klale or by Simon's spill. Toni swiveled in Simon's lap and put her hand on his upper arm.

"Simon, can you talk to me now?"

He nodded.

"Do you know what that countdown is?"

"It's a destruct sequence."

"For what?"

"The bunker."

Oh hell! And would that destruct sequence include Simon's fish-hook code? It would be like Choi to destroy all his property at once.

"How can we get out of here, Simon?"

"There are four exits with fourteen subsidiary escape routes," he told her. She grimaced and struggled up out of his lap, then reached back and took his hand.

"Lead us outside. Quickly."

Simon swayed slightly when he stood, but he seemed to recover as he strode across the room. Toni slung the carryall on her shoulder and followed, trotting to keep up. Klale jogged at her side, face pale.

Toni expected Simon to go up the stairs, but he turned down instead, dropping below the level of Choi's office. The staircase ended in another locked security door, beyond which was a seemingly endless concrete tunnel, low enough that even Toni had to duck her head and Simon moved in an awkward crouch. It looked recently built. One of Choi's private escape routes, no doubt.

They hurried silently. The tunnel turned inexplicably several times and finally ended in a metal staircase. There was no door, but Simon came to a sharp halt several meters from the stairs, crouched, pulled out his phone and entered a code. Somewhere in the distance Toni heard a smooth click. Simon moved forward again.

At the top of the staircase he paused by a rusted hatchway and turned toward Toni.

"This is the old transit tunnel," he said clearly, his voice sliding into Choi's. "Turn left and proceed along the walkway to the tunnel mouth. If the tide is in you'll have to wade until you reach a ladder."

He turned and it was Klale who caught at his arm.

"Simon! No! Come with us!"

The muscles around his jaw clenched, and Toni realized that he was struggling to refuse. She grabbed Klale's arm and pulled it away, then put her hand on his very lightly.

"That wasn't an order, Simon. It was a request. We're *asking* you to come with us. Please come."

His eyes were closed. He opened them and looked at her directly.

"Simon used you," he whispered. "To tap the KlonDyke."

"I know," she told him gently.

"You hate Simon."

"No, Simon. Think! Who told you that?"

Simon paused, then said slowly: "*He* did."

"He lied," she said urgently. "I don't hate you and I don't blame you for what Choi ordered you to do. I want to help. Please come with me and let me try to help you." If the fishhook isn't linked to the self-destruct, she added silently, but pushed that worry back. There was nothing she could do about it.

"Please, Simon," added Klale anxiously.

There was a very slight crease at Simon's brow.

"He lied," repeated Simon slowly, pulling away from Toni. "He lied." He spun and slammed his fist into the wall with sickening force. Then he hit it again, even harder. Toni winced at the snap of breaking bones and the blood on his knuckles, but she had no way of re-straining him. Klale clutched Toni's shoulder. Simon kept pounding—three, four, five more times, then stopped and spoke in an empty voice.

"He mutilated Simon. Tore everything out. It's all twisted inside."

"I know. I understand. I can help. You can hold onto me, Simon. I won't leave you alone. Please come."

He stood motionless and Toni tried to ignore the seconds ticking past. She could feel Klale's breath gusting against her ear. How long did they have left? Were they far enough away to be safe? No way to tell. They had to move! Finally she reached out.

"Simon, take my hand."

He turned slowly, staggering a little, then held out his bloody, misshapen hand. Toni swallowed and grasped it. He didn't seem to notice any pain. She tugged, wincing at the feel of bones moving against each other. He followed.

They were still groping through the dark transit tunnel when an explosion knocked them off their feet. Shards of rubble rocketed from the roof. Toni covered her head and lay huddled in terror for a few seconds, but the tunnel held. Next to her, Klale swore in a high, frightened voice.

"Klale? Are you all right?"

"Oww! It's my knee. I banged it right where I ripped it in the garbage chute. Hurts like hell."

"Simon?"

No answer.

Toni found her handlight and shone it through the dusty darkness at Simon's prostrate bulk. She couldn't see any injuries. She tugged his hand and felt a flood of relief as he started to get up.

They continued along the tunnel, wading the last few dozen yards through icy, gurgling salt water, then climbed a barnacle-encrusted maintenance ladder up into the night rain of Downtown. Toni didn't let go of his hand again.

33

"Was he in a fight?" Dr. Lau asked Klale.

"With a wall," Klale replied, studying the doctor curiously out of the corner of her eye for any resemblance to Simon. Were their noses similar?

"Well, the wall won," said Lau. He bandaged Simon's left hand with smooth, professional motions, but his voice was rough and his face was mobile with barely contained emotion. Simon sat oblivious on the couch, his head tilted back against a pillow, earphones on, and eyes closed.

"I've found dosage charts for Simon," said Toni. She was using her netset at the worktable, skimming through Choi's datacubes.

"Good," said Lau. "I'm doing what I can with the hand, but he has multiple compound fractures. He needs surgery."

Toni sighed and rubbed her eyes.

"It's going to have to wait until we get to Seattle. By the way, when you're done, please run a blood screening on Klale. I cleaned her knee, but she's had several rusty metal cuts."

Lau glanced at Klale.

"I'll be with you in a few minutes."

Klale nodded, then watched Toni pick up the netset and her carryall and move them over to the floor beside the couch. She took a medspray from Lau's kit, filled it, and passed it to Lau who administered it carefully to Simon's broken hand. Simon didn't flinch.

Dr. Lau handed the unit back and Toni reached into his kit again.

"Are you going to work on him now?" Lau asked unhappily.

"I have to. He sleeps under induction and REM controls. I've got to get him hooked up before he dozes off into nightmares." She loaded another medspray and gave Lau a tense look. "I'm giving him a mild tranquilizer and I've put a remote-activated knockout pack over his carotid artery, but it won't be enough if he goes berserk. Is your phone coded?"

Klale saw the muscles in Lau's jaw clench. He nodded.

"Don't forget the 'Dyke's jammers," Toni instructed as she administered the tranq in Simon's good arm. "You'll need a maxed tight beam, within five meters, aimed directly. Move back behind the couch and keep your eyes on him at all times."

Lau hesitated, looking like he wanted to argue. Toni ignored him and packed the medspray back in his kit with swift confident movements, then turned to the netset. Lau hovered over her for another few seconds, then clutched his phone and stepped behind the couch.

"Can I help?" asked Klale.

"No," said Toni, then looked up and met her gaze. "Truly. I'd prefer you out of this room, but if you must watch, stay over there by the bedroom door. No noise, no sudden movements."

Klale limped apprehensively to the door. When she was in position, Toni removed Simon's earphones, then sat down next to him, picked up his undamaged hand, and started talking gently, inducing hypnosis. It was like a standard first aid induction, only more focused and deeper, thought Klale. And Christ, Toni had stamina. An hour before they'd been running for their lives, but now Toni sat calmly, radiating a sense of professional competence, as if this was just another day at the clinic. Simon opened his eyes.

"Simon, you're going to stay very calm," Toni told him slowly and evenly. "I want you to focus on me, listen to what I say, and answer my questions. You can remember everything now—everything that happened when you were Simon, and when you were Blade, and when you were Choi."

He flinched at the last name, but nodded. Toni leaned forward.

"Simon, your master is dead. Choi Shung Wai is dead. Bentall is gone. You are never going back there. Do you understand?"

He held very still for long seconds, then whispered, "Yes."

"You're with me now, Simon. Do you understand?"

There was another pause, then instead of replying he sat up and moved forward. Klale flinched and saw Dr. Lau grip his phone tighter, but Simon simply slid off the couch onto his knees, then stretched out and abased himself to Toni facedown, the way he had after his punishment. Klale looked away, repulsed, then forced herself to look back.

"Simon, no. Sit up," Toni said firmly. Simon rose to a kneeling position in front of her, eyes downcast. "Tell me what you're doing."

His reply was so low that Klale could barely hear.

"I am grateful for your patience with such a miserable servant. I am grateful for . . ."

Toni interrupted.

"Do you recognize me as your master?"

"Yes."

She paused a second, then said harshly: "No."

Klale caught her breath. A jolt of shock and confusion ran through Simon. Toni reached for his right hand, voice gentle again.

"Easy Simon, easy. Stay calm. I won't leave you. I'm right here."

It must be hurting her, Klale thought, looking at how tightly his giant hand had wrapped around her small one. They were almost the same shade of brown, she noticed. Toni leaned forward.

"Simon, I'm going to explain something and it's very important that you understand. You are not a slave. You are not a tool. You are a person. You were a boy named Simon who was sold to Choi and altered, but Choi didn't destroy you. You arc still a person. You are still Simon."

Toni stared closely into Simon's eyes. Klale couldn't decipher anything on his face but she saw an unsatisfied frown on Toni's.

"Simon . . ." Toni's voice was soft and urgent. "Simon . . . tools don't dance. Only people dance."

This time Klale heard him catch his breath. Toni pressed on quickly.

"You're damaged, Simon. You know that—you told me so. I can help. I can help you relearn and rebuild until you become your own master."

Simon shuddered and Klale saw Toni wince—he must have grabbed at her hand—then she continued in a reassuring tone.

"It's all right. I understand that you can't do that now. You were conditioned to need orders. I can give you those, Simon. I can give you a structure until you learn how to make your own. But I won't do it without your consent. Therefore, I'm asking your permission to be your master until you're able to function by yourself." She paused, anxiety showing on her face. "Do you understand?"

Simon swayed slightly.

"I . . . don't know."

No wonder, thought Klale. That was a hell of a complex data spill for him to absorb.

"Simon, look at me. Look me in the eyes."

His head tilted upward.

"Will you allow me to be your master?"

For several long seconds their gazes locked and Klale wondered what they saw. Then Simon's reply came, unexpectedly firm.

"Yes."

Toni nodded, still remarkably calm, and Klale let out a long breath.

"Very well. I'm your master now, Simon. I give you orders and you follow them." She took a breath. "Give me your access codes."

Simon's muscles went rigid. Klale gripped the door frame.

"It is not permitted."

"It is permitted," Toni countered sharply. "I'm your master and I order it."

"Simon doesn't have the codes."

"Choi does."

Simon remained motionless, breathing fast. Toni held out the netpad and repeated the order. Finally Klale saw Simon's shoulders droop, then he reached forward and began entering a sequence. Toni exhaled and shut her eyes for a second, and Klale suddenly realized that Toni had been gambling. She hadn't known whether Simon had the codes. Mother!

Klale leaned limply against the door frame, feeling drained. After their escape from the bunker she'd thought that her body must have exhausted its adrenaline supply, but evidently she had unlimited amounts. In the background Dr. Lau wiped his forehead.

Toni dug in her carryall and produced the optic cables she'd taken from Choi's desk. Then she took out a curving piece of metal and began attaching the cables to it with quick fingers. Was that a training collar? Klale wondered, with a new surge of apprehension. Simon looked up from the netset, saw it, and flinched sharply away from her.

"Lie down here," Toni told him, but he was looking around the apartment in sudden, panicked recognition. Did he remember being punished? His gaze flicked over Lau and Klale and then stopped at the study door.

"Lie down, Simon," repeated Toni sharply. "That's a command."

Dr. Lau held his phone tightly, face taut. Toni took a cable from the collar and plugged it into her netset. Simon shrank back, tucking his bandaged arm protectively behind his head in a childish gesture. He was trembling and Klale could feel herself sweating with sympathetic fear.

"I won't punish you, Simon. I promise. I'm just going to do the assessment that you asked for. I won't hurt you, and I won't alter you."

Abruptly Klale found herself longing to pull Toni back. Didn't she understand how much she was asking? Simon was shaking violently now, his unnatural face gray and shiny with sweat.

"*Lie down!*" snapped Toni.

Simon's body jerked as if he'd been whipped. For a horrible frozen second Klale thought he would strike Toni, but he squeezed his eyes shut, then stretched himself face down onto the floor, breathing in panicked gasps. Toni reached forward and ran her finger swiftly over the back of his head, pressing a small plastic suction cup in place near the base of his skull. As she placed it with her right hand, she swiveled and hit a pad on the netset with her left hand. A cable glowed to life and Simon's body sagged. Air hissed out of his lungs.

Toni placed the other cups more slowly, licking them first, and then moving them carefully into position while she watched oscillating displays. When they were in place, she turned back to the set and started working on it. Was Simon breathing? Klale wondered anxiously. Finally she saw his chest move.

"It's all right, we're in." Toni reached over and put one hand on Simon's shoulder. "Easy, Simon, easy . . . I'm going to try to interrupt your fear response. It will take me a minute to find an effective pattern. There's some damage to the thalamic chip. Just listen to my voice and feel my hand on your shoulder. . . ."

She worked on the set for another minute, talking steadily. Lau let go of his phone with obvious relief and joined Toni at the set, watching over her shoulder.

"Simon, I can't find an easy fear block, so I'm going to use an existing subroutine to anesthetize your emotional responses. Your feelings will fade into calm, starting . . . now. Relax as much as you can. If possible, I'd like you to go back to the mountain. It will take me ten or fifteen minutes to run a general diagnostic, then I'll call you back and give you instructions."

Klale couldn't hold back any longer. Dr. Lau had pulled a pillow off the couch and was sliding it carefully under Simon's head. She joined them.

"Toni?" she asked anxiously.

"Mmm."

"How is he?"

"Ah . . . standard thalamic plug and five custom nine-filament arrays, some neural scarring . . . Wish I'd been able to get precoded apparatus from the bunker." Then she pulled her attention from the screen and focused on Klale. Her face softened.

"Fine, Klale. In fact, he's doing extremely well." She glanced at Lau and added quietly: "Simon's a very tough man and courageous as hell. I don't think I could have done what he just did."

Klale felt relief bubble up inside her chest.

"We did it!"

She drew a tired smile from Toni.

"At least we can treat him now, though I admit I'd feel better if I'd seen Choi's body—just to be sure."

"I saw it," said Klale abruptly, smile fading. She swallowed, remembering the corpse. "Believe me, he's extremely dead." And no point feeling sorry, either. He'd deserved it, she told herself. She gestured toward Simon. "May I touch him?"

When Toni nodded, she kneeled awkwardly on her good knee and patted Simon's shoulder, then reached down and placed her fingers against his upturned cheek.

"Simon, it's Klale. I just . . . I just wanted to say what I said before, because maybe you don't remember. I said that I loved you, Simon. I still do. I love you."

When she looked up, Toni was turning away, and Klale thought she saw a trace of sadness on the older woman's face. Then she realized that Dr. Lau was staring at her with startled curiosity.

She didn't feel up to explanations, so she gave him a cryptic grin, then moved over and put her arms around Toni.

"How are you?"

"Fine," said Toni shortly, though her shoulders were rigid with tension and she looked tired. She pulled away from Klale and forced a smile. "Perhaps after Dr. Lau checks you over you could call Ron. Tell him we'll need that boat after all. See if he can do it tomorrow night."

"Strat!"

Klale sat impatiently while Lau took a blood sample from her for his analyzer, then she bounced into the study, delighted to be calling with good news. She placed the call and got ready to speak, but instead of Mr. McCaskill's voice she heard the soothing tones of a reception protocol informing her that net traffic had temporarily exceeded local node capacity and only priority calls could be routed. Klale blinked at the set, astonished. Satellite links overloaded occasionally, but a local netnode? She'd never heard of that.

"This call is high priority!" she said.

In response she got a long pause, then an apology for "temporary difficulties." "Only calls to designated emergency IDs will be accepted at this time," the system told her. "We apologize for your inconvenience."

What, not even an offer to queue Klale's call? Then it finally hit her. Simon's data spill! She'd forgotten all about it. Hell, the Programmers must have shut down this entire local netnode to try and contain it. With sudden excitement, she switched to local news. The first site she tried was showing a creaky documentary on greenhouse gardening . . . and so was the next, and the next. Her schedule queries only produced more apologies for the downage. Finally she tore off her headset in frustration. This might be the biggest spill in local history, but she had no way to find out what was happening!

She paced the study a few minutes and tried again, then finally gave up and left. Staring at the set wouldn't bring it back up.

In the living room the smell of reheated chili and pompommes made Klale suddenly ravenous. Toni had Simon sitting up, still plugged in, eating from a plate in his lap. He seemed unaware of his surroundings. As Klale watched, he finished and Toni took his plate, then let him lie down on the couch, knees awkwardly jackknifed.

Klale dragged over the study chair and Dr. Lau spooned some chili into a salad bowl for her. They were eating out of an odd assortment of bowls and plates, Klale noticed, then remembered that Toni only had two place settings. They must be using all her dishes.

The chili was Toni's favorite—extra hot. It left Klale's mouth burning, nose running, and tears rolling down her cheeks. She finally pushed it aside, washed it down with a lot of cider, and filled up on pompommes instead, watching with fascination as Toni chewed without any apparent reaction. How did she do that?

"Right now he needs sleep and nutritional supplements," Toni was telling Dr. Lau. "We'll have to keep him as stable as we can until we can get him to Seattle."

"Are you sure we should take him there?" asked Lau quietly.

Toni shrugged.

"There's not much choice. There are only three research centers which could treat him, and Seattle's the closest."

"But you don't like their methods."

"It's all that's available."

"What's the problem?" interrupted Klale.

Toni looked at her.

"Klale, the state of the art in treating long term plug patients . . ." Abruptly she dropped her fork and leaned back, running a hand through her graying hair, and Klale realized that she was very upset.

"The easiest way to budge resistant patterns is by retraining— that means activating existing filaments or even adding more, and using many of the same chemical etching techniques." Her voice sounded brittle. "Simon will become more functional, certainly, but he'll never know for sure that anything he feels or thinks or does is really his own and not just an imprinted response." She looked down at her half-finished dinner, then added with sudden vitriol: "I couldn't live that way, I don't know why the hell I should expect him to."

Klale sat silent, shaken by Toni's vehemence.

"Then why take him there?" asked Lau calmly.

"He requires intensive twenty-four-hour care," snapped Toni. "I certainly can't handle him by myself!"

Dr. Lau leaned toward her with sudden force.

"You aren't *by yourself!*"

Toni looked startled, then uncomfortable, and dropped her eyes. Lau continued more calmly. "You and I have medical training. We can hire more help. I'll find the money. We'll use your methods— take all the time Simon needs."

"I'll help, too," added Klale.

Toni didn't seem to hear—her attention was focused on Lau.

"I'm sorry, I was forgetting..." her voice trailed off, then she said tightly, "You should probably get another evaluation. From a therapist who's more current and less . . . personally biased."

"I reviewed your papers," said Lau firmly. "And watched you with Simon. I also know that he is an unusual case. He will draw enormous attention in Seattle and I'm afraid we will lose control of his treatment." He paused, then added: "Also, I am guessing from what I read in your obituary that you aren't anxious to return."

"No."

Toni stared down at the table, then finally looked over at him.

"You do understand that he may not recover."

"Yes."

"And if he does, he'll never be completely normal."

"Yes."

Toni hesitated and in the pause Lau leaned forward and spoke with intensity.

"If you believe I will walk out on my son twice, you are very much mistaken." He held out his hand. "Simon has chosen to trust you with his life. Shall you and I trust each other?"

As they shook, Klale put out her hand to join theirs.

34

Six blue-uniformed Harbor Patrol officers waited stiffly in the street in front of Sisters' residence. Toni stopped when she saw them and looked over at Mary.

"What are they doing here?"

"Escorting us to the council meeting." Mary gave a wide smile that creased her brown face like old leather. "Today, dear, I saw something I thought I'd never see—a complete apology from the Harbor Patrol for the bar fight last month, payment for damages, and an offer of escort."

Toni couldn't help but return that smile. Mary looked radiantly confident as she strode forward in her royal purple outfit, with touches of lume in her hair that subtly highlighted the short tufts where they'd cut away riot glue. No doubt a deliberate reminder, Toni thought, with amusement.

The Patrollers saluted Mary formally, then fell in around the group of about thirty D.R.A. supporters. Toni walked next to Mary, with Dr. Lau on her other side. In the shade of the tall buildings the morning air felt cool, and Toni was grateful for the loan of Klale's heavy Indian sweater, although occasional gusts of wind blew right through the loose weave. It was probably great for sweaty work, she decided, but it was less than ideal for strolling. The light parkas worn by the Harbor Patrol looked far more practical.

"What brought on the Patrol's sudden change of heart?" she asked Mary quietly.

"Choi, of course."

"What?" she said, startled.

"Didn't you hear?" Mary asked, giving her a puzzled look. "Choi's bunker was bombed last night. It triggered a massive data spill."

"Oh . . . that," said Toni.

Mary looked at her sharply.

"Is our friend all right?"

"Fine," Toni assured her. "Sorry, I should have told you."

"Mmm," responded Mary, with a long, piercing look. Clearly she wanted to know more, but it would have to wait. "Well, embarrassing dossiers rained down over Vancouver last night and this morning, all of a sudden, councilors and Guild execs are lining up to be my best friends. It seems I couldn't have bought better publicity. Choi called me a useless blackmail target—honest, ethical, and loved by all my friends."

"Congratulations," Toni told her.

I should enjoy this, she thought, but instead she felt tense and anxious. She wouldn't relax until she got Simon away from Downtown. However, Ron wanted to wait until night to move him, and Mary so rarely asked a favor that Toni had agreed to go to her meeting at City Hall. Klale had stayed behind with Simon, though she should have nothing to do since Toni had left him hooked up, asleep.

She glanced back and caught Dr. Lau doing the same, but the KlonDyke was hidden behind other buildings. For a moment she worried about Klale, then she shoved her anxieties aside. Alberta was keeping a watch on the building, and even if the generator went down, the netset had enough reserve to keep Simon asleep for hours.

Their slow progress along Cardero Street halted and Toni glanced ahead. Violet, the tiny beggar, had stopped. She poked one of the Patrollers in the leg with her crutch and demanded to be carried. The man gave her a startled look and cast desperately around at his comrades before reaching down and lifting the little woman into his arms. D.R.A. members exchanged gleeful grins. Violet couldn't weigh more than fifty pounds, but she stank.

Two blocks farther north the street emerged onto Cardero Pier and a stunning view across Coal Harbor to the North Shore mountains, seeming very tall and close under a wind scrubbed sky. The harbor was dark blue and ruffled, noticed Toni, then she remembered Klale's indignant voice saying "Ruffled? Skirts are ruffled! Water is choppy!" All right, choppy, she thought with apprehension. And she faced another goddamned boat trip.

She stepped down the sloping ramp onto the private boat dock where three Patrol launches bobbed, looking appallingly unsteady. Catamaran-hulled ferries were bad enough, thought Toni miserably, but she especially hated small boats. She would never forget that nightmare journey back from the grain terminal with Simon and Klale in a decrepit hulk, crashing recklessly into a black void. At least Patrol boats were bigger than that.

Two figures jumped onto the float from a nearby launch and she felt an unpleasant jolt of recognition. Captain Dhillon and Cedar de Groot. Other Patrollers seemed surprised to see them and moved forward, but Dhillon hurried past and walked up to Mary. The captain's insincere smile seemed more forced than usual, Toni thought, and she looked like she'd been losing sleep. Beside her, Cedar fidgeted, twisting his coat sleeve with anxious fingers, seeming strangely deflated outside his usual setting.

Captain Dhillon saluted Mary, then de Groot stepped forward and spoke anxiously.

"I wanted to come myself, Mary, to see that you were fine and tell you how sorry I was to hear about the attack in the bar."

"Thank you," said Mary.

"I resigned yesterday, you know. I have nothing to do with the Free Vancouver League anymore. But Captain Dhillon thought—and I thought—that we should come and show our support. Of course, that terrible attack in the KlonDyke had nothing to do with the Free Vancouver League, but . . ."

Dhillon poked him and leaned forward, showing her teeth.

"We've come to escort you to City Hall."

There's something wrong here, thought Toni suddenly. But Mary thanked Dhillon and walked forward, with several others behind her. Toni hurried after her, unreasonably anxious to stay close. I'm just overreacting because I'm scared of boats, she told herself. Cedar was an ass, but not a tong operative. And the ride, however wretched, couldn't last more than half an hour.

Cedar helped Mary aboard Patrol Boat 7, and an officer offered Toni a hand. She took it, noticing automatically that it felt cold and sweaty. The man was nervous. She felt another wave of apprehension.

"I don't like this," she whispered as she joined Mary on the unsteady deck.

"I think Dhillon has been ordered to escort us personally and she's trying not to lose face," Mary whispered back. "I don't like it either, but we won't gain anything by offending her."

Toni hesitated, frowning, then clutched for a handhold as the boat tipped under the weight of more passengers. She wanted desperately to grab Mary and jump back to the float, but she fought the urge down, determined not to show her fear. Dr. Lau boarded, then Alberta's wife, Rill. A Patrol officer waved the next D.R.A members toward another boat. He tossed a rope up onto the launch and jumped easily after it, then the engines revved. Toni grabbed at the flimsy metal rail, then headed for the cabin. It probably wasn't any safer inside, but she'd *feel* safer.

As the Patrol boats cruised sedately through Lost Lagoon Channel, Toni tried to focus on the contrasting views—decrepit refugee floats to her left, lushly forested Stanley Park on her right. Local citizens were immensely proud of the park they'd defended for so many years, but Toni often wondered how many refugees had died for those trees. Emerging into English Bay from behind the shelter of the park, the boat was hit by strong winds and began pitching into whitecaps. The rest of the passengers clustered by the windows, evidently enjoying the experience. Toni gritted her teeth and tried to focus on the truncated bridge pilings marking the entrance to False Creek instead of her conviction that traveling on water was fundamentally insane.

A gust of cold air blew into the cabin bringing the roar of wind and engines, and Toni turned to see Captain Dhillon entering with her first officer, Neil McCaskill, behind her. They both held pistols and Baljeet's smile was much too genuine. As the door banged shut behind them, Toni felt a stab of fear.

"Excuse me, Citizens. Please place your hands on your heads where I can see them," ordered Dhillon. There was a stunned silence, then she barked "Now!"

Toni raised her hands with the others.

"But, Baljeet . . ." Cedar cried.

"Shut up, de Groot! You, too!"

De Groot stared down her gun barrel in stupefaction, opened his mouth, shut it, and put his hands on his head. Toni noted the pleasure on Dhillon's face and wondered if she'd shoot him.

"What's going on, Captain?" asked Mary calmly.

"I'm collecting your phones and your weapons. When I point to you, you will step forward and hand them to me very slowly, then stand still while I search you. Don't try any cretting heroics. You first, Miz Smarch. Step forward."

"Before you do this, maybe you'll tell us why," urged Mary. She fixed her eyes compellingly on Baljeet's. "This is very drastic. Maybe we can come up with another solution to your problem."

Dhillon's smile vanished. "Save your negotiating skills for Command!" she snapped. "If they cooperate, you'll all get home safely. Give me your phone."

Mary met her intransigent gaze for a second, then reached up and lifted her phone slowly from around her neck. She continued speaking to Dhillon, but Toni felt sure she was concentrating on Neil. Ron's grandson looked frightened.

"Obviously you're in some kind of smog, but it's not too late to back off. Nobody's been hurt. Just lower your guns and we'll forget about it."

"Shut up!" Dhillon snapped, taking the phone, but Neil wavered.

"Maybe she has a point . . ." he whispered urgently. Dhillon backed up until she stood beside him and then put her free hand on his shoulder. She spoke softly, but Toni was close and made out her words over the muted background roar.

"We're doing this for our families, McCaskill—think of your children. The Patrol won't protect them from a tong vendetta. Or us. Our only chance is to bargain for relocation—a fresh start somewhere new. Okay?"

Neil swallowed and then nodded. "Sorry, Captain."

"That's all right, I don't enjoy this either," Baljeet told him, but her eyes were hard. She stepped forward, patted Mary down and moved to the next hostage.

"Neil?" asked Mary urgently.

He didn't meet her eyes.

"Like the captain said, just do what you're told and everybody will be fine," he said nervously.

"Enough!" Dhillon ordered Mary. She moved to de Groot, who looked at her anxiously.

"Baljeet? You're not really going to do this, are you? I thought we were friends . . ."

"Friends? You pompous, feeble, double-fucking cret!" Her face twisted with venom, and Cedar flinched away, wide-eyed. "You humiliate me in front of my family, and run after that smut-licking bitch in the bar. You better hope the Patrol deals for you, de Groot, because I'd like nothing better than to take my honor out of your skin."

She shoved him back roughly, then moved to the next person. She searched Toni last, and with unnecessary force. Toni kept silent when a painful finger poked her armpit and a boot crushed her foot, then saw the frustrated fury in Baljeet's eyes and realized that she'd made an error. Dhillon badly wanted to hurt somebody and a whimper might have given her some temporary satisfaction.

Dhillon released Toni and gestured to Neil. They backed out, locking the door behind them. Toni took a deep breath and looked around. Rill stood motionless, white-faced. Dr. Lau stared grimly back at Downtown. Could we break the windows? Toni wondered. But then what? There was nowhere to go but into the water and she couldn't swim.

She had a sudden thought and poked Mary's arm. Mary looked around, met her eye, then nodded. Good. She'd triggered her subdermal emergency beacon. It was a slim hope, but it might be all they had.

35

"I don't suppose you and Toni are packed and ready to move to Sisters?" asked Alberta. The security chief stood in the middle of Toni's living room, legs planted firmly apart and arms crossed, looking as though she planned to stay forever.

"Uh, no," admitted Klale.

"I see. And are you going to tell me why that medic's been staying here?"

"It's very complicated . . ."

"No smog."

Alberta's questions could wait until Toni returned, Klale thought with irritation. Right now she wanted to get back to cruising the debris of the biggest data spill in West Coast history. Newsers were still clamoring over the failed inoculation response. When administrators shut down and vaccinated nodes, Simon had rerouted via rogue sites and satellite delay. As soon as local nodes came back up, the spill continued from global links. Adding to the confusion, thousands of netbums and data sniffers had jumped gleefully into the flood and abetted it.

And what a spill! Fifty years of tong financial accounts and secret Guild transactions, plus thousands of individual dossiers documenting everything from marital indiscretions to murder. Still more fascinating had been Choi's hoard of private security codes and account passkeys. This morning the entire west coast was scrambling to re-secure systems or to raid them, or both.

And Klale wanted to compile all the dirt she could find on her own Guild before security protocols cleaned up. Already she'd been delighted to discover that her personal nemesis, President Klassen, had been laundering Kung Lok funds through the Fisher Guild bank. Klale wanted all the details, and she intended to send them to every-body in Prince Rupert.

The netset buzzed. Klale left Alberta and rushed into the study to find Hans glaring at her from the screen.

"Did you see the spill . . . ?" she started excitedly.

"Damn right. I searched on your name and found out that you were nearly murdered a couple of weeks ago. Funny, you didn't men-tion it."

Oops, thought Klale. Simon must have been keeping Choi's files up to date. She hadn't realized that.

"Hans, I'm fine. You don't need to worry."

"You're expelled from your Guild, living in a slum in the middle of a gang war in a bar attacked by assassins, some sludge tries to kill you, and I don't need to worry?"

"Look, it's not as bad as you make it sound," she said weakly.

"I'll see when I get there."

"Hans! You don't have to . . ."

"I'm on the ferry now. I'll be there tonight. I'm taking you home."

"You can't!" Klale spluttered, although she'd just been thinking about going back to challenge her disbarment. "Hans . . ."

The signal cut and Klale found herself staring at a hold pattern. She hissed between clenched teeth, knowing that there was no point calling back. Some small part of her was pleased by his concern, but being trawled home by her big brother . . . ! How humiliating!

The netset buzzed again and she answered sharply, but this time it was Pum calling for Alberta. Klale stuck her head back into the living room.

"Alberta, for you. Urgent."

Alberta hurried over, and Klale eavesdropped with curiosity that rapidly turned into dread.

"Mary's emergency beacon triggered just a minute ago. We don't know why. She's on PBoat Seven heading for Cambie pier. We tried calling but we can't get anybody on that boat to answer."

"Keep trying," said Alberta curtly. "I'll call the Patrol. How many with Mary?"

"We're trying to find out. Five or six, maybe. Toni's with her." Pum hesitated and her voice dropped a little. "And Rill."

Klale saw the sudden fear in Alberta's eyes, then the security chief snapped into action.

"Round up volunteers and meet in front of Sisters. Armed. We'll need cabs."

"Where are we going?"

"I'll brief you when I get there," Alberta said curtly, then cut the channel.

Klale caught her arm with black premonition.

"PBoat Seven? Whose boat is that?"

"Dhillon's," said Alberta grimly.

"Oh no." Klale felt a surge of fear. "Alberta, I just read Choi's dossier on Dhillon. She's been doing business with the Viet Ching and she helped assassinate that Sun Yee On exec. She killed her own first officer, too."

Alberta's eyes widened, then she whirled to the netset and called Harbor Control. Klale barely noticed, stunned by a sudden revelation. Dhillon's officer had drowned on Pender Street wharf around the same time Klale had arrived Downtown. And Klale had seen Dhillon there! No wonder Dhillon had tried to kill her! And not once, but twice!

She forced her attention back to Alberta who was getting empty, patronizing reassurances from Patrol Command. Klale balled her hands into fists. They had to act! They had to help Toni!

Klale ran for the bedroom where Simon lay asleep on a futon, cables trailing from his head. She kneeled beside him, wincing as she landed on her sore knee, and studied the monitor interface on the set. It looked simple enough to wake him, but she hesitated. What would Simon do when he saw Alberta? And what would Alberta do?

She rushed back to the study and interrupted Alberta.

"I have to talk to you!"

"Not now!"

"*Now!* It's important!"

Alberta looked up at her for a second, then hit mute in the middle of a Harbor Control sentence.

"Taxing imbecile!" she snarled, then turned to Klale. "What is it?"

Klale led her to the bedroom and pushed the door open. Alberta took one step in and stopped dead.

"Jesus!"

"He belongs to Toni now," explained Klale hurriedly, the words feeling ludicrous in her mouth. "I'm sure he can help us, but I wanted to warn you first."

Alberta stared at Simon, then turned a hard glance on Klale.

"What about Choi?"

"He's dead."

"Yeah? And how stable is Blade?"

"His name is Simon. And—well, he's a little shaky," admitted Klale, then added: "But he engineered that spill, Alberta. He's clever and he knows Downtown. And I'm sure he'll do anything for Toni."

"That's what tools are for," observed Alberta acidly.

"He knows me," continued Klale urgently. "And Toni told him to do what I say."

Alberta didn't look convinced.

"Alberta, he traced me to the cargo hold! He can help us!"

"Well, he can't be less help than smogging Harbor Control," muttered Alberta blackly. "Wake him up." She reached for her pistol, which she wore today in a standard shoulder holster. "I'll cover you."

"No!" Klale took a deep breath and tried to sound calm. "He should only see me when he wakes up. We don't want to frighten him."

"Frighten him. Uh huh." Alberta stared down unhappily, then backed up. "Leave the door ajar. I'll be right outside."

"Right," said Klale.

She sat down on the floor next to the set, closed her eyes and took several deep breaths. Be calm and reassuring, she reminded herself. Simon is waking up in a strange place. He'll be scared. Then she told the set to start a wake cycle. It acknowledged, the screen flashed and a graphic countdown began.

Simon lay on his back, breathing quietly. Klale picked up his limp, warm hand, and cradled it, feeling an unexpected surge of protectiveness. How many hours had she sat beside her father listening to his labored breathing and wondering helplessly when it would stop? But even dying he had never been so vulnerable as Simon—so invaded, she thought, staring at the shining cables with revulsion.

As Simon's breaths grew shallower, Klale tried to remember all the things Toni had said about dealing with him. She wished like hell she'd asked more questions last night.

He opened his eyes.

"Simon?" she said softly.

A quiver of tension ran through him, and he glanced at her, then scanned the room. His face was immobile except for his eyes. He looked like Blade.

"Simon, you're in Toni's apartment," she said, trying to keep the anxiety out of her voice. "We brought you out of the bunker and Toni's your master now. Do you remember?"

After several very long seconds he nodded slowly, and she felt his hand squeeze hers. She let out a relieved breath, and told him to remove the cables. He sat up, peeling off the suction cups with practiced motions, then unclipped the collar. He was naked, Klale noticed suddenly, and he smelled sourly of old sweat.

"How do you feel?"

His eyes flicked past her nervously, then he tilted his head and replied cautiously.

"I don't know."

That wasn't promising, but she didn't have time to figure it out.

"Simon, I need your help," she told him, then explained the situation as coherently as she could. She finished without seeing any reaction in his face, and paused uncertainly before realizing that she hadn't told him what to do. Toni said he needed orders.

"Get dressed, come with me, and let's see what we can do to help Alberta."

Simon rose immediately, reaching for his weapons and equipment pouch first, and then dressing quickly despite the bandage on his left hand. His clothes needed washing, Klale noticed. And he needed new ones. Any color except gray.

Alberta waited at the study door. She gave Simon a long wary look before addressing Klale.

"Patrol Command still says they're having 'temporary reception problems'!"

Klale looked up at Simon. His eyes were moving rapidly, taking in the apartment. He stared at the couch, then the table, then over to the bedroom door.

"Simon, can you find out what's happened to Mary?"

He ignored her. Klale frowned, then realized that he was playing deaf.

"Simon!" She tugged his hand. "It's all right. Alberta is here to help us rescue Toni. Please speak in front of her."

For a moment she didn't think he would comply, then his head swiveled and he stared directly at Alberta with icy, assessing eyes. He drew himself up straighter and folded his arms arrogantly across his chest.

"Can you find out what's happened to Mary?" Klale asked again.

"I can attempt to do so."

"Then, do it!" she ordered, nervousness making her voice sharp.

Alberta stepped quickly out of the way as Simon strode past her to the study desk. He sat down, legs splayed awkwardly since his knees didn't fit under the desk. Klale moved to his left side, remembering to give him lots of room and not to stand behind him. Alberta took up a position on his right, keeping her hand near her weapon. Simon gave his bandaged fingers a brief odd look as if he hadn't seen them before, then started using pad and voice commands simultaneously. He worked with intimidating speed, even one-handed.

"What are you doing?" asked Klale.

"The Harbor Authority has changed its security codes. I am re-routing through a lesser defended access to their monitoring equipment."

The screen flashed onto an overhead view of Vancouver harbor. Simon zoomed in on False Creek, then zoomed again on three tiny boats inching across the screen with white trails behind them. The sim was superb, right down to the pattern of wind on the water and the splashes of foam at the boat bows. The first two Patrol boats were slowing to pull into Cambie Pier, but the third had changed course, accelerating east up False Creek. A babble of Patrol voices cut in from several different channels. After a second, Klale picked out Dhillon's.

". . . and if you pursue, I will shoot the first hostage."

No! Klale caught her breath. On the map, the other Patrol boats turned, but didn't follow. A calm female voice was attempting to persuade Dhillon to turn back.

"Where's she going?" muttered Alberta to herself, but Simon answered.

"Dhillon's launch is an easy target and its range is limited. She should attempt to reach a defensible location quickly."

Klale felt a chill of alarm as she recognized Choi's voice—higher pitched than Simon's, precise, and very ruthless.

Alberta bit her lip.

"Will she run to the Viet Ching?"

"She would be a fool to do so," said Simon. "She is not a tong member, and she is no longer useful as an agent. Also, her life is wanted as payment to the Sun Yee On for Kwong's blood debt."

Alberta stared at the map, her freckles standing out lividly against her chalky face.

"Where is she going?" she muttered urgently. "I want to get there first." She looked at Simon. "What about the piers?"

"Pier B-C is a possibility. She has access and she knows it well."

"Mmm. It's a maze, too. Easy to hide there. Can you get us a passcode from here?"

Simon manipulated the set for a few seconds, then sat back, shaking his head.

"Remote access has been suspended. They are using hard-wired backups."

"Damn!"

"What about Blade?" asked Klale. "Would they let you . . . him in?"

"Perhaps. The guards are unlikely to try to stop a tool. Also, with

Choi dead, the Kung Lok might decide to attempt capture. The success rate for retraining tools is low, but the investment is negligible compared to the cost of a new one."

Klale stared at him, horrified by his icy detachment. Alberta grabbed her shoulder and hauled Klale into the other room.

"We can't take him. We don't know what he'll do!" she hissed in Klale's ear. "He's as dangerous to us as he is to them!"

"Alberta, he wants Toni back!"

"Sure as hell doesn't sound like it!"

"Look, all he has to do is to get you into the pier. Then I'll bring him back here."

Alberta glared at her unhappily, then whispered: "Are you sure he'll follow your orders?"

"Yes!" lied Klale. She held her breath.

"Shit . . . Oh, all right. We got to try."

Alberta turned for the door. Klale caught her arm.

"Alberta. If anything goes wrong you can't let the Kung Lok take him!"

Alberta stopped for a second and glanced toward Simon.

"I'll do what I can," she said tersely. She picked up her jacket and started for the apartment door. "Get whatever you need and follow me. Quick. Meet in the lobby."

Klale nodded and turned back to the study. "Simon . . ." she started, then realized that he was staring down at the scars in Toni's parquet floor.

The apartment door snicked shut behind Alberta, and Klale felt a surge of panic. She forced herself to step closer. Simon's right hand was clamped on the desk so tightly that his fingertips were almost white.

He's frightened, she reminded herself urgently. Focus on what he said in the grain hold, or his gentleness when he made love.

She crouched down in front of him, blocking his view of the floor and put her hand over his. It felt like granite.

"Simon, please talk to me."

He stared through her.

"Simon?" She looked up at his rigid face and the angry red furrows of Choi's brand in his forehead. "Simon, what's wrong? Tell me!"

Abruptly, Simon gasped, then he spoke in a small, terrified whisper.

"She punished me. . . ."

That was the voice she knew, she thought with relief. She squeezed his hand.

"No, Simon! It was some sort of automatic punishment when you broke one of Choi's commands. Toni didn't do it!" His eyes winced shut and she studied him urgently, remembering how his fist had pounded the concrete wall. "Toni loves you, Simon. She would never hurt you. She promised, remember?"

She tugged at his right hand until he let go of the desk, then carried it to the back of her head. His fingers remained stiff, not curving to cup her head. Klale wanted to remind him of the grain hold and put her arms around him, but there was no time. She gripped his forearm.

"Simon, we have to help Toni. Quickly."

Simon flinched, then nodded, and rose.

Klale turned to wave the netset off and Baljeet's boat caught her eye, just passing the American floats.

"Lincoln!" she exclaimed suddenly. Should she call him? Well, he certainly was Dhillon's enemy. And the enemy of my enemy . . .

She sat down and made a fast phone call, telling Lincoln's reception protocol that she had an emergency and describing it as concisely as she could manage. Then she and Simon ran downstairs, taking the steps two at a time. After the first few floors the concrete treads started to blur together and Klale had to slow down so she wouldn't fall. At the bottom she staggered dizzily against the lobby door and peered out.

Alberta paced the lobby, alone. She saw Klale and beckoned.

"Pum borrowed a delivery van," she called. "Come on!"

In the loading bay Pum was dragging produce crates out of an ancient panel truck. She gave one startled glance at Klale leading Simon by the hand, abandoned her job, and ran for the cab. Alberta and Klale shoved out the last few crates and piled into the grubby box with Simon.

Alberta pulled the rear doors shut, motioning Simon and Klale to sit down with their backs to the cab wall. Klale grimaced at the slimy floor, all too reminiscent of the garbage chute, but she sat in the middle, groping for a handhold in the dim light from dirty rear windows. The truck bed was so narrow that when Alberta sat down the three of them were jammed together hip to hip. Klale heard a muffled shout in the distance that sounded like "That's my truck!," then the engine caught with a wheezing shudder and lurched forward.

"Can Pum drive?" yelled Klale, as the truck careened to one side, slamming Alberta's pelvis against Klale's, and Klale's against Simon's.

"She said so," grunted Alberta.

Klale looked up at Simon, wishing she could hold hands again, but his unbandaged hand was clamped around a tie-down. She felt his warmth against her and realized that she was cold. She'd forgotten her sweater. No, Toni had it, she remembered belatedly. And Simon didn't have his serape—it must have been left in the bunker. He'd also had nothing to eat or drink since waking, she realized suddenly. Damn! Toni said that was important.

A grinding screech of gears issued from the front of the truck, followed by the application of brakes too late to prevent a violent series of bumps which slammed Klale's spine against the floor. The van sped up again, then decelerated to a crawl. They must be caught behind a pedicart, decided Klale, straightening up again. Alberta was eyeing Simon's bandage.

"He had a little fight with a wall," Klale explained with attempted nonchalance.

Alberta gave her a sour look. Then Klale heard a tiny, peculiar voice from her other side.

"The wall won."

Klale blinked and turned. Simon was looking toward the rear doors, face blank, knees drawn up. She couldn't guess whether he'd been joking or making conversation, or just repeating what he'd heard.

Alberta's phone bleeped, and she let go of her tie-down long enough to answer.

"Score, Alberta! Looks like the PBoat's headed for Pier B-C."

"Good," she responded, falling suddenly against Klale as Pum accelerated into a turn. "Meet me on Hastings, out of sight of the main entrance."

Klale looked over at Simon again. He was staring at the ends of his fingers poking through the metal tie-down.

"Simon? Are you all right?" Klale whispered anxiously.

There was such a long pause that she didn't think she would get a reply, then he spoke in a bleak small-boy voice.

"The blood gets under my fingernails."

Klale fought down a stab of terror at his tone. "It's all right, Simon. Toni will be all right," she said desperately.

The van lurched to a stop and a second later the cab door slammed. Simon sat very still with his eyes closed, then he got up and propelled himself toward the rear of the truck, reaching it just as Pum yanked the doors open. He turned and Slanged "Five minutes, east gate," then jumped onto the pavement and strode away.

Alberta stared after him with an appalled expression.

"Jesus, he's going to go berserk!"

"No, he'll be fine, you'll see," Klale assured Alberta, but she heard the quaver of uncertainty in her own voice.

36

The docker in the security booth waved Blade inside with a white-eyed upward glance, then swung around in his chair, and Blade knew he was notifying security. Blade strode through the half-open cargo door into the cavernous interior of the freight deck. It should have swarmed with cargo pickers, but instead the concrete floor stretched empty ahead of him. Arc lamps were dimmed, trailer bays stood vacant, and a dozen cargo pickers stood in a silent line before towering rows of shipping containers.

Blade walked forward, then at forty meters cut abruptly to his left into a narrow alley between container stacks to a seldom-used maintenance door. He took a matchstick key from his pouch and inserted it. It didn't work. He pulled it out and entered a manual emergency code. The door opened. Security hadn't yet changed fire and evacuation procedures.

He moved quickly and silently along a corridor and up several flights of stairs, then stopped at a maintenance hatch between floors. It accessed a crawl space containing a blue-striped communications conduit. He kneeled beside the conduit and used his neural-linked stealth gear to set a hard tap. Once in, he infiltrated a low-level subsystem and triggered weapons detectors under the southwest side of the pier. Then he waited twenty seconds and interrupted all visual monitors on the south half of the pier, followed, in nine seconds, by toxin alarms on Level Two west. That should simulate a raid with gas grenades.

As Central Security responded to the alarms, he removed the tap and then traversed several lesser used staircases and maintenance halls to approach the east gate security booth. He had chosen the east gate because it was a small entrance, less heavily defended than the main gate, and hidden beneath street level. As he reached the security booth, he accelerated his pace and triggered a burst of adrenaline.

He hit the metal door of the security booth with his shoulder, slamming it inward on bent hinges. Inside two guards sat at consoles. As the first one started turning around, Blade struck the back of her head, then he lunged forward and pulled the other guard backward over his chair. The man fell hard. Blade rolled him facedown and dosed him with a fast-acting tranq.

He mirrored the gate window and removed the guards' weapons before checking the main console. Neither guard had triggered an alarm. Seven minutes remained until their next check-in with Central Security.

Blade mated his phone to a standard slot and called up a special executive voice code. The Kung Lok's Dragon Head feared internal assassination attempts, so his private passcode had overriding clearance. Fortunately, it was still active. Blade transferred the hub command path to the gatehouse, then canceled all other system access. That would leave security in chaos.

He glanced through the mirrored window and saw Alberta walking down the east gate ramp, her team behind her. She stepped firmly up to the window and stopped. Blade switched seats, located the controls to unlock the crew door beside the vehicle gate, then patched in a mike.

"Proceed inside to the first door on your left. Have your team wait while you come to the security booth."

Behind their chief, the KlonDyke bouncers exchanged nervous glances, but Alberta nodded expressionlessly and strode forward. Blade scanned as the group passed. Nine in the party. Eight armed. He locked the door behind them, unlocked the corridor ahead, then moved back to the other console to check the pier's status. On the west side of Level Two an armed squad in enviro suits jogged toward the freight complex. In the Central Security office, staff huddled in confusion over consoles as they tried to regain system access. Two ranking guards stood together, speaking urgently, and as Blade watched, one broke away at a run. Probably going to the data center.

A light flashed. Blade picked up a guard's pistol, and swiveled in his chair, covering the broken door. Alberta was approaching down the hallway, hands empty, with Klale behind her. She glanced at the broken door and the prone guards without expression. Blade turned back to the console and called up Harbor Control's Pier B-C datafeed.

He got a simmed eagle's-eye view of two freighters berthed on the west side of the pier and one tied up on the east side. The diagonally angled end of the pier stood vacant. That was a likely destination for Patrol Boat Seven. He stepped back to harbor view and saw PBoat 7 approaching with several patrol launches far behind it. He hesitated, then took a few extra seconds to switch from the sim to a live camera at the top of the office complex. His caution paid off as he discovered that the sim was inaccurate. Two decrepit-looking noahs, invisible to radar, were in pursuit of Captain Dhillon. American ghost boats. They were gaining on her, but Dhillon would reach the pier well ahead of them.

He called up a floor plan and marked a route for Alberta; then, while she studied the screen, he kneeled and searched the guards for keys. He was not permitted to kill without orders, except in self-defense, but he had to be certain the guards couldn't come after him, so he searched the drawers and found a wide roll of repair tape which he used to tape their mouths and wrists securely. Then he stood and stamped on the nearest guard's right knee, smashing down with his full weight. The woman woke, screaming under her gag. He moved to the second guard and repeated the procedure.

When he turned, Alberta had pinned Klale against the wall. The girl's horrified eyes were fixed on the writhing guards, then she looked up at Blade and her mouth moved.

"*Noooo!* Simon! No! No! No!"

Blade felt a distant twinge from Simon. He stifled it. Simon had no purpose here—Blade was needed to reach Toni. Klale also had no purpose, but Alberta might be useful. He held out a key to her.

"The emergency evac code is nine-zero-one-nine. It accesses all stairwells and common doors. The pier is on alert, but I will crash internal security now."

Alberta nodded and reached for the key, pulling back sharply as soon as she had it. She turned and pushed Klale ahead of her into the hall.

Blade went to the main console and ordered a full shutdown. The system queried him three times, but the Shan Chu code was good. Lights winked off on the big floor plan, then his screen blanked. Pier B-C was now blind.

Blade left the booth at a jog and entered the cavernous freight area of Level Two through a maintenance door. He avoided the main freight passage, running instead through narrow side aisles between tall container stacks. At a main cross-junction marked with broad white floor lines for the cargo pickers' navcomps, he paused and looked carefully in both directions, then used audio to check for sound. He heard voices behind him—Alberta's rough and forceful, Klale's high-pitched and frantic. He turned sharply and looked back, but saw no one there.

Alberta should be traversing a corridor on Level Three. The sounds weren't real—just echoes again, like the old screams. Simon moved forward, but he saw Klale's stricken eyes when she looked at Blade. He remembered how her hair felt against his fingers. So smooth . . .

No! Blade pushed Simon's thoughts away, and focused. Toni was his master. Her safety was imperative. He must reach Toni and protect her.

Toni's in danger, Simon whispered. She might die!

Blade's steps faltered, caught in Simon's wave of panic. *No!* Toni must stay alive. Toni's hand kept the world from spinning, kept black terror from swallowing him. If they killed her . . .

A deep bass organ chord swelled up inside him, lifting Blade's steps and pushing them faster and faster. The air pulsed G minor, and the old concrete floor beneath his feet throbbed with resonance. He remembered how the guards' knees had felt under his foot, how they bent and snapped. They had been strong and flexible, not like Choi's. The old man's brittle bones had crunched, like stepping on barnacles. But there'd been plenty of crimson blood beneath that desiccated skin—fountains and spouts and pools of it . . .

It felt like drowning in deep music, that beautiful thrumming in his chest and stomach. It took enormous effort to stop and push it back, but he needed Blade. Blade did not hear music. Blade did not feel music. Blade was stone. Blade followed orders. And his orders were to find Toni.

Blade gasped and shuddered with the effort of forcing white silence. He opened his eyes. He was leaning against a dented cargo container and the bandage on his left hand was stained with leaking blood.

He straightened and resumed his route to the north end of the pier. At the next intersection he saw an open cargo door with men standing by it, but no one looked his way. He broke into a silent run. Ahead were paired cargo and crew doors. He halted at a crew door, used the evac code, and inched it cautiously open.

Directly ahead, across several meters of concrete deck, he saw the mast and wheelhouse roof of Patrol Boat 7. The rest of the boat was below the pier level. Where was Dhillon? Abruptly he noticed the top of a companionway sliding into place. They were just docking. He looked in both directions. To his right, the pier superstructure came to a sharp point, and about ten meters beyond it the deck ended. To his left, the empty north deck of the pier stretched along for two hundred meters. He stepped through the door, let it shut behind him, and walked quickly to one of his usual positions, backing against the wall with arms crossed on his chest in his waiting stance. Blade was so often here that they might barely notice him.

He was just in time. Captain Dhillon came up the companionway first, herding Mary Smarch in front of her, and Cedar de Groot behind. Dhillon wore a heavy sweater instead of her uniform coat. She frowned down the pier at the closed bay doors, then she saw Blade and raised her pistol. Blade remained motionless. Dhillon hesitated. Another Patrol crewman came up the ramp behind her with two more hostages. Dhillon looked back at him, then lowered her gun, poked Mary, and started toward the building.

Blade studied the emerging Patrollers closely. All of them had exchanged their conspicuous blue parkas for the hostages' jackets but they still wore uniform pants. The last crewman herded a small woman wearing a uniform coat that hung below her knees. Toni. She appeared uninjured. Blade assessed the situation. Four well armed Patrollers, with six hostages. A direct assault had a low probability of success and would endanger Toni.

Toni looked at the pier and her gaze stopped on Blade. He studied her face and hands for orders, but she looked away without changing expression, so he did nothing.

Scudding clouds blew a sudden pool of sunshine across the pier, spilling over Toni's hair and shoulders. Simon had seen sunlight in her apartment, too, glittering in the windows and splashing gold and cinnamon on the floor. Toni lived where she could watch the sky. Music swirled in her rooms, emerald plants cascaded from red clay pots, and her fingers felt achingly soft against his cheeks.

She stroked his face after she put the collar on him, he remembered, then he felt a stab of fear. She was his master. She would burn thoughts out of his mind and twist obedience tight in his gut. She would splay his agony against the wooden floor . . .

No! She said she wouldn't punish him!

Choi had lied. Toni could lie.

No! Please, no!

Simon struggled with sucking, dizzy terror. Toni wasn't like Choi! Choi had never touched Simon, rarely talked to him, never let Simon's eyes meet his. But Toni looked inside him. She gave him a waltz drenched with honey. And she cried in warm, shaking gusts against his chest.

A blast of cold wind knifed against his neck and Blade blinked, realizing that he'd lost a piece of time. Captain Dhillon stood in front of a crew door, five meters to his left, listening to someone shout at her from inside. Blade accessed sound and identified Alberta's voice.

". . . have all the doors on this side covered, but I don't want a fight. Just walk in with the hostages one at a time, dropping your weapons."

Mary Smarch spoke urgently.

"It's not too late to surrender, Captain. Nobody's hurt. And my people will negotiate with the Patrol on your behalf. I give you my word."

Dhillon hesitated, her face indecisive. By blocking her access to the pier's interior, Alberta had left her in a weak position. There was a sudden roar beyond Dhillon and a loading bay door rolled swiftly upward, disgorging a large group of Longshore workers and security guards. They ran out onto the wharf, guns aimed at Dhillon's crew. In the midst of them Blade recognized Tommy Yip. Dhillon had hesitated too long.

Yip waved his phone. Dhillon's crew moved closer together, pulling hostages around them. Dhillon grabbed Mary Smarch, then shook her head at Yip and made the Sign for in-person talk. She took a step toward him, pushing Smarch ahead of her. Yip looked back at his guards unhappily. The fat restaurateur was a coward, but he would lose face if he didn't go to meet her. He stepped forward with a tight-lipped smile.

Abruptly his eyes focused on something beyond Dhillon and the smile vanished. Blade turned his head slowly to see a contingent of Bloods rounding the point of the pier, fanning out across the full width of the deck, with heavy assault weapons held ready. In their center, radiating arrogant confidence, strode Lincoln. His hands were empty, but he wore grenades on his bandolier.

The Kung Lok shifted their weapons to cover the Bloods. Tommy Yip stepped backward, breathing hard. Dhillon retreated, half running, to the center of her group, pulling the hostages into a circle around her crew. She was now directly in the line of fire between the Kung Lok and the Americans.

The Bloods halted several meters to Blade's right. Lincoln gave Blade a wary look, then walked forward, waving empty hands. He shouted.

"I apologize for arriving uninvited, Mr. Yip, but we were anxious to help you remove these taxers from your pier."

Blade could barely hear Tommy's response through the wind.

"Why the sudden interest, Mr. Lincoln?"

"Two things, Mr. Yip. I have a personal concern for Sister Mary, who has done so much work on behalf of Guildless Americans. And our friends, the Sun Yee On, are anxious to speak with Captain Dhillon."

"Friends?" Even from a distance Blade could see Yip's jolt at that news. "I thought you hated the tongs!"

"Times change," Lincoln observed.

"Then why not join the Consortium and have two allies instead of one?" tried Yip.

"Regretfully, I decline your kind offer. The Sun Yee On are the only tong powerful enough to offer the terms we require. And, with our assistance, they are the only ones who will survive this war."

Tommy's face showed fear.

"If anyone opens fire, the hostages will be the first to die."

"True. We would prefer your cooperation."

"You're in a bad bargaining position, Lincoln. This is our pier. We have you covered."

"Really?" said Lincoln. He looked up and waved. There was a sharply descending scream, then a body thudded wetly onto the concrete. It wore a Longshore shirt. Lincoln let a silence hang, then looked at the tense line of security behind Yip.

"It's one thing to work for the Kung Lok, but I wonder, Mr. Yip, how many of the people behind you are willing to die for your tong?"

Good tactics, thought Blade. Few of the Longshore Guild were actually tong members. And the security guards were not soldiers. Faced with heavily armed Bloods, they were likely to flee.

"We're not going with Lincoln," Captain Dhillon interrupted. "We'll kill the hostages first!"

"That would be sad," Lincoln told her, "but, unlike the Patrol, we won't bargain. We will deliver any of you left alive to the Sun Yee On."

"Lincoln! Yip!" came a shout.

Lincoln searched the faces ahead, frowning.

"Who's that?"

"Alberta from the KlonDyke. I'm inside, coming out." She emerged slowly from the doorway, her hands and holster empty. "Lincoln, I just want my friends back alive. If a fight starts now there's going to be lots of casualties all around. I'm sure the Longshore members don't want that. And I don't think Americans want to risk death on a Sun Yee On errand. Why not let me and my team escort

Dhillon's crew and the hostages into Patrol custody?"

An interesting attempt. Dhillon's crew was frightened and de-
moralized enough that they might comply. Tommy Yip would back
out if he could find a way to save face. Lincoln was the uncertain
factor.

Blade looked at Toni again. Still no orders. She stood beside a
tall Chinese man and Blade studied him with sudden intensity. He
had seen him beside sunlit water sometime before.... Had he
touched Simon with slender, gentle hands? But the man had been
younger, with sun-darkened skin and long shiny black hair tied back
with a scarlet scarf. And there had been a young woman. Toni! But
not Toni . . . Simon frowned. She'd looked different. . . .

They had held Simon, hugged him, and whispered to him in soft
voices. And they'd run hands across his head, through thick, curly
hair. Then they went away, leaving him alone. He cried and pleaded
but they didn't come back.

Simon concentrated, tugging at the strange, slippery images. He'd
been different then. Smaller, he remembered abruptly, and it felt like
a window opening. He could see Choi's mahogany desk—the same
desk, but much higher when he stood in front of it. His legs and feet
had been knotted with pain from standing still for so many endless
hours, and he'd been biting his lips, struggling not to whimper or
squirm at the piercing agony in his bladder. He couldn't hold on. A
warm trickle of urine dribbled down his leg, then a hissing stream
that pooled in his shoe and crept across the floor. The pressure less-
ened and the pain began to ease. Footsteps. A flood of terror. And
Choi's emotionless voice.

"You have been disobedient. You will thank me for enduring your
disgusting failure. Then I will punish you."

The air shimmered, and the organ's deep, wonderful chord swallowed the wind. Blade blinked and tried to focus.

He stood on the pier. Alberta was talking. Captain Dhillon was
talking. One of Dhillon's crew interrupted her. They argued. Lincoln
stepped forward. Dhillon grabbed Cedar de Groot and put a gun
against his head. Toni pulled lose and lunged, but Dhillon saw her
coming. The gun swung around.

No!

A scream soared inside Simon and he plunged forward into an
ocean of sound.

37

Maybe, thought Toni. Maybe Lincoln wants to be a hero more than he wants to give Baljeet Dhillon to the Sun Yee On. And just maybe he can hold back his eager gang. Another time she would have rejoiced in seeing Tommy Yip so cur-scared, but right now it was imperative that he keep his nerve, and that Dhillon retain her self-control. As long as everyone kept negotiating, the hostages were safe in the middle. Neither tong could open fire on Dhillon's renegades without risk of hitting the other tong and starting a battle.

Keep talking, Alberta! she urged silently. She risked a hasty glance at Simon out of the corner of one eye. He stood like a statue. Klale must have sent him, damn her. Toni could only pray that nothing jolted him.

Neil McCaskill breathed harshly behind her, fingernails digging into Toni's upper arm. He, at least, was desperate to surrender. Maybe, she thought, just maybe, we'll all live through this morning. . . .

Alberta was trying to get agreement from all parties to call the Patrol when Cedar de Groot's voice interrupted.

"Or I could call them, Baljeet. You know you can trust me."

Toni felt her stomach plunge as Dhillon whirled on him.

"Trust you, you feeble bastard? To humiliate me again? Like hell!"

Her gun swung toward Cedar. No shots! thought Toni desperately, yanking free of Neil's grip. She plunged forward, hoping to distract Dhillon, but Baljeet's trained reflexes were much faster than she'd counted on. The gun whipped around. Toni tried to duck aside. Too slow, she thought distantly. I'm going to die.

Bang!

Toni crashed to the ground, aware of someone screaming, then realized that she wasn't hit. She looked up, confused, and saw that Dhillon had dropped her gun and was clutching a long bloody gash on her arm. Her eyes were fixed with horror on something behind Toni. Simon!

Toni turned and felt a flood of terror. It was Simon screaming, his face contorted with murderous rage as he sprinted toward Dhillon. He'd forgotten his gun and was going to tear her apart with his hands. Toni shouted at him to stop, knowing it was hopeless.

"Get down!" Alberta yelled at the hostages, but Simon was already crashing through the confused group. The Patrollers, startled by his screams, hadn't reacted fast enough. He knocked two hostages aside and sprang at Dhillon.

Toni crouched in terror, braced for a hail of gunfire, but it didn't come. Tommy Yip stood frozen uncertainly on one side of the pier, and in the other direction, Lincoln had raised his arms, holding his men back. Three of Alberta's bouncers ran out onto the deck with guns raised, then hesitated, afraid to fire into the melee.

"Take Mary!" yelled Alberta, and climbed to her feet, pulling Mary up with her. Two bouncers ran to help, and another lunged for the next nearest hostage—de Groot. Toni caught a glimpse of Klale helping, then she looked back.

Baljeet lay on the pier while Simon slammed into another Patroller with a brutal two-handed blow. Neil fired at him, but the berserk giant didn't flinch or slow. He dove sideways with incredible speed, then picked up a Patroller and threw the man at Neil like a rag doll. Neil's bullets tore into his comrade before the two of them crashed heavily to the deck.

The fishhook code! Toni reached for her phone, then remembered in horror that Dhillon had taken it. She rose to her knees.

"Alberta!" she yelled. "Give me your phone!"

Alberta shoved de Groot through the door and turned, looking around blankly.

"Your phone!"

Alberta pulled the phone off over her head. She threw wide and Toni had to dive sideways to grab it, hitting the concrete deck with jarring force. She cursed and looked up.

A wounded Patroller ran for the launch and Simon sped after him with the same powerful, deadly grace she'd seen in his dances. The Patroller had no chance. Simon closed the distance, then leaped in the air and kicked out with lethal force, smashing his foot between the man's shoulder blades. The man's head snapped backward with a crack.

Toni looked down at Alberta's phone and tried to enter the long string of numbers with clumsy, shaking fingers, cursing herself for not putting it in her mailbox so she could access it remote.

"Toni!"

She looked up.

"Take off that coat!" she heard Alberta yell, then she realized with a sudden burst of fear that she was wearing a Patrol uniform coat and Simon was searching around with maddened eyes for another target. Rill and Dr. Lau were on their knees, stripping off blue coats. Toni sat up, too, yanking at her sleeves. Simon plunged into motion with dizzying speed.

"Get down!" Toni heard Alberta yell, but it was too late.

Rill was closest. Simon slammed into her, then turned and scooped the woman up by the back of her collar, swinging her into the air.

"No!"

Alberta ran at Simon, scrabbling frantically at her empty holster, then Toni heard two gunshots. She glanced wildly around as she flung off her coat, but the lines of tong weaponry were motionless. Then she saw Neil McCaskill, up on his elbows, firing.

Simon released Rill, sending her hurtling through the air while he dived into a roll. He was almost on top of Neil before Rill smashed onto the deck with a horrible crunching thud.

The fishhook code! Toni fumbled at the phone again. She entered the last digits and hit SEND, then looked up. Nothing. Simon stood shaking Neil like a rat. She cleared, and began again with clumsy fingers. Suddenly she became aware of a lull in the noise and looked up.

Simon had paused, staring around at the scattered, unmoving bodies. Neil dangled limply in his grasp. Toni held her breath and closed her eyes as Simon's eyes grazed over her, trying not to feel her own stabbing fear. All she could hear was the wind and a distant wail of alarms. She counted two and opened her eyes again. Simon's stare had moved past her. Nobody move! thought Toni desperately. If he loses momentum, he may simply collapse. As seconds crawled past, she felt a faint surge of hope, then a hump of gray and black wool lurched up. Dhillon in Klale's sweater! She was crawling toward her gun.

"Baljeet! Play dead!" Toni yelled, but Simon caught sight of her. He dropped Neil and leaped forward.

Toni forced her gaze down and tried to get the numbers right on the phone, distantly aware of a scream, followed by crunching noises. She pressed SEND.

Again, nothing. She glanced up. Simon had grasped Dhillon by the feet and was pounding her headfirst against the pier again and again.

Damn that code! Toni wiped her eyes, cleared and started again, then realized that the thuds had stopped. She looked up in time to see Simon drop Dhillon's body. He stood for several long seconds, swaying dizzily, then fell to his knees, head shaking from side to side.

Behind him Alberta rose to a crouch and ran three fast steps to the gun that Baljeet had failed to reach.

No! thought Toni suddenly, and she launched herself toward Simon, running into Alberta's line of fire.

"No!"

Alberta's face was red with rage, and her weapon pointed straight at Toni's chest.

"Move!"

Toni shook her head wordlessly, then Dr. Lau staggered to his feet and hurried toward Alberta, pointing to Rill's crumpled body on the concrete pier.

"I need a medkit!" he yelled at Alberta.

Alberta looked from Toni to Lau, then back at Rill. Lau jogged past her. Toni risked a backward glance. Simon was shuddering now, mouth half open as he gasped for air. The right shoulder of his shirt was a wet mess of blood. At least one bullet had hit him. When she looked back, Alberta was running to Rill's side.

Toni turned and bent forward.

"Simon," she tried softly, then called louder. "Simon!"

He started to focus and lifted his bloody hands, blinking at them in confusion. Then he looked down at the battered, misshapen corpse under him, with Baljeet's blood soaking through Klale's Cowichan sweater.

Oh no! thought Toni, and in the same instant she saw the horror light in Simon's eyes. He let out a terrible keening wail.

"No, Simon . . ."

She knelt, tugging urgently at his right hand, trying to get him to look at her.

"Simon! It's not Klale!" she yelled, but his eyes were already glassy and his face was going slack. She grabbed his head and shook it, only distantly aware that she was screaming.

"Simon! Don't leave me, damn it! Don't leave me!"

Gradually she became aware of a hand on her shoulder and a voice telling her to let go. It took all the concentration she could summon to make her hands stop their frantic, futile motions. When she released Simon, he crumpled to the deck and curled up in a fetal ball.

"Toni? Toni?"

She turned to see Klale looking at her with horrified compassion.

"I'm fine," she said, pulling away from Klale's hand, but unable to keep the hysteria out of her voice. She wiped her face, then kneeled and checked Simon's shoulder. Blood poured from the wound. She applied pressure and looked up.

"Klale, I need a medkit."

Klale was staring around at the carnage on the pier with dazed horror.

"He killed them," she whispered. "He killed all these people!"

"Klale!" Toni shouted. She waited for the girl to focus on her. "Get me a medkit!"

Klale swallowed and nodded, then after a second's indecision, sprinted down the pier toward Tommy Yip, who stood conferring with his security guards. There seemed to be fewer of them than there had been a minute before.

"Toni!"

Toni looked around at the urgent call and caught sight of Dr. Lau crouching beside Rill.

"Do you need help?" he shouted.

"No." Toni took a deep breath and repeated herself more loudly, then answered his unspoken question: "Heavy bleeding but not profuse. I can handle it."

Dr. Lau nodded, and turned back to Rill. What was he feeling about his son now? Toni wondered. She gazed around at the scene. Mary kneeled beside the unnaturally twisted heap that had been Neil. She seemed to be praying. Someone had draped a Patrol coat over Baljeet's bloody corpse and Pum was similarly covering the man by the companionway. Toni swiveled and looked back over her shoulder. Lincoln's Bloods stood with lowered weapons, and as she watched, Lincoln beckoned two of them and strode forward.

Lincoln looked satisfied, she thought distantly. And why not? Mary Smarch was safe. Dhillon was dead. And his gang members had been able to enjoy a vicarious bloodletting.

In the harbor beyond them, Patrol launches sped toward the pier in a white wash of foam. Too late. Far, far too late.

38

There shouldn't be sunshine today, Klale thought. She looked across the green carpet of Point Grey Park to a panorama of ocean and city, backed by a towering wall of mountains. The island of Downtown seemed just a tiny gray jumble in all the blue water. It should be shrouded in clouds crying onto the broken buildings, Klale thought bitterly—not bathed in crisp clear autumn sunshine.

The streets she'd seen this morning didn't even look like the same streets as yesterday. When they returned from the carnage on Pier B-C, Robson Street had stood empty, electric with fear, but today it surged with festive shoppers. On her walk to the ferry Klale had seen no sign of the tong war or the riots. Buildings blocked her view of the plumes of smoke still rising on the east side.

When Lincoln openly sided with the Sun Yee On, the Americans exploded in revenge against the Viet Ching and Kung Lok, lynching gang members and burning tong factories. The Council of Guilds had voted to send the Watch in, but the Watch prudently waited until early morning when the rioting waned before crossing Burrard into the east side with an escort of Bloods provided by Lincoln. Thinking about the people who had died last night made Klale feel sick. She could visualize with horrible clarity how the bodies must have lain sprawled and lifeless . . .

Klale hadn't been able to face Toni's apartment with the bloodied, mute specter of Simon. She'd spent the afternoon at the hospital with Alberta, and the night in Mary's suite.

Toni had warned her repeatedly that Simon was violent, but Klale hadn't really understood until she'd seen him smash the guards' knees. His brutality left her devastated and soulsick. How could she love Simon after that? How could Toni? She'd seen Toni's face on the wharf—crumpled with grief and dismay, but no surprise. Toni had understood all along.

And I was too stupid and naive to listen, Klale told herself bitterly. If I hadn't taken Simon to the pier with some tilted notion of him as a hero, Rill might not be lying in Vancouver Hospital with a broken neck . . . And Klale wouldn't be here, among the crowd of grieving people flowing out of the church after Neil McCaskill's funeral.

Klale hadn't cried until Hans found her. She'd retreated from Mary's gentle attempts to talk, and watched net reports on the spill while a knot of desperate tension built inside her. She'd utterly forgotten about Hans until she heard his voice say *"Klahowya"* and turned to see him—burly, hirsute, and very much out of place in Sisters—looking around with a slightly deflated expression at Mary's neat, homey apartment. He'd been braced for another confrontation, not the flood of tears that overwhelmed Klale when she saw him standing there, smelling of sea air and damp wool and Sundays at home. He looked startled when she rushed at him, but sat her down on the couch, patting her awkwardly and wiping her face with his handkerchief as he had when she was a toddler. She'd forgotten that, and forgotten how desperately she'd missed him when he moved away.

She couldn't talk about Simon, so she talked about everything else—the tong death squad, the funeral parade, the beggars. Hans listened patiently and his kindness had made her cry even more because she hadn't expected it. She hadn't bothered to look clearly at him since she'd grown up, still nursing a ten year old's resentment at her adored big brother's desertion. But how could she blame him for running away from her father and the Guild? She'd done the same thing herself.

Hans slept on Mary's floor that night while Klale lay awake on the couch, dozing into nightmares of Simon's screaming contorted face. At one point she heard the crunch of Simon's boot crushing the guard's knee, woke up, and ran to the bathroom to vomit up her dinner. Then she went back and listened to Hans's loud snores, somehow immensely reassuring in their normalcy.

"Klale. Thank you for coming."

Klale turned to see Ron McCaskill, wan and frail in an old suit of formal clothes, leaning heavily on his cane. He shook Hans's hand and returned Klale's cautious hug, accepting their inarticulate condolences with gentle dignity.

As he turned away, Klale felt a wave of desperate futility. She could almost see the waves of pain and violence spreading out from Simon's act like rings in a pond. Choi, Simon, the riots . . . Could it ever end? Could Mary or the D.R.A. or anything else make a difference?

Her own attempts to do good had made things worse. If she and Toni hadn't rescued Simon, Neil McCaskill and the others might not have died.

She and Hans walked through tree-lined upscale Guild streets to Twelfth Avenue and caught a tram to the Downtown ferry. While they waited at the Kitsilano ferry wharf, she called Toni's apartment, and was answered by a haggard-looking Dr. Lau. He said that Toni had been up all night watching Simon, and was finally sleeping. Klale explained she was coming by to pick up her belongings. She knew she should say something sympathetic to Lau about Simon, but she couldn't manage it and signed off with a surge of relief that she didn't have to face good-byes with Toni. Not yet, anyway. She'd call later.

Outside the KlonDyke's main doors they found four uniformed members of the City Watch standing sentry. Inside, the bar swarmed with activity. The staff were cleaning up, with the help of friends and customers, and the atmosphere was jubilant. Well, why not? Klale thought dully. The tong war was over, the bar was reopening, Mary was a hero, and it looked like the council would support the D.R.A.'s reforms for Downtown.

Klale stopped just inside the door and looked around. She saw Pum hammering a chair together and Val sweeping up broken glass. Bracken leaned against the bar issuing imperious directions. Alberta wasn't there—she'd still be at the hospital with Rill, Klale thought grimly. Bracken spotted Klale first and hurried over, threading her way fastidiously through the activity. She actually wore hempen work pants and flats, but Klale doubted she was in any danger of working. The pants were much too tight and if she bent over they'd probably split.

"Klale! Delighted to see you intact—well, safe, anyway. And you must be Hans." Bracken swept her eyes over him and simpered. "You're so much larger in person!"

Hans took that with his usual deadpan.

"Haven't we met some place before?" he asked suspiciously.

For a split second Bracken looked worried, then she recovered and thrust her hips forward.

"Not that I recall, but perhaps you'd recognize me from a different angle."

Hans scrutinized her crotch thoughtfully, then shook his head.

"Never mind. If I was that drunk, I wouldn't remember anyway."

Bracken scowled.

"I'm *always* memorable," she said archly, then turned quickly to Klale.

"I'm *so* happy to see you, sweets. Mary promised all these persons free beer in return for their services and it's going to be herniatic! We've got enough beer, but we're short everything else—servers, food, glasses . . ."

"I'm leaving," Klale blurted, unable to find any other way of saying it. "Going back to Prince Rupert on today's boat."

"Oh," said Bracken, suddenly deflating. In flat shoes she stood no taller than Toni, Klale realized, and when the animation left her face, all the heavy eye makeup made her look forlorn.

Pum strode up, looking self-consciously efficient as acting chief of security. She started to escort them to the stairwell, then Hans stopped and turned to his sister.

"Why don't you wait here while we go upstairs?"

Klale hesitated, then nodded with a rush of relief and shame. She kept remembering her promise to help with Simon, but she just couldn't face him. And the tension that had kept her going was draining away, leaving her exhausted. She watched Hans and Pum stride off, thinking distantly that Hans was in for another surprise when he saw Toni's apartment, but she couldn't summon up any amusement.

She stood near the bar for a long time, nodding without listening while Bracken delivered a rapid, high-pitched monologue about the deplorable damage caused by bullets and how it might nonetheless be an opportunity to refurbish the 'Dyke's turgid décor. I should pitch in and help, Klale thought vaguely, but she felt crushed with fatigue—as if it was too much effort to take just one more step.

"Klale!"

Klale winced and Bracken rolled her eyes as Cedar de Groot hurried over and wrapped his arms around Klale. She pulled away.

"Hello, Mr. de Groot."

"Oh, come on, you always call me Cedar! It's so good to see you! You look fine, well, a bit tired, and so am I of course, but I had to come in, you know, just to see how the bar was doing and say thanks to everyone who helped rescue me. I could hardly sleep last night, you know, kept waking up with nightmares. I've never been so scared in my life as yesterday. Seeing Baljeet was . . . I know she took some wrong turns, but she didn't deserve that—that horrible end. And I came *that* close to being killed, too . . ."

Klale nodded, with a grating sense of annoyance. How like de Groot to relate everything to himself. She stared at him, wondering how he could be so complacent, and so crass as to come back to Mary's bar after everything his tong-backed league had done to discredit her.

". . . and I don't know why they let Blade live. They should have shot that monster right there—humanely of course."

Yeah, a humane bullet to the head, Klale thought angrily. But she'd had similar thoughts herself. What right did she have to get angry at de Groot?

". . . unfortunate that something like that had to happen to make people realize how dangerous the tongs are, but at least it's made the city wake up and do something. It's just so tragic that people were killed by that terrible ghoul . . ."

Rising fury pushed words out of Klale's mouth.

"And what if Blade hadn't been there? Did it ever occur to you that he might have saved your life? That your friend Baljeet would have shot you in the head very humanely and thrown you in the harbor?"

De Groot stared at her in astonishment.

"Oh no, now, I'm sure that she wouldn't . . ."

But Klale couldn't stand it anymore. She clenched her fist, then drove her arm forward. The impact with Cedar's chin sent stabbing pain through her fingers and jarred her shoulder, but he hurled back with satisfying force, crashing against a table and then onto the floor.

"You self-serving cret! It was you and your goddamned Freevie friends that nearly got us all killed. And it wasn't Simon's fault he couldn't be a hero! He doesn't know how. But he tried!"

Her voice broke on tears of anger, but for the first time that day she felt really alive. A firm hand took her arm, and pulled her back, and Klale realized that Pum had returned. Cedar lay holding his jaw with a stupid, half-stunned expression. Bracken jumped up and down, clapping and cheering. Then Hans appeared at Klale's other side, with her duffel bag slung over his shoulder and her workboots hanging around his neck. He glanced down at Cedar with raised eyebrows, then looked at Pum.

"Guess he slipped," said Pum.

"Mmmm. Well, perhaps we'd better go before there are any more accidents," Hans returned, calmly. Then he took Klale's arm. "Ready?"

Klale nodded automatically, but she was still thinking about what she'd said. Without Simon, Alberta would never have got onto the pier. All of the hostages might have died. Klale shouldn't blame herself for taking him. If she hadn't, things might have been worse.

Hans took her arm and steered her toward the door. In the distance Klale heard Bracken's voice calling ". . . and come back and hit him again soon!" but she didn't look back. She was lost in the scene on the pier, remembering how Toni had kneeled over Simon, crying.

A pedicab waited outside. Hans threw the duffel bag in it and turned to Klale. She stared back at the KlonDyke, then said:

"I'm coming back. I'll go to Rupert with you and get my citizenship reinstated because I can prove what those bent nespots did to me and I'm not going to let them get away with it. But I'm coming back here afterward. Downtown needs my community service a lot more than the Fishers do."

She half expected an argument, but Hans peered up at the KlonDyke tower instead and grimaced.

"Sometimes you remind me of Mom," he said. "She never did anything the easy way, either."

"No smog," Klale said unevenly. "She married Dad."

"Yeah." Hans smiled, then reached out and gave Klale a bear hug that crushed her against his big shoulders. They climbed in the cab. The driver sounded her horn and leaned forward into the pedals. Klale turned and looked back out the window as the cab lurched down the potholed street. She watched the red "K" on the KlonDyke doors until it disappeared from sight.

39

"What are you doing?"

Toni looked up to see Mary, face flushed from the exertion of the long stair climb, peering in her bedroom door.

"Exactly what it looks like," she growled, turning her attention back to the section of parquet floor under her knees. "I'm finishing it."

There was a slight pause, then Mary simply said: "I'll make coffee and bring it in here so you can work while we talk."

How like her not to question or joke, Toni thought, hearing the gentle smile in Mary's voice. Mary was one of the few people she knew who wouldn't consider it absurd for Toni to be working on her apartment hours before she left.

It was a last minute impulse. Lying in bed that morning looking at her floor, she'd suddenly realized that she just couldn't leave it that way. She'd run away too many times before, leaving loose ends behind. And she had a few hours to spare. Dr. Lau was out buying medical supplies and spreading the story that he was taking his son back to Hong Kong, while Toni ostensibly watched Simon. But there was nothing to watch. She looked over again.

Simon sat on a futon near her bedroom window in exactly the same position they'd put him in hours before. His eyes stared vacantly out of a lifeless face. Toni had been able to plug him into neural software quickly enough to interrupt deep catatonia patterns, but he remained withdrawn and unresponsive. Well, at least it would make transporting him simpler, she thought grimly. Later, if he didn't start to recover on his own, she might have to force him back to awareness. It was an option she didn't like to contemplate.

She refocused her attention on sanding the edges of a small wooden block to fit in an irregular space next to the wall. It wasn't a perfect floor, of course. She had pieced it together in small sections over a period of several years, so even with careful masking and staining there were visible demarcations between patches, but the mix of woods and the parquet pattern disguised the unevenness. Probably no one else would ever notice. Not than anyone would ever see it.

She pushed the last piece of rectangle into place, eyed it critically, then pried all the segments up and applied a thick coat of adhesive to the concrete floor before setting them back in place. According to this antique parquet method, she should wait for the glue to set tight before sanding the completed floor with an abrasive pad. Then she should apply a coat of stain/finish, let it dry for a day, sand again, and then add a top coat. But she didn't have time. She had a meter-long strip left to do, then she'd sand and apply one coat of finish just before leaving.

Mary's footsteps approached and the aroma of fresh coffee overwhelmed the smell of sawdust. Toni sat up, straightening her sore back with relief, and wiping her dusty hands on a rag. Mary put two mugs and a plate of muffins on the floor nearby, then walked over to the window and crouched down by Simon. Toni watched her curiously. Mary took his hand and said hello in a soft voice, then after a long minute, reached out and touched his forehead.

Toni found tears burning in her eyes and looked down, trying to find something in the coffee to busy herself with, then wondered why the hell she was bothering to hide. Last night she'd cried on Mary's shoulder as she hadn't cried since she'd gone through withdrawal, and she'd found herself close to tears a dozen times since—as if something inside her had broken and all those unshed tears from a lifetime were demanding to wash down her cheeks. Nonetheless, she pushed them back, and didn't look up again until Mary came and sat on the end of her bed.

"Did you feel anything from him?" she asked.

Mary shook her head.

"Nothing at all. I'm sorry. Why do you have him wearing head-phones?"

"It's dance music. I doubt it will do any good, but picking out music gave his father something to do."

Mary nodded.

"What time are you leaving?"

"Eleven. The streets should be reasonably quiet by then. Ron found a fast boat and two friends to help us. If the weather stays calm, we should reach your cabin before dawn."

Please gods let it be calm and let it be the last goddamned small boat trip! Ever! She forced back her dread and added in a lower voice:

"I'm very grateful to Ron. Without his help, I don't think the families of Simon's victims would ever have agreed to this."

"As much as he grieves for Neil, he can't find it in his heart to blame Simon," Mary said quietly. "We talked it over yesterday. Ron considers himself partly responsible for Simon, you know. He'll do whatever he can to help, so long as you and Rigo ensure that Simon doesn't harm anyone else."

Those stupid tears were close again, so Toni sipped her coffee. Mary passed her a muffin. She took it automatically and nibbled without appetite.

"I'm afraid the cabin won't be very comfortable, Toni. It's never been properly finished and the pipes are in terrible shape. Pack plenty of warm clothes and all your tools. I wish I could come along to help you settle in, but I've got a council meeting on Monday that I simply can't miss."

"Of course," said Toni, relieved for a change of topic. "How did this morning's meeting go?"

"Magnificently. The same councilors who wouldn't talk to me a few weeks ago are my long lost friends, and the newsers are building me up as a folk hero. Lincoln's behind a lot of the flash, of course. He's the rescuer of the hostages and the noble leader of the oppressed Americans."

Toni grimaced slightly, without surprise. The Harbor Patrol wouldn't comment on the hostage-taking incident, nor would the D.R.A. De Groot was ducking questions, and Tommy Yip had vanished. Lincoln was taking full advantage of the silence and public curiosity to retail his version of events.

"He's a dangerous ally," she commented.

"Very, but at the moment he's also invaluable. We're teaming up to negotiate with Cascadia Rail and the city. He's a sharp bargainer and I'm a strong mediator. I think we're going to get a better deal for Downtown residents than I ever dared hope for."

Mary finished with a sigh that contradicted her optimistic words and Toni raised a questioning eyebrow. Mary caught her look and smiled tiredly.

"I was just thinking about all the work ahead of us. I have no doubt that the railroad will be approved now, Toni. The revelations about tong corruption in the local Guilds and their connections to the Free Vancouver league have gutted the opposition. And we'll get Maglev jobs for the Guildless, but it'll be six months at least before any of them materialize. In the meantime a lot of factories and stores on the East Side were destroyed in the riot. Many people have no homes, work, or food, and we have to deal with several hundred suddenly unplugged blissers. The Americans are the worst off. It's going to take everything that Lincoln, the D.R.A., and the city can do to keep the lid on."

"It doesn't sound like you'll be spending much time at the bar."

"No." She paused a second, then added with an edge of fresh pain in her voice, "I'm going to miss you very badly, Toni."

Toni paused uncomfortably, then cleared her throat.

"How's Rill?"

"Stable and her neural signs are good, but it's a serious injury. She'll be permanently disabled."

Mary stared at the floor and Toni studied her face. The beautiful wrinkles were deeper than usual and Mary had dark smudges under her eyes, but she still projected a strong sense of resilience and purpose. It was her faith, Toni thought, feeling a trace of envy. When Toni was young, she used to despise religious people as hypocrites, weaklings, and fools, but she'd come to realize that faith could be a strength.

Mary looked up and caught her eyes. "Do you have enough money?"

"I haven't checked. But yes, I will accept a loan, so you don't have to bother being tactful." She reached for the netset, lying on the floor by Simon, waved it to life and called up her personal file on the 'Dyke's net account. Wrong file, she thought, looking from the balance to the ID. Then she blinked. This was her subaccount, and the balance read $GD 103,912. Her stunned look attracted Mary's attention.

"What is it?" asked Mary, moving up behind her, then she caught sight of the screen. "Gracious mother!"

Toni scanned back over recent entries with sudden suspicion. Four deposits had been made in the last two days, all from sources she'd never heard of.

"It had to be Simon. He must have launched a subroutine liquidating Choi's holdings into my account."

"If that's true, Toni, this will be just the start. Commodities and venture shares have a two-year-minimum turnover. Properties start at five. I remember it took us almost seven years to settle my uncle's estate."

Toni blinked and swallowed, then decided that she didn't want to think about it. Not now. Thank God she didn't have a personal ID. Large sums of money would be slightly less conspicuous in a trade account. Another thought struck her and she checked her mailbox.

"No messages." She hadn't expected any, but she nonetheless felt an irrational stab of disappointment. She didn't want to lose Simon without having said . . . something. Even good-bye. She closed the account abruptly and made her voice dry. "Well, I believe I can turn down your offer . . . Oh!"

"What?"

"Klale. If she doesn't get her citizenship back, she can still apply for an independent slot at university. I'll pay her tuition . . ."

She felt Mary's hand on her shoulder.

"She'll win back her citizenship. And she won't forget you, Toni. She'll be back."

She should hug Mary, Toni knew, but she felt too fragile—as if her tears might never stop once she let them start. She patted Mary's hand, then lifted it gently off her shoulder, and moved back to her parquet work. She asked a question about the bar. Mary answered calmly and they discussed the KlonDyke for a while, then fell into a companionable silence in which Toni's thumping and sanding overlaid the faint street noises echoing up between the buildings. Simon made no sound. He might have been a holo-sculpt.

"Soothing, isn't it?" Mary said finally. Toni looked down at her hands and nodded.

"Yes it is. Satisfying, too. Everything fits neatly into place. Not like patients." She paused, remembering, then pushed past her reticence. She had no secrets to protect now.

"We used to joke about therapists' hobbies. Perpetual home renovation was one of them. You can succeed at building a floor if you just follow the right procedures and persevere, but people aren't like that. Sometimes you do everything possible and fail, and sometimes you succeed without understanding why. We can do a great deal, but we still can't mend a human soul. A floor, on the other hand, is a permanent, visible success. I think I prefer floors." She slid another block into place. "I've always assumed that you felt the same way about baking."

"Mmm. But I don't prefer baking to people. Toni, love—if I put batter in the oven I get muffins out every time. But people are a constant surprise. It's like opening up the oven and finding orchids or emeralds or a rainbow. I'm always astonished by the magic in people and the power of love to bring it out. And of all the examples I've come across, I think Simon is the most extraordinary. If you hadn't shown me that dance I would never have dreamed that he could have such joy in his heart. What's more, I believe that he will survive. He's endured so much, Toni. And he loves you so deeply."

Toni shook her head with irritation, not raising her eyes from her work. "You're an incurable optimist."

Behind her Mary sighed.

"I don't want to be cured of optimism. And I wish I could give you more of it."

"I never had any optimism," Toni replied, unable to keep the bitterness out of her voice. "I make do with rage and stubborn persistence."

"I know. But right now you need hope and so does Simon.

Toni . . ." Toni turned and saw Mary watching her with deep brown eyes. "He's going to need everything you've got—you know that, don't you?"

It was hard to meet those eyes, but she did, answering as steadily as she could.

"Yes. And you should know that I don't quit, even when I should. I'll take care of him."

"Take care of yourself, too," Mary said softly.

40

Maybe I should have arrived earlier, thought Klale, shifting the heavy pack on her shoulders. She hadn't realized how difficult it would be to find Mary's cabin without directions. Though gray afternoon light still filtered through the trees, the winding, narrow road was already deeply shadowed in December dusk. She'd passed the last visible house and now only occasional gravel lanes led off to either side, marked by old delivery boxes and hand-lettered boards tacked on trees. When she'd called up an island map on her phone, she'd been stunned to discover that the island not only lacked street addresses, but locations of private residences weren't publicly posted. Evidently they didn't encourage visitors. Klale sighed and trudged up a steep hill to the next sign.

BLUE ELYSIUM, SARA & MAPLE, PHONE: SCHMIDT.CORTESI.NA.

That wasn't it. She paused for a minute, giving herself a breather, then moved on. She'd continue for another twenty minutes, she decided stubbornly. By then it would be too dark to find the signs and she'd have to call Toni.

More signs appeared at a junction of two lanes just over the crest of the hill on her left and she hiked closer, squinting to make them out. The first, ornately carved, said only ANDERSON. A much smaller plastiche sign tacked underneath read SOUTH TESLIN, SMARCH8.NA. Klale smiled in relief and started down the nearest lane, her breath steaming in air that smelled of damp earth and fir needles. A few

meters along the lane her phone bleeped, so she stopped and identified herself to the security system. It acknowledged and invited her
to continue.

The lane dipped downhill, then turned sharply. Rounding the
corner, Klale saw a ramshackle cabin with a wide sagging porch and
a stone chimney rising from a mossy shingled roof. Light and music
flowed from the windows into the dusk. Toni's jazz, thought Klale
with a poignant wave of emotion. She hesitated for a long moment,
trying to sort out her feelings. She hadn't been able to speak freely
with Toni by phone because of security worries about Simon. Toni
hadn't precisely invited Klale to come, nor had she ever asked for the
help Klale was about to offer, and Toni could be prickly. Then there
was Simon. Klale still found it difficult not to feel fear and repug-
nance when she remembered him.

Well, better to face him than stand here worrying, she told herself. She hitched up the pack again and strode determinedly forward
along the lane and then up a path through tall, wild grass that would
be loud with crickets in summer. At the porch steps she hesitated a
little, then trod as quietly as she could on the creaking boards and
peeked in through the open curtains.

She saw a shabby, comfortable living room, with a stone fireplace,
old patch rugs, and a big shapeless sofa. Dr. Lau stood with his back
to her, setting an extra place at a long, green-painted table. The room
looked peaceful and homey, but she saw no signs of Simon. Klale's
eyes went back to the table. Four places.

She stepped to the door and knocked. Almost instantly, Toni
threw it open, letting out a rush of warm air, redolent with supper.
Klale dropped her pack and wrapped her arms around Toni's shoulders.

"I missed you!" they both said at once.

Toni pushed her gently out to arm's length and Klale's appre-
hensions vanished as she saw Toni's smile. Dr. Lau stepped up, hand
outheld, but Klale went past it and hugged him, too, enjoying his
instant of surprise. She grinned and backed away.

"I should have given you more warning, but I got a last minute
ride. This friend of mine got a sleek trade on a rebuilt trawler engine
from a guy in Campbell River, and she offered me a ride down on

her boat if I'd come and help her load it. We made Campbell River yesterday night, loaded the engine this morning, and then she dropped me at Manson's Landing on her way back north."

"We're delighted to see you, Klale," Toni said warmly. "How's your brother?"

"Oh, Hans hasn't stopped snickering over the Fisher Guild's forensic audit. I guess everybody figured Klassen and his friends were bent, but we had no idea just *how* bent. Maybe it wasn't much compared to some of the Vancouver Guilds, but it shook our people up. Did I tell you I've been offered a full scholarship on top of the apology for unwarranted withdrawal of citizenship?"

She shrugged ruefully at Toni. "I know I should have appealed things before, but I thought people wouldn't back me because of Dad. Should have had more faith, I guess."

"Well, come in and sit down," Lau told her. He hefted her big backpack and staggered sideways. "Ah . . . I see you packed light."

"Well . . ."

Klale ran a nervous hand through her tangled hair. Toni gave her a sharp look.

"Precisely how long did Mary send you for?"

Klale grinned.

"Well, she explained the problem with the island council—how they've got steep service tithes and don't want to waive them. So I said, I'll work it."

She raised her voice over Toni's attempt to interrupt.

"See, with four of us living here that's forty hours a week Island service, and if I do all forty hours myself, you two are freed up for Simon. I can take a few nights with him, too—give you both a break. I packed everything I need; even a tent in case the cabin's too squish. And don't even try to say no. I moved my university slot back to next summer. I'm yours until June, like it or not."

She crossed her arms and stood grinning saucily at Toni. The older woman sighed.

"You're quite finished . . . ? Well . . . I was going to say thank you. We do need the help and we're pleased to have you."

"Extremely pleased," added Lau, perhaps a little too forcefully.

"Strat! And it looks like a great cabin!"

Lau and Toni spoke simultaneously.

"Yes."

"No."

"It's rustic," amended Lau, "but we make a fine medical team. Toni fixes pipes and I cook."

"It's a smogging prehistoric hovel," said Toni darkly, "but Rigo's cooking makes up for a lot. That's borscht you smell. I didn't believe that I'd enjoy cabbage soup, but it's wonderful. Without those stairs to climb I'm going to get fat."

Klale caught the flash of sadness in her eyes.

"How's your apartment?" she asked.

"The building isn't demolished yet," said Toni shortly.

There was an awkward pause and then Klale realized that they were all circling the unspoken question.

"How's Simon?"

"Still very withdrawn," said Lau, abruptly somber.

Toni nodded.

"He hasn't regained the mass he dropped that first month. It's his damned metabolism—he loses weight very easily."

"He's . . . he's still *there*, isn't he?"

"Oh, yes. Lots of neural activity. He seems to be daydreaming. We don't want to force a response from him, so we're going to wait him out."

"We won't to use Choi's methods," Lau interjected with quiet bitterness.

Toni glanced at him, then at Klale.

"We studied Choi's training records. They're appalling." She looked closely at Klale and added: "Simon's on the porch."

"I didn't see him," said Klale, startled. She turned around immediately, then felt Toni's hand on her arm.

"He's quite safe—we installed a neural restraint—but I'll go with you if you'd like."

"No, it's all right. Really."

Nonetheless Klale's stomach churned as she opened the door and stepped back outside.

It took her a moment to see Simon. He sat on the floor at the very end of the porch, hidden behind an old rattan chair, gray clothes blending into the shadows. His arms were wrapped around his knees and he stared out at the yard with unmoving eyes. His left hand was still bandaged, Klale noticed. She approached cautiously, startled by how gaunt he looked. Bones and veins stood out under his skin, making his face look more skull-like than ever. In the center of his forehead a pink-brown rectangle of new skin marked the site of Choi's brand. She paused for a second, finding it hard to speak.

"*Klahowya*. It's Klale."

She could have been talking to a statue. Even in the bar his eyes had been more alive, she thought. She spoke to him again, then reached out and touched his right hand. It felt cold despite the blanket draped over his legs. Her fear ebbed in a wash of sadness and pity. She pushed the chair away and kneeled down, then put her arms around him as best as she could. It felt like hugging a tree, but she held on for a long moment, then pulled back a little and kissed his soft cheek.

"I missed you, Simon," she said. She felt awkward talking aloud into his silence, but she needed to say it and he might hear.

"I found out something about myself after I left. I found out that I couldn't stop loving you, even when I was horrified and frightened and angry. It was caring so much that made it all hurt even worse. I couldn't stop thinking about you. And after a while the anger faded, and I began to remember the beautiful man I met in the dark."

She watched him for a long minute, then on impulse, wiped a couple of tears off her cheek onto his. He still gave no response, only the very faint steam of his breath in the cold air. Something about his stillness reminded Klale suddenly of the way he'd stood on the pier and she had to fight down a surge of fear. That's stupid, she told herself. You weren't afraid of him when you should have been, and now that it's safe you have jitters. Better get over them. They won't do Simon any good.

A weather-stained cushion lay on the chair. She tossed it on the floor and sat down against his tall, hard side, burrowing under the lap rug for warmth and trying to remember how she'd felt in the cargo hold the first time she'd talked to him. She reached up under his unresisting arm and pressed her hand over his cold fingers.

"It felt strange going back to Prince Rupert," she told him. "It seemed so different—smaller, greener, richer, more peaceful. But it hadn't changed—I had. You changed me, Simon. Toni did too, and everyone Downtown, but you most of all. You changed my world." She squeezed his arm, feeling her throat tighten. "I wish I could change your world," she whispered.

Tears misted Klale's eyes. She snuggled closer, gazing out under the porch railing, then caught her breath. Simon's hand was moving. Ever so slowly, it turned palm up, then his fingers curled gently around hers.

EPILOGUE

The boy danced alone in the most beautiful place in the world. The joy of the green-soaked glade ringed with soaring trees made him leap and sway and somersault in the fading light, buoyed by the music pouring from the house into the tall grass.

A crescendo rained down and he spun with delight, reaching his hand out to brush soft branches. He had never imagined that trees would smell so wonderful or that they would roar so loudly in the wind. The music ended and he stood still for a second, then threw back his head and looked up, hoping that there would be stars tonight. The sky here was dusted with them, like glittering snow.

As the next piece of music began he heard movement at the door and he looked over, expecting Toni to step onto the porch, and take the silent tool's hand. But it wasn't Toni—it was a beautiful ghost with wind-tossed red hair spilling onto a blue roll-neck sweater. The boy watched for a few seconds as she walked over to the tool, then he ran lightly through the long grass and climbed onto the porch to see what she was doing.

She was talking to the tool, stroking its ugly face, and her fingers were as warm as if she was real. The music leaking through the windows suddenly ached.

A papery voice breathed venom in his ear.

"You know she's not dead. Neither am I. I'll never die. And I will use you to kill all of them."

Choi! Old terror tried to grab him, but the boy leaped from the porch, fled through shadowy plumes of grass and wrapped his arms around the biggest fir tree, hugging its deep-rooted calm.

Slowly his fear ebbed. Soft cool sounds of evening enveloped him. A long distance away he heard footsteps on the porch as Toni led Choi's slave inside the cabin, then the clink of dishes and snatches of voices and laughter. After dinner the handsome doctor would take out his guitar and sing by the fireplace. The boy couldn't resist that. He'd go inside then, and curl up by the couch to listen. And Toni would hold his hand—anchoring him safe in her beautiful, astonishing world.

In Toni's world the boy who danced was free.